Michael Cumiskey was born in Stockton-on-Tees to parents both from immigrant stock – his mother's family originating from southern Italy and his father's from County Cork in Ireland.

He is a graduate of Middlesbrough College of Art and Design and in the past worked as the Resident Artist with the Skelmersdale New Town Development Corporation.

Currently, he lives in North Devon with his wife, Sue. Their three children have now left home and live in other parts of the country.

Michael Grainger is a born opportunist. Selfish to the core, he scorns his parents' value system and initially, along with two school friends, imagines himself better than all those around him. Not surprisingly owing to his attitude he finds it impossible to find suitable work. After a limited foray into petty crime he eventually signs on at the local art college where he hopes that after gaining a reasonable command of the jargon, a minimum of effort might secure for him a reputation as a creative artist. Part of the attraction, of course, is the possibility of high financial rewards and an association with attractive, available females.

His application of somewhat sharp practice quickly establishes for him a local reputation, which in turn enables his access to a London college. The new context only causes further distortion of his objectives and this is reflected in both his treatment of female friends as well as his putative art works. Indeed, the exhibition of pieces he eventually sells to an advertising executive mainly comprises work he has bought from other students. Despite being 'caught out' several times, once obliging him to spend time abroad, another – a legal conflict – making it impossible for him to sell his works for a decade, he nevertheless continues to practise his own form of advantage-taking, both in regard to the art and with his associates on both sides of the law. He is particularly vindictive with those who might have crossed him, however long his vengeance might take.

Sorry, Picasso

Michael Cumiskey

Sorry, Picasso

Vanguard Press

VANGUARD PAPERBACK

© Copyright 2014
Michael Cumiskey

A CIP catalogue record for this title is
available from the British Library.

ISBN 978 1 84386 945 0

Vanguard Press is an imprint of
Pegasus Elliot MacKenzie Publishers Ltd.
www.pegasuspublishers.com

First Published in 2014

Vanguard Press
Sheraton House Castle Park
Cambridge England

Printed & Bound in Great Britain

Disclaimer

This book is one of fiction. Suffice to say, however, that, although it is an invention, some of the incidents described are derived from actual experience. Nevertheless, there was/were no particular artist(s) in mind when it was written and no particular college referred to. As far as its subject matter is concerned, given the continuing interest in the Conceptual Movement and the attendant advertising associated with it, it seemed like a topical target that might lend itself to a degree of lampooning. It should be remembered also that the behaviour of Mick Grainger and the value system he exhibits throughout the book have been created as an entertainment and were not intended, necessarily, to reflect the same in any actual artist living or dead, no matter how similar they may appear.

Artists and non-artists alike will read this book and hopefully enjoy at least some part of it. To the artists, I say – should you find any of the notions or ideas for work described in the text appealing, please feel free to use them either in part or whole, according to your personal needs or requirements. To the non-artists, I can only add that perhaps, after reading the book, you might indulge yourself in a little creative endeavour of your own. In the words of Wilfred Pickles, a once well-known radio artist, why not, 'Have a go.'

Acknowledgements

Thanks are due to my good friend Phil Anastasi who helped in the resolution of this book, and others by questioning my motives, the direction of my narrative, and my spelling. It is therefore only fair to dedicate this effort to him, to his patience and his skill.

Introduction

Mine is a success story. Success achieved through raw talent and an ability to rise above whatever difficulties and unfairness I was faced with. Without doubt, therefore, I see myself as one of life's winners. Or, as one might say in the Madison Avenue parlance of the marketing culture that dominated Thatcher's 1980s, 'I've arrived,' 'My eyes are blue and my balls golden'. Moreover, in the orbit of that creative universe in which I chose to work I've been recognised as a star. Through my own effort, a modicum of good fortune and just a minimum of jiggery-pokery, I've acquired the fame, the money and a secure and well-deserved place in the history books.

Consequently, I feel no qualms about describing my life in that kind of unexpurgated detail seldom admitted by most public figures. I therefore intend this to be a no-frills account of my life's experiences: one that will inevitably describe the rude, juicy bits and place the sticky hairs of my intimate relations under the microscope. I will describe my strokes of genius and my *coups des magnifique*, my mistakes, my prejudices and my errors of judgement. Everything will be exposed, as it were, down to the bum-fluff on the baby's scrotum.

What the reader might or might not make of it is left entirely to their taste and perspicacity. In all honesty, I've reached that stage in life where I don't give a flying fuck what people think. I might add that this is a happy, euphoric state and one that prompts a profound feeling of freedom from always being overviewed and of worrying about the sensitivities and opinions of others. Not that in truth such sensitivities ever made much difference to me actually. On reflection, I suppose it was the pretence that they might make a difference that proved the chore.

Sincerely,

Michael Grainger.

Chapter One

1972

There were those who believed that the quantity of bitter beer consumed in my hometown was qualification enough for a special status award from the Duke of Edinburgh, or at least a blue plaque from the Prince Charles Trust. Indeed, if any of the major brewery companies had been inclined to sponsor such a competition, there is little doubt that Stockton-on-Tees would have been a leading contender. In the regular weekend quest for stupefied insensibility however, any local referendum on the subject would need to have precluded the hours immediately after closing time. On reflection, given the vegetative state produced in so many of the denizens after 22.30 hours, the most appropriate award might have been one from the Royal Horticultural Society.

In those days in the place where I lived, drunkenness was and always had been part of the culture, not so much a leisure pursuit as an occupational necessity. Particularly amongst the participants, the only time when objections might be heard was when the lack of focus impaired the throw of a dart or the turn of a domino; complaints usually made using the bluntest of language. These situations often prompted some to exercise the second most popular group activity, namely street fighting. Needless to say, for many alcohol clearly obviated the need for other cultural activities. Not surprising then, that the eventual loss of three cinemas and a theatre in favour of bingo halls and a cheap-jack auction house went without significant protest. The same was also true when, in order to accommodate a riverside development in grotesque concrete, one whole side of a fine Edwardian high street was vandalised to destruction. This was my heritage.

At that time, as far as I was concerned, the most significant cultural achievements to be found in Stockton comprised four accomplishments. The first was the Stockton to Darlington inaugural journey by rail, made by Stevenson's steam train, known as the *Rocket*. (Presumably securing its place in history on account of the provision it made for a hasty departure.) The second was the invention of the safety match (due to its continued importance to smokers the world over). The third, the Parish Church, designed at least in part by Christopher Wren (on one of his 'off' days) and arguably, the fourth was the date of my birth: October 25th 1953. I am forced to admit that, despite the fact that October 25th was a birth-date I shared with Pablo Picasso, on the occasion when I first identified this hierarchy of achievement, I still had no clear notion of how my own ultimate fame might be realised.

The beginning I choose for this account is during the month of December in 1972. This was an occasion when, due to a series of worse than usual political cock-ups, the approaching Christmas holiday period had been left in disarray.

That year, through their strike action, the miners had rendered life after dark almost impossible. A post-war society that had grown relaxed through having instant access to electrical power for lighting and central heating was now suddenly tensed, subject to a new capricious austerity. Overnight, pubs throughout the town switched to candle-power and those that could, reinvented hand pumps. On the streets, a Victorian gloom settled after dark, crime increased and some locations became no-go areas once the sun had set. Further afield, the IRA bombing campaign made travel to the London region a life-threatening gamble. The lunatics were clearly in charge of the asylum at last.

In all honesty, however, the root of my personal complaint was not typical. At that time as far as I was concerned, if London and its immediate environs had vanished overnight in a nuclear mushroom, the only difference to my world would have been the resultant (welcome) gap on the nightly TV news-caste. And, as I was seldom at home in the evenings to feel the effect of the power cuts, the miners could continue their march into the English Channel and stick their pit-heads as far up their arses as possible. I argued that the sooner we converted to nuclear power, the sooner those same miners could be retrained to do proper jobs. My complaint was more a matter of principle. The damned cheek of the Irish in bombing the mainland made me think it was time they were left to shoot one another to bits without British help.

I suspect, therefore, I was not the only person in Britain to imagine England was on its way to a richly deserved pit in deepest hell-fire. On top of that – my face had suddenly sprouted a collection of aggressively red spots, some with disgusting yellow heads.

Every conversation I had with that face in the bathroom mirror is etched forever in my memory by the acid of my pubescent discontent. I was then just nineteen years of age and experiencing an unusual bout of insecurity. I say unusual only because I had never before lacked confidence in myself. Indeed, if my teachers were to be believed, I was seen as being overconfident almost to the point of arrogance (a patent nonsense). That day things were different. The one-sided discussion in the bathroom led me to believe secretly that I was either a complete failure or a very late developer. A conjecture not helped by the spots.

I remember every pimple, every postulating, suppurating yellow head, every critical scrutiny, and every application of whatever patent nostrum boasting alleviation that happened to be in the bathroom cabinet. The ointments found there appeared as if by osmosis, a tactful kindness by my mother who was too conscious of my delicate sensitivities ever to mention the skin patination that then plagued me.

Unfortunately nothing worked. Nothing had worked for nearly two years. And, as my dad was wont to observe (being far less obliging in respect of my feelings than his wife), it was nearly as long since I had worked. He failed completely to understand that you don't launch a proper career by taking the first job offered – or for that matter the twenty-second or twenty-third. Due to the nature of my existence at that time, I had developed a low threshold for boredom and, as far as I had been able to ascertain, most jobs available to me on Teesside looked to be exceptionally boring. I wanted to do something exciting but did not yet know how to identify the excitement I sought. I felt an urge to reject all that was ordinary and pedestrian but could see nothing with which to replace it. Most of all I longed for recognition but could not identify any talent by which I might achieve that kind of celebrity.

Spotty and insecure I may have been but I was convinced nevertheless of my special individuality, just as I was also in the eventual manifestation of a unique skill – one that would guarantee a life of excessive comfort. The constituents of this comfort (I believed) would include the company of attractive and willing female companions and unlimited access to soft drugs. Needless to say that although I was uncertain what my talent might consist of, or under what circumstances it might appear, I was nevertheless certain of its existence.

After breakfast I was collected by my friends Bruce and Tony and taken in Bruce's car to sign-on. For those unfamiliar with this obligation, it is the fortnightly shaming process designed by governments to inhibit creativity, to limit freedom of movement and to apply vinegar to the wounds of the unemployed.

As we turned into the High Street, part of the number plate of the car in front said TOM. Very unusual to see anything so easily pronounceable let alone a complete name. It reminded me of a kid called Tom Bluer who had been in our class at junior school. Tom had achieved the rare privilege of being killed by the steam train called the *Flying Scotsman* when he was only nine years old. He was also the first one in our gang to go to London. It was 1963 and the old express was on its last trip south. For his friends, keen train spotters to a man, myself included, this equated with the noblest departure imaginable – as evocative as a Viking funeral. Sadly Tom's Valhalla was an involuntary, hundred miles per hour trip south to the capital.

There was this bridge over the main line where we used to play 'dare-do' whenever we got the opportunity, usually at the weekend and on school holidays. It was a simple enough game of childish machismo, the sort of activity popular amongst those still too young to smoke cigarettes in public or to gain admittance to public houses. To qualify you had to climb the barrier and stand on one of the curved iron crossbeams while the midday express train passed underneath. In truth it was enough to put the shits up anyone. A fact made all the worse when, still blinded by smoke, your mates grabbed the back of your jumper as if they were about to push you into the path of the train. The sound was ear splitting and, as your nose and eyes filled with acrid smoke, the old metal bridge shook as if it too wished you gone. We did this regularly, taking turns to taunt one another to brave the train. Then one day when it was Tommy's turn, the smoke cleared and Tommy had disappeared. It was a good game but we never played it again. To be honest, I could never be certain whether or not it was my jumper grabbing that had tipped him over the edge or if his fall was due to his natural clumsiness. All I knew was that what was left of him was on its way to London. Poor sod.

His mother could never look at me after that without her eyes filling with tears. Whenever we met, she would cry, mutter her son's name and place the flat of her hand on my chest. I grew to wonder if her action was to push me and the memory of her Tom further away, or if she was demonstrating a wish fulfilment – symbolically pushing me also from the bridge.

A moment later I saw NEL and thought that it was odd how once you saw a car number-plate that rang a memory bell, you started to see others. NEL equated in my mind with the obliging, Nelly Withwaites. She had moved to Tees-side when she was ten ... .u the old Plaza cinema near Her family had moved all the w... ...ed a whole generation of boys to with ICI. She talked funny, ... 'cherry-picker' par excellence. And, as due to her generosity d- ..inority sport, twelve months after Tom had the river. Single-b..e found a new activity to engage our attentions. It the damp my..m scribbling down numbers in notebooks and the thrill train sp..as anything but vicarious. However it did supply a sense of ma..albeit that the detail was unidentifiable to the innocent.

At the crossroads I noticed an old Volvo boasting PET, the surname of my mate Bruce who was driving his old Citroen and finally, just as we pulled into the DSS car park, there was a Y-reg Standard with the letters BAR rearranged to spell: BARY.

My favourite primary school teacher, indeed everyone's favourite teacher and the one who taught us in the scholarship class, had been Mary Bary. She had been a real cracker. The lovely Mary Bary (who always smelled of something nice and who wore very thin, provocatively thin, flowery dresses) was the fantasy figure in the masturbatory dreams of every lad in our class. Whatever Nelly Withwaites had, Miss Bary had more of it. We would compete to stand close to her as she sat at her teacher's desk marking our books, struggling for a glance down the front of her blouse. A seminal influence, for twelve months Miss Bary proved the model definition of desirable womanhood for almost every boy in the class, surely providing an image that would excite and torment us all for years to come.

Miss Bary lived alone with her mum in Hartburn, just a couple of roads away from my mate Bruce. In those days Hartburn was very posh, an area where the business community in Stockton was able to express its preference for an absence of net curtains, for open-plan living rooms and for large, well-tended gardens. The residents of Hartburn didn't work in factories, they owned them. If you stood at the end of Bruce's garden on a wooden box, preferably in winter when the trees were bare, we discovered it was sometimes possible to see Mary Bary's knickers hanging on her mother's washing line. Unlike her mother's huge white sacks, hers were small and lacy and often in exotic colours. To the envy of the uninvited, Bruce's back garden thereafter became a Mecca for his closest friends. No matter that the cold Siberian winds were sufficient to freeze brass monkey's balls, when the

conditions were right, a ...
the holly bush and take tur...
twenty five yards distant. Bruce's ...
were led to believe that we had develo... ...ies would assemble behind
birds...
                  ...r's scanty underwear
    That morning the three of us travelled to the ... real intentions,
an old Citroen Light Fifteen. It was a stylish model ...ching winter
French police and one that, despite its age, was still capable o...
and all three of us enjoyed turning heads. We liked to boast that ...car,
individuals and aggressively so.

    Twelve months before, despite having achieved A level results that we were told would have guaranteed us a place at university, we had jointly agreed to reject the option of higher or further education. As 'confirmed individuals' we chose instead to leave the sixth form at St. Mary's Catholic Boys' Grammar School to seek our fortunes in the world of work. That being said, none of us had so far been able to find sufficiently well-paid employment that would satisfy the model that we had chosen for ourselves. Our needs were relatively simple – we thought. We wanted work that would permit some extended freedom of movement, that would require little effort but that would provide the status and the financial rewards we all felt should be our destiny.

    To some large extent therefore, the world of work had so far eluded us. Principally to satisfy parents, there had been a few half-hearted attempts made in menial jobs but none of these had lasted and, at my prompt, we consoled one another with the old adage that, 'There had to be something better round the corner.'

    The only problem with 'waiting to be discovered', however, was the lack of spending power and the constant nagging we suffered at home. The pressures on each of us varied enormously. Bruce's family was by far the wealthiest and as a consequence, the stress placed on him was minimal by comparison. Tony's situation was a different matter. His dad was, in the language common amongst American movie cops, a 'three-time loser'. Currently he was serving an eight-year stretch in Durham prison for GBH and burglary. Tony would often joke that his father was away at their place in the country, a reference to the fact that their surname was also Durham. False optimism, as I was to discover later in life, is frequently one of the saddest traits endemic in the criminal classes, part of the same paranoia that leads them to believe they are invulnerable and therefore undetectable.

Despite his sense of humour however, there was no disguising the fact of Tony's family circumstances.

Their home was situated on a newish housing estate; one of the council projects conveniently located two miles out of town. Convenient some said, as it removed a large section of lower working class people out of the town. Hardwick, as it was called, was a soulless, new brick and concrete affair bereft of architectural character where public open space equated with somewhere to dump rubbish. Local wags would have one believe that the architects had seen fit to design the estate as a wind tunnel testing site and the accumulation of the community's flotsam, blown to fill any available corner or cul-de-sac, seemed to confirm the claim. Public entertainment facilities were notable only by their absence. For amusement, tenants were confined to drinking, watching television or witnessing the street fights that inevitably occurred outside of the pub after closing time. Some of the more perverse folk on the estate viewed the fight participants' supporters' competitive pissing against backstreet walls as further entertainment. Not surprisingly juvenile crime rates were as high as the feeling of disaffection amongst their parents.

If Bruce and Tony's home backgrounds described opposite ends of the social spectrum, mine more nearly approximated to the middle. I lived in a privately rented, corner-terraced house in Russell Street, only a short walk from the town centre. My Father had once been a floor manager in a big department store in Newcastle but after his motoring accident he had been made redundant. In their wisdom and to satisfy the needs of the job, his employers decided that floor managers needed two whole legs. One and a half legs would definitely not do. It was a welfare policy more suited to the kind of equal opportunity scheme as that practised in South Africa under apartheid. Thereafter, 'unsuitably' retrained, he worked in a Remploy factory near the river, binding books. A place where a man boasting one and a half legs might be seen to have distinct physical advantages over most of his workmates. I have a vague memory that he had once been a kind, tolerant dad. Unfortunately, the absence of one foot and half a shin seemed to have distorted his temperament, turning him into a bitter, frustrated tyrant who ruled his home domain like a Russian Czar.

On his return from work each evening, the pungent, clinging smell of leather and glue accompanied the clump of his prosthesis down the passage and would herald a change in my mother's mood. His arrival seemed to sap her confidence, visibly weakening her resolve. His view was that housewives had an easy life and should therefore observe an agenda entirely designed to satisfy the needs of their working husbands. Subsequently, should any small detail of his expectations not be met to his satisfaction, his exercise of moral blackmail and exhibitions of self-pity would be presaged by raging fits of bad temper. On these occasions the variety of his venom was encyclopaedic.

The lack of his understanding as it was applied to me was equally blatant. Mostly, he hid his disappointment with what he perceived as my lack of ambition behind a repeated emphasis on work ethic advice that was entirely alien to me. He would focus repeatedly on the need, as he put it, to 'apply oneself with real commitment,' as though by repeating this key phrase I would imbibe his meaning in one gulp. As though commitment was the key to success and as though 'luck' played no part in one's ultimate achievements. Needless to say, he was a seriously dissatisfied man. The only solace he found was in the strictest application of his religious practice. He was more Catholic than a cartload of Popes. Unfortunately it was a penance in which the rest of the household was obliged to share.

By the same token my father applied strictures to the economic management of the household that might have been more appropriate had we been at war or under siege conditions. Every penny had to be accounted for, every purchase justified. His perennial concern was waste and it was not unusual to find him scrutinising the contents of the dustbin seeking evidence of our profligacy. In the days when I was the recipient of pocket money, I was expected to explain my spending each Friday evening before the following week's allowance was allocated. Apparently the only way he could see of acquitting his financial responsibilities was by demanding that my mother and I were scrupulously prudent.

"Are you seeing that Miss Libby today?" Tony asked, whispering in my ear as we waited in the queue. "Cos if you are, you'd better have a good story ready. She's a real stickler."

I shrugged pretending I couldn't care less.

"He's right, Mickey," Bruce added, "I had to see her the last time I came and she sent me to the bloody Mallable – as if someone like me would work in a fucking factory."

In fairness, the visits we were obliged to make to the DSS offices were the only regular trial we had to suffer in this respect. And, whilst we made a pretence to one another of anarchic indifference, every visit nevertheless proved a test of nerves. Having been drawing benefit for more than three months without a single job interview, I had been notified by post that I was to see Ms Libby to discuss my prospects – Social Security code speak for 'explain yourself and show willing or lose your dole money'.

Ms. Libby proved to be the surprising exception. A small woman with grey, bespectacled eyes she had a friendly disposition and seemed genuinely to want to help. Reading from her notes, she first recited the litany of my qualifications and then made polite inquiries regarding my interests. There was no intimidation, no transfer of guilt and no mention of me not trying to find work. She referred to an aptitude test I had taken weeks ago and, based on the results, without any malice she described to me both my strengths and my weaknesses.

"Michael, you have well-above average intelligence but I'm afraid you find difficulty in dealing with authority figures," she said smiling. "Just between you and me, I understand how you feel as I have the same problem myself."

I grinned back and agreed that one of my pet hates was anyone who flaunted their status. She conducted the rest of the interview in a fairly light-hearted manner after that and, although later, she said I had a tendency to be self-indulgent and was inclined to be lazy, her pronouncements were not accusatory. In fact the accuracy of her analysis surprised me and, despite myself, I found I was beginning to like her. At some point I made her laugh when I commented how she might make herself wealthy by opening a counselling service in Harley Street, rather than doing fortune telling for the DSS.

In all, the interview lasted forty minutes but before I left her desk, Ms Libby had persuaded me to fill out an application for a fine art course at the local art college. Of course I had no intention of attending such a place, going back to a school of any description was a non-starter – and more importantly, as far as I was aware there was no money to made being an artist.

Back in the Citroen minutes later, I was careful to avoid telling my friends about the application form and justified it to myself as being the only way to keep Ms Libby off my back. Tony and Bruce had a good laugh at what they imagined was my discomfort in the interview but then we adjourned to the welcome midday quiet of the *Castle and Anchor* on the High Street. This was our regular watering hole after signing on, a place where we could commiserate with one another and an oasis of calm with alcohol as the universal palliative. Our visits to the DSS always left us feeling depressed. The regular money orders allowed us only a modicum of financial freedom and our dependency on the state left us subject to the close scrutiny of social services staff. We felt we were at the bottom of the social hierarchy.

Inevitably, the subject of money was the focus of our attention on these occasions.

"We've got t'make some cash," Tony said, sipping his pint of bitter.

"And quick," Bruce added.

"Then we'd better consider a life of crime," I answered, "cos it seems there's no way we'll get hold of any money otherwise."

My suggestion was made only as a joke but the others responded to it seriously, proving once and for all that it had long since been a consideration at the back of their minds also. They began to itemise the possible options.

"There's no way we could organise a bank job," Bruce offered unnecessarily.

"Or any kind of stick-up," Tony said. "But we might want to consider burglary."

Now given his family history, Tony's solution surprised no one and as there were no alternatives on offer, we began to examine his suggestion more carefully. The problem was – who to burgle and what to take should we manage to get into whatever establishment we set our sights on. Being the self-confessed expert, Tony took centre stage. He was a mine of information. He told us that there was big cash to be made and that he knew someone – a 'fence' – who would buy anything we got hold of.

"Me dad uses him all the time – a Jew-boy – but a nice guy nevertheless. And he gives a fair price. It's a piece of piss."

His confidence however, was not infectious. I didn't want to remind him that his dad was currently serving a term, having been caught in the act. And, if being caught doing it wasn't enough, Tony senior had not thrown up his hands and called it a fair cop like the cinema-going public were led to believe all burglars did, instead he'd beaten the shit out of a security guard with a club and been done for GBH as well. 'A piece of piss' was not at all the way to describe the way he practised his profession.

Bruce was not quite so sensitive.

"Your dad's in prison isn't he?" he asked meaningfully.

Tony wasn't fazed at all. "That's no surprise, he has no idea," he said, "like a bull at a tea party he is – always comes unstuck. He's only been home for three Christmases since I can remember. Any time there's a break-in accompanied by violence the coppers come round for him – and most of the time, they aren't wrong. I wasn't suggesting we follow his example – just that we use the expertise I've acquired from watching him."

Bruce was still unconvinced; "Yeah – but just so we understand one another – let's make sure there's no violence. Eh, Mick?"

I struggled not to smile. Bruce stood six foot two in his socks but had no stomach for a fistfight. He had always relied on a silver tongue and long legs to get him out of trouble ever since primary school. However, I nodded my agreement without comment. Unlike our tall friend, Tony and I didn't mind a punch-up when it was warranted or when we had the advantage – but like both my friends I had an aversion to the very idea of going to prison.

"And if we have a no violence rule," I added, "let's also have an agreement those no one talks either. I mean – if we got nicked, let's agree that we keep quiet – eh?" I said meaningfully.

Nobody argued with that but I had my fingers crossed.

Having agreed basic ground-rules we spent the next hour or more trying to decide on a suitable focus for our first 'job'. Still imbued with childish, Robin Hood-type romantic notions, we agreed that we should target only the rich. In practical terms we said this made sense.

"It wouldn't be much use burgling poor people", Tony rightly argued.

The problem was that most local rich people were, to our knowledge, neighbours of Bruce's family. It seemed that anyone worthy of our attention lived in Hartburn. As a consequence, Bruce naturally found fault with every suggestion. He claimed first-hand knowledge of neighbours with sophisticated alarm systems, about others who owned guard dogs and still more who possessed shotguns. One name was rejected on the basis that the man of the house had once been a professional boxer and another, on account of the security shutters he knew were in place at all the downstairs windows. Indeed, although he denied it, eventually it seemed to both Tony and me that such was Bruce's intimate knowledge of his neighbours' crime prevention details that he must have considered burglary before. In the end we had to agree that finding a sufficiently ill-prepared, rich victim was a good deal more difficult and time consuming than any of us had ever imagined. We parted company without having resolved the conundrum but agreed to meet again that evening in *Jock-o-Browns* to consider the matter further. On my way home I found that suddenly I had a growing respect for Mr Durham senior and began to understand some of his frustration at being caught.

I spent the remainder of the afternoon as usual, in front of the TV. Bored with the reports of the Vietnam War and Nixon winning the presidential election, I slept off the beer and watched most of an old black and white movie, a cowboy, with Randolph Scott playing the hero. Mam worked away steadily in the kitchen preparing the evening meal and doing the ironing. She woke me just after five with a cup of tea and a couple of chocolate digestive biscuits.

"You look whacked, son," she said, brushing my hair back from my brow. "Did you see anything worthwhile this morning?"

It was a standard issue inquiry made in the hope that one day I might find paid employment. From my point of view however, it was a comment made to emphasise that finding a job was becoming an emergency. A matriarchal pressure I felt I could well do without.

"Oh yes, Mam," I replied, honing the sarcastic edge of my voice to just within acceptable limits. "I found lots of possibilities – that is if you want to see me working a till in Woolworths or investing my A levels in becoming a caretaker for some shitty printing works. Sure there were lots of grand openings."

She looked hurt.

"I only asked, son," she said defensively. "You know your dad and me only want what's best for you." She paused and then added, "It's just that, at the moment – money's a bit tight…"

I sat up quickly. That was a foul – below the belt. All well and good reminding me about getting a job – but to get all sly and critical just because I didn't contribute to the family budget – yet. That wasn't fair. "Then you'd better have my dole money," I said. I struggled unconvincingly to reach my trouser pocket but my mother protested. She laid a hand on my shoulder and said something about not wanting to take money from me, especially as it was so little anyway. This was just as well as I had little more than small change left anyway. Her eyes were damp when I looked and I hoped she wasn't going to turn the tears on. I can't stand tearful demonstrations. In the end, thankfully after only brief reassurances of her continued support, she kissed me on the cheek and left me to my TV cowboy and my snack.

This little episode gave me food for thought. It was my firm belief that parents should keep their children for as long as it was necessary. Otherwise – don't have children. This much was common sense. Clearly her petition was the first explicit sign that they did not want to continue to be financially responsible for me. Needless to say, I had not asked to be 'born' into a family where the father went and got himself crippled, or to have parents with a joint IQ less than their shoe size. Their problems were not of my making, so why should I suffer. In my view they had never properly understood me. No surprise in that as I was not their 'natural' child.

On my twelfth birthday, perhaps as a treat for passing the scholarship, they had announced to me that I had been adopted. Although this shocked me, it justified my feeling that I was a foreigner in their midst. This news had changed everything and afterwards, although the lovey-dovey stuff was still practised occasionally, I knew that all the sloppy kisses and Christmas hugs in the world would never make me a blood relative. It followed that they'd deliberately spoiled my chances of being adopted by a rich family and such selfishness was unforgivable. Now apparently it was 'crunch' time.

I knew from one of the Asian kids at school that in some societies, just like in pre-nuptial agreements, offspring are brainwashed into promising financial responsibility for their parents when they get old. They had to guarantee a provision for the old folks. Like you had to ensure that your mam and dad's last years would be encased in a rosy glow of mandatory, feet-up TV watching and paid-for holidays abroad; waited on hand and foot with à la carte meals-on-wheels on constant tap. Like hell! How primitive can you get? And if you devoted years and years to looking after your parents it would be unlikely that you would have children of your own – unless you adopted some. The point was well made and the jury's verdict had to be guilty as charged.

I rested the case for the prosecution and sipped my coffee. I was satisfied that such a scenario would not – could not – apply to me. There was no feeling of guilt in my resolution, and no regrets. I knew that even if my adoptive parents were to pop their clogs that very night, other than a meagre inheritance, it would mean little or nothing to me.

An hour or so later I heard my father arrive home. He shuffled past the front room dragging his gammy foot. I heard him mumbling to himself complaining about the weather, about factory politics and the vagaries of the local bus service – the usual moans and groans. But just before the kitchen door closed behind him I heard him ask if I was home. The rest of what he said was lost. Doubtless he was checking to see if his son had achieved the impossible and obtained work – checking on his investment, looking forward implicitly to an easy option. Once complaints about the weather and the job were aired, his next gripe was inevitably to query my activities. An interest, I grew to believe, that was entirely derived from the vain hope that one day I would assume sole responsibility for his financial welfare.

"Don't hold your breath – bastard," I muttered.

To make matters worse, my parents were increasingly obsessive about their Catholicism. The ardour of their mode of observance was little short of ridiculous. Their brand of religious fervour was taken almost to the point of fanaticism and the symbols of their religion permeated every facet of our daily lives. There was, for example, an element of ritual associated even with mealtimes, an emphasis that reduced the more normal atmosphere of such a social gathering to one more appropriately redolent of a church service. Having been raised in this ethos, I was well used to the symbolism, versed in the associated meanings and entirely familiar with the faulty reasoning. However, by the time I reached my teens, I could no longer share the beliefs implicit in my parents' actions. It was yet another area of divergence. Not surprisingly, my feelings of alienation in this regard were always greatest at the dinner table. The evening meal was an occasion when the thanks given to God both before and after eating, often took longer than the eating did. Then there was the Kafkaesque emphasis placed on the number three.

It had been explained to me when I was still in the infant school that in our home, evening mealtimes would seek to echo the mystery of the Holy Trinity: the 'three men in a boat' syndrome designed to confound the best brains in Britain and further confuse the worldwide uninitiated. Typically, no explanation regarding why this should be so was ever given. It was a fact and, like other dictums of faith, it could not be questioned. Consequently, at dinner there would be three courses for three people, three vegetables with the main course and three pieces of tinned fruit submerged beneath evaporated milk as the pudding (it was usually tinned fruit). The father was always served first and the son next, a further enhancement of the religious imagery. Leaving the Holy Ghost to serve herself last.

Naturally, I was ever reluctant to accept confirmation of my role in this hierarchy. After all it was the son who had ended up losing the argument, getting a real kicking and being nailed to a cross. I had no intention of satisfying that role.

In my view the religious metaphor was ridiculous. Eating was essentially a body refuelling exercise. At best a social occasion. You want to pray – go to church; you want to eat then sit at a table – some hope. To make matters even more uncomfortable, we were constantly overlooked by images of Jesus and Mary His Mother, pastiches of which were hung either side of the fireplace. I remember them well. In one, a sadly demure Caucasian Mary casts down her eyes whilst her exposed heart – torn in half – floats between the merest suggestion of breasts hidden beneath the folds of a white nightdress. With her hands outspread it was hard to decide if her obvious pain was generated by her concerns regarding her son's terrorism, her virginal state or through the failure of her abortive heart transplant operation. In the other, a thoroughly blood-soaked, hippie Jesus with looks not too dissimilar from those of Cary Grant the movie heart-throb, pointed to his own transplant. His heart dripped gore due to it being encased, as his head was, in a thorny twig from somebody's prize floribunda. His T-shirt was also bloodstained and the gashes in the palms of his hands really needed several stitches. At aged seven, I once asked if there had not been Elastoplasts in those days, a question, I recall, that had cost me my pudding that day.

The lesson learnt; subsequently I kept such inquiries to myself.

On the other hand, I might well have found the ethos of the evening meal more tolerable had the quality of the food been more exceptional. Unfortunately the denizens of my home had yet to discover healthy eating, still less to value festive foods. Pedestrian is the word that springs to mind and any similarity to those feasts referred to in the Old Testament were entirely accidental. In this instance, my parents' enthusiasm for making the Good Book a reality ended with the theoretical. On this particular occasion for example, I observed that there was no fatted calf as enjoyed by Moses, no sweetmeats or larks' tongues as in Biblical feasts of yore, still less the guinea fowl and stuffed swan of the traditional medieval Vatican court. Instead we were served an anglicised rendition of pasta: an anaemic macaroni cheese garnished with chips and frozen peas.

What could one say? Bad enough to pervert the pasta – sufficient to make it a solid mass – but the addition of soggy chips and frozen peas was to make a meal that one might find objectionable in any 'greasy spoon' down any motorway. It was the kind of culinary treat that, for generations, has subjected the digestive tracts of lorry drivers to acid more corrosive than that found in car batteries. A black comedy. Furthermore, the 'Italian' dinner was sandwiched between much-diluted mushroom soup, courtesy of Campbell's as the starter and three pieces of sliced Del Monte peach, as ever, swamped in evaporated milk that posed as our pudding. "You'll like this, Michael," my mother said as we sat down, "I did it special because I know how you enjoy foreign food."

There was little I could say.

By far the most irritating condition imposed on the family's evening meal however, was the rule of silence. Whilst food was being eaten no one was allowed to speak. It was an addition invented by dad, obviously meant to raise our spirits and jolly along the occasion. Conversation was permitted only when coffee had been served. That evening, as soon as the cups were filled, the interrogation about my job prospects began in earnest. This sequel included an impromptu rehearsal orchestrated by my father, for an imaginary interview for a job with Barclay's bank.

It appeared that working for a bank or building society was seen by both my parents as the highest possible pinnacle of achievement to which I might aspire. Presumably a notion founded on the importance they placed on thrift and 'the ability to apply oneself with real commitment'. In his previous place of work, due to a temporary absence of the personnel officer, dad had once been responsible for staff in-service training and, although it had been for only a short period of time, he claimed thereafter to have specialist knowledge of that area. It was often a weakness of his to lay claim to expertise in all sorts of different areas after only the briefest association, a sure sign of his chronic arrogance. On this occasion, he had clearly spent considerable time inventing the most obtuse interview questions his imagination could conjure. He had not however, developed his theme far enough to decide what the ideal answers might be. The only conclusion reached in that respect was that those I offered were totally unsuitable. When for example I was asked why I wanted a job with the bank, the reply I made, "Because I'd like to handle other people's money," was seen as flippant. Equally my interest in seeing the private accounts belonging to our neighbours was thought to be unprofessional. The fact that I had no interest in Banking and no intention of ever applying for a job in that sector failed to impress or influence the occasion and I was able to escape the flow of endlessly boring clichés and homilies, only by volunteering to do the washing-up.

From my position at the kitchen sink I was able to listen in to some of the conversation between my parents in my absence. It was a rare treat to have the unedited version first hand. However, it was not so much an exchange of views that I heard, just the machinegun-like diatribe of abuse from my father to Mam. Typically once his critical engine had been fired up and without me to harass, George Grainger brought what passed for his critical faculties to bear on his wife. In the first instance he commented on her cooking, and however accurate his reflections they were a cruel and unnecessary series of sarcastic comparisons that soon had her in tears. Undaunted, he applied the same level of caustic acid to her appearance, comparing her to some "handsome woman" he had seen in a big car near his works that day. It was not long before I heard her leave the dining room to sniffle her way upstairs to the private sanctuary of the bathroom.

Cruelty, I decided, was a characteristic of George Grainger, a trait he had honed to perfection. And, although he liked to imply that his attitude was rooted in his disability and the disappointments he had suffered professionally, these were only excuses.

"I get so frustrated, Nell," he would say to his wife a little later through the bathroom door, "and I suppose it's that, that causes me to be so bitchy."

'Like hell,' I thought.

As usual Mam quickly forgave him, so becoming a co-conspirator in his justification fantasy and therefore an equally culpable participant in her own abuse. Despite my vague recollections of better times, I was quite prepared to believe that Dad had always been an evil old sod and that his accident, his physical impairment and the ensuing loss of status he suffered were just pegs on which to hang his hat of aggressive ignorance.

In my experience he was not the only one to exhibit such a tendency. In fact his behaviour was typical of his kind. I had noticed, during my occasional visits to his place of work, that a similar cruelty was apparent in the behaviour of many of his workmates both to their family members and to their colleagues. Indeed, as a consequence, I had grown to believe that those affected by serious disability were often so bitter that they turned their latent anger on those nearest and dearest to them. It was as if they sought to lay the blame for whatever had happened to them on someone else – or, however irrationally, as a revenge on society at large.

My private response was to emphasise the most irreverent and, I believe, the most honest reaction of which I was capable. And this despite the popular climate of so-called, 'political correctness'. Who could doubt that a man with one leg – or even one and a half legs – was funny? So many comedy sketches on TV and cartoon characters make the same point. Or that a birthmark, especially on the face, was ugly. If beauty can be defined as often as it is in the press, then no one can surely deny the fact of ugliness. It's just the opposite end of the same spectrum. Equally, in shopping areas, a wheelchair is undoubtedly a bloody nuisance and those people with a stutter aren't worth wasting one's time listening to. These are opinions that simply reflect my judgement call and are my reaction to the grossly bad-tempered behaviour exhibited by those afflicted by these various complaints. In my view it does no good pretending that cripples and freaks are normal. They know, just as we do, that they are anything but normal. I left the house as soon as the pots were done and without a backward glance I went out to meet my mates.

Chapter Two

Our initial criminal act had been rehearsed until we were step-perfect and, like a football team revving up confidence for the big game, once the strategy was agreed we had reassured one another with guttural air-punching gestures and cries of "Yeah" and "But Right-on." Despite the preparation however, I was secretly glad that it was nearly dark when we made our move. When it's cold and dark people don't pay too much attention to their neighbours or their surroundings – I reasoned.

Bruce acted as the lookout, positioning himself at the corner whilst Tony and I walked briskly into the car park. Our walk said it all. We didn't just stroll; we walked with purpose, like we had somewhere we had to be. I wore my suit and carried a Times newspaper under my arm, Tony carried a briefcase. To the casual observer we belonged in the car park, we had business there. We were used to parking our cars in posh car parks and nobody was about to challenge a couple of guys with such obvious justification. Ninety-nine percent confident of success we toured the ranks of cars in the late evening gloom.

Half way down the second row of cars, I looked at my watch and shook my head. Actions that implied Tony had forgotten where he had parked the car. I acted angry and Tony performed apologies. It was an understood scenario and anyone who might have been paying attention would be left in no doubt about what was happening. A moment or two later I followed my friend to a big Ford that he had picked out. A new top-of-the-range model, polished and well cared for. There were a couple of suitcases on the back seat and a handbag, prizes for the taking. Tony took only seven seconds to get the door open. As smooth an operation as the workings of a Rolex watch. He even shut off the alarm.

Back at the corner moments later Bruce took one of the cases and we toed the pavement back to the Citroen parked across the street. It was a perfect job. We didn't speak until we were half a mile down the road. The loot was driven round to Tony's house to be examined secretly at our leisure in his bedroom.

His mam was a right character. When she saw the suitcases she asked if we were moving in. Quick as a flash her son said, "Don't be daft, Mam. Bruce is off for the weekend. He's just called round here before he goes to the railway station."

She just smiled. She'd seen it all before.

The cases were opened quickly and the winnings spread across the single bed. The clothing was okay, two men's suits and a variety of women's dresses – some expensive looking, plus underwear and shirts and the usual stuff people pack for a holiday. However, the handbag proved to be the real prize. It contained a wallet with thirty-five quid in it and a leather pouch. The pouch held seven rings, a thin gold chain and a bracelet studded with what looked like tiny diamonds.

It had been my idea but once we had agreed to target cars rather than risk a break-in, it had still taken us four days to find a likely place to strike. Four days equal to eight sessions in the pub to work up sufficient courage – now we'd done it. More importantly we'd done it successfully and without being caught in the act.

Our escapade was small beer by comparison to the crimes that other miscreants regularly enacted. Nevertheless I still choose to believe that the feeling of satisfaction associated with breaking the law – and not being captured whilst doing it – was one of the greatest. It confirmed a sense of superiority. It made us imagine that we were cleverer than our neighbours were and it allowed us to enshrine a secret more precious than any we had previously shared. Successful thieving was a narcotic and that night we were all high on its effect.

Once the initial euphoria had passed however, we were faced with the final task of selling anything of value for whatever we could get.

"So – how do we get shot of the jewellery then?" Bruce asked.

"We'll take it to Jack Zimmerman like I said we should," Tony replied. "He can be trusted and he'll give us cash straightaway."

"You sure about trusting him?" I asked doubtfully.

"Completely certain. He's gold-plated," Tony said quickly. "Me dad used to take everything to him."

"How about the threads?" Bruce persisted. "Does he do clothing?"

Tony looked uncertain.

"If not we'll have to dump 'em," I added.

"To be honest – I don't know if he'll take clothes… mind… some of this is good clobber."

As he spoke this time Tony picked out one of the jackets and slipped it on. It might have been tailor-made for him.

"Smart eh," he said doing a twirl. "I might keep this one for myself."

"Never mind all that," Bruce snapped. "We didn't do the job just so we could get new suits. More importantly what are they worth?"

"More importantly still – we don't want to keep anything that can finger us for the job. It's crazy to keep stuff," I said. "Anyway, the real value is in the trinkets not the old clothes."

I picked up the bracelet for the tenth time and looked at it closely. It contained a collection of green stones set against smaller white ones against a heavy gold strap.

"I mean these could be emeralds set with diamonds. It's got to be worth a few hundred."

The others fell silent at the mention of such a sum. Money had been a scarce commodity in recent months and the thought of sudden wealth left us imagining what we could do with our individual shares.

"So…" Bruce whispered, "we might be talking about more than a thousand quid – for the lot."

The pause for consideration lengthened. Suddenly this first crime held the prospect of a new reality – a possible solution to all our economic conundrums

"Course – we'll have to be careful," Tony started to say.

"That goes without saying," Bruce interrupted.

"No, what I mean," Tony went on, "what I mean is – if someone had a thousand quids' worth of stuff from my motor, I'd have all my friends take a serious look for them."

That was a sobering thought. I did not realise until then that we had no idea who our victim might have been, or how much influence he might have. If it turned out that he was well placed then the police would be extra keen to get his gear back. Things could get very busy.

Privately, I decided there and then that I would not be the one to negotiate a deal with Mr Zimmerman. As a precaution I would encourage one of the others to trade the stolen goods in order that Mr Zimmerman at least would not be able to identify me – even if he were 'gold-plated' as Tony claimed. Clearly Bruce was thinking along the same lines.

"I think we should ask Tony to do a deal with this Zimmerman character. What do you say, Mick?" he said.

I nodded, "Makes good sense. We don't want to go in there mob-handed and he knows you – doesn't he, Tony?"

Tony looked pleased, "Sort of. I met him once – but I'm sure he'll remember me."

The meeting was arranged by telephone and two nights later Bruce and me waited across the road from a pawn shop on the edge of a shopping area close to the town centre in Middlesbrough whilst Tony did the business. As scheduled, Tony had entered the premises at six o'clock carrying the goods in their original cases. It was cold sitting in the car and, although our anticipation of the result was high, the longer we waited, the greater our discomfort and the deeper our concern. Earlier in the day snow had fallen and as the light disappeared the temperature dropped below freezing. The pavements shone and the ruts left in the road were soon hardened troughs. I sat on my hands and tucked my chin deep down into the neck of my sweater.

"He's been a helluva long time," Bruce muttered for the fourth time.

Unfortunately, as we were still only embryonic criminals, neither of us had any idea how long such a negotiation should take. Moreover, our initial confidence in Tony's ability soon began to wain. It sagged increasingly as time passed. Clearly there was no set price for stolen jewellery and we expected Zimmerman to pitch his first bid as low as he thought he could get away with. How low that might be however, we had no idea.

Meanwhile the wind-chill factor increased and the two of us in the old Citroen struggled to maintain our circulation as much as we did our confidence. In fact it was fifty-five minutes before Tony reappeared, by which time the cold having tested our humour, we were in no mood to tolerate what he had to tell us.

"Well," Bruce demanded as soon as Tony got back into the back seat, "how did we do?"

"First off he said the clothing had no street value – but he said he would get shot of it just to save us the trouble."

Tony's half embarrassed opening gave me a premonition of failure. It left me with a kind of weakness in my bladder; a sure indication all had not gone to plan.

"So you left them with him anyway?" I asked, already knowing the answer.

"Yeah – well, no good us toting them around..."

"And the rest – the rings and stuff – what about them?"

Tony's response was to pull a bundle of bank notes from his jacket pocket. "I got us two hundred and seventy quid for the lot." he said.

Now, if someone had told us a week before that we would have that kind of money, what amounted to almost a hundred pounds each, handed to us for a couple of hours work, we might have seen it as cause for celebration. Now however, we had been touched already by the greed and suspicion inherent in our chosen profession. Bruce's mouth acquired a twisted wrinkle of disbelief and he stared hard into Tony's face

"Are you asking us to believe that you let the old bastard have all that gear for a miserable two-seventy. Cos if you are me old mate, you must think we're just off the banana boat."

"Are you accusing me of trying to fiddle you?"

"Oh – when I get to that part – you'll know all about it I promise. Tell us exactly what Zimmerman said."

For the next thirty minutes or so Tony was subject to the kind of cross-examination more usually reserved for the prime suspect in a murder inquiry. With respect to the bracelet, it appeared that our Mister Zimmerman had said the white stones were only 'brilliants' – tiny diamonds with little real value and, far from being emeralds, the green stones were peridots. He told Tony that the poor settings in both the bracelet and the rings detracted from their resale value and that he would probably have to break them up to get his money back.

Throughout this investigation I argued and Bruce objected every time Zimmerman was quoted. We cast doubt on his skill and then questioned his honesty. We even raised a question about Tony's negotiating ability and then finally, Bruce lost his temper. But none of it made any real difference. Nothing anyone said could change the outcome.

Tempers eventually cooled but the atmosphere in the car was still charged with suspicion and disappointment and as the focus of this was indistinct there was a feeling of unease. Once we had time to consider the situation, I'm sure neither of us actually believed Tony would cheat us. The worst he might be accused of therefore was a lack of skill in dealing with Zimmerman. From his silence however, it became obvious that his pride had been badly fractured. His face was white and he sat slumped back into the seat chain-smoking, taking long drags on his cigarette and blowing a thin stream of smoke at the roof of the car. It was finally up to me to play the peacemaker.

"Anyway – what if Zimmerman has ripped us off – what if Tony was brow-beaten into taking a bad deal – it isn't the end of the world… and for a change we've got some money."

My proclamation did the trick and the others nodded their accommodation.

"All it means is that we have some readies," I said, "– some real cash in our pockets – and that can't be a bad thing. Can it?"

The nodding heads continued to nod.

We soon forgot our complaints and cheered considerably when we set about dividing the bundle of five pound notes into three equal piles. Afterwards we adjourned to the pub back in Stockton and began to do some serious drinking.

We left the bar at nine thirty and on an impulse agreed to hit on another car that same night. Fortified by the alcohol and feeling high on success, this time we were more confident than ever. We marched into the same car park laughing and joking and, after picking out the biggest, most expensive-looking car, we went to work as though it was the most normal thing in the world.

*

Although it may have few claims to fame, Stockton-on-Tees can still boast one of the widest high streets in England. Its dimensions are such that on two days every week, it hosts an open market along its central reservation without restricting the dual carriageways that run along either side. Each Wednesday and Saturday street-traders come from far and wide to sell a variety of goods that encompass the whole spectrum of foodstuffs, of hardware, textiles, electrical and paper goods and household effects. Needless to say, on market days the town bustles with visitors. Parking becomes impossible but the pubs stay open all day.

Two mornings after our latest escapade was a Wednesday and therefore a market day. Consequently, it was a day that we intended to spend drinking. I was in the act of opening the front door that morning when Mam shouted to me from the kitchen. A letter addressed to me had arrived from the principal of the art college. It arranged for me to attend an interview on the following Monday morning at ten a.m. My mentor Miss Libby had clearly forwarded the application and with impressive results. Mam was delighted.

"Won't your dad be pleased," she cooed, taking the letter to read it for herself. "He always said you were talented. Just think – you could become a real artist."

I found her emphasis on the word 'real' irritating, as though 'real' artists needed confirmation of the fact from the education system.

"Van Gogh never went to art college, Mam, neither did Michelangelo, nor for that matter any of the…"

It was an excuse for me to apply my usual brand of cynical sarcasm but, in this case, it went unnoticed. Nothing could dampen my mother's excitement and, as I left the house, she was cheering herself by imagining me being called to paint portraits of the Royal Family.

The town was crowded. As usual on market days, it was a Mecca for all the fervent shoppers in the region and some would make the trek from as far away as Dormanstown on the far side of Middlesbrough. However, not all the visitors were interested in shopping; some came to indulge in the more than usual lengthy opportunity afforded by the extended licensing laws. Not surprisingly therefore, another characteristic of market days was the frequency of drunkenness. Often by the time the pubs eventually closed, the High Street would be populated by groups of men, many of whom found it difficult to stay upright, see straight or, still less, avoid involvement in fights. The sobriquet of 'Dodge City' most often applied to the town by local sages was therefore one commonly accepted as regretfully most appropriate.

I would not normally have been up and about quite so early in the morning and, had it not been for the turn of events the previous evening, I would certainly have remained under my eiderdown until well past midday. However, as a consequence of our latest foray into the world of petty crime, Bruce and Tony had agreed to meet me that lunchtime in the bar of a pub well away from the main thoroughfare, one in which we were almost strangers. Bruce was already there when I arrived and I ordered him a pint of Bass. He looked worried when I returned to the corner table.

"What a fucking cock-up," he whispered. "A bloody good job I had the motor running, or else we'd all be behind bars."

I could not disagree, "Fair play though," I replied. "We weren't to know that the bastard driver would be sleeping it off in the back of his car."

Bruce pulled a face, "Of course not," he hissed back. "Not as though either of you had eyes, not as though the car had windows either." He gulped his drink, "My God – fancy breaking into a car when the owner is still in it. It qualifies for a Goon's script."

The taproom bar was crowded and as usual Tony was late arriving. I was ordering another round at the bar when he came through the door and we exchanged nods of acknowledgement as he went to Bruce's table. I had just paid for the drinks and was in the process of organising the glasses to carry all three together when a guy who had followed Tony and stood alongside me at the bar, spoke. He was a man in his thirties and his accent was bog-standard Sunderland.

"I bet that third pint is for Tony." he said with a sly grin.

I had little or no patience when it came to smart arses in bars so I ignored the comment. It was not a pub that I'd used often so I couldn't say for certain where or if I'd met the guy with the grin before. However, as I set the glasses down on the corner table I found that the grin had followed me.

"And you must be Bruce," he said still grinning, nodding in the direction of my friend.

"Who's your mate?" Bruce asked.

"Never saw him before," I replied, feeling my irritation rate increase… "But if he takes my advice, he'll fuck right off before I have to find out."

Tony laughed and picked up his glass. He sipped the beer and then turned to the man, "Take my advice, Geordie, and make your exit whilst you can still walk."

*

I recognised the car driver immediately. The image of his expression was etched forever on my photographic memory plates recording our recent trauma. It would be hard to forget him – ever. Tony had just snapped up the driver's side door-lock when his white face had appeared from behind the back seat – like a bloody ghost. Shock set in. I couldn't believe it and my reactions had gone into automatic. I caught my breath, a sweat broke out and my bowels began to move of their own accord but I was three strides away already when I heard Tony yell. I turned to look back, just in time to see my friend struggle to release the hand that gripped his jacket. Suddenly he punched the white face. A solid bone on bone contact, a right hook efficiently delivered. The face disappeared. Now, it sat staring at me across the other side of the police inspector's desk. This time sporting a bruise that spanned the bridge of the nose and encompassed both eyes, making its owner look surprisingly like the Lone Ranger.

The loudmouth in the pub had finally declared his interests by flashing his warrant card and introducing himself as DI Causer from the local CID. He told us we were required to accompany him to the Station where we would be charged with attempted theft of a car and with aggravated assault. It was a nightmare come true. Bruce was so upset he spilt his beer – and Causer had continued to grin.

Save for Tony's juvenile record, none of us had ever been arrested before and if anyone had proposed such a possibility I would have probably argued that escape would be high on my list of options. Since childhood I'd watched Jimmy Cagney, Humphrey Bogart and a long line of other heroes all make good their escape from law officers in black and white. I'd seen the car chases and the rooftop shoot-outs, the precarious struggles on narrow ledges and the lucky break when the sheriff passed by. Faced with the same situation, I found that real life was very different. We went quietly.

Once we were seated in his sparsely furnished office, Detective Inspector Causer called on the victim to identify us. However, before the man could react, Bruce suddenly became hyperactive. When our arrest had been announced in the pub, his face had gone blotchy and he'd said nothing since then. I thought it was just nerves but it went deeper than that.

"Just a minute Inspector," he said loudly, his blotches joining up to produce a fully reddened face, "if this is some kind of identity parade – then it's illegal."

The proceedings halted for a moment and then Causer asked quietly, "And why would you imagine that?"

"Because in an identity parade, those arrested need to be kept separate from…"

Causer did not let him finish. "Young man," he said brusquely, "I hope you aren't trying to instruct me as to the legality of ID parades. For your information, you were not actually arrested – but asked to assist in our inquiries. And this is not a 'parade' as such."

"So we're not under arrest?"

This time it was Tony who asked the question. The Inspector looked him in the face; "Not as yet, Tony – but I suspect out of the three of you, you will be the one to be charged. You could be soon keeping your dad company."

"In which case I want to consult with a lawyer," Bruce demanded.

"As you are not under arrest – as yet, there is no requirement, no onus on the police to allow that facility. Now – as I was about to say…"

"Well if we're not under arrest then I presume we are free to leave?"

This time Bruce's question made the policeman flush in anger.

"Okay," he muttered, "as you insist on the full formality, I am arresting you…"

He completed the official warnings required under law and Bruce promptly asked again to see his lawyer. He was quickly escorted to another room to use a telephone. The Inspector turned to me and asked, "And do you want your solicitor as well Mister Grainger?"

I shook my head. I didn't know any solicitors so I didn't have one to call. Instead I replied, "I am entirely innocent so I don't see the necessity."

For a moment Causer studied me then he turned to the Lone Ranger and asked him if he could identify me. The man looked at me, a long look. He dabbed his swollen eye with a white handkerchief before he replied.

"I can't be one hundred percent. The trouble is – I didn't see that one's face – not clearly anyway. Sorry."

The uniformed constable who stood at the door made a sigh of resignation and Causer's mouth tightened. Identification was clearly the whole basis of their case.

"Okay, Grainger, I want you to go and wait in the other room. There's another matter that you may be able to help us with but that can wait for the moment."

On the way out I bumped into Bruce. His mouth was set in a determined line and his face had paled. He ignored me like his mind was elsewhere. Apparently the advice from his solicitor had been to say nothing. Causer talked to me later on my own, appealing to my good nature as evident in my family background and trying to get me to admit to the previous car theft. I told him I didn't know what he was talking about but, as a sop to his sincerity, I added that maybe Tony had done both jobs on his own.

It fact it turned out that Tony was the only one who could be identified. His juvenile record for shoplifting had provided a recognisable description and, as there were two characters seen with him, we were judged guilty by association. It had not taken an investigation of Maigret proportions to discover all our identities and we'd been easy to find simply by following Tony. The upshot of this episode was that some days later Tony appeared before the Magistrates where he was found guilty of assault. The Beak was sympathetic however. Having been plied with stories of Tony's home situation he gave our friend a three-month suspended sentence and bound him over to keep the peace. As there was no evidence of any substance against us, Bruce and me got off, virtually scot-free.

Fortunately, at the time of our arrest none of us had any unreasonable amount of money in our possession and, as there was no request made to search our homes, our previous 'winnings' went undiscovered. The only penalty imposed on me and Bruce was a tortuous lecture, delivered by Inspector Causer, on the dangers of choosing a life of crime. He told us finally that he had a suspicion that we were involved and that he had no doubt that we would meet again.

Despite our bravado at the police station, in a funny kind of way Causer's warnings did have the desired effect and we agreed to suspend our criminal operations for the foreseeable future. I believe that, like me, my friends were horrified by the prospect of being locked away and were only too pleased to return to the straight and narrow path. It was odd however, that each of us should fall so short of our own self-image. Odd also that on the way home from the court that day, I saw DUD on an old Ford Prefect. I couldn't decide if it referred to me or to one of my friends.

As a matter of course, all our parents had been kept informed of developments and, judging by their reaction, I was left in doubt as to whom the DUD referred. Subsequently, I was subjected to a series of warnings and threats from my father, as it were, the voice of God warning an insignificant Israelite to mind his behaviour. The fact that I had not been charged was immaterial in the eyes of my parents. They were convinced of my guilt and certain thereafter of my place alongside Hitler and Jack the Ripper in the deepest pit of Satan's inferno. I was confirmed as the black sheep, the sinner and had at last realised their worst fears about my character. That day and for some days afterwards, my father wore an expression in my presence; similar to that one might associate with the look of hopelessness seen on the faces of the relatives of the condemned man. He summed up his obvious disgust by telling me that now I'd never get a job with a bank and, although I made no comment, for me this was a disappointment on a par with a football pools win. My parents had overreacted as usual – wasn't I innocent until proven guilty? Didn't the burden of proof lay with the prosecution? But it was to get worse before it got better.

Amongst those of the Catholic community who still practised their faith, it was common for requests to be made to the parish priest to dedicate a Mass for a private intention. Sometimes the intention was specified and sometimes it was kept secret. In both instances however, the dedication of each daily Mass in the coming week was announced after the services on a Sunday. It was generally a sad litany of hope for lost souls made by penitents who were still sufficiently gullible to imbibe the dogma and this group was supplemented by a gang of 'wannabes' trying to extort a favour from their imaginary God. Mrs Carson offering a Mass for the souls of the deceased members of the Carson family; Mrs O'Rourke offering a Mass in thanksgiving for the safe delivery of her sixth grandson (the subject of a previous petition) and sundry others all equally embarrassing. On the Sunday following my 'brush' with the law, after the nine o'clock Mass my own embarrassment was made complete. Father O'Brien declared to the whole assembly that on the following Thursday, a Mass would be said for… "the soul of Michael Grainger, a sinner of this parish".

It would have been simpler to dress me in a white sheet and give me a bell to ring.

Not surprisingly I decided that that would be the last time I would ever attend Mass. It proved the last straw to break the back of my religious practice, a camel that had faltered under the yoke for years in the increasingly arid desert of my growing irreverence. And, as Christmas approached, I was left to dwell on the degree of Christian charity evident in that kind of public humiliation. With hindsight I believe that my rejection of the Roman faith was inevitable, I have never been one to join clubs or organisations. When institutions such as that Church apparently take such pleasure in the castigation of its members, it is surprising that any members remain members.

Chapter Three

1973

The festive season came and went, characterised as usual by bouts of over-indulgence and sanctimonious clap-trap. On the one hand, the broadcasting authorities typically used the opportunity of a more than usual captive audience, to transmit as many repeat shows as their archives could muster. On the other we were subject to a marketing invasion planned more carefully than the Normandy landings. Inevitably by New Year's Day the surfeit of cold turkey and Sergeant Bilko drove me to spend what was left of my ill-gotten gains in the pub.

I have grown to believe that occasionally life sends us messages and that should we ignore them we do so at our peril. Consequently, after such a near miss with the law on only our second job, it was abundantly clear to me that I was not about to become any kind of Mister Big in the criminal underworld. I'd got away with it – but only just. Other than the money I had stashed away however, there were some other advantages to be gained from the experience. The very fact that the victim's perceptions were so badly faulted that he could not identify me was one interesting fact. Then there was the business of the law officers being hidebound by the system they represented. In this case, rules designed to protect the innocent had instead protected the guilty. It seemed to me that in a general sense, the application of rules, however well intended, inevitably caused some level of distortion in practice. And this caused me to think more seriously about the world of fine art.

I concluded that both in the pursuit of a life of crime and in that of an artist, a necessary dependence on credibility is obviously evident. The differences exist only in the penalty to be paid by each in the event of disclosure. One requires the perpetrator only to face the possible antagonism of the critics whereas the other is obliged to face his accusers in a court of law. And, whilst they may both be guilty of playing confidence tricks, the criminal found guilty might well lose his freedom, the artist has only a reputation at stake.

The development of my thinking in this regard had come about as a result of the pending interview at the art college. For the first time I had begun to take the prospect of potential studentship seriously. There was still however, a major obstacle – there was a mandatory requirement on all interviewees to show a folder of work and I had little or none to show. I had done well in art classes at school, even acquiring a grade 'B' at advanced level, but I had never taken it seriously. If I were to gain a place at the college, I had to revise that opinion. As a result, I spent a lot of that weekend trying to identify an angle on the situation.

I listed the advantages of being a student – especially an art student. These I identified as:

(1) I would qualify for a grant, that much was certain;

(2) I would not have to do much work – well students don't, they just doss about most of the time drinking coffee, chatting up women and smoking spliffs; and finally

(3) (and perhaps most significantly) there was an abundance of attractive females readily available at the college – and, if the gossip was to be believed, I mean really available.

There was only the admission hurdle still left to jump.

Initially, I calculated that if I did a concentrated work schedule – day and night over the weekend – I might just be able to produce enough work to convince the lecturers of my artistic integrity. I could still draw tolerably well and, even though my colour sense was doubtful, the week-end purge was a possibility. I recalled from my art history lessons that Henri Gaudier-Brzeska once did two stone carvings in a weekend so as to convince Jacob Epstein of his virtuosity in that medium. He had never worked in stone before. Unfortunately, I am no Henri Gaudier and good drawings can take a long time to develop. It would also have meant that I would need to work through Saturday night after my statutory nine pints of bitter – an unlikely option.

Instead, by a lucky chance, I chose to read up on the Conceptual art movement. This became immediately attractive. I discovered that mostly those artists did not actually make anything of any substance. They were responsible it seemed, only for having good ideas. That is good – obtuse – ideas. The credibility of their offerings hinged on persuading their contemporaries and some of the critics that they were serious contenders in

47

some kind of aesthetic ideas marathon. An apparent race in which no one seemed to know where the winning post was located or how far one needed to run. Now I was, and had always been, full of good ideas. I knew equally, if I turned my mind to it, I could come up with all sorts of way-out, off-the-wall notions that would/could surprise and shock the establishment. This was obviously the way forward – no clay behind my fingernails, no need to spend long hours at an easel and no rules that could be applied reflecting traditional values.

I spent half of Saturday at the public library. I read everything I could find on the exponents currently in the public eye. I learnt something about their philosophy and examined the degree of exaggeration in their claims. It was necessary evidence and time well spent. I didn't want to be caught out should some smart arse start to ask me questions about artists such as Richard Long wandering the countryside making stone circles or that guy Carl Andre who did the bricks at the Tate. My research enabled me to put together a journal-type notebook and even though it took me most of Sunday, I still had time for a couple of pints before bedtime.

The pretence I intended to adopt was one in which the journal was a constant companion. One that recorded ideas consisted of cut-out pictures from magazines, photographs taken by me and jottings-cum-drawings. I would claim that I had kept it diligently over the last two years as a sort of reference system for future development. It was a fabrication of course. If it was simply ideas they wanted – then it would be ideas they'd get.

I was up early on the Monday morning in question but, despite Dad's advice, I chose not to wear a suit. I dressed in a T-shirt and trainers with my jeans. I didn't shave and left my hair as it was – straight from the bed. It was a 'found' image, similar to that which I had seen worn by any number of students. A mean average of what the college authorities had grown used to. At eight thirty with my 'evidence of study' tucked under my arm, full of confidence I took the number 11 bus from the High Street in Stockton to Middlesbrough.

*

"And what-th do you imagine you might-th have to offer the college?"

The question came from the principal of the art college a Mister Evelyn Bernard. An insignificant little man whose legs were as short as his speech impediment. His delivery was made all the more confusing due to a lowland

Scottish accent, obliging me to listen carefully in order to avoid asking him to repeat everything. He was proving to be the smart arse I'd worried about meeting.

On my arrival at the college I had been conducted to a waiting room along with two other hopeful applicants. They were both dressed for combat. The male, John Turner wore a suit with a sharp tie and highly polished black shoes but the female – and Ruth Menzies was all female – wore torn jeans and a loose cotton top under a heavy sweater. The delineation between their approaches was significant and I was not surprised to discover that John's intention was to enter the fashionable world of Graphic Design or that Ruth simply wanted to paint. To begin with Ruth had kept on her heavy sweater but, in the cloistered atmosphere of the college's central heating, she took it off leaving her small audience with a delicious memory of a taut, pink midriff. The glimpse of bare flesh, topped with just a hint of unsupported breasts lasted only a microsecond but, as far as I was concerned, it was love – or maybe – lust, at first sight.

Ruth, I discovered, was terminally shy, speaking only when a question was aimed at her directly. The tone of her voice was as duskily promising as any blues singer and I spent much of the waiting time, imagining it whispering intimately in my ear. The thought of those pale pink lips so close to me was tantalising. John was a different matter. A dour Yorkshireman, whose accent belied his smart suit, he talked continuously in a loud voice about drawing nudes and his belief in something he called the new technology of computers in design. In my limited experience computers were just adding machines so I couldn't quite see what he was so excited about. However, his repeated declarations about life drawing caused the principal's secretary to glance disapprovingly over her spectacles and I liked him immediately.

"I'm sorry – thought it was the college that was going to do something for me." I replied.

There were just three of us in the room and my response made the other person present, a senior lecturer called Joss Pruitt, begin to grin. The office itself was a big uncomfortable room without any sign of paintings or sculpture to relieve it. Other than the desk, three chairs and a small bookcase it was devoid of furniture. Consequently, I imagined I could hear my voice ring and echo when I spoke. I had tried to answer some of the silliest questions imaginable from Mr Bernard employing the level of tact and diplomacy I thought might be expected, during which Pruitt had sat there in silence. His reaction at last was a welcome relief. The grin spoke volumes.

"It has' th to be a two-way process," Bernard replied frostily, "and you should underthand that in our little community, the students have a responsibility to the college as well as to themselves."

Naturally I agreed, "Of course sir," I said reverentially, "I was only implying that the guidance received here would represent the major influence in whatever artistic future I may have."

He looked sceptical but my reply seemed to satisfy him. After studying me for a moment he turned to Pruitt indicating it was his turn to apply the thumbscrews. The senior lecturer flicked through my journal, which he had on his knee.

"This sketchbook of yours – there isn't much evidence of observational work – drawing that is."

I said nothing, pretending I didn't recognise his comment as a question. "Are there reasons for that?" he asked.

"I thought you would be more interested in ideas rather than skills. I have some more traditional things – I suppose I could bring them along if you wish…"

"Okay," he said, "so tell me about your ideas… this one for instance." He turned the book towards me showing some diagrams of a body displayed in squares. This was the acid test.

"Oh that – I was playing with the notion that as the human form has played such an important part in art, it might be interesting to isolate the constituent parts – examine them singly – study actual relative values rather than symbolic worth…"

"And how would you make the parts?"

"I wouldn't – I thought they could be real body parts."

Now that stopped him in his tracks. He grinned, shook his head and flicked a page over.

"I see – and how about this one?" he said.

This time he showed me a sketch of a hole drawn in exaggerated perspective. It was situated next to a piece of simplified architecture of exactly the same dimensions.

"Public art," I said, "positives and negatives – things are usually built 'up' not 'down' – space displacement. Don't we sometimes look down on architecture…?"

The grin came again.

"So what kind of course do you think you would most benefit from?"

Now he closed the journal and looked directly at me for the first time. This was the main chance, the opportunity for which I had rehearsed a suitable 'pitch'. I gave him a practised smile.

"Interesting you should ask that – I intended to ask about the options available. I think there should be room for a course of study that isn't defined too closely by the traditional skill bases. I think I would prefer an opportunity to diversify across the whole spectrum – tackle the problems from different viewpoints."

He was nodding now, "A combined course?" he offered.

I agreed, trying to look enthusiastic.

"That's interesting, Joss – don't you think?" Bernard said to Pruitt interrupting the flow. "Wasn't that exactly the subject raised at the last staff meeting?"

Clearly I had tweaked a topical nerve.

The rest of the interview was much more relaxed and less gladiatorial. Much of it was spent discussing what such a course might include and from the discussion I gathered that the principal was all in favour of change, despite the opposition of some of the older heads of departments. I gave private thanks to whatever deity had directed my reading to this subject. One of the art college's publications had suggested that this might be the way forward for foundation courses, as had been the case with some of those at degree level.

Before I left the room I made reference to the recent aeroplane crash in the Andes, the one where the survivors became cannibals in order not to starve. I said it could almost have been a Conceptual art event and although Joss Pruitt laughed, I could see he was impressed. He said he would like the opportunity to discuss some of the ideas in my journal at greater length and I took this as a good sign. I left the room feeling quietly confident.

As arranged, I met up with Ruth and John in a pub round the corner at lunchtime to compare notes. I arrived and found the bar was already full of students from the college, the usual mix of long hair and beards, braless girls and 1950's fishnet tights. We found a table and John got a round of drinks, pints of bitter for him and me and a cider for Ruth.

"What did you reckon on the principal?" he asked sipping his beer.

I shrugged my shoulders and Ruth said she thought he was okay.

"Silly bugger asked me if I could stretch a canvas," he added answering his own question, "and I'd just shown him slides of several oil paintings."

"I must admit, Joss Pruitt seemed to look on Bernard as if he was a bit of a fool," Ruth said.

Each of us gave a précis of our respective interviews and soon we were discussing the idea of combined, less structured courses. Ruth and I agreed wholeheartedly with the notion but John favoured a more traditional approach. He wanted to specialise in graphics from day one – he said.

I watched Ruth carefully as she spoke. She was animated for the first time and clearly took the prospect of study very seriously. I found her very sexy. Unfortunately the sweater was back in place but the rise and fall of her generous breasts still teased my imagination. I had always enjoyed the company of females but in recent years had not had much opportunity to indulge myself. It was obviously an aspect of my formative education that needed further research.

Since my initiation by Nelly Withwaites back in junior school, there had been only a few occasions when I'd had the opportunity to fumble with girls – usually in the back row of the local cinema or the rear seat of Bruce's car. None of these had actually resulted in a proper fulfilment, by which I mean the kind of knockdown drag-out sex as seen in the porno movies. Truth to tell therefore, my experience had thus so far been limited. This was to be remedied at the soonest opportunity – I decided. Ruth focused my thinking in this regard and each time I looked at her my imagination went into overdrive.

I was increasingly aware of what might be described by some as a character fault in my make-up with regard to girls. It's one I first became aware of around the time I identified my attraction to Mary Bary, my teacher. I find myself going to any lengths to please – to be agreeable, even when such agreement contradicts what I might believe myself. As a child the fault was insignificant, my views were still emerging and my opinions unfounded. More importantly, at that stage the girls I tried to impress were inevitably unimpressed, apparently immune to my chameleon behaviour. As an adult however, the results could be catastrophic. I nevertheless found myself agreeing with everything Ruth said. She could do no wrong and I didn't care what anyone else might think. Unfortunately, the contrariness inherent in most young women often means that they do not want a complete endorsement of their views. Apparently on occasion, they enjoy being argued with. I was yet to understand female masochism or the apparent need so many women have to be dominated.

After a while a couple of older students at the next table insinuated themselves into our conversation. Clearly they had spotted Ruth and fancied their chances. The one with the greasier hair struck a pose as some kind of intellectual and, supported by his friend, argued vehemently against combined courses. To my considerable irritation Ruth took his position on board and changed sides. With hindsight I realise that the attraction of what might appear to be a more mature opinion can prove an undeniable force, especially where young women are involved. I could hardly contain my annoyance.

There have been occasions, usually when, due to the effect of strong drink, I have used violence as a method of resolving such arguments and it is something I usually regret afterwards. But the instant gratification of seeing my opponents fall or, still better, back down in the face of unpredictable insults, is ever a temptation. This was proving to be just such an occasion. With four faces arguing for the status quo, my responses became less and less reliant on logic and more dependent on personal insults. As expected my venom was returned with interest by long hair, although his imagination was limited in this respect. He ended one sentence with, "…and arseholes like you have been the cause of so much trouble in art colleges' curricula. You're a fine art fascist and should be treated as such."

"And how would that be?" I asked. My question was deliberately provocative. It left him no way out.

"Stepped on," he said.

"And do you see yourself being the one to do the stepping?"

"Mick," Ruth interrupted, "I think this debate is getting silly."

"If one party opts for a violent solution, it can hardly be termed a debate anymore," I replied.

It was a nice switch of responsibility, I thought, placing blame on long hair and his friend. But I wasn't yet content, "They do say that violence is the last refuge of the ignorant," I added, "so I suppose I should be tolerant of these two."

That was the last straw. Long hair rose up like an avenging angel and breathlessly tried to relocate blame but the game was lost already. I ignored him and directed further insults about him to John and Ruth as though he had disappeared. He wanted to hit me, I could feel as much in his tension but he didn't have the balls. When eventually I suggested we might take it outside, he left muttering the fuck word between every noun.

Ruth took the bus with me back to Stockton and, although she agreed to go out with me the following weekend, I could tell she was still unsure about me. I didn't care. She was prime meat as far as I was concerned – and I was long overdue a main course barbecue.

Chapter Four

1973

I was motivated at last and in the summer of 1973 I took a job labouring at blast furnaces for a firm making pig iron in Stillington, a summer job that was hard work but well paid. Now, whilst I am not usually one to seek out hard physical work, this time there was a clear objective. This was an exercise designed to raise enough cash to buy a car. My relationship with Ruth had reached that stage when we wanted to have our own transport and a place, hopefully, to enjoy those corporeal delights that only total privacy can afford. In other words, you couldn't fuck your girlfriend unless you have access to somewhere quiet where there are no witnesses.

Consequently each morning that summer I would catch the seven a.m. bus from the High Street and forty minutes later would begin to barrow scrap iron into a convenient furnace mouth. Basically my activity was a simple process. Mounds of scrap metal were loaded via a magnetic crane onto barrows. The barrows stood in turn on a huge weighing machine and once an agreed weight was recorded, the barrow 'lads', of which I was one, would wheel them away. Working in groups of four we would take our loads on a lift up to a gantry some fifteen feet above ground. The gantry led to the mouths of three furnaces and whichever one was operating that day would be the place we would tip the scrap.

During the course of the day, the furnace in use would be tapped at its base, allowing the iron residue to run, molten hot, into moulds. Once they had cooled, the moulds were opened and the ingots or 'pigs' of iron were removed. Needless to say the temperatures needed to accommodate this process were excessively high, a fact that only the barrow lads fully appreciated. By the early afternoon, after the furnace had been tapped, the electric fans employed to drive the furnace would direct the flames out through the furnace mouth. At that time our job became a dangerous adventure. Body hair was often scorched away, eyebrows disappeared and on one occasion I saw a woolly sweater burst into flames. Consequently, to save us becoming burnt offerings, whatever the weather we always wore gauntlets and caps, scarves and heavy, protective clothing.

The ethos of a well-paid, macho activity suited me and I was able to fit in without any problems. To some extent this was due also to the fact that the camaraderie amongst the barrow lads was typified by an irreverent sense of humour. To kill the boredom throughout the day practical jokes were their main preoccupation. To create a 'good laugh' was seen as the pinnacle of anyone's achievement. The methods employed in this quest demonstrated a level of creativity my 'arty' friends could hope only to aspire to. The best one I witnessed was when Jimmy Dell, an eighteen-year-old, pissed into the furnace. How he knew – if indeed he did know – that urine subjected to high temperatures creates the most perniciously obnoxious stink that would permeate every nook and cranny of the whole site, was beyond my understanding. Even the boss came down from his ivory tower to complain and a rumour went round that he was considering closing the factory for the rest of the day – but it remained a rumour only.

During a ten-day period when the furnaces were being re-bricked, I was relocated to the engineering shop where evidence of the same mischievous humour persisted. One of the welders, a guy called Mo, showed me some of his favourite tricks. I discovered that if an acetylene torch was left to leak slowly, either into a bucket of water or into pipe-work under construction, minutes later the application of a match – from a safe distance – would create an impressive explosive flash. I saw blackened faces, I saw workers flung backwards onto the floor and I even saw a passing secretary throw an armful of files into the air.

These distractions helped the working day to pass more quickly. And, as there was no doubt in my mind that I wanted the whole episode to pass as quickly as possible, the jokes were a relief. However, despite the humour of my workmates, I hated every minute spent at the factory and it was only the prospect of buying a car and the opportunity it would afford regarding Ruth's secret delights that kept me focused.

By then, I had agreed an arrangement with Ruth. We determined that we would not make an exclusive commitment but that we would nevertheless see one another on a regular basis. What that meant in practice was that she would continue to see her regular boyfriend and, had I been similarly blessed, I could do the same. It goes without saying that I was not similarly blessed. She had been friendly with an old school chum of hers for over a year; a spotty character called Dean who was training to be an accountant. She assured me it was not a physical relationship and having met Dean, I could understand and believe her. He was a wimp. Accordingly, my pose was as the laid-back, easy-going type without a jealous bone in my body. I led her to believe that I was still in demand and that I had a few female friends whose favours were available. Unfortunately, the truth was that the last time I was in demand was when the police were looking for me.

I worked on the principle that if one takes an equation that includes a car-owning male and an attractive girl, often one will find that this will equal lots of opportunity for sex. I had to have a car – consequently – six weeks of hard, tortuous work.

The other high spot of that summer was the way that my stock on the home front had suddenly soared in the market index. When the offer of a place at the art college had arrived on the doormat, Mam and Dad's attitude to me underwent a complete transformation. I was legitimised. I was seen to be casting off the stigma of being unreliable, unemployed and untrustworthy. Suddenly I was not that 'lazy bugger upstairs,' I was a student.

"Mick is studying Fine Art... He's always had a talent for Art... They offered him a place straight away..." Mam would boast – and so on.

And when I took the labouring job, it was as if I had been awarded a Nobel Prize for Endeavour. Suddenly Dad had always known what a hard worker I was.

"The lad knows the value of hard work... He doesn't mind getting his hands dirty... He's always been a worker."

The move from parasite to paragon was instantaneous – the joins seamless – the mend invisible. However, if they had known that the student option was the lesser of several evils or that the labouring job was simply to enable easy access to Ruth's knickers they may not have been quite so happy.

In the event however, although I was able to satisfy my carnal appetite on a couple of occasions with the lovely Ruth, the 'dreadful' Dean eventually outbid me for her affections. My old banger, all I could afford even after six weeks' hard labour – a Renault 10 of indeterminate age – was eclipsed by his newish MGB, a purchase supported by a bank loan guaranteed by his wealthy father. Henceforth the exploration of Ruth's private parts would be confined only to real leather seats. She was whisked away each weekend to join the quickstepping sporty set at the Spa Ballroom in Saltburn and thereafter no doubt, to the car park in Marske where the joys of fully-reclining seats could be enjoyed with the sound of the sea as a backdrop. Now it seemed, she was always otherwise committed and after several refusals, reluctantly I decided to cut my losses and seek pastures new.

Other than the irrefutable fact of Dean's MG I concluded that my fatal mistake was in treating Ruth like a lady. I'd been that bit too agreeable. I'd been so obsessed with her that my sex drive had been left in neutral for most of our association. This was a mistake I would not repeat and the failure coloured my judgement of the fair sex for evermore. Armed therefore with my old but reliably portable shagging facility, I set about to lay waste to the female student population.

As a result of my new hobby and given that I had spent the major part of the summer labouring at the furnaces, I had lost touch with Tony and Bruce. Just before the start of the new college term therefore, I renewed contact with my friends down at *Jock-o-Browns* one Sunday morning.

I was amazed to discover that the summer had changed them also. In the interim they had both taken full-time jobs. A development that I claimed was as a result of my good example, but in truth was probably more to do with the shock of our near miss with the law. Tony now spent his days working in a factory as a trainee manager. He wore a suit, a short back and sides and boasted that now he shaved every day. Presumably to mitigate the effect of his new status, when we met he swore more volubly and drank to greater excess than ever before. It was much the same with Bruce who was employed as a draughtsman in a large architectural practice in the town centre.

In many respects the change in lifestyle of my friends was more difficult to accommodate than that affecting my own circumstances. It was the shift in their value systems that proved hardest to understand and this was most especially true of Tony. He appeared to have changed character overnight. The debonair, establishment-hating anarchist had given way to someone who complained about the timekeeping of his minions; a man with a Building Society Savings Account and a credit card; a tie-wearing customer of Burton's and, to cap it all, someone who was apparently about to become engaged.

It felt like the end of an era and the rift that developed between us was finally completed when I started to attend the art college that September. The difference in our interests prompted their criticisms and an increasingly perverse disapproval of my activities. Suddenly they began to sound like the people we used to laugh at and their devotion to conservative values proved the last nail in the coffin of our friendship. We had nothing left in common except a secret history.

Life as a student, on the other hand, was everything I had imagined it might be. There were infrequent periods of activity when the production of something resembling an artefact was required but, as long as these were carefully managed, the effort needed was minimal. The majority of my time was therefore spent talking, drinking and experimenting with seduction techniques.

With hindsight, it's fair to claim that the community I joined represented a sub-culture situated on the fringe of normal society. A group whose reason for being depended on broadly agreed terms of reference, the meaning of which was largely unintelligible to the general public. It was therefore true that communication between members of the art college community was possible only when the newcomer had acquired the requisite language skills. It was therefore essential to become as thoroughly familiar with the approved vocabulary as it was with the detail of the subject's history. It came as no surprise to me to discover that the incidence of confidence-trickery in the world of fine art was as high as one might find in any group of insurance salesmen. The only differences being that shyster insurance salesman are found out sooner rather than later, whereas artists seem to go on forever.

The death of Pablo Picasso in April that year confirmed my argument. He was ninety-one when he died, never having done a day's work in his life. He was nevertheless able to leave an incalculable fortune by virtue of the high price his works could bring. In effect he printed his own currency. In life he afforded himself several wives and numerous mistresses and was a frequent client in some well-known French brothels. In death he acquired the status of a saintly cultural genius. I rest my case.

With the passage of time, I was able to identify three sectors that made up the student body. There were those with no skill or talent – some of whom could only talk a good 'art talk'; there were those who had imbibed the 'Art for Art's Sake' philosophy with their mothers' milk and who dedicated all their time to acquiring a deeper understanding – usually through work; and finally, there were those who saw an opportunity that could be accessed through a minimum effort and with a modest talent. I myself belonged to the latter group but, in the necessary quest for credibility, spent my time in the company of the second who were by far the most talented and clearly the most intelligent.

Eager to find a niche, I made few public pronouncements during my first year, spending my time instead listening. I avoided taking sides and made sure my opinions – when called for – were consistent with those of the majority. And when I was not drinking beer at the pub or coffee in the common room, I spent my time reading. I absorbed anything and everything associated with art history. Unfortunately this left little time for making art and towards the end of that first year the paucity of my production became a bone of contention.

Joss Pruitt called me to his office one afternoon to warn me that I was about to fail my annual assessment.

"You fit in well, Mick," he told me, "but with so little work to show, the principal could easily put you on a warning – a yellow card. You need to do something fairly major to redeem yourself."

Joss told me this in the privacy of his office as an act of kindness and I knew I would need to act on his advice as quickly as possible. The stories about the long slow slide to course termination were legion around the common room and it was a path I did not want to follow – could not afford to follow.

That evening I spent an hour or more chatting to Pete Westly, one of the advanced students. He was a mine of information and whilst his work was a complete mystery to me, he was well respected by both the staff and students alike. Indeed, if art colleges had gone in for having head boys, he would undoubtedly have filled the role. In our discussion about the state of art, he argued for what he saw as a return to basics. However, as his latest pieces were colour-field paintings – enormous canvases filled with only one colour, I could not equate his argument with his product. There was one called *RED* – and would you believe it was red – all red? I offered little to this discussion but I remember thinking it was a bit like saying sand is sand or concrete is concrete – or was I missing the point. Nevertheless, it was as a result of talking to Pete that I began to realise that rules of logic need not apply and that originality was everything. It was also as a consequence of my discussions with Pete that I spawned my first real art idea.

The next morning I was in the studio very early and by the time Joss and the other students had arrived, I had completed a large floor sculpture (– I said). I'd covered the whole floor of the small studio with builder's sand and, working back towards the door in order to maintain the integrity of the surface, I drew a series of lines. I worked with a pointed stick and a rake and the effect was similar to that found in some Japanese gardens. Finally I wrote some words on small sheets of paper and scattered the sheets across the sandy surface of the room. Words such as 'death', 'thought', 'vagina' and 'hope' all figured.

Before lunchtime my 'sand-drawing' was the subject of heated debate throughout the building. Due to the limited access – there were only two doors to that studio – students and lecturers queued throughout the day to view the work, some of them photographed it. Joss was delighted. I took care to avoid his questions however, allowing my answers to depend on description rather than explanation or justification. It was a strategy that paid dividends and before the day ended, the philosophical roots of the sand drawing – having been designed and amplified by the staff – were agreed by all.

I received an 'A' in my assessment.

More importantly, the attention created by the sand drawing promoted me to a higher status amongst my fellow students. Now, suddenly, I was a force worth listening to. At last my opinion counted for something and my responses were weighed carefully. In fact it was the principal who suggested that I should develop the idea. He had the department furnish me with six enormous sheets of marine plywood and asked me to work on the back lawn. The ensuing pieces – variations on the same theme – appeared as photographs, first of all in the local press and then in one of the better-known national art magazines. Suddenly I was a celebrity. I didn't like to tell anyone that I'd been drawing things on beaches in sand since I was a four-year-old.

I did not understand half the things that were claimed for the drawings or even the references made – but that did not matter. I simply sat nodding in the right places trying to leave the impression that the explanations made only scratched the surface of what the work was about. After my conversation with Pete, I decided to work big – like he did – and to title things simply, without explanation. The sand works were thereby entitled: 'Sand I', 'Sand II' and so on. I also took his advice and never talked about the content of the work.

"The work is its own explanation," he said, "so justification isn't needed."

The reaction was remarkable and I felt I had discovered a formula, a guaranteed mode of operation that was fail-safe. At some stage, I even began to believe that I was actually an artist and that my work had some significance. My detractors were few but they included a journalist on one of the local papers that called me a charlatan and did his best to expose what he saw as a completely meaningless exercise. However, possibly because so many other people enjoy sand and remember drawing in wet sand on beaches, I was able to curry enough support to persuade everyone else that he was an old fogey and hopelessly out of date. And, whilst at least some of the public at large may well have shared his scepticism, no one could affect the impetus of the interest generated. I was, as they say, on a roll.

*

The following year, 1974 was hectic from day one. Letters to write, ideas to process – girls to enjoy and drinks parties to attend. There was a real temptation to dwell on the fact of being a big fish in a small pond but I resisted. Now that I had experienced a small taste of celebrity status, I wanted more but I wanted it on a national if not an international scale. I read about the prices being paid in fine art auctions down in London and realised fully for the first time that there was money to be made. The pity was that most of the artists whose work fetched ridiculous prices were dead. It was nevertheless a proven fact that if one wanted to make money, then one needed to be in a place where there was plenty of it about. London was obviously the place to be.

In April I was advised by Joss that I should stand a good chance of early entry onto a degree course. He said I should apply to some of London colleges. He was not to know that one college had already been in touch with me suggesting exactly the same thing. The South London college in question was not best known for its student product or for the exceptional quality of its teaching. As far as I could gather, its lecturers comprised a group of elderly failed artists. It was a place that survived under the banner of being a centre for creativity, the kind of smoke screen that proved irresistible to the world of education snobbery. As such, it sounded like just the place for me – easier to shine amongst dross than amongst bright sparks, I reckoned.

The following month an agent telephoned me to ask if he might represent me. He said he was already in contact with several London galleries who had expressed an interest in exhibiting my work. This was a huge compliment but neither he nor they knew that I did not have any work to show. The sand drawings had been a lucky one-off and since then I had been reluctant to chance anything else for fear of failure. There had been spin-offs, the photographs, the sketches (done afterwards) and the articles and interviews but that had all dried up. I knew then that if I were to capitalise on my new reputation, I badly needed another big idea.

One of the fringe benefits of my newly found status was the increased attention I received from the local female population. I seldom sat alone in the coffee shop and was in continuous demand in the pub. It was during this period however, that I began to worry about my drinking habits. I'd always enjoyed a few pints and on occasion would drink a little too much. But beer had none of the long-term effects as the drink that I now chose to make the subject of my main social activity – namely whisky. To order a large scotch was somehow much more chic than to ask for a pint of bitter. At least in my imagination, it placed me immediately alongside the 'super-cool' stars of the silver screen, the Humphrey Bogarts and James Deans of the world. Also, and this was not insignificant, its effects were more immediate. The throat-burning liquid lifted my spirits and etched a path to my brain, making my perceptions that much more acute and my arguments so much more convincing – I thought. The hangovers I wore as a badge of maturity, the lost evenings as a sign of not caring what people thought. It was only when the drink began to affect my performance as a stud that I became aware that the habit was debilitating. I discovered that dropping off to sleep between the soft and willing thighs of the latest fleshy acquisition was not the best marketing ploy for my charms. The drinking had to be controlled. Access to so many obliging female bodies however, tended to keep me fully occupied and it was through my pursuit of corporeal satisfaction that eventually gave rise to my next art venture. The idea actually germinated in the midst of a bout of very energetic love-labour with a well-endowed girl called Mandy.

Mandy was a big girl and at some stage I remember I became aware of the actual extent of her curves. Immediately my imagination projected a series of images that caused me to smile and I found myself having to assure the subject of my attentions that I was not laughing at her.

I took the idea to Joss and through him managed to obtain a small grant from ICI. He was well connected with the firm's plastics division whose directors were ever keen to patronise worthwhile cultural causes, often at his behest. On his say-so they took the project to their hearts and agreed to underwrite all my costs – an unusual coup and one worth its weight in gold. I had some invitation cards printed and, at lunchtimes, I gave these out to likely looking individuals in the town centre. It was a time when the office workers were out and about, and an occasion when the selection of body shapes available was at its most varied. I made it clear in the text of the invitations that, should they agree, they would be assisting in an art installation and also that they may be required to do some unusual tasks. I was careful not say precisely what I might want them to do.

As a result of the sixty invitations I gave out, twenty-six people turned up one Friday night at college for a briefing session. I had not emphasised the fact but every one invited was overweight. Some were just flabby, some gross and one or two, gargantuan. This was to be my *Fat Art Project.* I did not try to justify my reasons to the volunteers; I simply described what I would require them to do. One or two asked questions but the majority sat in stony silence throughout giving no sign of their approval or their agreement. I'd calculated that if only ten or more appeared on the day, I would be able still to complete the exercise.

On the day in question, a Saturday morning, nineteen bodies arrived, mostly males in their middle years. We assembled together in the same studio where I had created the sand drawing and I asked them to undress, leaving their clothing in the room next door. I had removed all the furniture and covered the floor with sand yet again. For the next two hours I arranged and photographed the bodies in a variety of the most unlikely postures and whilst the proximity of one to another varied, none of them actually touched. Each volunteer was given an egg-shaped piece of white card, which they either held in front of their face or wore, tied back with elastic bands in front of their faces. Accordingly they were unidentifiable. In the second part of the exercise these white cards carried a photograph of my face. In this way I became the *Fat Art Project.* The whole thing was over by midday, at which time the participants were treated to a finger buffet with wine courtesy of ICI. I was intrigued by the degree of seriousness in the room whilst the photographs were being taken. Indeed the participants treated the project with far more sobriety than any group of students would have. By the same token, everyone present did their level best to assume the various – often silly – postures I demanded of them.

It was fortunate that Joss had reminded me to secure signed release statements from everyone involved. Fortunate because, once the pictures were printed, some might have claimed embarrassment leading to claims for compensation. The photos appeared eventually in a wide variety of newspapers and magazines and, although my models were unidentifiable, several did call to make complaints. I bought Joss a bottle of Scotch as a thank you.

I called the piece – *Indoor beach wish fulfilment in the sub-conscious minds of naked sun-worshippers: Fat Art Opus 1.* A title that was predictably misrepresented by one of the tabloid 'rags' as 'The Fat Arse Project'. A sound bite that I had calculated would appear and that I hoped the public might adopt. It was, and the newspaper in question printed various letters complaining about the apparent absence of morals, prompting the age-old question, 'Is this art?' It was good stuff and amazing publicity in the cause of Mick Grainger's career in the art world.

The photos were variously enlarged for some publications and reduced for others, sections were extracted, detail was examined and scrutinised and I even did some drawings from them. There were so many spin-offs that I had no need to concern myself with any other work for the duration of my stay at the college. I concluded that from that time, my college life was to be one long holiday.

I could not have been more wrong.

Chapter Five

1975

Celia was hot – and I really mean hot. A new student – still wet behind the something or other – still wanting it and still so easily impressed. She arrived late, weeks after the rest of her year group had enrolled, on account of her parents living abroad. She was high-profile from day one. I first noticed her as she walked ahead of me down the main corridor and was stirred by the plasticity of her moving parts. Her figure was generous and therefore unfashionably robust, promising more than most fellers could safely manage. A challenge therefore, and one that I immediately took up. Her personality proved to be loud and uncompromising and her skimpy tops and slit skirts were an invitation for tongues to dangle rather than wag – they did both. Even in the most liberal of environments – which was certainly true of the college – Celia managed to shock the community. I took her out on a date the first day I saw her and immediately we became an item.

By then I had dated a variety of females, even including one of the younger lecturers. But that had been a mistake. Shirley – a fashion lecturer – fancied that she could defy the age gap by baiting her hook with the promise of being easily accessible and especially submissive. In the throes of her pleasure, her appreciation often took the form of sustained screams, loud enough on occasion to threaten the sound barrier. Needless to say, our sessions in her little apartment in Redcar were characterised by her lewd cries of enjoyment, sufficient on one occasion to cause her neighbours to call the police. Shirley was a genuine masochist. She liked pain and sought it in ways I had never imagined possible previously. Conversely, her classical good looks were complimented by an accent owing its roots to a variety of public schools, an image of superior sobriety that could not have been further from her actual character. To make our association even more complex, she had a casual penchant for having more than one partner simultaneously. This practice accentuated the element of risk that she so enjoyed but necessitated my drinking even larger quantities of whisky than normal in order for me to accommodate the situation. And when the alcohol no longer worked its magic, she introduced me to a variety of consciousness-expanding drugs.

The thrill of exercising the kind of control she required in the sexual arena eventually wore thin, especially when her orgasm could only be achieved after repeated applications of senseless cruelty. I warned her repeatedly, but to no avail, that however perfect her body form, the treatment to which she subjected it would eventually affect the quality of its appearance if not its responsiveness. Ignoring me, she would only smile beneath the pleasure-induced perspiration that blurred her vision and demand more. Shirley sickened me. I returned her whip and her handcuffs and left her to find someone else to perform her ritual punishments.

I had also had an opportunity for a rematch with Ruth, albeit a brief one. In her case however, my motive was as much one of vengeance as one of passion. Dean, the improbable accountant, had apparently faded into the grey, numerical background to which he belonged and the lovely Ruth let it be known through mutual friends that she would look favourably on my attentions. She had changed substantially from the shy girl of my earlier experience; used to getting all her own way, now she was a control freak with a superiority syndrome. Her attitude typified a level of condescension that I recognised immediately. A 'Lady Bountiful' mentality that took no account of her previous rejection of me. There was every expectation that I would come running should she indicate her willingness. I came running all right. I took her to a party and, after giving her a severe shagging, I offered her services to two of my mates. She left hastily and never came back.

Celia was different. Celia would shag anywhere and she made no secret of the fact. Inevitably there were those amongst my contemporaries that claimed she was a nymphomaniac but that was not the case. There was no doubt that she had experienced the joys of conquest and pleasurable capitulation between the sheets before she met me but once we took up together, she obliged only me. Having said that, I must admit she had an appetite for physical enjoyment at least equal to that of any man I knew. I never knew her to refuse me.

Around the time we met, I was serving out my last term at the college, a period traditionally of soul-searching prior to my move. Unfortunately, like most young people then, my value system would hardly bear close scrutiny. Possibly a reflection of that evident amongst our world leaders, it comprised a series of contradictions. Messages involving morality from that leadership were very mixed. Harold Wilson had been elected to number 10 Downing Street and was dishing out money to strikers and honours to his mates like it was Christmas whilst the American President, Mr Nixon, was about to be impeached. No one, it seemed, could be trusted and within some circles of the college community I was almost equally unpopular. The success and attention I had earned also earned me the enmity of some members of staff and this was particularly true of the head of fine arts. In that last term he insisted that I should conform to a curriculum comprising entirely of skill-based exercises. He told me bluntly that if I were to miss any of the set classes or lectures he would torpedo my application to the London colleges. He did not care how much I drank, or how many girls I slept with, he did not mind if I upset members of his department or that what I produced was below par, he simply wanted my attendance. Joss Pruitt spoke up for me but to no avail. Mr Bernard was not about to overturn the instructions of one of his department heads no matter how much his institution may have benefited from the publicity related to my activities. I was therefore obliged to attend life-drawing classes, to perform mindless exercises in basic design and spend hours, painting still-life groups. None of which could I do with any kind of virtuosity. In fact my skills, as far as traditional modes of art-making were concerned, were poor. But who needed them!

Consequently, I'd quickly become bored. I concentrated all my efforts therefore on my female companions. My old banger became the stage set for innumerable pas de deux, occasionally even, pas de trois – a palace of delights. Celia came along at just the right time.

False modesty was entirely foreign to Celia. She saw something she wanted and she said so – a breath of fresh air. Her favourite position was doggy style but due to the geometry of my old car, this was one contortion that could not be easily accommodated. It was our practice then to drive out to a certain beachside car park at Marske, a bespoke shagging site where the deed could be safely enacted after dark. There were other places, leafy lay-bys and wooded hideaways that we frequented but, compared to the sand dunes at Marske, they were just the entrée. Marske was the meat course. Naturally the site was popular with other members of the screwing-after-dark public but there was an unwritten etiquette signifying the importance we all laid on the need for privacy and cars parked after dark were, therefore, judiciously placed at a discreet distance from one another.

The only inherent disadvantage of this location was the sand. The same medium that had helped establish my small reputation now became a nuisance. And the use of a travel blanket and/or various types of plastic sheet never seemed to make much difference. Needless to say, the inconvenience of finding sand in one's picnic sandwiches on family holidays paled into insignificance when one considered the places it found its way into during the process of sex-on-the-beach. However, it was a small price to pay and, had we not been disturbed one night, we may well have happily continued using the car park ad infinitum.

The disturbance I refer to happened one Friday night, an occasion when, for the best of reasons, Celia was being particularly voluble during our coupling. The remoteness of the spot normally allowed her to indulge herself in this regard. She was a noisy fuck – she said so herself. That night however, the screeches of her approval were louder than ever. Unbeknown to us they were sufficiently loud to carry as far as the road and to attract the attention of a passing police patrol car. Before I knew what was happening, the two constables from that car were viewing the scene and making encouraging noises from only yards away. Celia had her head in the sand – so to speak – and remained unaware of our visitors. She was therefore able to maintain the level of her obvious enjoyment unaffected by any feelings of embarrassment. My positioning was less fortunate. I knelt behind her actually facing the 'sheriff's' men – and, if anything was ever designed to kill off sexual passion, it is certainly the close proximity of two grinning policemen.

"Go on, son – give it to her. Look at those tits…"

The comments, whispered as encouragement, acted like a cold shower.

Suddenly Celia heard them and realised we had an audience. Cool as the proverbial cucumber she looked up and said, "Gentlemen – there's a charge for simply watching."

The taller of two 'boys in blue' stepped forward at this and quipped, "Then maybe we should join in." As he spoke he began to loosen his tunic. By now I had disengaged myself but had begun to wonder where this might be leading. The young policeman advanced and Celia, unperturbed as ever, viewed him with a cheeky grin.

She caught my eye, "But only if my boyfriend doesn't mind?" she said

What could I say – given the liberal stance of which I had always boasted and the deviant streak endemic to my sexual preference, I felt I could hardly raise any real objection. The girl was willing and the guy was keen – so – what the hell. I nodded my agreement.

"Just watch her on the bends," I quipped, "sometimes she accelerates too quickly. She needs a firm hand."

A moment later the constable was mounted.

I stood with his colleague watching the spectacle with a curious mixture of feelings. Despite those occasions afforded by Shirley, voyeurism was a relatively new experience still and, as I discovered, one that could generate reasonably pleasant sensations. In the back of my mind to start with, the appearance of the law officers had caused me worry that they might arrest us for indecency. This was hardly likely now. The big guy presented himself unashamedly and performed with admirable enthusiasm. He rode Celia hard and quickly and she took it without complaint.

Amazingly, when it was his turn the other policemen reneged, claiming he had a problem. He did not define the nature of the problem but from the attitude of his companion, I deduced there might be a question concerning his sexual preference. As they returned to their patrol car however, I hear him mutter something about being a good Catholic. The other one just laughed.

Long after their departure, Celia laid with me on the blanket looking at the night sky, laughing. We coined phrases such as, "abuse of the law", "wasting police time", and "truncheon charges". Celia was certainly no worse for her adventure. She said she had experienced a perverse thrill at being taken by a complete stranger, especially with an audience looking on.

"But how was it for you, Mick?" she asked. "Weren't you just a tiny bit jealous?"

"Why would I be jealous?" I replied. "It's not as though I was excluded – I had a ring-side seat."

And in truth, I did not feel jealous – just excited. Indeed I made a mental note for future reference that this act might be one to be included in our repertoire for the future. In the past I had occasionally been involved in situations with two women but only Shirley had shared herself with more than one man before. The possibilities were provocative.

*

During my time at the art college my home environment had changed completely. Almost overnight it seemed that I had acquired a new status. The attention I attracted from the media allowed my parents to revel in my reflected glory. My father's sarcasm had all but disappeared – replaced now by tentative enquiries about how the work might be going and had my latest assessment proved successful? Due to the celebrity of his son, at work he was regarded differently himself. Benefits seemed to accrue on all sides. Mr Grainger senior was offered a promotion to the position of foreman. Typically, in the first instance he refused it. However, presumably in the belief that my talent was due to his genetic influence, he found he was now consulted regarding certain design matters: the size and typeface used on book jackets and the most appropriate motifs. At one stage he was even asked if he might redesign the company letterhead. Thankfully he resisted the temptation.

In a similar fashion, Mam's stock had also risen with her neighbours. Without warning one day she was invited to join the Catholic Women's League. As I understood it, this was an organisation ostensibly devoted to good works, to cleaning the church and arranging the flowers there. However, it was also the kind of society that some upwardly mobile working class-women aspired to, as the pinnacle of local Catholic society. Given her natural shyness and a distinct lack of any sign of upward mobility this was an opportunity that my mother had previously only dreamed of. As far as I was concerned, I could never understand why she might even contemplate joining such an association. Their right-wing tendencies, particularly in respect of their 'respectable xenophobia' would not have been out of place alongside the Brown-shirts of Nazi Germany before World War II.

I was interested to note that during this period no reference was ever made to the fact of my adoption. That particular piece of information was apparently swept into the domestic 'wait and see' file along with my father's scepticism.

I never bothered to try and discover how this change in our social standing might have affected the family income, still less our credit worthiness. The only sign that the situation had become more flexible was that, for the first time in ages, I found it considerably easier to borrow money from my parents. I needed only to intimate that I was short of funds and money appeared – paper money – as if by magic. There was no more talk of my making a contribution to the household budget and no more suggestions that there was a need for me to take a part-time job at weekends. In the same vein, whenever I was alone with my mother, she would insist on telling me, in a confidential tone, how Dad wanted me to – 'make something of myself'– whatever that meant. Why she was needed to interpret his aspirations on my behalf was never made clear. Neither could I recall a time previously when he was prepared to trust her with any kind of representation on his behalf.

One morning I received the long-awaited invitation to an interview at the South London college to which I'd applied and my parents' joy was complete. Dad noticed that the college in question was affiliated to London University and thereafter told his friends that I was going to study at London University. Needless to say, no one from either side of the family had ever had the benefit of further education, let alone a university place.

"We knew you'd make good, son," Mam said, devouring the letter for the umpteenth time as Dad nodded his agreement over the Saturday breakfast. As a consequence, on the morning in question the breakfast table was like a Christmas morning and for once the number three did not figure in any of the arrangements. The Holy Trinity was consigned to limbo and I was served my eggs and bacon first.

"So, son," Dad said through a mouthful of best Danish bacon, "supposing they offer you a place at this – this university – what will you get when you finish?"

"A degree – I suppose."

"A degree," he smiled at the thought, "and what sort of degree will that be?"

"They are graded according to how well you do – there's a first class, then a 2:1, then a 2:2 and…"

"No, no I didn't mean all that stuff – I meant what letters will you get after your name?"

I smiled appreciating for the first time what he was getting at. "First degrees are always Bachelors, so I suppose I'll get BA. Fine Art."

They both fell silent behind smiles of satisfaction. Eventually Mam said, "Michael Grainger BA," and Dad nodded repeating it quietly to himself.

I tried to explain the hierarchy of degrees to them but my efforts could not dint their preoccupation. Their son would one day have letters after his name and that was about all they could grasp.

After breakfast Dad informed me that I should go and see the manager of Burton's – a friend of his – and get measured for a new suit and no amount of argument could persuade him that a suit was unnecessary. In his eyes, an interview for a place at a university made a 'smart new suit' a mandatory requirement. And when his proposal was endorsed by Mam who explained, "Your dad will pay for it," I let them have their way.

The following afternoon I went to the High Street and picked out a dark blue, double-breasted pinstripe suit. It would at least suffice for funerals and weddings I told myself. I should nevertheless have to pack my jeans and sweatshirts when I travelled south as I planned to change my outfit on the train.

Despite my previous resolve, I was persuaded to attend Mass the following Sunday and after their continued kindness to me I couldn't refuse. After the service the priest announced that a mass would be said in thanksgiving for the favours received by Mr and Mrs Grainger. There was no mention of me this time, confirming the practice of naming the sinners but not naming those who might appear to be reformed. Advertising obviously worked – even in the Catholic Church. I don't know why it rattled me so much given that I couldn't care a fig what the church, the congregation, or for that matter, my parents thought. I had long since decided that, should I secure a place at a London college, a significant aspect of my freedom would be never to attend a church service of any sort ever again.

My original plan was to take my jeans and sweat shirt in my bag and change from the suit on the train. However, when the day came, the suit felt so cool – with an open-necked white shirt and trainers – that I decided to wear it instead.

There were fifteen other hopefuls assembled in the reception studio when I arrived. Each of them carried a bulging portfolio of work and every one without exception wore jeans and T-shirts. A few smiled at my suited splendour but I ignored them. After a while two lecturers came into the room and announced they would collect the work that we'd brought with us. When I handed in my small folio of photographs, the guy doing the collection stopped and stared at me.

"And that's it?" he asked in a loud voice.

"That's it," I replied in an equally loud voice.

He smirked and asked, "Is the suit part of it then, as well?"

I felt myself flush. He was dressed to the same standard as the others in the room.

"Sorry," I said," sorry if I'm not wearing the approved uniform – but I find it hard to conform – you'll find that artists are like that."

As I spoke I deliberately looked the length of him – like he was a cow's dropping. His jaw fell and he immediately turned and left. An Asian lad who sat next to me laughed as the door closed.

"Wow – you don't care do you. You made him properly pissed."

"He's a prick." I said.

"Aye but a prick who might be somebody deciding your future."

I was a little surprised to find anyone among the opposition worrying about my future. It was most unusual and I liked him because of it. His name was Ram and he told me he was from Wolverhampton. He actually said he was, "A painter from Wolverhampton," and that made me like him all the more.

He asked me what I wanted to do and I told him honestly.

"I want to make a lot of money," I said, "and I don't much care if I paint, sculpt, or even knit socks to do it."

A couple of nearby faces looked up having overheard my comment. Their disapproval was explicit in the look they gave me but what did I care.

None of us knew that the time we spent waiting to be interviewed was being taped. If we had known, perhaps some of us might have been more circumspect in the comments we made – but I suppose that was the point. It was only when I was called in for the formal session and I was faced with the video of myself, declaring my manifesto that I began to see how it might be interpreted.

There were four interviewers; all lecturers save one who was the head of fine arts. The prick was amongst them wearing a substantial sneer. They played the video without comment and when it was over, the head of department asked, "So, Mick – how will you go about making a lot of money?"

I answered promptly, "Ideas," I said, "people pay for good ideas."

"But is that art?" another one asked.

"Yes," I said. By then it was too late to try and dress it up. I had to be positive.

"What kind of ideas?" This time it was the prick.

"New ones."

There was a pause and I could see a couple of them smiling – patronising bastards. The one with a beard whispered something to the head of department who then asked, "So – can you tell us – or better still show us – a new idea?"

"There are several in my folio and…"

"So you can't actually produce one – now?" The prick again.

I took a deep breath. This was the acid test, "I can – but I'd need your co-operation – the co-operation of all of you."

One or two sniggered but the head of department looked thoughtful – then he said, "Okay. We'll co-operate."

"You'll do as I ask?"

Heads nodded, some reluctantly. I stood up and moved my chair away. Now I was in charge, this was what I was good at.

"Would you please arrange your chairs in a semicircle well away from the desk gentlemen," I instructed.

They did as I asked but for two of them at least, clearly against their wishes.

"Now – would you sit on the floor in front of your chair and take off your shoes and socks."

This brought protests from the prick but he did it finally. I then made them put their feet up on their chairs and lay back on the floor and once they were in position I went round tickling their feet. There was almost immediate chaos. There was laughter and some swearing some struggled to get up before I got to them but I reminded them of their promise. I could not however, keep them under control for long and the situation soon deteriorated. The questions and objections came thick and fast.

"What the hell do you call that...? Are you taking the piss...? Is this just a silly joke...?" and so on.

When order was finally restored the head of department asked me to explain, so I did so, "We've just made, what I would call, a Laughing Stock Sculpture."

The arguments began immediately but no one could deny my claim that it was a new idea.

One week later I was awarded a place on the fine art degree course due to begin in September 1975.

Chapter Six

1975

I had attended the college of art in Middlesbrough for two years – two formative years. Years that charted a progress from ex-sixth former/unemployed person cum part-time thief in a forgotten northern town, to undergraduate at London University; from cultural cynic to minor cultural icon, and suddenly all that was over. I still had no illusions about the quality of my creative abilities, however. I realised that my good fortune so far was derived only from my instinct for survival and a small talent for making the ridiculous appear acceptable. It was the irreverence of my humour that had carried me forward. The originality of my ideas bore no relationship to the level of their intellectual novelty and little mental rigour was needed to comprehend their purpose. Mine was a reaction to the institutionalised idiocy so often found in those educational establishments claiming to be able to 'teach' young people to become artists rather than to teach them to make art.

I nevertheless found that sometimes I was beginning to take criticism of my work rather more seriously than I once might have done. There was a developing side to my thinking that quite enjoyed the psychobabble often applied to what I did. This prompted a growing conviction that my work might have more significance than I had once thought possible. Not surprisingly, I found myself studying the lives of famous artists and the movements, to which many of them once belonged, looking for common ground. I reasoned that there were probably many others who had begun their career seeing the Art Game for what it was and whose work initially was produced with tongue in cheek.

I reasoned that the critics and other non-participating observers had self-evidently inspired the degree of sophistication and significance attributed to works of art – particularly in the last fifty years – observations made after the event, rather than whilst work was in progress. Few would chance their reputation applauding the work of an unknown – but once they became established, then it was a different matter. These were people who tried to make original comments only in order to outdo one another as well as the artist under scrutiny. They employed obtuse classical references and claimed to identify psychological motives to qualify their claims Such cod expertise, I decided, needs only its own justification.

The paint 'splashers' and 'dribblers' of the 50s and 60s were certainly dependent on outsiders to define their philosophy, as were the 'found object' crowd. The abstract expressionists couldn't draw so they made squiggles; they couldn't paint so they went for gestures, some claimed their work was derived from that of children and some never got their hands dirty, preferring to become 'architects' of their product rather than 'makers'. I decided that in the main, art as we know it is clearly a confidence trick, one that has been practised for generations but one nevertheless proving a far more effective larceny than stealing from cars.

There was some satisfaction in being able to conclude that the Art Game was simply a means of extracting hard cash from those who pined to join in the apparent mysticism of the art insiders. Social mores concerning good taste inevitably imply that the owners of artefacts are knowledgeable and refined – when in fact the only pre-requisite is that they are rich. And with the advent of increased patronage from institutions such as the Arts Council, local authorities, and new town development corporations, it seemed that the culture of deception was prospering, its currency was rising. It was all about money and I wanted a piece of that action – a slice of the profit, and if that meant marketing my work alongside frozen peas – then that was what I was prepared to do – and more.

With my newly acquired access to the capital city, I knew that if my objectives were to be realised I needed to attract attention. The certain way of accomplishing that was to be controversial – and I had already learned how that was best achieved.

I was relieved and delighted finally to receive the offer of a place in the London college. There had been moments after the interview when I thought that perhaps I had gone too far. I had guessed beforehand that the question of proving my creativity might be asked – not an unreasonable guess given the limits of what work I had to show. Clearly I knew also that I needed to make an impression by doing something no one else would dare to do. That there would be limits to the patience the interviewers would be prepared to exercise on my behalf was obvious, but I appreciated also that the degree of their willingness to participate would restrict the success of my venture. I knew that lecturers in art tend to treat the formal interview situation very seriously – almost as though they see it as a recompense for their more usual laid-back attitude. I felt therefore, that if I could get them to laugh, it would make all the difference. Laughter is always a good catalyst, inevitably generating a feeling of well-being and the notion for the 'Laughing Stock Sculpture' came about as a consequence of a conversation with Celia the night before my interview. At some point during our discussions she had warned me dolefully that, "Whatever you do, you mustn't make them a laughing stock!"

Afterwards, when I reported back to her she could hardly believe I'd actually done it.

"You've got the balls for anything, Mick," she said, laughing at the same time.

This was a statement I was not prepared to argue about, particularly as she was so well placed to make such an assessment – she was holding the items referred to at the time in her hot little hand.

Needless to say, preparations for my migration south began as soon as I received the letter of acceptance. The subsistence grant would be small but the college was able to offer me a scholarship that made some small difference. The generous financial arrangements provided by the state promised me a standard of living roughly comparable to that of a homeless person. However, there were lots of part-time jobs available in London and I felt sure I could find something to supplement my income sufficient to accommodate my modest needs.

With the administrative arrangements taken care of, my last months in Tees-side were devoted to a round of farewell parties. These were 'show-stoppers' the like of which the town had not seen before. They ignored the passage of time and the quantity of alcohol consumed; they paid scant respect to noise abatement regulations and none at all to the social mores that determined acceptable sexual behaviour. Some of these parties were hosted in private houses but the best were those that took place high up on the moor above a market town called Guisbrough. A sufficiently remote location to guarantee us non-interference from respectable society, still less from the police.

Perhaps the most memorable of these celebrations was one night when it rained. And when it rains on the North Yorkshire moors even in summer, the water arrives in quantities seldom seen since Noah. Apparently designed to confuse all animal life in those parts without the advantage of gills, it is also known to be delivered horizontally, expertly seeking out those small gaps between collars and necks. Not surprising then, that the local rural community always look so clean or that they seldom part their lips when they speak.

The derelict farmhouse where we had stored the food and drink that night offered little or no protection as its roof was missing. Consequently, most people left early. Seven of us remained, erecting a makeshift shelter and zipping together seven sleeping bags next to the bonfire. It is worth mentioning that five of the survivors were females and, with a ratio of five to two, the games we played beneath the covers may well have been silly but they were certainly satisfying.

One of the more difficult farewells I had to make was to my old schoolmates, Tony and Bruce. Our agreement to meet on an ad hoc basis, usually at weekends, had quickly fallen foul of other demands in our new lives. Weekly had become monthly then bimonthly and later still – only by arrangement. In the end we rarely met anymore. I telephoned them on this occasion and arranged to meet at what had been our local pub, the scene of so many other meetings in the past. Sadly I found them to be even more changed than before. In the short space of time since we last met, they had imbibed the middle-class creed of hypocritical respectability – swallowed it whole, along with the various prejudices endemic in small minds. They both boasted a job with a view to career, the savings account with a view to a mortgage and the ubiquitous fiancées with a view to in-laws for Christmas week-end. They used expressions like, 'time to grow up', 'getting a grip', 'a foot on the ladder' and so on. They had begun to sound like schools' careers officers, the people no student worth his salt ever listened to. The worst aspect of Bruce's new persona was that he now drank halves instead of pints. A practice once seen as being sacrilegious. Clearly he no longer qualified as a virtual extra in our once favourite movie – *Saturday Night and Sunday Morning*.

"So," Bruce said, sounding like his father, "you're off to the big city then – maybe it'll help you sort yourself out."

I hardly dared answer. I was only two pints in but already my comments had met with obvious disappointment and not a little derision from my friends.

"Are you courting yet?"

This time it was Tony who asked and I really had to bite my lip. The emergence of his BBC accent took a lot of getting used to.

"Courting?" I couldn't resist, "Courting – who the hell 'courts' anymore. I have girlfriends – one in particular – but I certainly don't 'court' her. I fuck her occasionally. Is that courting?"

They exchanged looks that said 'poor bastard'.

"Oh come on fellers," I snapped back, "do me a favour. Courting went out with words like snogging and bobbysoxers."

"You really haven't changed at all have you, Mick – still loud and still as vulgar as ever," Bruce replied in the pained voice of an agony aunt.

"If you mean I still don't pose and posture – and pretend to be what I'm not – then no, I haven't changed at all. But you have old mate. If you're not careful you'll become a bad joke."

Tony immediately sprang to Bruce's defence, telling me how rude I was and that my comments were uncalled for. In no time at all we were into a real argument, all pretence gone. It was personal and vindictive, increasingly foul-mouthed and full of recrimination.

"You were always the yob. The one without manners…"

"And you were ever the one with pretensions – with or without manners."

"You're a wanker, Mick."

"Coming from you – being the local expert – that's a compliment."

"If this wasn't a leaving party – I'd leave right now…"

"Well leave if you fucking want to. No one is stopping you."

"What a bastard you turned out to be."

"Whereas you were always a bastard."

"A cunt of the first order."

"Maybe, but I doubt you've seen a real one – in the flesh so to speak."

And so it went on. The difference this time was that whilst I was enjoying myself, my companions were clearly taking it all to heart. The only saving factor was that, as the argument progressed, their language and their accents slipped back into pure Teesside – but they could no longer laugh at it.

Tony was the first to leave and despite the polite effort he affected to wish me well, his flushed face made it clear that he would not want to maintain contact. After that, Bruce stayed only long enough to say that I had ruined what should have been a good evening. He could not resist a final reference to my recent publicity and to my, "senseless attempts to make art". These he blamed for my, "ego trip".

I let him have the last word.

I watched him go with a certain amount of regret. It was so sad that he and Tony should regress so quickly, should forget where we all came from and all that must still be contained in our respective hand luggage.

My imminent exit generated another oddity also, this time at home. My parents decided – without reference to me – that a ritual family gathering should mark the occasion of my departure. Therefore, they gathered together a disparate collection of distant relatives the night before I left and invited them to share jam tarts, butterfly cakes and small talk in the parlour. They even supplied a limited amount of supermarket 'sweet' sherry, not sufficient, I hasten to add, to enable anyone present to approximate to a state of intoxication, enough only to generate stomach acid. One glass was more than enough to raise bile in the throat and make the digestion heave. Typically, I was the last to know about the party. Indeed I knew nothing about the gathering until it happened and, although I might have stayed had I been warned, I had already made my own arrangements.

"Just a few friends and relatives," Mam said, "they've come to see you off."

I'd been 'seen-off' by most of them in the past and had nothing to say to any of them anymore. Uncle Derby had tried to get his hand down my pants when I was only seven years of age – dirty old sod. His wife Molly – a simpleton kitchen robot – had dismissed my complaint arguing that, her husband hadn't meant any harm; cousin Billy was a scrounger and a lout – always picking his nose, borrowing money and smoking my fags. I'd once thought there was some hope for him – the hope that he might emigrate to somewhere boring like Canada. His mother, Aunt Gemma, was a secret drinker – one that everyone knew about! Her best claim to fame to be to fall senseless at the altar rail just as the priest was offering her Holy Communion. The vomit stains on the church carpet could never be removed. On the other hand, Billy's sister Patricia used to be a tasty bit of stuff; she was three years my senior and a real tease. When I was fifteen she caught me in the dark passageway at their house and before I knew what was happening she had my dick out. I was never given the chance to find out what her real intentions were, as Aunt Gemma put in an appearance at the front room door at the same time as my member appeared in her daughter's hand. For once I was the innocent party – but of course no one ever believed me. Thereafter, Patricia and me were never allowed to be alone together.

Patricia eventually fell pregnant by a guy working on the oil rigs, shortly after her twenty-second birthday. Within months of the birth, her lover disappeared down an oil pipeline and was never seen nor heard of again. None of this came as a great surprise and, like so many others, she quickly became respectable. For public consumption she henceforth favoured an apocryphal tale about how her husband had died at sea.

Did I want to spend my last evening on Teesside with this crowd? No I did not. However, given the gravity associated with the occasion by my parents, I felt I had to put in an appearance at least. Consequently I suffered the half-hearted congratulations, the nudges and the winks about being a student in London and the thinly veiled suggestions that 'it might be nice' if one or more of them visited me – when I eventually got a flat of my own. Fat chance – I thought. I even ate a jam tart.

Given the accident of their biological relationship, families often demonstrate a curious psychological construction when they herd together. Publicly they will claim the allegiance traditional amongst those sharing a gene pool whilst privately they will criticise and castigate every other individual present almost to the point of destruction. On this occasion the lack of strong drink limited the gossip and intimate asides to a significant degree. As a consequence the resulting social situation was pallid and half-hearted without even the possibility of a disagreement let alone a shouting match. It would have been almost worth investing in a few bottles of Scotch if only to see them perform.

Those qualities of personality particularly evident in my family, are generally and most obviously apparent at funerals or weddings. These are times when any strangers present can be treated to a dose of the peculiar brand of embarrassment in which my relatives specialise. The characteristics they regularly employ on these 'family' occasions include unashamed greed, vitriolic jealousy, the cruellest vindictiveness and lechery that would make the Marquis de Sade blush. I concluded that without doubt my closest relatives were ignorant, obvious and totally lacking in style. In a word, they were boring bastards destined forever to be losers.

I excused myself after a short stay, telling them that I had been invited to my tutor's home for a farewell drink and, as I had not been warned of their coming, there was no way I could fail to attend. I don't know if they believed me but I was able to leave by eight thirty nevertheless.

Instead, I drove Celia to the car park on the coast and shagged her till well past midnight.

My relationship with Celia had been special from day one. We shared a number of interests but concentrated mainly on those concerning the giving and taking of pleasure. Our understanding was not however, in any way seen as contractual. It was neither a prelude to marriage nor did we see it in any way as an impediment to sexual contact with others. Nevertheless, save for the episode with the policeman, we had both remained faithful. My departure to pastures new was not therefore an occasion for regret – that much was logical, we told one another – but relationships have a way of defeating the most ardent logician.

After the intrusion by the policemen, I had managed to remove the back seat of the car, allowing for the most athletic contortions either of us could devise without having to resort to the sand dunes. The inclusion of some extra blankets provided the basic comforts and we were able to enjoy a degree of privacy the open beach had never been able to afford.

That night it was warm and after the umpteenth session, we lay back on the blankets and rested. Celia had been unusually quiet, creating an atmosphere between us and I was expecting a reaction. The car slowly filled with the smoke from our cigarettes and the windows steamed up before she finally broached the subject.

"Are you going to miss me?" she asked in a small voice.

"Of course – what do you think."

"So – do you mind – if I come and visit you sometimes?"

I rolled over to face her and was surprised to see a tear roll down her cheek, reflected by the distant streetlights.

"Hey – what's all this?" I asked – knowing full well what it was.

"Just me being silly."

I ran a hand down her smooth flank and across her buttocks. A constant temptation such proximity, full curving flesh and a slim back, monstrously ripe fruit. Celia had a wonderful body.

"It's not silly at all," I whispered, "and if you want to – you could come down and stay."

Her muscles twitched under my hand.

"Really, you wouldn't mind?"

The soft skin of her inner thigh was like silk.

"Of course I wouldn't mind. In fact – if you wanted to – you could probably switch to a course down there and be with me all the time. Have you thought about that?"

She rolled over grinning, "I've thought about nothing else for weeks," she said.

Despite our agreement there was still no talk of any greater permanency to our relationship. Having already seen the landscape of female students in

London, there were mountain peaks there that I might still like to climb. Celia was a familiar delight but I did not want to feel restricted.

I had given little thought to anything at that time, other than ways of establishing my personal comforts in my new location. I was so confident about being able to satisfy the course requirements that I'd given little consideration to those particular needs. I preferred to see my time in London as an opportunity to find a profitable niche – my very own lily pad in a much bigger pond.

My first task however, would be to find accommodation.

Never having spent any time away from home before, never therefore having had to fend for myself, the prospect needed careful analysis. Clearly I would need access to cooking facilities and somewhere to sleep. I'd like a bit of space where I could store a few books and possibly a wardrobe. The only other consideration was cost. My budget was severely limited and, if I were to retain money for socialising, I needed to keep my outgoings as low as possible. I soon realised that the only way to find a suitable place would be by making an extended visit to the city before my course started and so that is what I decided to do.

Naturally, after our discussion on the night of the party, Celia wanted to come along but I persuaded her otherwise. It would be hard enough trying to concentrate on the task in hand without her easily accessible charms I telephoned Ram, the Asian lad I'd met at the interview, and he kindly arranged for me to stay with his relatives for a couple of nights. He told me he was also looking for a move away from the family so we agreed to look together.

Chapter Seven

The Singh family lived in an Edwardian terraced house comprising five bedrooms, two reception rooms a kitchen and two bathrooms It was situated in the heart of the Asian community in Southall. The father and mother both worked in a restaurant on the High Street and Ram's two cousins were employed in a local bank.

It was the first Asian household I had ever visited and in terms of culture shock, it was a leap in the dark. My first impression was a cacophony of colour, pattern and texture. Rich silks and heavy cotton fabrics meshed with highly decorated, embossed wallpapers from around the world, unashamedly proclaiming a very different cultural heritage and making explicit the religious beliefs practised by the household. Images of Hindu gods were evident in every room, posturing on shelves, in corners and in window spaces. In many respects, other than the frequency of religious icons, it was an environment as far removed from my own home, as it was possible to imagine. I felt like Sinbad discovering a new and exotic land.

The welcome I received was equally rich especially in the texture of its generosity. I was treated as an honoured guest. Surprisingly however, once we were alone in his room Ram began to apologise for his relatives, claiming that they were sometimes an embarrassment.

"They still behave like they're in India," he said, "and they haven't made any attempt to change."

"Why the hell should they change?" I asked.

"Because we all live in England now," he said. "This is a new country and they should pay respect to the local culture, instead of harping back all the time to 'the old country'." He pronounced the last bit of this judgement with bitterness. I suspect he was afraid I might find his relatives and the home he shared too foreign and it made me begin to think about the similar criticisms I applied to my own parents.

Often, since the announcement of my adoption on my twelfth birthday, I had spent a lot of time wondering about my natural mother and father. And, whilst I understood George and Mary Ellen Grainger's need to want to tell me the actual truth, I could never properly comprehend why they refused to discuss the matter thereafter. The argument they posed was that, as my natural parents had played no part in my upbringing, their identity should be of no significance. The implication being, that if I wanted to pursue the matter, I was in some way being disloyal to their efforts. It was a very Catholic 'spin'. Guilt is a significant strategy employed by that church, a means of control that has proved highly successful on generations of adherents. In my own case however, it provided one of the first fractures in my belief system. The need to know – to identify one's origins is strong and I could not understand how such a good Christian couple could want to leave their child – even their adopted child – in such a psychological dilemma.

Privately, I imagined all manner of different possibilities regarding my natural parents. By turns depending on my mood, they were rich and famous, wealthy landowners, even aristocracy, and they would be delighted when I discovered them again. On other occasions they were homeless down-and-outs, living hand to mouth, without any conscience concerning their lost offspring. It was a fruitless exercise but one I felt compelled to return to. I also reasoned that my increasing determination to be successful in the material world could be attributed to the vacuum left by this – not knowing.

Given the dubious nature of my own origins, I was therefore surprised and grateful for the kind attentions the Singh family lavished on me. This was most especially true in respect of the money I was able to save by lodging with them. Mr Singh erected a camp bed in Ram's room for me and Ram proved to be as easy to get on with as I'd imagined he might be – a really nice guy. He was clearly very serious about his painting and his art works lined the room with stacks of canvases in two corners. His interests in art however, were the complete antithesis of mine. His had a traditional approach, skilful in its method and punctilious in its attention to detail. I nevertheless chose to reserve my comments at least in part on account of the generosity I'd received.

The evening on which I arrived we spent hours scouring the Accommodation To Let advertisements in the *Evening Standard* – a thankless task. This episode was followed by numerous telephone calls asking for more detail, making appointments to view and haggling over the rents being asked. The following morning we went off to look at some of the flats, flatlets, rooms, and house-share facilities we had arranged to see the previous evening.

That day we saw twenty different places, some of which were in a terrible condition. It was a long day spent meeting with landlord's representatives, talking to solicitor's clerks and estate agents, arguing with landladies and negotiating with caretakers. It was not until mid-morning of the second day that we finally agreed to take two separate bedsits in what had once been a mansion block in Nottinghill. The road was called Copeland Gardens and it was located just off the end of the Portobello Road market, as cosmopolitan an area as one was likely to find anywhere outside of Lisbon or Cairo. On our floor – the second – there were seven bedsits and one bathroom. Each room was equipped with a tiny electric oven with a hotplate and a spare power point, presumably for an electric kettle. Ours were two of the smallest rooms. They boasted only enough space to squeeze past the single bed to reach the full-length window overlooking a communal garden facing west. There was just space at one end behind the door to stack suitcases and a modest amount of possessions. Clearly these rooms were not designed as places where one might host a dinner party but when I remarked as much to the caretaker, he was not amused.

Mr Finney, the caretaker, showed me that outside of my window there was a balcony but he warned me that he could not guarantee its structural integrity.

"If 'n' you go out there, yer on yer fuckin' own. All I'm prepared t'do is call a fuckin' ambulance," he told me sympathetically.

Obviously not a man to pull his punches, Finney was a foul-mouthed old bastard of indeterminate age. An Irish immigrant of some thirty years before, I discovered from my neighbours that he had a chequered past involving a period in prison. Some said he had once worked for an Italian vice baron, pimping for girls at King's Cross railway station and enforcing his master's requirements. It was impossible to determine the degree of truth in these stories but after having met the man, I could easily see him in just such a role. The caretaker's job was apparently his retirement perquisite, a golden handshake when his Italian boss was finally deported.

Ram's room was a few doors away along the corridor and it offered an almost identical quality of accommodation. However, whilst the lack of usable space hardly affected me, Ram needed studio space if he was to continue to work on large canvases. He therefore regarded the room as being only a temporary arrangement whilst he found somewhere more appropriate.

We signed some kind of agreement with Finney that day. These were contracts without the benefit of any legal status but we pretended to be impressed. He produced two grubby bits of hand-written paper for us to sign and embellished the almost unreadable regulations with a verbal explanation. "Y' don't do any kind of work from here – they're not commercial premises y' understand – an if 'ny have tarts visiting then y' make sure they're out by eleven. We don't want any women staying overnight else y' forfeit the deposit and yer out the next day."

I did not argue the point but had no intention of being bullied by this gnome of a man still less of abiding by his silly rules. I gave him the fifty pounds deposit and insisted on a receipt only to find that he could neither read nor write.

It was three weeks before I took up residence at Copeland Gardens and as Ram was not due to arrive for another few days, my arrival proved an opportunity for me to take stock of my situation. I stretched out on the lumpy mattress, tuned my transistor radio to a pop music station and had a good think.

I had grown used to having lots of people about me and I began to appreciate that the solitude might be one the things that caused me concern – at least initially. Living alone would be a significant contrast with what I was used to. I determined therefore that in future I would spend my evenings out and about. The neighbourhood was full of character and as a consequence the pubs and café catered for a wide range of food and drink. Then there was the market. Portobello market was known internationally as an antiques market. However, it was also every other kind of market as well, boasting some of the best fruit and veg one might find anywhere on the planet.

Typically, it was only when I came to calculate the actual detail of my income that I first perceived a chronic problem. Unless I lived like a hermit, I would need to find part-time work immediately. There was no point in living in one of the liveliest, busiest cities in the world and staying home every night, but in order to enjoy the facilities I knew I would need a fairly substantial injection of weekly cash. I was not depressed by this realisation, I had always believed that you needed to be amongst rich people to have any chance of becoming rich. In that respect I was in the ideal location, London certainly had its fair share of wealth. There was plenty of money about; I had only to devise a method of acquiring some. I spent the rest of the evening studying the job advertisements.

The following morning I registered my presence at the college. I received copious bits of paper and met the rest of my year group at an inaugural lecture given by one of the tutors. In the afternoon I was awarded a space in the main studio and told that I would work there. Finally, I took part in a group debate, chaired by our tutor, to discuss 'the place of the artist in society today'. I considered this a complete waste of everybody's time and concentrated my comments on derision, trying my best to alienate those who took it seriously. Surprisingly, the level of disagreement I was able to generate appeared to meet with the tutor's approval, if not with that of my fellow students.

In the evening there was a reception held for all the newcomers. Thankfully this was a relaxed affair – neither best frocks nor suits. There was a buffet and a bar, the food, beer and wine were free and everyone took advantage of the fact. A four-piece band kept the noise level just above 'unbearable' and after an hour or so various couples began to dance.

A limited number of older students attended this first social gathering, apparently, according to the official view, to offer the hand of friendship across the age groups. In fact they were there to size up the new talent and to have their pick of the fresh flesh. It was an exercise at which I have to admit they excelled. A careful scrutiny of the people present led me to believe that the gender bias amongst the new students favoured attractive young females. This led me to suspect that in their case, the admissions interview technique employed was more to do with the length and smoothness of legs and the cup size of bras rather than an aptitude for making art.

At some stage I was talking to a girl, a brunette called Julie, when a bearded third year student who introduced himself as Henry joined us. He told us he was currently exhibiting work in a gallery in Camden.

"What sort of work do you do?" I asked innocently.

"Situations." He said without looking me directly in the eye.

"And what the hell are 'situations'?" I asked.

Without preamble he then ran straight into a sound bite that could have come straight from his catalogue. A splurge of art double-talk obviously designed by a wordsmith from his agent's office, probably fresh from a red brick university and clearly without any respect to what might pass for the English language. There were vague references to Freudian and Jungian theory on social interaction in what simply amounted to a marketing exercise. He said nothing at all, however, about the work itself. It was a prime example of the codified system of communication employed by critics and aimed at the cognoscenti, one that I knew I would eventually need to practise myself. It was amusing and irritating almost to the same degree, the latter the more so when Henry eventually went off with Julie.

I strolled into the corridor outside and studied the noticeboard there. Amongst the more usual proclamations there were also advertisements for job vacancies. Most of the part-time work advertised was for cleaning staff. Despite my need for extra cash, somehow I just could not see myself with a broom and mop. There was one advertisement, however, that caught my eye and that was from a West End night club asking for waiters. The money wasn't great but there was a free dinner included in the package. The hours were from four thirty to midnight and the number of nights worked was apparently open to negotiation. I took down the telephone number and resolved to ring them.

"You looking for work then?"

A tall guy stood behind me looking over my shoulder.

"Well – I need to make some money, if that's what you mean," I replied.

"Don't we all," he muttered glancing round, "but would you consider something that wasn't quite kosher?"

Did I look like I was still green? Did I leave the impression I was just off a banana boat? This was the drug pusher's dirge in a million pubs and just as many college bars throughout the length of the land. And most usually made to pimply- faced youths, innocents who didn't know any better, the kind that ended up taking the macro-risk for the micro-return.

"What sort of money are we talking about?" I asked keeping a deadpan face.

"Could be as much as forty quid a trip – plus expenses of course."

"And what would I be carrying – from where to whom?"

"No need to worry about that – just a small package you'd pick up from a friend in Dieppe once a week – then drop it off with me. Easy money. What d'you say?"

I gave him my most angelic smile, "Okay. But forget the forty quid – I'd want twenty percent of the street value. What do you say?"

His smile was slow to come and when it did he nodded knowingly.

"Well – you can't blame a feller for trying – can you. Maybe I could supply you. What d'you use?"

"I used to use Brilliantine but I found it left marks on the pillowcase – now I just use my wits – like you do."

My response made him smile the more, "Not even a bit of grass?" he persisted.

I laughed and stuck out my hand. "Mick – Mick Grainger – fresh from Tees- side and pure as the driven snow."

He took my hand. "Gerry Jones from Brighton. Nice to meet you, Mick."

Gerry was also a final year student and had subsidised his studies for the last three years by occasional work for a major importer from South London. He would not divulge the name of his employer but promised me two hundred quid for every student I could recruit.

"You'll be amazed how many take the bait – and after all it isn't hard work – just a bit of a dodge."

"Especially if you get picked up at customs," I added.

After the reception we joined a group of students and went to the pub together. Gerry wanted to make an impression and insisted on buying drinks for everyone. He paid from a roll of notes that would have choked a cow. Not surprisingly, I got pissed.

Back at my room the electricity had run out and I didn't have any change for the meter. I tiptoed down the hall to Ram's room to borrow from him, hoping that he had arrived at last. It took a few minutes for him to answer to my timid knock and a little while more before he opened the door to me.

"Come on – come on in," he said glancing down the corridor as he spoke.

Inside I saw he had a girl in his bed. He closed the door quietly.

"Mick, meet Fay."

I nodded at the mound of hair and grinned. "If Finny catches you, there'll be hell to pay."

"Don't even think about it," Ram replied, "we've been avoiding him all day."

Fay was a nurse and had met my friend only that morning when he'd gone into St Mary's hospital for an X-ray.

"An X-ray?" I asked.

"My doctor is an old fanny," Ram said. "I've had trouble with my bowels for years and now he packs me off to the hospital for tests. He's from the 'you-can't-be-too-careful' school of medicine."

"So what did the results show?" I asked.

"No one will tell you that – you're just the patient. So I've got to go back to my own doctor to find out."

Fay appeared from beneath the duvet and confirmed this view whilst Ram made coffee for us all. Typically he had equipped his room already with most of the additives that make life comfortable. There was a coffee maker, an electric kettle and a toaster. Later when the coffee arrived it was sweetened with whisky and accompanied by digestive biscuits. Fay sat up to accept her drink and the fact that she was bare-breasted did not seem to cause her any embarrassment at all.

"Fay has agreed to pose for me," Ram announced through a mouthful of biscuit. "She has a great figure – show him Fay."

"It's not a peep-show," Fay snapped back pulling the duvet closer.

"Don't be silly. Mick's an artist too, he's seen dozens of naked women – anyway you should be proud of what you've got. Go on stand up and let him see you."

Reluctantly Fay stepped out from under the covers. She was stunning and I could not resist the temptation to touch. I stood near her and put my hands on her shoulders whilst I studied her... like sex was the furthest thing from my mind.

"See, I told you," Ram boasted.

"And you weren't wrong," I said softly, "turn round will you, Fay?"

The girl turned slowly. She was still a little red-faced but obviously delighted with all the attention. Ram was right; she was beautiful, perfectly proportioned and unblemished. I ran my palm down the crease in her back, stopping just above the buttocks.

"Such a sway," I said to Ram.

He smiled back perfectly aware of the game I was playing and clearly willing to endorse my participation.

"And she's half French," he said still smiling. The implication was not lost on me.

"Do you paint?" Fay asked as she completed the turn to face me again.

"I make situations – sort of new sculpture," I said, stealing a phrase from earlier in the evening. "I use the human scale as the basis for the relationships I create – you don't mind if I touch you – do you?"

She paused for only a second before agreeing. So I continued to touch her.

I never did discover how Ram managed to pull such a smart piece of choice flesh in such a short time, still less how he persuaded her to model for him – but it didn't matter. The touching turned to fondling and in no time at all the three of us were in the narrow bed with Fay providing all that two energetic young men could ever hope for in matters of the corporeal pleasures. Given the recent admission of Britain into the European Common Market, the fact that Fay was 50% continental also made me feel that I was 'doing my bit' for international relations – at least that's what I told Ram later.

The following day I telephoned for an appointment at the club where the waiter's job was on offer – a place calling itself the *Studio Club*. Miss

Winterness, the club secretary, said she would talk to me at four PM that afternoon. The solution to my cash flow problems was about to be solved – I felt it in my bones.

I left Ram and Fay clutched in one another's arms at about ten that morning. Their appetite for each other seemed insatiable and, although I had taken my pleasure with Fay's indulgence, I knew that it was Ram she preferred. I regarded the episode therefore as simply a fortunate meeting – especially on my own part.

Chapter Eight

Miss Winterness was a tall woman boasting a large stature with Edwardian bosoms – great bulbous forms that sloped away from her crisp white collars in an incline, steep enough to defeat the most accomplished downhill racer. The severity of her appearance was exaggerated further both by the tightness of her hair drawn back across her head to culminate in a tiny bun and the concentric creases caused by her chins being forced back into the starched white collar of her blouse. She sat, glass in hand, behind a small desk in a half-glazed cubicle that occupied a far corner of the cellar that housed the club. The scale of the tiny office was diminished further by the size of her physical presence, leaving her hardly enough room to turn round. Her proportions dwarfed her desk, the safe, and the filing cabinet.

My first impression was of a character from a Dickens novel and whilst she fitted her environment perfectly, both she and the club were strangely at odds with the contemporary bustle of Regent Street only a stone's throw away. I decided that had she been swathed in dark velvets and silks rather than in the flowery prints she chose to wear she would have been more consistently in character. By the same token, to my reckoning her voice should have had the timbre of a rich baritone instead of the 'little girl's' voice, which she employed. She was bizarre in every aspect.

"Come in, Michael," she said softly, studying me from head to toe, "come in and tell me all about yourself."

I had arrived a little early, as befits anyone seeking casual employment and had it not been for difficulty in finding the place, I would have been earlier still. I finally located the entrance hidden between two brown-painted doors of indeterminate use in a side passage just off Regent Street. Once I had descended into the depths of a dimly lit foyer, I was stopped by the tall, thin figure of the doorman.

"We're not open yet, Sir," he said in an authoritative tone, pronouncing the 'Sir' as though it were a threat.

"I'm here to see Miss Winterness," I replied defensively.

"And do you have an appointment?"

"Yes – for four."

"And are the other three outside still?"

His humour was lost on me and before I had time to form a suitable reply, a thin, high-pitched voice called from the office beyond, telling him I was expected.

Due to the space being so limited, for the duration of my interview, I was obliged to sit on a barstool just outside of the open office door, almost an observer rather than a participant. At her request, I described the detail of my background and consequently, she seemed reasonably satisfied that I was not an undesirable. The moment I stopped talking, however, she took up the conversation and talked for the next thirty minutes, hardly pausing for breath.

She described the constitution and history of the club, explaining that it was a member's club – owned by the members and administered by an elected board of major shareholders. She even outlined the detail of the lease on the property and the fact that it only had another few years left to run. She ended by telling me the names of some of the more notable members. Some were from the world of television and show business then there were lesser-known artists who were Royal Academicians and finally a sprinkling of aristocrats, none of whom I had ever heard of before. It was only when this list of celebrities was finally exhausted that she began to describe the nature of the job for which I was applying and, in order to expedite her description, she then took me on a tour of the facility. The space was split into four main areas: the entrance foyer, which also housed the tiny office; the dance floor with a bar at one end and a small stage at the other; and the restaurant, at one end of which was the fourth – the kitchen.

"The kitchen is where you will work – for most of the time," she said showing me a small 'L' shaped working kitchen, tightly packed with ovens, fridges and sinks.

"Chef is very particular about her kitchen so you must take special notice of her rules – Mrs Barnes is a treasure – irreplaceable and whatever else might happen here, no one must ever upset her."

I nodded enthusiastically, as if I would rather assassinate the Pope than upset Mrs Barnes and my assurances were apparently accepted.

Although it was never stated outright, I gathered from the discussion that followed about wages and which nights I would work, that my application had been successful. Contrary to my first impressions, I was to learn in time that Miss Winterness did not have an authoritarian bone in her large body. She was generous to a fault and always willing to listen to any kind of hard luck story. She was also prepared to tolerate the most outrageous behaviour from staff and although, for example, she would complain daily about money missing from the previous evening's till receipts, I never ever heard her accuse anyone of stealing. The club was clearly her whole life and she treated it as she might an only child. Sometimes it was noisy, sometimes nasty but she was always there to wipe its nose and apply plasters to its minor injuries.

Once the agreement was made and I had accepted the terms and conditions of the job, Miss Winterness took me to the bar and offered me a celebration drink. I chose a Scotch, which she poured generously for me. She poured herself a large Brandy – a Remy Martin. I was to discover that she never spent any longer than twenty minutes without a glass of brandy in her fist. It was her practice to drink steadily throughout the long evenings and late nights but seldom showed the worse for wear. I never saw her collapse through drink and I never saw her lose her temper because of it. Needless to say she was never rude or abusive.

On the other hand, I never saw her refuse a drink either.

That evening I dashed back to Nottinghill to tell Ram and Fay my good news. At last I had a source of income readily available and beyond the clutches of the Inland Revenue. Equally, my outgoings would be reduced due to the free meal and it did not take a rocket scientist to see that I would also be able to subsidise my grocery bill with tasty bits from the fridges in Mrs Barnes' kitchen. For the first time since I'd arrived in the capital, I felt confident that I could manage my finances.

I found the door to Ram's room locked. More than locked, it was barred. A hasp had been screwed onto the jamb and a huge brass padlock prohibited entry. There was no answer to my knock and no other sign of where my friends might be. I assumed that the worst had happened and Ram had been caught in flagrante delicto. I was about to retire down the corridor to my own room when Ram's neighbour, a mousy girl in a nurse's uniform poked her head out of the next door along.

"I think they've gone," she said apologetically.

"Gone where?" I asked.

The head came out a little further. "There was a terrible row. Mister Finney came round this afternoon and they shouted at one another for ages…"

"And what were they shouting about?" I asked feigning ignorance.

"Your friend had a girl staying with him and Finney said he'd broken his contract so he had to go."

As I'd suspected, Old Finney had caught Ram and Fay together.

"Did they say where they might go to?"

She shook her head. Just then the door opposite opened and an older woman stepped out. My first impression was of a tramp, that is – a sort of bag-lady; I wasn't wrong. Ram's neighbour turned out to be an interfering old bag, a harridan and one well-versed in gossip and domestic slanging matches.

"You a mate of that Paki?" she asked in a loud aggressive voice ruptured by years of woodbine smoking.

I bit my tongue and nodded, "Yes – do you know where they went?"

Obviously she took this to mean I could be easily browbeaten and stepped out confidently into the corridor. On closer inspection she was in a state of some severe dilapidation almost equal to the building in which she lived. Her hair was tangled, obviously uncombed for days, her dress crumpled, as though she had slept in it and her fingers were stained dark brown. Despite this however, when she looked at me she wore an expression, as though it was me that belonged in the cat's litter tray.

"Mister Finny came round and your Paki friend wouldn't open the door at first – but when he did and Mister Finny saw the tart he had in there, he was told to get out. The Paki's bit of stuff gave him a mouthful – a right dirty whore she was with a mouth as big as her arse. They only left when Finny threatened to call the police. They said they'd be back for their stuff later."

"But did they say where they were going?"

"No. He just up and left with his slag trailing along behind him."

I'd got as much as I was ever going to get from this old bag, so I dropped the pretence at politeness.

"Thanks a lot for your help – incidentally you might like to know that Mr Singh isn't from Pakistan, he was born in Sheffield and his parents came from Durban in South Africa. His girlfriend is the daughter of a merchant banker and a qualified nurse..."

"I don't give a fuck about all that. As far as I'm concerned he's a dirty Paki and she's no good if she sleeps with the likes of him."

"Dirty," I said loudly, "did you say dirty? Have you looked in the mirror this – this year? You appear at the door of your hovel, looking like you haven't washed for months and you call him dirty. That has to be a joke. And as far as sex goes, I bet the only sex you get is from stray dogs and then you'd have to pay for it. Now piss off you – you dirty old sack of shit."

White-faced, the young nurse opposite suppressed a grin. In her doorway the bigot turned a light shade of purple. Clearly unable to think of a suitable reply she retreated back into her room muttering obscenities and slammed the door. I thanked the nurse and went to my room. However, when I opened the door, there was Ram sitting on my bed next to Fay. The grins on their faces indicated that they had heard my comments.

"The keys are all the same," Ram said, "and I knew you wouldn't mind."

Once Finny had gone, they had apparently returned to my room to wait quietly for my reappearance.

"Trouble is," Ram said, "the old bastard has fixed a lock on the door and all my stuff is still inside. He claims I owe him a week's rent and that he'll keep my gear if I don't pay up."

We'd each given the caretaker a deposit of one week's rent when we signed up and we'd also paid a week in advance. The deposit was justifiably forfeit – but to ask for more – that was completely out of order.

"We heard that you met Mary 'the mouth' from the room opposite," Fay said.

I nodded. "Oh yes, we met. She retired badly bruised in the second round. If she'd owned a towel she'd have thrown it in."

"We think it was Mary that blew the whistle on us," Ram said. "Some guy down the hall reckons she's Finny's week-end lay. Apparently she lives rent free – for services rendered."

This news did not surprise me at all; the bigot looked like she'd once worked the streets – at the poor end of town. No wonder she was so twisted.

Later, after the building had quietened down for the night, I undid the hasp on Ram's door with a screwdriver and retrieved his things. I worked quietly so as not to alert Mary and by the time I left, the hasp had been restored sufficient to look as if it hadn't been tampered with. In a modest celebration, the three of us went out to a local café for a serious fry-up and then on to a pub for a couple of pints. As there was no chance of them finding alternative accommodation that night Ram and Fay joined me in my room. However, this time the noise of our activities were severely limited. We did not want another visitation from Finny.

There was no reaction from Finny regarding the break-in and the next morning Ram and Fay went on their way to seek another flat or a room. Ram's old room was let the same day.

The work on my new course followed much the same practice as it had back in Tees-side. Typically, the proscription was defined in terms of skills rather than ideas. Each of the students had a weekly tutorial with a lecturer appointed to be their mentor and this was the only forum for philosophical discussion. As we expected, as the term progressed, the meetings became more lax and less frequent. The life drawing classes eventually stopped and my tutor found better things to do than to offer any kind of dialogue about my work. Older students told us that it was a pattern we could rely on throughout the course, referring to it as, 'art college wilt'. The absence of tutorial guidance however, had little or no effect on my time or my activities. The simple truth was that I did little that could be termed work and devoted myself instead to the pursuit of money. The so-called university was all that I had imagined it might be – namely a soft option designed for 'dossers'.

I quickly became well established at the *Studio Club* and regularly worked three nights each week. Miss Winterness soon adopted me as one of her favourites. Also, through an assumed politeness, a keen observation of her rules and not a little toadying, Mrs Barnes the chef began to treat me like a long lost son. Meanwhile, Fay and Ram found a two roomed flat over in Camberwell and, although I saw less of them than before, we kept in contact, albeit infrequently. By then there were other distractions to keep me occupied.

I attended college only spasmodically and then only after midday. I made certain that I was always present when staff were about to make one of their spasmodic visits or when the administration were making spot checks. The rest of the time was my own – an urban honeymoon without the responsibility of a bride. Infrequently, I considered ideas relating to those projects I'd begun in the past but this was only to safeguard against cross-examination by my tutor. I rehearsed a statement in which I claimed to be working on a new idea and employed a carefully practised argument using art 'double-talk' to support the lie. My grasp of art language was improving daily and I began to carry a small notebook and a camera – in most people's eyes – the tools of the keen observer. They were not to know that there was seldom a film in the camera and that my scribbling generally amounted only to lists of things I needed to take from my employer's fridge.

Otherwise my time was spent exploring London, once known as the swinging city and probably then still the most exciting capital in the world. I got to know its markets, its night life, and the full range of its entertainment industry as well as something of its history. I was always a committed people 'watcher' in much the same way that I enjoy noticing odd number-plates on vehicles and I began to collect a memory of the strange folk with whom I came in contact. In this context, the club proved a main source of reference. I struck up an association with many of the regular members – hardly a friendship in the true sense, sufficient only as a clearing house for club gossip. As a consequence, in a surprisingly short time, I felt that I had accommodated my new environment successfully.

Celia had written a number of letters during these first weeks and eventually at the end of October, she wrote to say that she wanted to visit me. Our exchange of letters had been spartan offering only the briefest glimpse of our individual activities but this was not surprising. Our friendship derived more from the physical side of our relationship than it ever did from conversation. Naturally I did not describe my various peccadilloes with Fay and one or two other young ladies. I was pleased however, when Celia told me that, despite our agreement, she had remained faithful. As far as I was concerned, my adventures made no difference to my feelings for Celia and I looked forward to her company with the same degree of anticipation as ever. The only problem with her impending visit was how to accommodate her. I did not want to have to start and look for new lodgings just yet, so I decided to try and do a deal with Finny.

It was the old man's usual practice to bring out a deck-chair and position it in front of the building each afternoon to catch the last rays of the autumn sun. A ritual that inevitably included a sun-screen that consisted of several bottles of Guinness. It was also from this position that he would hold court – discussing mutual interests with friends and neighbours and listening to petitions from his tenants. One afternoon I made certain that I was already sitting on the entrance steps before he appeared. I also made sure that my holdall bag was stuffed with his brand of sunscreen. We chatted and shared a drink, I told him a couple of off-colour jokes that I knew he would appreciate and he reciprocated with some of his own that were even cruder than mine. This led naturally to a discussion about sex.

"Tell me, Mick," he said, "that girl – the friend of your mate the Paki – did you give her one yourself – by any chance?"

"Several times," I answered honestly.

He shook his head jealously, "Lucky bugger – if she'd been a bit more co-operative that day, they could have stayed on in the room."

"You didn't try it on yourself – did you?"

He gave me a secretive look and grinned, "When he opened the door she was there behind him buck naked. Calm, as you like. Full fanny frontal – didn't care a toss. But as soon as I began to talk about 'favours' for 'favours' she was at me. She had a mouth on her that girl."

He waxed lyrical about how he would have enjoyed Fay's company down in his basement and when he was in full flow, I introduced the problem about Celia. I told him about her visit and the difficulty in finding somewhere to stay.

"She'll only be staying over a couple of nights and, if you could bend the rules a bit – I wouldn't mind paying double rent for that week. What do you think?" I said.

As expected, he muttered a bit at first about the danger of being caught out by the owner and losing his job but then, just as predictably, he accepted the proposition. He said it wasn't the money so much that made the difference in attitude – it was him being asked in advance that counted. He claimed that it showed some respect for his position and if I could add another fiver to the rent then Celia could stay as long as she liked. We opened another couple of bottles to seal the deal and by the time I left him he was well pissed.

*

Celia arrived at Kings Cross station on October 24th, the eve of my birthday. I had all but forgotten about the birthday but she had a card and a present in her luggage and made a big fuss about it. She looked as good as I remembered her. Her newly blonded hair was cut in a bob and beneath a denim jacket, she wore a dress cut short to just above the knee. The thin fabric of the dress did nothing to disguise the fact that she was braless. Like a gust of fresh air she took my arm and marched me towards the taxi rank at the entrance. In the taxi she kissed me and let her hand stray onto my lap, whispering promises in my attentive ear the while. Naturally, I was very excited.

Her train had arrived just before lunchtime and by the time we got back to Nottinghill the afternoon was still young so I took her to *Hennecky's* pub on the Portobello road for a ploughman's lunch and a drink.

As luck would have it Finny was at the bar when we arrived, drinking with a couple of his cronies. I could therefore do no other than make suitable introductions and watch the hungry eyes of the older men, greedily searching her body. Finny's orbs almost popped out when she stood before him and he held on to her hand rather longer than necessary when they met. We got away to a side table eventually but I was conscious of the eyes at the bar throughout our lunch. At every opportunity one or another of the viewers would wink or nod in our direction and before we finished the cheese, a tray of drinks appeared, courtesy of the lechers. Clearly, on account of Celia, Mister Finny's status had received a considerable boost amongst the clique of his grubby friends.

Later, back at the room, we lost no more time with conversation and jumped into bed together. Celia was special, of that there could be no doubt. She had an instinct for pleasure that allied itself to an aptitude for the exotic. The evening was one to remember. It brought back memories of nights in the sand dunes facing the cold of the North Sea, of struggling for position in a cramped car, and most of all of her high-pitched gurgles of delight echoing the deserted beach. If fucking was an art form then Celia was a maestro without peer.

The afternoon grew dull and the room faded into the dark of the evening as our struggles continued. How long we actually devoted to the exercise of mutual satisfaction I do not recall. Neither can I remember how many times we coupled. It seemed to be a continuous activity, punctuated only by the briefest periods of rest – a cigarette or a cup of coffee. Long after dark Celia arose to visit the communal bathroom leaving me exhausted. She pulled on an old dressing gown and crept out along the corridor. She had been forewarned about Mary and the possibility of confrontation but was unconcerned at the prospect and I was confident that she could hold her own in any exchange of vitriol.

She was gone for quite a long time and when she did return, her face was a little flushed. She closed the door and I could see her grinning despite the lack of light.

"I've just been talking to your friend," she said mysteriously.

"Mary the mouth?"

"No – your Mister Finny."

She climbed back next to me beneath the duvet and put her face next to mine.

"He's a randy old sod. Asked me if I fancied paying him a visit down in his basement flat."

I propped myself up on one elbow, "He what?"

She laughed, "No problem, Mick, he just tried his luck. I refused of course and then he tried to make a grab but I was too quick for him."

"You mean he was waiting in the corridor when you left?"

"Yeah – just outside the door. And then he waited until I came out of the bathroom and tried again."

"The dirty old bugger, I'll smack him next time I see him."

"There's no need for that. I doubt he could manage it anyway. I put him off finally by saying he'd have to ask you for permission to shag me. It worked and he wandered off muttering about how lucky you are."

I grumbled aggressively about geriatrics and their fantasies but she just chuckled. She stretched out alongside me and threw one of her legs across mine, "Do I take it then that you're not prepared to share me anymore?" she asked mischievously.

"Well – he's hardly a policeman – is he?" I replied.

She poked me in the ribs with a hard finger.

"On the other hand," I continued, "it might be good for you to have an older man – and we could negotiate a rent rebate if you were nice to him."

"You are a pig," she snorted. "And as you get older, you'll be a dirty old man just like Finney."

Now it was my turn to laugh and I turned on my side to face her, still chuckling.

"It's a thought though – isn't it?" I whispered. "You could earn quite a few quid if you realised your assets – and – as I'm doing my bit by working as a waiter, why shouldn't you find some part-time employment?"

She laid there quietly for a while and then replied, "It wouldn't bother me too much you know," she said at last. "I could easily go on the game – if you wanted me to."

The turn in the conversation involved a detailed discussion about the possibility of Celia working the street. It lasted about a half-hour before the stimulus proved too much. Another round of sexual activity followed leaving me totally exhausted and I went to sleep with my head full of pornographic images.

Chapter Nine

The activities of those students, with whom I shared the main studio, made the atmosphere there resemble a cross between that of an abattoir and a sewage farm. The stench that filled the air was sufficient to cause any passing heath inspector to order immediate fumigation, if not to order the building to be condemned. My fellow first year students appeared to be obscenely preoccupied with the prolific use of human waste and dead animal life. I wandered past their cubicles, therefore, trying to determine their motivation and at the same time, trying not to breathe the air.

It had been nine days since I last visited the college, an absence due entirely to my involvement with Celia and my job at the club. Fortunately an absence that had not been noticed or recorded. My appearance however, was only on account of our termly assessment being almost due and the fact that I had nothing tangible for anyone to assess.

Given the atmosphere I found, I concluded that either a miniature revolution had occurred whilst I had been away or that the department had been infected with a virus affecting the students' mental stability. Gone was the pleasant aroma of oil paint and turpentine only to be replaced by the foetid stink of human excrement, the malodorous damp of stale clothing and those pungent chemical smells associated with an undertaker's parlour. It was a revelation akin to that of Dante's visit to the Inferno.

Nearest to the double doors, I found Kim, a pretty Eurasian girl, dipping a large spatula into a plastic container, attempting to coat a dinner service with shit – human shit (as it transpired – her own shit). Oblivious to my disgust, she told me that the main problem was one of achieving a consistent thickness.

"You couldn't make the plates in different thickness," she said, "and it's doubly difficult ensuring the cups maintain the same capacity... the stuff hardens so quickly..."

I chose not to ask what might happen if it did harden too quickly or how she kept her bucketful of the medium consistently moist. Thankfully she observed a modicum of hygienic control by wearing rubber gloves. She tried to recruit my approval by telling me what she intended. "Imagine a dining table," she said, "covered with a crisp white cloth. The silver shines and the freshly cooked greens contrast with the dark brown of crockery." She glowed with enthusiasm, "'Kim's Feast' is the title and it says something about junk food, about chemicals in food, about greed, about hygiene and about society's obsession with stuffing their bellies whilst the Third World starves."

I nodded politely as though we were in harmony but rejected the mental image her description prompted and moved on.

In the next space another girl, Hilary from Slough, sat diligently mixing a bowl of silicone rubber solution. Her project concerned pumping the solution into dead animals, the insides of which, having been removed, were displayed nearby in glass carboys.

"I need to be able to put them into strange positions," she told me seriously, "as if they were part of a fashion show."

She emphasised the words 'fashion show' as though this would impart the meaning of her endeavours.

"I will probably give each of them masks – masks of the faces of famous fashion models – get it?"

I made noises as though her intentions were as laudable as they were obvious but left thinking that she had serious mental problems I discovered later that Hilary was in fact a refugee from the Dress Design department and that since she'd been told she was too 'big' to model dresses herself, she wanted to do something more 'serious' than dress designing. Poking fun at dress design presumably fitted the bill.

Across the room two lads from Hackney, Dean and Jeff, had teamed up in a manner closely resembling that of Gilbert and George. They were busy with a very large canvas. They refused to discuss the work in progress and despite my questions they continued in silence to stick large rectangles of paper to the canvas.

The problem, as I saw it, was that the paper and the canvas were exactly the same tone of aubergine. It was obvious that, given the precise proportions of the paper, it would eventually cover the whole canvas obliterating it. Naturally I asked why it had been necessary to paint it the same colour in the first place but they ignored me. I enjoyed watching them at work nevertheless and was especially impressed with the care they took in positioning the paper pieces. It was only after a long scrutiny of their efforts that I observed that a very fine gap had been left down the centre of the canvas. It bisected the surface precisely down the centre with all the care of a surgeon's scalpel.

I resisted the temptation to tell them that they'd missed a bit. East End lads are not best known for their sense of humour.

Alongside Dean and Jeff, Julie McGregor sat amidst mounds of old clothing – or at least that was my first impression. She looked rough. Her hair was a tangled mess and she had bags under her eyes that could well have served as skips for a building site.

"Hi Mick," she said as I poked my head round the corner, "how are things doing?"

"Fine," I said, "couldn't be better."

She grinned, "Short of ideas are we?"

I bit my tongue, ignoring the crack and looked critically round her space; "You've been busy. What's all this about?"

"It's about me," she said defiantly, "these are all the clothes I ever owned – everything is here." As if to prove the point she rummaged through a nearby pile and pulled out a pair of children's knickers. "My first proper knickers," she exclaimed proudly. "Mum kept 'em. She's like me, she keeps everything."

I nodded trying to appear thoughtful.

"So, this is all about me – I suppose it also says something about my family – especially my mum, a kind of family history. Not a perfectionist piece – except maybe my own kind of perfection. Yes?"

I'm not sure if this is a question so I nod again – slowly this time.

"Went to the *Groucho* last night," this time she smiled – clearly more than a very happy memory, "everyone was there of course – pissed as a rat – but I scored with this performance artist from Canada. And did he perform! A dick like a horse's – ooh."

She lit another cigarette to compensate.

"Got any booze on you?" she asked suddenly.

"Sorry. When I have it – I drink it."

"Know what you mean. I gotta cut down. Spoils the shagging."

She got out of her chair and rearranged one of the mounds of clothing. I could not tell what difference the rearrangement made but when she stood back to admire it, I nodded again, this time in unison with her.

"That's more like it," she said with a smirk, as if some great improvement had been achieved. "Have you seen what Dean and Jeff are doing next door – its magic eh?"

"Yeah heavy," I said, "that purple is so concentrated – and the line – eh?"

Julie nodded this time, "The galleries are onto them already. Jacobson was here yesterday and that woman from the Serpentine telephoned. They're going to be big – real big."

I left Julie wondering about big ones and strolled over to see Ram but he wasn't there. There were a couple of big paintings turned to the wall in his studio; I left them as they were, not wishing to seem nosy. The place was certainly alive with activity – what kind of activity was a different matter – but what the hell. They were happy and they were doing what they wanted to do. My space was next to Ram's and by comparison to the others, it was still virginal.

Next door to me a guy called Tommy was sticking condoms onto a fashion shop mannequin. Thousands of rubbers, colour coded and dangling from their packets, leaving an impression like that of a buckskin shirt. I hardly knew Tommy so I just glanced in. He caught my eye, "Like it?" he asked.

"Interesting," was all I could offer.

"I get them for free. Lovely aren't they?"

"Beautiful."

"I'm into all that stuff about paradox," he said, "ambiguity and paradox – like there are some tarts who put out the high-class image – but they still get fucked... like no matter how well-dressed we are, we still get done over by the establishment."

Not knowing how to respond to this I just stood and stared.

Untroubled by my silence he continued, "So the rubber appendages represent fucking in both senses – but they're on the outside not the inside – cos they're for birth control as well and that's not profitable fucking. See – a paradox eh?"

I left shortly after Tommy's thesis. I had to be at the club for five and I didn't think I could take any more superficial intellectualism, however well meant.

On the other hand it was good to see that I was not alone in rejecting the traditional value systems or the established ways of working. However odd some of the work might appear, I concluded that this was the cutting edge. And the more I thought about what I'd seen, the more inspired I felt. So much so that I decided that as soon as I got back to my room that night I would begin to develop some ideas of my own.

It was also interesting that after spending an hour or more in the studio workspace, I could not smell the shit at all.

On the tube I found myself wondering why so many of my peer group were preoccupied with human waste. A new movement perhaps, one that could be reasonably called sewagists or shitists perhaps. I appreciated as much as anyone that funding one's projects was always a problem and this perhaps justified those with an obsession about bodily excrescence. After all they were for free. However, to hope that by exhibiting your own waste products were to imbue them with special significance greater than their parts, I believed was arrant nonsense. As Gertrude Stein might have put it: 'Shit is shit, is shit, and is shit.' However beautifully it might be presented. The same was also true for mounds of old clothing – when did a pile of clothing become more than a pile of old clothing. And because the old clothing had all belonged to one person made no difference at all – in my view. Even with my jaundiced perception of the world of fine art, I believed that such attempts as I had witnessed in the college that day could never transcend the banality of the muddled thinking that had produced them. The philosophy was fine but the product was disappointing.

I determined that I would begin to make real art. Art that made a difference – something truly original?

That night we were busy. Sixty-four covers before ten o'clock and that included two large parties consisting of six and nine diners, respectively. My timetable for the night had followed its usual pattern. I arrived around five p.m. and laid the tables, then I had my dinner. Mrs Barnes was already in situ having all manner of pots and pans bubbling away on the three oven tops. She had delivered the evening's menu to Miss Winterness who typed it out and photocopied it before putting it into the plastic covers on each table. We opened the doors at six p.m.

The diners ordered their meal from me. I copied their request on my pad and then transcribed it onto bits of paper, which were pinned to a board in the serving hatch. When Mrs Barnes filled the order, I would then cross it out. I was also responsible for most of the cold puddings, the cheeses and the coffee, and had the delight of clearing away the used crocks before resetting the tables. As customers left they would approach my station and settle their bill – mostly in cash. Often, diners would ask the waiter to obtain wine for them from the bar and, if the restaurant was quiet, this proved no great hardship, otherwise the wine waiter from the bar needed to be called. Most members were considerate and patient with waiters and difficulties arose only when visitors affected offence when the service was not quick enough for their purposes. Food was seldom returned for whatever reason but when it was, it was replaced immediately without argument.

I had adapted quickly to the needs of the job and took some pride in having the restaurant organised efficiently. Customers left generous tips and the atmosphere was generally relaxed and light-hearted, a welcome relief from that in the college studios.

Mr Bonphiro was a regular customer, dining with us at least three evenings every week; consequently a friendly relationship was established between us. He would ask about what I was doing, about my love life and about the gossip at college and in return he told me about his own life. He had been a professional tennis player in Portugal but currently he was a senior partner in a large advertising agency. He was unmarried and lived his bachelor existence in a luxury flat near Regent's Park. A quietly spoken man, he nevertheless exhibited a healthy sense of humour and seemed to be seriously interested in modern art. This was not unusual amongst the membership and the management board encouraged a host of 'artistic' activities in the club, including exhibitions of small paintings – usually watercolours, a poetry evening and occasionally an afternoon drawing class.

This was also reflected in the preference shown by Miss Winterness in employing those involved in the arts as waiters. She said it helped encourage the club's ethos and I was not surprised to discover that in her youth, she had herself been an artist's model. Indeed, if the rumours were to be believed, she had been one of the mistresses of a very well known painter in the 1950s. A fact that she eventually confessed to me one night, after a particularly heavy bout of drinking. I was always cautious about receiving information that might otherwise have been too personal to tell, as it was inevitably the cause of some regret once the hangover had passed. Shared secrets can prove the most destructive force between employers and employees.

That particular night I was exhausted by ten thirty and to make matters all the worse, the little woman who normally did the washing-up had called in sick. Even after the final table was cleared, therefore, I still had a mound of dishes to wash. As a consequence, the casual orders for late-night sandwiches could not be satisfied and various people complained. Miss Winterness soon appreciated the scale of my dilemma and rolled up her sleeves and helped clear the backlog. Chaos was thereby averted and order restored. However, although the club closed at midnight, that night it took another forty minutes to get the last members to leave and this meant that I had missed the last tube. Fortunately Miss Winterness lived in South Kensington and took a taxi home each night. She offered to drop me at Nottinghill on her way home, a treat for me that was to prove even more fortunate for her.

The taxi was just turning off the Edgware Road into Praed Street when she suffered a heart attack. One moment she was extolling the virtues of my diligence at work and in the next she was making a deep-throated gurgling sound. Her eyes rolled and she slipped back into the hard seat. I cleared her airways but as her body convulsed, I called for the driver to stop. Once he realised what was happening he drove us quickly to St. Mary's hospital next to Paddington train station. I dashed up the steps and called for a doctor. A moment or two later and an emergency team ran out to the taxi. Miss Winterness was hoisted onto a trolley and whisked away in seconds. The club contracted the taxi on her behalf so I did not have to pay for the fare; however, the driver had been so helpful I felt obliged to tip him.

I sat in the reception area for the next hour waiting for news. Not knowing sufficient about Miss Winterness' personal details, I was unable to satisfy the requirements of the admissions clerk. Instead, I handed over her purse in which they found her driving license and that appeared to satisfy their immediate needs. It was almost two a.m. before the doctor emerged to tell me that she was as comfortable as could be expected in the intensive care ward.

"Would you like to see her before you leave?" he asked finally and although I was reluctant to spend even more time in the hospital, it seemed the thing to do. I allowed myself to be led through the long white corridors, past lines of equally pale sleeping faces to stop at last outside a pair of double doors.

"She's in here for the moment – don't stay more than a couple of minutes she needs her rest. Okay?"

I agreed and went in quietly.

I find there is often sameness about the appearance of people once they are admitted to hospital, as if the first injection fills them with an obligatory uniformity. Almost, as soon as they become prone, they seem to lose their individual identities. Add to this a collection of tubes and monitors, a few bedside machines and what looked like a drip and Miss Winterness was almost unidentifiable. It took me several seconds to see where she was. Her eyes opened when I approached, dull grey stones in a mound of cracked pastry.

"Ah, Michael," she said in an even smaller voice than usual, "you saved my life…"

The embarrassment of unearned thanks was magnified when she took my denials as modesty but whatever my reaction, I had obviously made a new friend. Our conversation was brief and she fell to sleep in mid-sentence after only a minute or so. I waited only a moment or two more before I was glad to creep away.

Unfortunately my return journey did not include the help of a nursing guide. Add to that the fact that a sense of direction was not one of the attributes with which I had been blessed and inevitably I got lost. The reception area at the hospital entrance eluded me therefore for the next twenty minutes. Eventually a night nurse who stood on guard in the doorway of a large ward stopped me. Obviously suspicious, she cast a hooded eye over me and began a cross-examination. The nurse was an older woman; the folds in her face were almost as numerous as those in her cloak and in the half-light, almost as blue. I was questioned as to my business and it took some time before she reluctantly accepted my explanation. She was in the act of directing me to the entrance when a voice from a nearby bed just inside the ward door spoke my name. I turned and found Ram lying there.

"Ram – what the hell are you doing in here?" I asked, astonished to find a face I knew.

Before he could reply the nurse took my arm and pulled me away to one side and whispered, "I'm afraid Mr Singh is quite ill – are you a friend?"

Chapter Ten

Perhaps the most seminal influence throughout my early childhood was that exercised by an involvement with the Roman faith. And despite my rejection of it, it proved to be a value system more difficult to displace than cat hairs on a woolly blanket. Significantly, as my parents first represented it to me, the depth of its hold was as systematic as it was profound. To dislodge it was therefore a slow process. Eventually, however, the percolation of logic through the fine gauze of a personality intent on physical gratification, achieved a predictable and entirely desirable outcome. Despite the years of brainwashing, it was never part of my nature to pay respect to the holy insurance men in white collars. And however comforting it might have been to pray for the things I wished for and thereby to defray responsibility for failure, I chose instead to bite my tongue and do the best I could on my own. Sadly none of this applied to my friend Ram.

Ram's family were Hindu and they were as devout in their belief and in their practical observances as any Christian family might be in theirs. Naturally he had resisted the influence himself but due at least in part to the depth of his relationship with his parents, when the chips were down as it were, the belief proved too pervasive. Not surprisingly therefore, when he was diagnosed as having bowel cancer, the relatives looked to their gods to find a cure.

Some days after finding my friend in the hospital, I persuaded a staff nurse to talk to me about his illness. According to the nurse, the prognosis was fairly good. Tests showed that so far the tumour had not spread and that if it could be reduced in volume by radiotherapy and chemotherapy, an operation to remove it was feasible. In the meantime, there would be severe pain and discomfort, some of which would be caused by the necessary introduction of a colostomy bag. This, I was informed, was a temporary measure designed to reduce the danger of further infection via the bowel.

Before the fateful night at St. Mary's hospital, I had not seen Ram or Fay for a couple of weeks. The distance between our accommodations proving too great to make easy socialising possible. Added to which, my infrequent attendance at college had increased the difficulty. It had therefore proved all but impossible for anyone to communicate the onset of Ram's illness. Once I discovered him however, I made regular visits to his bedside.

During the next three months Ram underwent several operations. A slow painful process of therapy apparently made little difference to the size of his tumour and finally the surgeons decided to remove it as it was. By this time my friend was only a shadow of his former self. He retained his hair, which was a blessing, but all his body fat disappeared and his eyes became like pebbles. He looked beaten. In terms of his psychological welfare however, the worst blow was Fay's increasing reluctance to visit him and long before his final operation she had stopped coming altogether. Not the expected behaviour of case-hardened nurse, still less that of a lover.

One night as I sat reading to him – he loved to be read to – he suddenly declared that he did not believe he would ever recover. I objected of course but he was adamant, "Honest, Mick," he said, "I don't see an end to this. The bloody thing has fucked me good."

"Get out of it," I said, trying to sound as upbeat as possible, "you've done well. The treatment seems to have worked and they got the bastard thing out – in its entirety. What more do you want."

He studied me from beneath heavy lids. "I'll tell you," he said softly, "it'd be nice to do a few things for myself for a change… I can't even wipe my own arse."

"I thought you'd stopped using it for the time being," I replied trying to make him smile, "And you should complain – even the Royal Family have to wipe their own arses. You've got it made."

The weapon – the only weapon in my arsenal was humour and for a while it seemed to work. I told him that cancers hated being laughed at – so he had to laugh at his. I said he should devote at least five minutes every day laughing and making fun of his cancer and assured him that, just like policemen and college lecturers, cancers hated to be ridiculed. During my visits I did my best to make him laugh – but I could be there only four or five times a week and according to the nurses, for most of the rest of the time he was deeply morose. The medical staff came to believe that the biggest impediment to Ram's recovery was his attitude, arguing that post-operative depression killed as many patients as did their original disease. It was deeply depressing.

Christmas passed and the year ended almost without anything worthy of note happening. I took Celia to Trafalgar Square on New Year's Eve and we both ended up dead drunk in somebody's private house party but none of that was too unusual. Naturally I chose not to travel home for the holiday and instead opted to suffer a long maudlin conversation with my mother on the telephone. In the process she extorted a promise from me that next year I would trek back north to share their celebrations. It was a promise I had no intention of keeping but my agreement made her happy nevertheless.

At that time, my concern about Ram needed to be carefully matched against other worries. The more immediate problem was the fact that I had no work to show for the coming spring assessment. There were rumours that, due to a possible visit from HM Inspectors, the staff were about to be particularly invasive in their questioning and that they would be looking for an excuse to expel one or two students from the new intake, just to prove their toughness. Therefore, as the date approached my panic increased. I recognised the familiar feeling of alienation – as if I'd been disenfranchised.

In the early days, I had gained so much mileage from the projects done in Middlesbrough that it would be impossible simply to repeat them. Also, there was an emphasis currently placed on the need for evidence of a development in skills and this would apparently leave those old projects sadly lacking. My worst fears were confirmed when, one week before the assessment, staff let it be known that they would be looking for signs of an appreciation of traditional techniques as well as originality.

As usual it was Celia who came up with the idea that was to save my neck. She pointed out that, due to his illness, Ram would be excused the rigours of a formal assessment and that most of his work had been done outside of the college studios – so it was as yet unknown to the tutors.

"I'm sure he wouldn't mind you if you borrowed his paintings," she said. "He'd probably find it a huge joke."

It was a touch of genius. Ram had been absent almost as much as I had myself and consequently, no one had any idea what he had done. We went to his flat the next morning and let ourselves in with the key he'd loaned me. It was an Aladdin's cave. There were seven large canvases, each finely painted in an increasingly surreal theme. The attendant drawings were neatly filed and accompanied by notes about his point of departure. I took the lot. From the state of the place, it was obvious that Fay had not been there for some time, so there was no one to witness my actions.

The following week I received a commendation from staff and was awarded a small cash bursary as a prize.

By now Celia had successfully negotiated a place as a late entrant onto the foundation course. Given her gregarious nature, not to mention her obvious good looks, she was quickly accepted by staff and students alike. There had been some initial difficulty regarding the payment of her fees but this had been sorted out by the kindly intervention of Ken – one of the foundation lecturers. Ken was another of the tutors who took a particular interest in new female students. He sometimes took Celia out for a drink and although she always denied the fact, I was certain he had propositioned her. She claimed that she always resisted staff blandishments, especially those involving a bed for the night, but knowing her unusual appetites, I could never be sure of her truthfulness. Not that it mattered a great deal. Celia still proved the best of company and the most versatile of partners in bed so I had little to complain about.

Although we spent most of our free time in one another's company, Celia seldom came down to the club when I was working. This meant that for three nights each week, she was free to make her own social arrangements. On those rare occasions when she did call to see me at work, she was inevitably the centre of attention amongst the old guard of middle-aged 'chancers' at the bar.

On those nights when the club was quiet, I often found myself in conversation with Mr Porphino. He was an art buff, he said, specialising in the early Renaissance, particularly the work of Giotto. He was a mine of information and, although he listened carefully to what I had to say about modern art, it was his detailed knowledge that provided the most interest in our discussions. He knew all about Michelangelo and Leonardo da Vinci, the Medici and the Borgias. He talked convincingly about patronage and argued that it was only through the financial interest of patrons that many artists ever became known. At some point one evening he asked me if I had ever considered trying to acquire a patron myself.

"It can make a huge difference, Michael," he said meaningfully, "opening doors for you, ensuring publicity and marketing your product."

I pointed out to him that whilst the idea had obvious merit, there was little opportunity for someone like me to meet anyone like that.

"You must remember, Mr Porphino, I hail from a very different background in the working-class wastelands of the north. It is most unlikely that I will ever meet socially with any big-money men…"

He smiled as he interrupted me, "Now that is exactly what I wanted to talk to you about, Michael. How would you like to attend a reception at the National Gallery – say, next Friday evening?"

"That's a bit like asking if I'd like to win the football pools," I replied.

He smiled again and continued, "Well – next Friday, the Friends of the National are hosting a small reception to welcome the new director. Nothing too special – just a glass of wine and a chat – a chance to meet a few people. What do you think?"

"I'd be delighted," I said, "as long as you don't mind being seen with an unknown like me."

"Silly boy. More importantly there is someone I want you to meet. I've talked to him about you and he would like to meet you also."

"Who's that?"

"His name is Manny Hume – one of the Hume twins – arguably the biggest collectors of modern art in Britain... And he is currently interested in seeking out new talent. He is very well connected and, if he likes you, he could prove a powerful friend."

This was the most exciting break so far in my short career, an opportunity to rub shoulders with the people who mattered. About as far a cry from my Teesside origins as it was possible to get and I agreed immediately. I was told to meet Mr Porphino outside the side entrance at seven the following Friday evening. He emphasised the need for me to look smart and seemed pleased at my enthusiasm.

I could hardly wait to get back to the room that night. I badly needed someone to share my news with and Celia was the obvious choice. However, the room was empty when I got back there and it was two in the morning before Celia reappeared. At first I thought she was a little drunk, her speech was slurred and she was unsteady on her feet.

"Had a bit too much, have we?" I asked.

She looked at me and grinned. Her efforts to unbutton her blouse failed and she eventually gave up, fell back onto the bed and began laughing – as though I had just said something really funny.

"Never touched the stuff," she said at last, "but I did have a little smoke... and a pill or two."

She closed her eyes and put her head back and a fraction of a second later her skin colour changed. Before I could do anything she was sick – a magnificently challenged digestive function – sufficient to gain a gold medal in any freestyle projectile-vomiting competition. It is odd, if not interesting, how small spaces seem to magnify unpleasant smells and this occasion proved the rule. I am not, nor have I ever been the tidiest of people. Celia and I had therefore reached an agreement that, if we were to reside in the small room without the bloodletting small living spaces impose on their occupants, we would need to engineer the most careful space management. Shelves had been located judiciously above eye level, plastic boxes were slid beneath the bed and every available surface top had its own articles situated in precisely equal arrangements. There had been no accommodation left for vomit. Vomit had never been on our agenda.

Needless to say, Celia's late-night performance rendered the majority of these considerations a waste of time. Matters were made all the worse by my girlfriend's apparent need to roll about on the rapidly saturating sheets. The mess was indescribable. I was very upset – in fact, I was fucking furious. However, I was obliged to spend the rest of the hours of darkness trying to clean the room. And, whilst I applied the limited resources afforded by a cold water wash-hand basin, a box of paper tissues and a bottle of antiseptic, Celia slept.

Due to Celia's indisposition, the curiosity natural to any boyfriend about a female partner found in such a condition could not be satisfied. This was another frustration on which I had time to dwell in detail during the night. Her slumber may well have been that of the innocent but I needed convincing. At first light I repaired to the bathroom. As any kind of sleep had proved impossible, I imagined that a shower and a shave might be a remedy for the feelings of aggression that filled my soul. I had a need for self-indulgence, a desire to lavish some care on myself by the generous application of hot water and sweet smelling-soaps – and so I did. I ran off more than my share of the hot water and shaved twice to produce the smoothest finish possible; I used Celia's shampoo and shower gel and I finished with an aftershave lotion of which even Barbara Cartland would have approved. By the time I had finished the other tenants on that floor were lining up in the corridor, already late for their morning tube trains and buses. My apologies were vague and the scowling faces of my neighbours etched their disapproval into my back as I retreated to my room.

The room door was ajar and the bed was empty. Celia had gone.

I dressed quickly and before leaving, gave the space a final burst of lavender aerosol to mitigate the last memory of Celia's evening meal. By now my fury was enough to crack my teeth. Running away would not suffice and if Celia imagined that… Half way down the staircase I met the object causing my irritation, on her way back up.

She gave me a weak smile. "Sorry, Mick," she said in a plaintive voice.

"Where the hell have you been?"

"To the loo downstairs – I couldn't get in ours – you were in the shower."

It was difficult to decide at this point if I was more annoyed with her or with myself. I could not trust myself to engage in any kind of conversation so I left her on the stairs in her dressing gown, saying that I was in a hurry and that I'd see her later. It was only when I arrived at the tube station that I realised that I had locked the room door. If Celia did not have her key with her she would be locked out. Maybe Finney would achieve his ambition and get her to visit his cellar after all. At least that made me smile.

Chapter Eleven

1976

As luck would have it, at the very moment when Mr Porphino decided to introduce me to Manny Hume, I had just filled my mouth with a fistful of tiny delicacies from a passing tray. Doesn't it always happen like that? You go to any lengths to seek out the right contacts, you dress in your best bib and tucker, shave carefully, and arrive in good time, you even forego the copious supply of free alcohol in order to maintain some semblance of sobriety, however unaccustomed, but the moment you decided to eat – that is the moment someone attempts an introduction.

A hand fell on my shoulder and a voice in my ear said, "Michael – I'd like you to meet Manny Hume."

I turned to find Mr Porphino standing there smiling, accompanied by a large heavily built man with black hair and even blacker eyes. I coughed a spray of fine pastry in their direction and retrieved the situation only by the use of a large white pocket handkerchief.

"Excuse me…," I mumbled. "Sorry – so sorry. Delighted to meet you, Mister Hume."

I took his hand and even then, at our very first meeting, I became conscious of the big man's awkwardness. Not so much an absence of social grace, rather something to do with a disconnection in his movements – a physical discordance, as if he had been assembled from disparate parts. Manny was the personification of a 'found object'

"I've heard so much about you from Charlie," he said, "it's a real pleasure to meet you at last."

They do say that the most lasting impressions are made in the first moment of meeting someone new, as though the essential ethos of a person's character is fractionally more exposed in those first few seconds. If that were the case in this instance, it is a wonder that any kind of relationship was ever formed between Manny Hume and me. From his point of view I must have appeared the most gauche and ill-mannered pastry-splutterer of his considerable experience. Equally, my first impression of him was of a very odd man indeed.

He wore a pair of thickly elasticised cushions for lips and even when these were not used to emphasise his stream of mostly irrelevant anecdotes, they were ever mobile. They stretched into large smiles; parted in quick grins; they pursed thoughtfully, grimaced sympathetically and pouted questioningly. It was just as if a third party had their hand up his neck, working the features in a practice session for real-life puppetry. Quick glimpses of Hollywood-perfect teeth repeatedly flashed a dazzling artificial whiteness, hypnotically distracting my attention. Moreover, his lips were where his face ended – the verb at the end of the Latin sentence – a perimeter after which a small chin receded to marry seamlessly with a fleshly flapped neck.

By contrast, densely black eyebrows circumscribed the other end of his long face and I was to learn that, if a clue was ever needed to his moods, these inevitably proved the best reference points. Unusually the eyes told you nothing, their immobility proving to be a severe contrast within the constant flexing of their surrounding context. The eyes were as a quotation from the man's inner self, held in parenthesis by his brows and lips.

"So," he said raising one of the black eyebrows, "Charlie tells me you're an artist – what kind of things do you make?"

It was the first time I had heard Mr Porphino referred to as Charlie and I had to suppress a smile.

"Situations," I said, "like visual puns – witty comments in which things are a bit short of normal."

"I like that," Manny proclaimed loudly, "did you hear that, Charlie, 'a bit short of normal' – nice one. And what are these situations worth, Mick?"

"In cash terms – they're only worth what someone is willing to pay for them."

My quick response was appreciated – as I'd expected it to be. It was a predictable question from someone in the world of commerce and to make vague claims of intrinsic value would have been a pointless exercise.

"Exactly," the big man said, "so now we're agreed about value systems – when can I see some of your stuff?"

Charlie Porphino stood smiling alongside his friend. He was well pleased with himself. He had told me that if I hit it off with Manny Hume, he could easily become an important patron. What neither of them knew at this point was that, despite my marketing pitch, I had nothing of any substance worth offering for sale.

"Manny has been a collector all his life and he already has some modern pieces."

"And I intend to have a lot more. I like the things you young guys are about. You're making the classic pieces of the future – and it goes without saying – if I keep ahead of the market, then I'll reap the biggest rewards."

This creed was typical. According to rumour in the press, Manny Hume's practice was to promote and direct markets. He was a trendsetter rather than a trend-follower and if the prices he had achieved recently at auction for some more traditional art works were any guide, he was able to manipulate the Art world, just as he did the commodities markets.

"Tell you what, young Mick," he said, "take my card and when you next have a batch of works to show, give me a bell. I know a lot of gallery-owners so maybe we can organise an exhibition for you."

I took the card and thanked him, promising to get back in touch as soon as possible. My fingers tingled; this was the break everyone imagined might happen. If Manny was willing to invest in my future, we could take the world by storm. And the tiny problem posed by my not as yet having produced anything was actually in line with the best business practice – namely, get your order books filled before you spend money on production.

As if he read my mind, Manny turned back before leaving to tell me that if I needed working capital, I should ring his secretary, "We can deduct the cash outlay from sales at a later date – no problem."

Charlie Porphino told me later that Manny had been very impressed with me. He added that I should regard his patronage as a major coup – as if I needed telling.

It was not obvious at this time – especially to me – but apparently Charlie Porphino's exceptional interest in my career and welfare was not motivated solely by a commitment to fine art, neither was it the action of a philanthropist concerned that young people should reach their potential. I was to learn later that Porphino was gay and the crowd that represented most of his closest friends were well-known sexual predators. They were described to me as the equivalent of kerb crawlers, seeking to take advantage of immature flesh by any means possible. In the first instance I thought this judgement was more than a little harsh. Charlie had shown me nothing but kindness without any trace of an alternative agenda. However, when he began to bring his friends to the restaurant as his guests, they soon betrayed their preferences. By then it was too late to distance myself from him. To be fair, however, I did not care a fig about his sexual proclivities as long as he did nothing to try and include me in his activities. There had never been any conditions attendant on the introduction he made to Manny on my behalf but eventually it became obvious that he had hopes nevertheless for a quid pro quo. It became increasingly difficult to refuse his continuous invitations to join him for dinner at his home and the attention he lavished on me soon became a standing joke amongst other staff at the club.

Harry the wine waiter cum bouncer was especially amused by my predicament and teased me whenever the opportunity arose. If he saw Porphino enter the premises he would rush to the restaurant and suggest that I should comb my hair. Often he would ask Charlie if he thought my bum was cute and sometimes he would pass on faked messages just to confuse the situation further. Eventually I decided that one way to stop the situation becoming a perennial problem was to make enough money so that I did not need to work at the club. Manny Hume was therefore the key and consequently I began to formulate a plan to take advantage of his interest.

*

One evening after college, I took Dean and Jeff for a drink at a wine bar just off the Strand. It was situated in a side street and accessed via a steep flight of stairs, letting down into a warren of old vaults beneath the road. The variety and quality of the wines on offer however, was not reflected in the price charged and it proved the most economical drinking place in London. Jeff told me it was one of their favourite places but best avoided at lunchtimes when it was crowded by city staff from the offices nearby. On those occasions the toilets were a no-go area, apparently confined to those wishing to snort cocaine, shoot up heroin, or sell their rear end. There were one or two such customers evident that evening but other than their ability to drink copious amounts of red wine and talk in loud voices there was little evidence of obvious brain damage.

"So," Dean asked, "are you going to tell us?"

We'd just opened our first bottle when he posed this question and I pretended that I had no idea what he was talking about.

"Tell you about what?"

They exchanged grins.

"Come on, Mick. You know we're dying to hear about what you're doing. You were the one to make a big impression when we all arrived and we know you have somewhere else to work – else you'd be in college with the rest of us."

I paused for a moment to think. There was an idea germinating in the back of my head but it was too soon yet to declare the detail.

"I can't say too much just yet – but how would you like to help me out with a project?"

"For money of course?" Dean asked.

"Of course," I agreed.

They both laughed, "We'll do almost anything for money," Jeff added.

"Is it legal?" Dean whispered.

Now I laughed. "It's legal – and what's more you're both good at it."

Before I left them we'd agreed a deal and I bought them another bottle as a token of good faith.

Unusually I had been ignorant of their admiration but it made recruiting them all the easier once I realised. I was pleased with myself. Why had I not thought of the idea before? It was an obvious solution. And if their attitude were typical then it would not prove difficult to recruit others from the year group.

By now I was in danger of being late for the club and I knew I would have to run if I were to catch my train. I dashed through the two rooms leading to the staircase and in the process bumped into a couple just behind one of the brick columns. They were locked together like limpets in a throat-tickling contest with the usual sound effects. The young woman turned to complain as I hurried my apology.

"Hello, Fay," I said, unable to keep the caustic edge out of my voice.

Her embarrassment was little recompense and, after the briefest conversation in which I described Ram's state in as much lurid detail as my imagination could muster, I left her to enjoy the rest of her evening.

During the next month I was busy trying to 'sell' my idea. Kim was the only one of my contemporaries who was not tempted by my offer. She maintained that her 'After Dinner Service' of shit-lined crockery was too precious to part with. The integrity she assumed annoyed me and in the end I decided to leave her to wallow in the material she spent so much time playing with. As there was no such thing as copyright, there would be no problem in reproducing the work. On the other hand Hilary and most of the others had no problem with my request – money was a great motivator. As

123

a consequence by the end of August I had enough work to fill a modest exhibition space. And if I wasn't the originator of it, at least I was its manipulator – and wasn't that justification enough to claim it as my own.

The notion of employing other artists to do the work was derived from the old atelier system – an apprenticeship scheme. My development of the idea only took it a small step further. Instead of them working to my specification, they worked to their own – but I paid for it so it became mine. Artists are increasingly once removed from the production of their work, even most of the most famous artists employ assistants – why not remove oneself one stage further I argued. I was happy with my resolution.

The idea had sprung from the necessity to take advantage of Manny's offer. It was essential that he should not go wanting and as I did not have work of my own, I obtained some. What it consisted of was immaterial – so who had produced it, didn't matter. It was art and Manny wanted to buy art. Bearing in mind the advice once given me by Joss Pruitt in a similar situation, I took the precaution of getting each of the artists to sign a release form denying any interest in their work and promised them various sums of money – once Manny paid up.

My next task was to find studio space. I needed an environment sufficiently large both to house the art works I had acquired and to live in. Celia and I had outgrown the tiny room we rented from Finney and since her late night adventure, things had been a little difficult in our relationship. We needed a new start. It took us a further month of searching before we found somewhere suitable, a place that we could almost afford. The result was a run-down warehouse in Hackney. The group of empty, semi-derelict buildings waiting for redevelopment stood just off Urswick Road. There was electricity and water laid on and even an ancient gas cooker that stood in a far corner facing a space as big as an aeroplane hangar.

I reckoned that if I could not get enough cash from Manny, I could always return the work and nothing would be lost save the time spent moving. On the other hand, if he bought me out, we would be set up and financially secure.

As usual it was Celia who came up with the idea to put the finishing touch to the scheme. She suggested that I should have some work in progress as well as that which was finished.

"If you want to convince Manny then you should have something ongoing – something started – and the bigger, the better. He'd like that I'm sure."

She was not wrong.

I did some soul-searching and counted my money – our money, before deciding that the only option was to have something 'ready-made' and the only 'ready-made' of any size – that we could afford – was a scrap car. I promptly went down to the breakers yard and selected an old Ford Estate car and the foreman promised to deliver it the following day.

Now I know perfectly well that a scrap car isn't a work of art but neither is a set of handlebars and a bicycle seat – not until Picasso put them together like a bull's head. And in the sphere in which I had chosen to work, giving whatever I chose a name like, *The Bull's Head* was unnecessary. With a few minor adjustments, I could coin a title such as, *Turning onto the slip road one Saturday night* or, *A petrol engine dreaming of Oxford's spires* or any of a million other expressions implying complex philosophical ideas.

The space we'd rented had a side entrance consisting of two enormous double doors and it was through these that I had the bulk of the work delivered. The various pieces were distributed throughout the space and by the end of the following morning it was beginning to look like a proper studio. I used my credit card – a newly acquired facility – to hire a collection of heavy tools such as a chain saw, power drills, a nail gun and a variety of others. And whilst I arranged the heavy stuff, Celia mounted groups of newspaper clippings, magazine pictures and bits of notes from my journal. These made for an apparent collection of source material and the fact that they were as random as they were confusing only made the final effect that much better. Shortly after the old Ford was delivered and sited, I telephoned Porphino and then Manny Hume.

I was unable to speak directly to either of them. Both secretaries claimed they were busily engaged in meetings and, although promises were made to alert them to my call, I was left in no doubt that my message would have little or no priority. Now this was the cause for some real concern. How long I could maintain the new studio with such limited means was questionable and I had no doubt that my student friends would not wait indefinitely for their money either. Privately I began to re-examine the sanity of my gamble.

I had explained to both secretaries that it would be impossible to contact me by phone, as there was no such facility at the studio. Instead I'd suggested that it might be a better idea for either of the principals in this matter to try and contact me at the Studio Club. I knew also however, that private incoming calls at the club were not encouraged. Fortunately Manny had placed his return call before I arrived for work that evening. He had left a message telling me to phone him at home before ten o'clock that night. It appeared that his legendary charm had worked its usual magic on Miss Winterness and, at his suggestion; she agreed that I should make the call from her office just before the restaurant closed that night.

I have no doubt that Miss Winterness's attitude was coloured at least in part by the fact that she still felt that she owed me a debt of gratitude. On her return to work she had advertised my part in the swift treatment she received at hospital to anyone willing to listen. I was the local hero according to her. In the event, she had made a surprisingly quick recovery after her 'incident' – as she liked to call it – and now regarded me as some sort of guardian angel. Each evening when I arrived she would report me on her progress with her diet, her exercise plan and the limit she now applied to her drinking. She would also confess to me on those occasions when she had transgressed. I was nevertheless aware that her claims did not always reflect the accuracy of the facts. I knew for example that as soon as the restaurant was busy and I was fully occupied, she would go to her office for a sneaky smoke, a sure sign that she was also cheating on the other aspects of her health regime. Other than to offer her encouragement and to give tacit approval of her efforts, there was little anyone could do under such circumstances. If she was intent on committing suicide who was I to try and change her mind.

That night the club was busy and by ten o'clock I was exhausted. For much of the shift I was distracted by my concerns over money and this caused me to make a number of errors leaving several customers upset. However justified, their complaints put me in a bad mood and I began to question if the job was worth the hassle. The pay was only minimal in relation to the degree of effort required and I started to wonder if there might be some other way of supplementing my income. It occurred to me that, as I was the one handling the cash, it might be possible to fiddle the takings in my own favour. Consequently, I devoted some time to an examination of the procedures employed in the restaurant, trying to see ways in which they might be adulterated.

Due to the chaos caused in the kitchen, I did not get to phone Manny until twenty minutes after ten. However, when I rang his home he answered immediately and greeted me like a long-lost friend. I lost no time in telling him about the studio and the work on show there and invited him along to see for himself.

"I'd love to visit, Mick," he said, "but not in the too near future…"

My heart did a cartwheel.

"Unfortunately I'm off to the States first thing in the morning and I'll be gone about three weeks. But as soon as I get back, I promise to drop round."

After that the conversation dragged. We discussed some of my ideas for big projects and the kind of technical expertise I would need to accomplish them but I was preoccupied throughout with thoughts of bankruptcy. My worst fears were realised. Three weeks delay would mean financial disaster. There was no way that I could continue renting the studio without help and no possibility of settling my debts with the other students.

Money was mentioned for the first time towards the end of our conversation when, thankfully, Manny asked how I was fixed for cash. My pause must have told him the truth of the matter and he quickly offered help.

"If you need a little something to tide you over, I can let you have something on account as I promised – say as a down payment on one of your pieces. What do you say?"

What could I say? For once in my life I was tongue-tied. He didn't wait for my reply.

"Now – if I get my secretary to make you out a cheque for – say – five thousand. Would that help?"

"That would be a life-saver."

He laughed and told me he had suspected that I might be in financial difficulties.

"You mustn't be too shy to ask for help, Mick," he told me, "we have a business relationship now and I'm only too pleased if I can make life a bit easier for you."

He told me to ring Julia his secretary the following morning and he promised to contact me as soon as he returned.

I put down the phone and sat back in Miss Winterness's chair. A flagstone had been lifted off my shoulders.

"Did it go well, dear?" Miss Winterness asked from the doorway.

"Very well," I replied, "very well indeed."

Whether it was the stimulus provided by my conversation with Manny or not, I do not know but as soon as I returned to the kitchen, I saw a way of improving my take-home pay. The order pads used by the waiters were inevitably dog-eared with pages missing both from the front and the back. If I were to take a sizeable order – say once per evening shift – on a page at the back of the book, it would prove a simple matter to remove it at the end of the evening and take the sum of that bill from the till. At the other end of the transaction, orders taken were written up on scrap paper for the Chef and mounted with a paper clip on a board in the serving hatch. As each order was filled, it would be scribbled out. If I removed the scrap of paper with the targeted order at the end of the evening then there would be no record of it, leaving me free to take whatever sum had accrued on account of it.

It was foolproof – a brilliant piece of creative innovation. And if I selected a group of four diners who were likely to spend in excess of twenty pounds per head then my weekly pick-up could increase by between two hundred and forty to three hundred pounds. Now that was a worthwhile sum. The likelihood of discovery was remote and, save for the occasion of stocktaking, which was carried out only every six months, I could see no way that the loss could ever be detected.

At that time there were other waiters employed also on a part-time basis. Only two of us worked alone, however. The others provided a safety valve, to ensure that on party nights or when a particularly large group of diners booked tables, we would have sufficient help readily available. I nevertheless hatched a plan to convince Miss Winterness that we didn't need the extra waiters and that two of us could handle all the work. Trevor was the name of the other waiter who worked solo. A student from the Midlands, he was currently studying at the Royal Academy School and he boasted a sense of humour similar to my own and a problem with a cash shortage also almost equal to mine. We had worked together several times and it took no time at all to persuade him of my plan.

However, Miss Winterness took a little more time to accept our new idea and it took a last minute refinement to finally persuade her. We offered to guarantee that the takings from the restaurant would never again be short. If they were short, we agreed to make up the difference out of our own pockets. Miss Winterness found this a most compelling argument and agreed immediately. We also promised that one or the other of us would always be available whatever the occasion and that on extra busy nights we would both serve on tables. She bought us both a drink at the bar to celebrate and promptly fired the other two waiters. It was a major coup.

Chapter Twelve

Manny Hume's offices were situated in Duke Street. Having said that, they were not at all what I'd expected. The accommodation consisted of a collection of sober rooms in what had been a Georgian house. The décor was simple — inexpensive even — the detail mostly original, the furniture bland and non-committal, the carpets corded and the lighting direct. The only memorable things were the art works. The place was stuffed to the gills with twentieth century art. Matisse, Degas, Van Gogh, Picasso, Sisley and Monet filled the waiting rooms with colour, and inside Rembrandt, Goya and van Dyke provided a more serious urbanity to the office itself. I did not yet get to see the inner sanctum but learned later that Manny kept only a small collection of drawings in there, including works by David Hockney, Henry Moore, Ben Nicholson and Henri Gaudier-Brzeska.

The reception space was quiet, almost the acoustics of a bedroom (not my bedroom I hasten to add) and if more evidence was needed to further this illusion it was provided by Julia, his secretary. Unlike the business-suited, crystal-tipped ladies who populated the city office byways, those who clinked their cocktail ice-cubes in an equal-opportunity, digital heaven of profit and loss, Julia's presence was unashamedly feminine. Androgyny had no foothold here. Her voice was soft and her manner uncompetitive. She afforded herself an easy smile without damage to the aura of competence obviously apparent in her position and a welcome greeting equal to that of a friend. Best of all she had great tits.

I was smitten. Not to be so would have implied a dangerously low blood pressure or the kind of immunity to stimulus that could be caused only by castration.

"Good morning," she said, fixing me with eyes as green as any tropical sea, "and can I help?"

The temptation to itemise the many ways in which her kind assistance would be gratefully received was difficult to resist. Instead, however, I stepped smartly forward with my best smile and offered my hand. "Michael Grainger. I think you're expecting me – yes?"

Her touch was warm and brief but the green eyes clouded momentarily.

"Can you tell me why I might be expecting you, Mister Grainger?" she said.

"Manny asked me to call by this morning – to collect a cheque."

She referred to a shorthand pad and then to her VDU. The screen's reflection lit her face as she studied it.

"I'm awfully sorry, Mr Grainger – but I have no record of a cheque for you from Mr Hume. Can you give me a little more detail?"

My breath shortened as I tried to explain. It sounded weak if not implausible and when I finished Julia looked more than a little sceptical.

"And you are Mick Grainger – the artist – yes?" she asked.

I nodded feeling the credibility gap widen still further.

"I'm sorry, but it appears to have slipped Mr Hume's memory. He's been very busy of late and the trip to Boston was so unexpected it left him with a busy schedule, having to deal with a whole complex of business matters in a very short time." She paused leaving me space to develop an alternative theme. I failed to respond so she continued, "I can only suggest that you wait for his return and deal with him directly."

My empty stomach sank and the tensile strength of my patience reached its limit.

"You may suggest that – but it hardly satisfies the situation. Can't you issue a cheque on Mr Hume's behalf?"

"Sorry but under the circumstances – no I can't."

"Which circumstances are those?"

"Simply the fact that I have no record of Mr Hume's intention in your regard. He left no instructions about a cheque so there is nothing I can do."

I could feel the perspiration drip – the lifeboat had left without me. If I didn't get the cheque before Manny returned I'd have nothing to show him and nowhere to show it to him.

"Look Julia," now I was plaintive, "if I don't get that cheque today…."

She cut me off, "You'll not get a cheque from me without an instruction from Mr Hume today or any other day."

A familiar panic took root.

"Okay – I understand that. Is it possible to contact him? Get him at his hotel? Do you have a copy of his itinerary?"

A small doubt appeared in her face for the first time. Maybe this wasn't some whacko straight off the street trying for a handout after all. She glanced down at her pad and then back at me.

"He hates being disturbed when he's off on a trip. I'm only to telephone him in an emergency and..."

"I promise you – this is an emergency – honestly it is. He'll tell you as much himself."

She studied me briefly, sighed and picked up the telephone.

"If I lose my job over this, you will not be my most favourite person, Mr Grainger," she said as she dialled a long number.

Thirty minutes later she finally gave up. Mr Hume it seemed could not be contacted via either of his hotels, or at the office where his meeting was scheduled. Julia was sympathetic and promised to continue to try and reach him. She pointed out however, that when he wanted to remain out of touch as he did sometimes; there was little anyone could do. I thanked her and left.

Manny Hume's failure had left me in severe difficulties and for most of my tube train journey back to Hackney I examined ways that would enable me to hold out until he returned. To some large extent the situation had been alleviated due to the prospect of higher earnings from the club but three hundred pounds per week was not going to solve all my difficulties. I needed some three thousand pounds plus to pay off my student friends. If that were not available then I suppose they would have to wait. I would save a little cash as soon as I gave up the room in Nottinghill and returned the hire tools. If I purchased a few bits and pieces, a fridge, a bed and a couple of cupboards, Celia and I could operate just as successfully from the studio as we did currently.

When it was described to her however, the plan to move house did not meet with Celia's approval. Suddenly she could not see why we shouldn't rent the studio and keep the room in West 11 as well. She had settled in Nottinghill, she said, claiming it was a fairly central location and she had become familiar with the shops and the market.

"It's not as though we're hard up any more," she said, "all that money you rip off from the nightclub should be more than sufficient for our needs."

My explanations were ignored and my protestations dismissed as penny-pinching. I was accused of being more like a bank manager than an artist and of devoting all my waking moments to the pursuit of cash. The implication of my being greedy was the last straw.

"It's a bloody good job one of us thinks about money," I snapped, "You never give it a second thought."

The notion of budgeting was always anathema to Celia. She calculated the extent of her financial worth by counting the money in her purse. If she had enough to buy the basic essentials, she considered herself well provided for. There was never any thought for the future – it seemed. The idea of moving to live in Hackney had always been a strong possibility but her opposition to it was only made manifest when it was described as a money-saving exercise. As if money saving was something we should not have to consider.

"Celia, the art business is just that – a business. Don't be fooled by all that crap about inspiration and ways of changing the world. The only thing that changes the world is currency – and the more you can acquire, the greater the changes you can make."

She sulked for a while but by the late afternoon she had accepted the inevitability of the change of address. At some stage she sat beside me on the bed and made her peace.

"I'm sorry, Mick," she whispered. "I'm just an old bag when I get started. Take no notice. I know I don't contribute much to the pot – the trouble is I have no real skills – certainly nothing I could do to make some cash. I design hats – and who the hell wants to buy hat designs from me."

I put an arm round her and kissed her on the neck.

"You'll like it over in the East End. There are street markets galore over there and…"

"I suppose I could become an escort."

"A what?"

"An escort. One of the girls in my group at college has signed on with an escort agency. She gets a hundred quid every time she takes a client on the town – and all she does is look good and let the guy chat her up."

"Prostitution. It's just prostitution with a veneer of respectability. I bet she fucks some of her clients too."

"She doesn't – at least she says she doesn't. She's married with a kid."

"And when did that make any difference!"

The strangely familiar stimulation provided by this conversation eventually left us both excited. We kissed and my hands went to work.

"I always said you'd make a great hooker."

"I know I would – even old Finney thinks so," she laughed.

"And what the hell has Finney got to do with anything?"

"He's always trying to touch me up. He grabbed me on the stairs the other day and invited me down to his basement again – dirty old sod – said he'd let us off the rent for a month if I was nice to him."

"Got to give him an 'A' for effort though. I wonder how many of the females living here pay their rent like that… So – did you do him a favour then?"

"No I did not."

"I bet if he'd been a policeman you might have, though."

I received a slap for my teasing and we ended up rolling on the bed together. It was not long before our clothing was cast aside and we were struggling together in our bare skin.

Celia's appetite for sex was as keen as ever. Much like a man, once she was stimulated she would go for it whatever the time of day or location. This occasion was no exception and what started as a silly romp soon turned into a frantic coupling. There was never any doubt in my mind that fucking was Celia's real forte, it was an activity in which she was able to express all her creativity and originality and one which she never seemed to tire of.

Before I went to work that evening Celia joined me on a visit to see Ram. It had been three days since I last visited him and to be entirely honest, the infrequency of my trips to the hospital was largely on account of my dread at seeing him. His condition appeared to be deteriorating. His colour was worse, his weight loss greater and there was a smell about him that presaged fatality. I was horrified to find that now he was fed through a drip and, according to the ward sister, he had stopped taking solid food completely.

Sister Thomas took me to one side, to tell me that his doctors were more seriously worried about his condition than ever before.

"Is that a polite way of telling me that he's dying," I asked.

Her lips were tight, "I'm sure you understand," she said quietly. "I cannot say that – not categorically. All I can tell you is that the tumour has migrated to his liver and he is in a great deal of discomfort."

"Is there anything, anyone can do?" I asked feeling thoroughly depressed. She shook her head.

Back at the bedside, Celia sat holding Ram's hand. He watched me with his dull eyes sunk into hollowed cheeks and tried to smile.

"How's he doing then, nurse?" I asked Celia, winking at Ram as I spoke.

"He tells me that he'd like me in the bed next to him," she answered faking a laugh.

Ram grinned, flashing a set of teeth apparently too large for his face, "She fancies me, Mick – sorry, mate," he whispered.

His voice was dry and distant, a file on steel plate sound. My friend had acquired a delicacy that one normally associates with old people, fragility like that of some spindly legged insect whose structure threatens to collapse if touched. I sat down and took his other hand.

"I don't like coming here anymore, Ram," I said. "You never have any grapes for your visitors."

"Funnily enough, Mick, I don't like being here either," he replied, trying to smile.

"So – when do you get back on roast dinners?" I asked.

"Sometime – never," he said seriously.

Celia kissed his hand, the tears running unashamedly across her cheeks. I tried to keep his attention in case he noticed but he'd seen her already.

"Hey," he whispered, "you're supposed to be here to cheer me up." He turned to me again. "Give this woman of yours a big kiss will you and tell her that as soon as I'm out of this place, I'll give her a right seeing-to."

We stayed with Ram for about an hour, leaving only when the nursing staff came to give him his medication. It was obvious to all of us that he understood his condition perfectly well and before I left, he had me bend over close to him for a private message.

"Thanks for everything, Mick," he said, "but don't come back. I hate to see you both so upset."

Ram was one of the bravest people I ever met. Ignoring his own discomfort, he continued to maintain the pretence for another five days, just to cover the embarrassment and hurt in the faces of his relatives. He died on a Monday morning just after dawn and later that week Celia and I joined his family for the funeral service. Afterwards, his parents asked me to dispose of all his art materials and canvases. They told me that they had never approved of his chosen career and wanted no memory of that part of his life. It was a very sad occasion.

The sudden death of close friends provides the impetus for an examination of one's conscience – sometimes. A timely opportunity to assess the path one has chosen, to calculate the value – the true worth of life left. This was certainly true in my own case after Ram's death.

The dogma that was the essence of the Catholic faith had long since become a thing of the past for me. However, it was difficult to decide honestly if my rejection of that creed had been more from convenience than through philosophical or spiritual disagreement. There could be no doubt that I had found it inconvenient; equally, however, it had always been foreign to my way of thinking. Like most established religions, Catholicism was in many of its aspects, primitive. It kept a foot firmly in a previous century and its symbolism was therefore often inappropriately referenced. Undoubtedly there had been good people – sometimes even holy people, associated with that church, but these were more than evenly matched by legions of those whose hypocrisy, greed and self-indulgence defied definition.

I was not certain any more if I even believed in an after-life. Notions that the good would be elevated and the bad punished were, it seemed, designed to support an earthly class system rather than to satisfy any need for universal justice. Then there were the anomalies: the God of Love and how he allowed the suffering of the masses; the last-minute, perfect act of contrition-reprieve for despots, and then that category known as martyrs – the justified killing of innocents, a failure to survive being raised to special status. The promises of holy insurance men in white collars rang hollow and their assurance of better things to come was a simple marketing device aimed at getting the punter to commit to a policy.

Better, I think, to rely on oneself in a survival system that puts 'self' top of the list. This life may be all we get and existence at the meanest level is not good enough therefore. In my mind the survival instinct is closely linked with a need to prosper, to increase one's wealth, to aspire, to influence, to seek power. It's associated with increasing comfort and easement of effort, with pleasure and satisfaction. The Bible tells us that, 'Man is born to labour and the birds to fly'. Conversely, I choose to believe that if man needs to fly – then fly he must, even if he has to hijack the aeroplane.

I had decided some time ago that no matter what opposition I might meet with, no matter how hard the decision required or unpalatable the actions resulting from those decisions, I would not be a martyr to any cause other than my own. I would never negate the responsibility I felt for myself. I concluded therefore, that Ram's death held no significant message for me. He died simply because he contracted a killer disease and it was immaterial whether the cause was genetic or environmental. No one was sending any kind of message to anyone else by Ram's death and, other than the obvious, there was nothing to learn from it.

I never had a proper opportunity to talk to Ram about my borrowing his paintings. I was certain, however, that he would not have objected and, since his parents had asked me to dispose of his work, I saw no value in attracting any more attention to the fact. This was a convenient solution to what could have been an embarrassing situation.

Chapter Thirteen

Since my arrival in London, I had had little contact with my home. At that time in my mind, Teesside equated with a claustrophobia of the spirit, a 'downstream' situation to which I had neither inclination nor no good reason to return. Just before the Christmas season that year, things changed. It had been a busy year bringing the promise of real independence and the prospect of exhibitions that bit closer. Not that I paid much notice to it, but the rest of the world outside the art establishment was still on its way to a well deserved hell. Wars had occurred all over the place including Angola, the Lebanon, Rhodesia and in Palestine. Terrorist movements of various sorts were attempting to hold the civilised countries to ransom for all manner of obtuse political reasons leaving me to conclude that they were all mad. Meanwhile the revolution in the art scene reached new levels of its own idiocy at both ends of the spectrum. The pile of bricks by Carl Andre was shown at the Tate amid objections from the public and old Lowry, the painter of industrial scenes in Manchester, died. He never did learn to draw or if he did he hid the fact. His work was sort after nevertheless – there was obviously still hope for the rest of us.

In anticipation of Manny's eventual return from the USA, Celia had moved with me into the studio. We said goodbye to Finny's hovel in Notting Hill and I for one had few regrets at leaving it. The plan was that we would move again – to more comfortable quarters – as soon as Manny could be persuaded to part with a sufficiently sizeable chunk of cash. Unfortunately as the weeks passed and Manny's return was delayed time after time, we had to accept that the studio had become our home. To make matters worse still, the winter cold came early that year and, as the studio proved to be impossible to keep warm, we spent our time either in the local pub or crouched round a small electric fire wrapped in blankets. I avoided college altogether as my colleagues there were always asking for their money.

Naturally I kept in touch with Manny's secretary Julia, phoning her on a weekly basis. She kept me fully informed about her boss's travels and to her credit made a large number of transatlantic telephone calls on my behalf. Recognising the extent of my needs, she said she was prepared to issue the elusive cheque just as soon as he gave his approval. However, it became increasingly clear that for Manny, out of sight meant out of mind and the necessary approval was always somehow avoided. His visit to Boston was first extended to New York and still later to California, and it seemed that he had meetings scheduled for almost every minute of every day. Consequently any conversation Julia managed to have with him was brief and inevitably focused on his business interests. When the cheque was mentioned, he would sweep aside the subject saying he would deal with it personally – when he returned. Julia was apologetic but, as she said, her hands were tied.

We had set up a bed in the far corner of the studio, next to the wash-hand basin. We also installed a small electric oven with two hot plates, a tiny fridge, and a wardrobe. Initially there was no other cupboard space, no work surfaces and nowhere to store provisions. All our facilities had been purchased through second hand furniture shops and at auctions. This provided only the meanest level of accommodation and the lowest level of comfort. By now we had a little money put by and could have easily invested it in more appropriate and more user-friendly equipment to make ourselves more comfortable. We resisted the temptation simply on account of the belief that any day – as soon as Manny returned – our fortunes would experience considerable change. We would rather spend our money on a nice meal in an Indian restaurant than buy a pressure cooker or deep fat fryer.

However as the weeks passed, the privations we suffered living at the studio began to take their toll and we decided that we could not tolerate the idea of spending Christmas in such surroundings. Despite the inconveniences we knew we would suffer, we finally agreed therefore to trek north and spend the holiday with my parents.

Ever conscious of the cost of travel and only after we'd priced both train and coach services, we finally decided to hitchhike. The club was about to close for two weeks to be redecorated so there was not a problem in that regard. I would certainly miss the income but felt that we both deserved a break. For some time I had avoided any contact with the students whose work I had obtained. As I could not yet settle my debt, I avoided college altogether. Instead, I left messages promising payment in the near future. As yet there had been no reply from my year group and I took this to imply that either they were content to wait for their money; else they could not discover my new address. Whichever it was, I was relieved when we finally set off for the North.

We left one Monday morning and took the tube as far as we could, arriving at Apex corner the traditional starting point for hitchhikers going north, at eight o'clock. Our first lift arrived almost as soon as I stuck out my thumb – a good sign. A lorry stopped and the driver said he was delivering bathroom equipment to Northampton and was prepared to take us that far. He dropped us on a slip road just before the town and a school minibus picked us up within ten minutes.

The bus was half full of fifteen-year-olds returning with their teacher to Thirsk, after a visit to the museums in London. The teacher proved to be their art master, a stocky Greek Cypriot whose hair was as black as his sense of humour. He had driven them down to the capital to look at paintings in the National Gallery, a welcome break he said, from the proscription endemic in the school timetable. He was obviously popular with the teenagers and told us that away from school when he was 'off-duty' he allowed them to call him by his first name – which was Phil. He said that he had enjoyed the trip but was nevertheless glad of some adult company on the journey home. When he discovered that we were art students he began immediately to cross-examine us, obviously for the benefit of his pupils, some of whom would undoubtedly choose a similar career. The kids joined in and from the nature of their questions it was obvious that they were kept well informed about the next step in their Art Education.

Inevitably a debate started concerning traditional values in art and the bus split into two camps. The pile of bricks at the Tate was demolished and Rembrandt was resurrected; Conceptualism was crucified and easel painting ridiculed. This was by far the best part of the journey and both Celia and I were impressed with the range and quality of the argument put to us, particularly those that questioned the Conceptual Movement.

Phil was a chain-smoker and the majority of his pupils also smoked. Presumably this was another privilege of being 'off-duty'. As a consequence, we were obliged to drive for long periods with all the windows open. The wind whipped through the bus and the temperature dropped dramatically. Scarves and woolly hats were pulled over freezing faces, gloves appeared and coats were fastened tightly. The stop for refreshments at Ripon was a welcome relief and hot coffee accompanied by bacon sandwiches soon restored the circulation to frozen extremities. I was surprised to find that Phil treated his pupils out of his own pocket and it made me wonder if I had

had a teacher of his calibre who obviously cared as much about his pupils, perhaps I may have had happier memories of my own school days.

Eventually we were dropped off in the middle of Thirsk. Phil told us that this was a regular stopping point for the long-distance lorries that came through the town and that, if we went to a particular café, we would be certain of getting a lift to Stockton. The minibus left to a disjointed chorus of 'Leaving on a Jet Plane' – obviously Phil's idea, echoing his preference for antique pop music. We waved until they turned the corner.

The café turned out to be a traditional 'greasy spoon'. One of a dying breed made almost extinct by the Formica and cellophane-wrapped sandwich variety promoted by big business and now exclusive to the motorways. It was a place where dark brown tea was served in pint mugs, where everyone took at least four spoons of sugar and where the average fry-up looked like it was sufficient to choke a carthorse. We were both hungry and the tempting aroma from the kitchens proved too great to avoid, so we sat down to a 'travellers' breakfast'. A snack consisting of double fried eggs, bacon, chips, kidney, and baked beans with fried bread on the side. The tea was as bitter as sour mash whisky but it went down a treat and the cost was only about twenty percent of that charged by the plastic food palaces. After I settled the bill, I asked the woman at the till if she knew anyone who might be travelling to Teesside, as we needed a lift. She called out to a group of drivers sitting in the corner and we immediately had several offers.

We travelled the last leg of the trip with Bill. Bill was an independent haulier and the owner of two vehicles (tractors he called them). His main contracts were with a chain of builder's merchants and he carried a variety of heavy goods for them the length of the country. In the café he seemed a reasonable enough guy but my suspicions were raised as soon as we climbed into his cab. Every available space was filled with pictures of female nudes. And these weren't the nudes of Rubens or Ingres, still less the amateur attempt to make a girlfriend or wife seem more sexy than she was; they were eighteen carat, 'in-your-face' porno queens, heavy-duty women whose proportions were almost as vulgarly artificial as their poses. Like well-worn tyres, the faces of these ladies had recorded every tortuous mile their bodies had travelled.

After we were seated Bill grinned at me as if I was a co-conspirator, "Like the girls then?" he asked, winking and licking his lips. I said it must be difficult to concentrate on driving with so many hairy arses pointed in your

139

face and added that I preferred girls to the baggy old women he had on display. My obvious criticism was ignored.

Once behind the wheel he insisted that Celia sat between us, her legs either side of the central console – "Just so you don't both get all crushed up," he said to me.

It wasn't an unreasonable suggestion given the limited space, except for the fact that each time he changed gear his arm rubbed against her thigh. I suppose we should have expected the worst. However, we had travelled only about four miles before he declared himself.

"I pick up a lot of hitchhikers on this run," he said, looking at Celia's legs, "mostly they're not as nice as you though – Celia isn't it?"

Celia said nothing.

"Sometimes I let them have a kip in the back." He glanced over his shoulder, "there's a bunk back there – very comfortable it is too," he laughed, "and convenient too – if you see what I mean."

"No I don't see what you mean – actually," Celia replied coldly.

Bill drove in silence for a few minutes then, without warning he pulled over into a lay-by and stopped. He turned to face us with a sick smile.

"It's this way, kids," he said, "there's an unwritten rule for hikers in these parts that goes like this – if I give you a ride then – you give me a ride. Now that isn't too unfair is it?"

His left hand rested on Celia's thigh and as he spoke it moved fractionally, in tandem with his grin.

"We can do it in the bunk, its cosy back there – and your boyfriend can go for a short walk – or if he likes he can watch – I don't mind."

Celia turned on her most wicked smile and reached across to put her hand over his crotch. Thinking the argument had been won, Bill adjusted himself in his seat, making his sensitive regions more accessible. It was only when she took hold that he realised his mistake.

"Oy!" he shouted, struggling unsuccessfully to distance himself.

I saw her grip lock on.

"Oy – yourself, shit-for-brains," she said quietly, tightening her grip. "I wonder what makes you imagine that this little dick would satisfy a girl like me, eh?"

Now his face was strained and he suddenly became short of breath.

"I... I... I was only kidding. I didn't mean..."

Her knuckles whitened and he looked like he might be sick.

"And I'm only kidding," Celia said, "if I thought seriously that you were the kind of guy who'd take advantage of young women hitchhikers... I'd squeeze these nuts till they popped."

On cue Bill squealed like a pig. "Now then, Bill – if you have any more bright ideas, I suggest you keep them to yourself."

When she released him his face was white and for several minutes he was doubled up in pain.

"You're a right bitch that's for sure," he muttered at last, still holding himself, "and I want the pair of you out of my cab – go on fuck off, both of you."

Celia turned to me.

Her wink was enough to alert me.

"Okay, Billy-boy, here's what happens next," she said. "You kick us out and I'm going to telephone the police. When they get here, we'll tell them how you assaulted me – in front of my boyfriend. They'll pick you up before you get more than a few miles down the road – and you can say goodbye to your business after that. Your choice."

Our driver said nothing. A moment later he put the engine in gear and we moved off. During the rest of the trip he turned up the radio and listened to sixties pop music. He never spoke to either of us again.

It was snowing when we arrived in Middlesbrough, big flakes like five pound notes. As directed Bill dropped us in Roman Road in Linthorpe. We had decided to get off near the art college and take a bus the rest of the way. I got out first and just as Celia stepped down, the vehicle lurched, almost causing her to fall; the final act of a mean-minded man.

"Fuck you both," he called as he turned the wheel and we watched him speed away.

"What a bastard," Celia said, "I should have castrated him when I had the chance."

I laughed. "I thought you did. His face remained a funny colour even when you let him go."

We walked round to Linthorpe Road and took a red United bus to Stockton. Thirty minutes later we were walking through Stockton High Street. It was only a short distance to my parents' house and as we approached I began to wonder what our reception might be. Since I'd moved to London I had not been back. I had written spasmodically and had received replies in equal amount but the communications had been of a pedestrian nature – idle chat about where I was living, the weather and what I was doing. I had no idea how they might react to Celia and as we approached the doorstep I began to wonder if it might have been better to stay on in London after all.

We were half way down the passage before Mam poked her head round the kitchen door.

"It's Michael," she shouted. "George, it's Michael. Didn't I say he'd come home for Christmas? He promised last year..."

The second part of her statement was directed at the kitchen behind her, obviously to Dad who would be feet-up in front of the fire at this time of the evening. A moment later and I was in a steely embrace. Dad appeared a second later and stood there smiling in his slippers waiting for Mam to exhaust her welcome.

"You've lost weight, son," she said.

"Looks fit enough to me," Dad added.

"Now you are staying for Christmas, aren't you, son?" she asked.

"Of course he's staying," Dad replied, "why else would he be here?"

Throughout this domestic salvo, Celia stood quietly behind me. I felt her increase the pressure of her grip on my arm, a sure sign that she thought it was time for an introduction.

"Mam, Dad," I started," this is Celia... a friend. I thought she might stay too – if that's all right."

The duo paused to scrutinise the first girl I had ever brought home to meet them. Only a CAT scan could have been more searching. Eventually it was Mam who broke the silence.

"Hello, Celia," she said, like she was addressing a five-year-old child, "and do you go to college in London too?"

"Yes I do. Actually, we go to the same college."

Then it was Dad's turn, "And are you 'actually' in the same year group?" His sceptical-cynical approach was a programmed ridicule, implying – how would a mere girl with such airs and graces dare to be in the same year group as his son. I felt the grip tighten again and feared the worst.

"Actually – I'm a year behind Mick," she smiled and I saw my parents grin the family blessing in unison – but Celia continued, "however, as we live together, I do see a lot of him."

The best part of the next hour was spent trying to persuade my parents that I had not sold my eternal soul to the powers of darkness and that, despite first impressions, Celia was not a twentieth century manifestation of the Whore of Babylon. To say that they were shocked was to understate the obvious – they were horrified. I had a premonition of another announcement after Sunday Mass!

Once Celia had made the declaration there was no way that I could deny it. I was therefore left to defend it. However, to start with all my attempts to play down the normality of our relationship were met with a tide of accusations. There was the 'marriage is a sacrament' routine followed by a whole series of Biblical references and ending with the full spectrum of Catholic dogma on the subject. Only when the heavy-duty religious big guns were exhausted, was I then subjected to the, 'Where did we go wrong' and 'How could you do this to us' appeal. I had to listen to claims that they had, 'set my feet on the right road', 'shown me the way' and given me 'every chance'. It was a performance without any recognition that by implication Celia was just as guilty as I was – and Celia was present throughout. Fortunately, I saw her smile at some point and realised she had seen the humour in what was happening. Had she taken offence the outcome could have been quite different.

In the end, both sides accepted that we were sinners and, whilst this was not likely to make the ten o'clock Vatican newscast, still less stop the traffic on the motorway, it was at least an agreement of some sort. And, as the Inquisition informed us that repentance was a matter for our consciences alone, we were content to accept the criticism.

Mam nevertheless pointed out to us that under her roof we would need to behave ourselves and would, of necessity, occupy separate bedrooms. Her concern that neighbours might discover our secret paid scant respect to the fact that in living memory, no one in the neighbourhood had ever been given access to the house, leaving us to wonder how they might discover our shameful practices without being told about them. My father's response was simply to shake his head and retire to his chair, a gesture implying parental shame, as if all his efforts to instil a spiritual dimension in his son had failed. Later, he would occasionally refer to a time when we might have children of our own and would therefore begin to appreciate the disappointment they could bring. After this and fortunately for the duration of our stay, the matter was never referred to again.

Paradoxically by the time we sat down for our evening meal together the atmosphere had changed completely. Far from being an instrument of the devil and the root cause of my fall from grace, Celia became the life and soul of the proceedings. She and Mam chatted like old friends, comparing critical notes about my personal habits and debating what might be done to improve them. More importantly, thereafter my nocturnal visits to Celia's room each night and the unmistakable sound of our physical exertions were ignored. Having stated their case, clearly, the judicious application of a blind-eye was employed.

The following afternoon I took Celia to visit the Wednesday market in the High Street. That year Christmas Day was to fall on a Saturday, so the mid-week market was the last before the celebration. The town was filled to capacity and the market stalls were festooned with decorations and coloured lights. Public spaces were filled with a festive atmosphere, made all the more seasonal by the sound of carols and a thin layer of snow. Various shops played music through open doors and the Salvation Army's best brass band, located at the far end of the High Street, blasted their version of 'Good King Wenceslas'. At the opposite extreme some two hundred yards away, the Round Table had gathered a disparate collection of musicians who competed with mournful 'Silent Night'.

"It's very Hollywood," Celia said, obviously amused by the efforts of the stall-holders, "I almost expect to see Jimmy Stewart appear with a big white rabbit."

I told her she was a terrible cynic and also that she was confusing two quite different movies. "The white rabbit was in a film called *Harvey* and that had nothing to do with Christmas. The famous Christmassy one with the angel was, *It's a Wonderful Life.*"

Whatever our scepticism, we enjoyed the feeling generated amongst the crowds and in no time at all had imbibed the spirit of the season. Despite the crush, we wandered between the stalls, examining bargains and exchanging good will messages and banter with the stallholders. In the middle of our trek through the market, I was suddenly stopped when a young woman put out her hand out to me. I looked up to find that the hand belonged to Ruth. The very same Ruth that had shared my initial interview day. It seemed like a long time since we'd shared secrets.

"Mick," she said, grabbing me as I passed, "how are you?"

We exchanged the kind of pleasantries one might expect to exchange with an ex-lover whilst in the company of the one currently in vogue and pretended a polite interest in each other's news. Eventually I introduced Celia and Ruth pulled her young man forward to shake my hand. His name was Gordon and he worked in advertising, she told me.

"He's doing rather well," she said, raising her eyebrows as though sharing an indiscretion, "recently, he was made a junior partner… we could end up in London ourselves."

It was a middle-class performance by a middle-class lady. We were being let in on the secrets of a promising career but in the best possible taste without the merest hint of a boast. I recalled that Ruth had dropped out of college amid gossip that told of an unwanted pregnancy and I wondered if Gordon had been the father.

"So – if you're up for the hols," she gushed, employing my most hated diminutive, "you should drop round for drink one evening. Eh, Gordon?"

Gordon smirked.

"We'd love to," now it was Celia putting on the 1940s cocktail party accent, "wouldn't we, darling?"

Although I could not be certain, I suspected that Ruth appreciated that the piss was being extracted. Gordon on the other hand had no idea.

We duly scribbled our address on the back of an envelope and in return received a nicely printed card – with a logo – from Gordon. He took the initiative for the first time as this exchange was made, telling us to, "Give us a bell to arrange a date – sometime after Crimble, preferably."

Celia was in stitches for the next twenty yards and for the rest of the market tour she adopted a crude if effective imitation of Ruth, dredging up a series of antiquated expressions made popular by the likes of Noel Coward in which 'giving a bell' and 'Crimble' figured continuously.

It proved to be a day for meeting old friends. Outside of the Odeon cinema we crossed paths with Tony and his new wife Mona. Clearly he had achieved the transformation started around the time of our last meeting. He was no longer the smart-talking, foul-mouthed Tony of yesteryear; the streetwise thief had become respectable – in extremis. If appearances were criteria for assessing success, Tony was doing very nicely indeed. The Durham family had been Christmas shopping, he in a smart, well-cut suit and she, in a fur coat. And whilst the sartorial splendour of neither would ever be mistaken for Bond street still less Saville Row, they nevertheless stood out from this environment like the proverbial 'sore thumbs' they were.

The social history of Stockton once-upon-a-time was more concerned with keeping a job and maintaining the essentials of getting enough to eat rather than with the ephemera of the fashion world. A bias that was still in evidence generally despite any new-found prosperity. The contrast provided by Mr and Mrs Durham was therefore sharpened all the more. I thought it was sad. Tony had once represented the third side of a resistant square peg that had deliberately avoided trying to fit into the establishment's round hole. And whilst Bruce and I had offered culture and science to the partnership, Tony had been our tutor, responsible for educating us in survival techniques on the street. We had been close friends and, even in spite of the strain placed on our friendship by him the last time we met, I still harboured happy memories of our time spent together.

We all shook hands and exchanged the shorthand personal histories that people do on such occasions. He had done well for himself (the second old friend to claim as much that day) He had left the management scheme and joined the staff at a bookmakers. Now he owned his own betting shop and enjoyed a level of wealth he never previously imagined possible. Significantly, his newly established confidence had allowed for the rediscovery of his sense of humour. He could laugh at himself and showed no embarrassment when the subject of his family was raised – progress indeed. Mona was the daughter of a bookmaker and although she was used to an affluent life-style, she still managed to retain a reasonable perspective on life and a down-to-earth attitude about money. I came to the conclusion that she was the ideal partner for my friend and as we all got on so well together, we arranged to meet for a meal the following evening.

We'd not been back in the house for more than ten minutes when Dad asked if we were going to attend midnight Mass that year. Clearly it was a matter that had been discussed in our absence.

"We could all go together," Mam said, letting her excitement at the prospect show, "like we used to do."

"The trouble is I'm not Catholic," Celia replied trying to ease the refusal.

"That doesn't matter," Dad said, "everyone's welcome on Christmas Eve. In fact I'd like to bet half the congregation won't be Catholics."

"So you'd be more than welcome," Mam added, "unless that is you don't want to go."

Employing this tactic they made it impossible to refuse. We agreed and in the process provided Dad and Mam with the best of Christmas presents. Suddenly, they imagined there was light at the end of the tunnel, hope of redemption perhaps even the possibility of a conversion. Some bloody hope.

*

The Golden Bamboo was more popular now than it had ever been in the past. When I lived in the town its sole function was to service the drunks and the late-night leftovers that hadn't managed to get a girl to take home when the Palais de Dance closed its doors. The 'Pally' as it had been popularly known was the forerunner of 'Spin Disco' that now occupied the premises next door to the restaurant. The most significant difference being that Spin Disco seemed to attract a more affluent and certainly a more respectable crowd than the 'Pally' had ever done. The social interaction that used to take place most often in the Golden Bamboo was usually in direct proportion to the quantity of beer that its patrons had ingested earlier in the evening. And, if that had been followed by a failure to 'pull' a bird at the dance, dulled wits turned frustration into short tempers and fights often broke out. But apparently all that was a thing of the past. Peace had come to Dodge City.

Tony and Mona were already seated when we arrived. They greeted us and after the usual arguments – who would have what and how many portions were required – we finally agreed what we wanted to eat. When all this was settled we ordered drinks and settled to chat.

I had always imagined that if Tony ever did get married, he would probably end up with someone from the rough end of town. I couldn't have been more wrong. Now that I had an opportunity to study Mona more closely, I saw that she was much more attractive than I'd first imagined. Moreover she was generally well informed and her comments implied a thoughtfulness that was entirely unexpected.

"So," Tony asked, sipping his pint of lager, "what do you two get up to down in the Smoke?"

"We're still at college," Celia replied, "but Mick is working hard to get himself a patron."

"A patron?"

"Someone who will help foster his art," Mona explained.

"Foster his art!" Now Tony was mocking his wife, "And how will he foster his art?"

"He'll buy it," I said

Tony's face showed that he understood at last, "Ah – that's different. So this – this patron has lots of cash – yes?"

"Lots," I replied, "he's probably the richest person I've ever met."

"What's his game?"

"He's into marketing, advertising – the media generally – fingers in lots of different pies."

"So why would he want to invest in you?"

"Because he knows a good thing when he sees it," Celia interjected, "And Mick is a good bet."

Tony laughed, "Aha – loyal as well as sexy eh!"

147

Celia blushed and Mona sprang to her defence, "Don't be a pig Tony."

The meal arrived before he could respond and for the next forty minutes or so, the conversation focused almost exclusively on the food. We were enjoying our last course, a favourite of mine called Toffee Banana, at about nine thirty when a group of young men arrived. From their behaviour, the loud voices and bleary eyes, it was clear that they had been drinking heavily. They took a nearby table and began a loud conversation.

"I thought you said this place had grown up," I commented to Tony. He looked up, apparently noticing the men for the first time.

"Are they bothering you?" he asked.

I grinned, "No of course not – but..."

He didn't let me finish and spoke as he pushed back his chair.

"Enough said."

Mona put a hand on his arm, suddenly she was concerned, "Don't make a fuss, Tony – please," She said quietly.

Now he was standing, loosening the middle button of his jacket. This was déjà vu. I'd been here before. Typical of those men of modest stature, Tony had always been aggressive. In our previous life, he had boasted the shortest fuse, always the quickest to take offence, the first to hit out. Bruce and I used to believe that Tony's aptitude for imagining insults was based on the insecurity generated by his family background and that his penchant for violent reaction derived from the length of his legs – or rather the shortness of them. In the years between, whilst he hadn't grown any bigger, he had certainly acquired all the attributes needed to provide better security making me conclude that his performance now was designed only to show me that he was still physically capable. He was showing off.

"Not me that's making a fuss and a nuisance of myself sweetheart," he said, in a voice loud enough for the whole restaurant to hear.

The man sitting nearest looked up, just as Tony leaned to whisper something to him. The effect was instantaneous. He stood, knocking over his chair in the process and grabbed Tony by a lapel pulling him closer. Hammers were cocked.

"And you can fuck right off, smart arse – else you get yourself a smacking."

A sentiment thoroughly and obviously approved of by the man's friends. It proved just the provocation my old friend had hoped for.

Chapter Fourteen

The man's name was actually George, the same name as my father but there the similarity ended. Amongst the other claims he made during the hours of darkness that night was that he held the title of being the heaviest drinker in the County of Durham. This was a claim I was far more inclined to believe. Testimony to support it was demonstrated at around three in the morning when he rose from the bottom bunk and proceeded to regurgitate the copious contents of his stomach on the floor of our cell. And if that were not bad enough, he then attempted to wash away the steaming deposit by emptying his bladder into the mess. Although he was still unsteady on his feet, as he stood at well over six feet in height with a physique that Rocky Marciano would have been proud to boast of, I did not feel it was politic to make my complaints to him directly. Instead I turned my face to the wall and pretended to be asleep. It was the culmination of a night to remember.

To start with, the fight in the Golden Bamboo had followed a predictable form. Hoisted to his toes by the man he had clearly insulted, Tony responded with a head butt. It was a crisp well-delivered crunch to the bridge of the offending nose, ensuring his attacker of both a lengthy visit to the accident and emergency unit of the local hospital and possibly years of enforced nasal congestion. Naturally the victim let loose Tony's lapel and staggered back only to trip on the table behind him. The table tipped and the man fell. His fall generously included the next two tables and in quick time the restaurant was a shambles.

Sensing, as one might, that this was not the end of the confrontation, I was actually in the process of advising our escorts that we should leave when one of the man's friends decided to help clear the wax from my left ear. He hit me so hard that I was also airborne, albeit for a second. In maintaining the spirit of the occasion, my flight path ended by demolishing another two tables, the occupants of which quite understandably, became agitated. In language decorated by a liberal sprinkling of less popular adjectives, they argued loudly that their chicken curry had been meant for eating and not

149

wearing. To press his point home one kicked me in the ribs whilst the other punched my original attacker in the side of his head.

The disturbance spread quickly. It was enjoined also by several of the Chinese waiters, polite young men who only a moment before, had been content to deliver the egg fried rice, the noodles and the sweet and sour king prawn dishes to some of the people they now sought to strike down with bamboo poles. Cutlery was strewn everywhere, crockery smashed and furniture broken. The screams of women, the shouts of men's threats and the dull noise of bone meeting bone quickly drowned out the background musak. In such circumstances it is always difficult to gauge the passage of time but at some stage someone must have called the local constabulary. Amidst the melee, I heard the sound of police sirens – a warning of what was to come. However, at that moment having recovered sufficiently at least to wreak my revenge on the man who had used me as a football, I was too preoccupied to take too much notice.

My claim to the desk sergeant later that I was in fact one of the injured parties fell on deaf ears. Unfortunately, just as two heavily built constables had entered the restaurant, I was seen in the middle of the wreckage, to be punching the face of a fellow diner. As eyewitnesses, the constables proved to be unimpeachable. Their evidence was given preference therefore and I was kindly invited to spend a night in the cells. There was no choice of accommodation and the room in which I was eventually located consisted of bunk beds, a bucket, a small window, and George – allegedly the Prime Minister's cousin.

On the occasion of my arrest and once the smoke had settled, I was surprised to find that Tony did not also find his way into the Black Maria. I presumed that he must have warranted more singular transport, probably in a police car, but that was not the case. When he did not appear at the desk sergeant's reception area, as I was concerned, I even asked after him. I was told that as he was the first person to be attacked, he would not be required to put in an attendance unless called as a witness.

So much for justice.

In keeping with my limited knowledge of the system, I imagined that I would be released the following morning with a slap on the wrist. Wasn't this the usual practice for minor disturbers of the peace? Apparently not. At six a.m. we were served strong tea and bacon sandwiches and an hour or so later George was sent on his way. The young policeman who delivered the tea dismissed my questions with a grin.

"I hear they're going to charge you. You destroyed that Chink's restaurant and they're bound to want a pound of flesh."

For a while I was speechless. I had destroyed the restaurant. If they thought for a moment I would cough to a charge like that then they must be under the influence of some illegal narcotic. I spent the next four hours planning my defence. Celia and Mona would testify I felt sure – and what could they say. They'd surely seen the attack on me. One minute I was sitting there enjoying my toffee banana pudding and the next, I was suffering earache in the lap of some frustrated football star. I tried to recall if I'd ever known a lawyer in the town. I'd certainly need a lawyer if I were to be taken seriously in court. And what of my friend Tony? He'd started the trouble after all and whilst I was here in jail, he was no doubt off somewhere doing last-minute Christmas shopping. It dawned on me at that moment that this was Christmas Eve.

Christmas Eve was always a big time in the Grainger household. There would be cold meat and pickles for lunch and I'd brought a couple of bottles of wine from London especially for the occasion. But by now my parents knew about my arrest… the consequences weren't worth thinking about. I could just hear them tell how 'Mick had spoilt the holiday', 'Couldn't stay out of trouble for even one evening', 'Disgraced the family – ended up in prison.' It was a nightmare.

It was three in the afternoon before the situation was resolved. The cell door opened and I was told to get my gear and follow the young constable to the desk. A plain-clothes officer accompanied the sergeant this time. The man looked vaguely familiar but it wasn't until he spoke that I recognised him as DCI Causer, the nemesis of a previous incarnation. He smirked when he saw me.

"Well what a surprise – Mr Grainger – yes?"

I tried to adopt an upbeat attitude, "Hello Detective Chief Inspector, how nice to see you again."

The sergeant looked surprised. However, he pushed a book and a large brown envelope across his desk in my direction and told me to sign for my belongings. It took me a second or two to appreciate that I was being released.

Causer said, "So – you're still as lucky as ever I see."

"This isn't luck – its justice," I replied as I signed my name.

"If justice was served young man, you'd be appearing before the courts sometime after the holidays. And if the owners of the Golden Bamboo had taken my advice they'd be pressing for damages. If they hadn't dropped their charges you'd be spending your Christmas behind bars."

This was news of course. So they'd refused to press for damages. But what of 'affray' of 'disturbing the peace' and all the other catch-all descriptions of charges the Police could bring under their own volition. The sergeant filled in the gaps as soon as I'd collected my money and my lighter.

"You should understand, Mr Grainger, that we are only dropping the other charges because of some discrepancies concerning the start of the fight. If we were a little more certain, we would certainly put you up before a magistrate." His tone was severe, much like a teacher talking to a miscreant in the head's office. "You should therefore consider yourself very fortunate – on this occasion," he said.

"Not for the first time," Causer added.

"This time we are binding you over with a caution. If we have reason to bring you in for whatever reasons in the near future, the charges from now will be resurrected. Do you understand?"

"Perfectly."

"In which case you are free to go."

At the swing doors I stopped and wished them both a happy Christmas but my goodwill was not reciprocated and I left them scowling at my back.

A car was parked at the kerb outside and as I came down the steps, I saw Celia in the passenger seat alongside Tony. They were both grinning like Cheshire cats. I got into the back seat and Celia turned to greet me, "Hi, lover," she said, "you okay?"

"I'll be a lot better when I give this little shit a good thumping."

Tony was still grinning into the mirror but said nothing.

"He was the one who got you out," Celia protested, "he settled with the restaurant for the damage and got them to drop the charges – otherwise you'd be hanging up your stocking in a prison cell."

"And whilst I am forever in his debt," I snapped back, "it shouldn't be forgotten that it was him who put me in there in the first place. Him and his bloody machismo."

Now Tony laughed, "But it was a helluva scrap wasn't it and – let's face it, Mick, a night in a nice warm cell must have done wonders for your arts' research programme."

On the way back to my parents' house, to my friends' amusement, I told them about my cellmate George and my reunion with DCI Causer. They laughed all the way and although I joined in, the memory of the situation was still too fresh for me to be completely relaxed about so near a catastrophe.

As expected, my parents gave me a cool reception. Nothing too obvious this time, just the usual shaking of regretful heads and the deep sighs of disappointment. The copybook had once more been thoroughly blotted and it would take a considerable effort to restore my status in their eyes. In the meantime, in order to give myself a break from their disapproval and to wash away the feeling of invisible prison grime, I went upstairs for a shower. When I emerged I found Celia sitting on the bed waiting for me. To my surprise her intention was serious rather than frivolous.

"What did you get for your parents for Christmas?" she asked.

Her question stopped me. I hadn't given the idea of presents a second thought. What was more to the point, my financial situation wouldn't allow any real level of spending – even if there had been time to do any shopping. My face must have given the game away.

"You didn't forget, Mick," Celia was as disapproving as I'd ever seen her. "How could you? Didn't you get them anything at all?"

I shook my head. "I didn't think that any of us would be bothering – not now we're all grown up and…"

"Well they've certainly bothered," she interrupted. "There are parcels under the tree for both of us."

It was a real bind and although I wracked my brains for an easy solution I couldn't come up with anything. Not surprisingly, it was Celia who eventually found the answer. She was often able to solve conundrums on my behalf and this was no exception.

"Have your parents ever been to London?" she asked.

She knew the answer already; we'd talked about their unwillingness to travel outside of their home region on many occasions.

"Of course not," I replied, "it's hard enough getting them to go to Middlesbrough let alone take a train south."

She look mischievous, "How if you were to offer to pay for them to come down by train – and stay in a hotel and promise we would show them the sights – take them to see a show and all that?"

The germ of her idea grew. This could be the Christmas present I'd forgotten to buy and as handsome a present as you'd find – for most people. The big difference was that I knew categorically that they would refuse. They'd say no – but they would be so impressed with the offer. It was the kind of thing that they would tell all their friends about – how Mick had offered them an all-expenses-paid-for holiday in London. It was truly a touch of genius. We talked it over, embellishing the detail as we went, trying to decide the best presentation, rehearsing the disappointment when they refused and practising responses. Disaster and embarrassment were suddenly turned around, transformed into a significant achievement. Christmas morning would be better then I'd feared.

We were half way through our evening meal when Mam first mentioned Midnight Mass. She suggested again that we should go together as a family. Celia exchanged glances with me, warning me not to make an objection. We had discussed the matter of Midnight Mass several times and couldn't agree. She was inclined to believe we should attend, if only to satisfy my parents, whereas I thought otherwise. On this occasion, without further reference to me, she took executive action.

"Michael and I talked about that," she said, filling the silence that occurred after my mother's declaration, "and we thought it would be nice to go – all together too."

Dad smiled into his meal and Mam glowed like she'd been awarded an Oscar.

"That would be really good. It's been such a long time since we went to Mass together. And I suspect that Michael sometimes forgets his religion when he's down in London."

I wasn't sure if this last comment was a question or simply a probe to test for my reaction. Whichever it was, I ignored it and continued to glower at my girlfriend.

Midnight Mass in the Roman Catholic calendar boasts a special occasion. In religious terms it is the first opportunity to celebrate the birth of Jesus. It is therefore a joyous occasion and usually accompanied with the full panoply of rich organ music, stirring hymns and a High Mass with three priests and a coterie of altar boys in attendance. It is also, however, a significant social event. One of a limited number of times when those of other faiths are made – obviously made – welcome. The doors are open to anyone on Christmas Eve. Having said that, many of those who attend do so for a variety of reasons, most of which have little or nothing to do with celebrating the birth of the Son of God.

Other than the devout, regular church-goers, there are those representing so-called 'lapsed' Catholics (and I suppose I fall into this category myself – although the epithet, 'lapsed' is one I never agreed with, as it implies that the failure was by accident – when my rejection of Catholicism was definitely on purpose). Anyway, it's my belief that the lapsed Catholics attend often from feelings of seasonal guilt. It goes without saying that if there is guilt to be felt in this context, it will be felt most acutely at Christmas. The 'curious' crowd swells their numbers – those people with nothing better to do, usually older folk without the prospect of family company, who always wondered what this well-publicised and very different Catholic celebration was all about.

The most unwelcome visitors to this late-night ritual, however, are without doubt the drunks. Like moths around a flame, those that have taken on an excessive fill of alcohol seem to collect in surprising numbers at Midnight Mass. Some observers have argued that the inebriates probably arrive by mistake, imagining that the brightly lit entrance and the sound of music promises access to another late-night bar. I am not convinced however. For much the same reason as the 'lapsed' Catholics, I believe the drunks collect at that time in that place due to qualms of conscience. This is not an unusual state in those whose brains are addled through drink. I see them, smitten with some degree of remorse, attempting to assuage their guilt through a once per year confrontation with a sacred setting. Further to this, I suspect that the mentality they demonstrate at this time is not too different from that seen amongst devout, regular churchgoers. The only differences being in the frequency of their attendance and the quantity of alcohol in their blood streams

As expected, my parents insisted that we arrived early for the service demonstrating a propensity for timekeeping apparent in no other aspect of their lives. Unwilling by then to spoil their enjoyment more than I had already, I conceded the point and accompanied them and Celia in the mile walk to the church. It was bitterly cold and the pavements were like a skating rink. Needless to say, although I expressed regular concern on behalf of my mother's stability – she often lost her footing even in dry conditions – it was me who ended up on my arse. And although the others in our little party found something amusing in my fall on the ice, I could not laugh along with them. It was surely a sign that the evening was to be just as much of a catastrophe as the prison cell.

It had been quite some time since I had entered St Mary's Church and despite the warm welcome implicit in the multitude of lights, the smell of wax candles and the organ music, memories of a childhood spent reciting Latin responses at the foot of the high altar prevented my immediate enjoyment of the occasion. This had been the scene of some of my worst nightmares. As a tiny five-year-old in the process of being trained as an altar boy, I'd once been caught short and shat myself during a Benediction service. Too shy to leave the side bench where I knelt, I suffered the trials of my overloaded underpants for the duration of the service, providing for the benefit of the congregation a pungent aroma much stronger than the traditional smell of incense. Fortunately, the parcel remained intact until I was well on my way home with my mother. The deposit I then left in a side street however, was rumoured to have played a significant part in the eventual demolition of that area. On another occasion, aged seven, I'd fainted during an early morning Mass. Other than my mother and the priest, there was no one else in the church that morning and had she not looked up from her devotions, I may well have remained prone, spread-eagled on the steps until Father O'Brien turned for the final blessing. His fury, expressed in the loudest terms at finding my mam behind him tending to her little boy, should have given both of us a better understanding of religious priorities. Much like any theatrical performer, his attitude was that the 'show must go on' even if one of the chorus is rendered unconscious.

As far as I could tell, nothing much had changed. Mam led the way down the central aisle and we took seats, two pews back from the altar rail. "Ring-side seats", I whispered to Celia. During the next half-hour the church slowly filled to capacity. Soon there were so many people that chairs, normally reserved for use at the annual garden fete, had to be brought from the sacristy. These were placed in the aisles and yet still there were people standing at the back. As the numbers increased the noise level of half-whispered conversations rose also, almost drowning out the medley of Christmas carols issuing modestly from the organ loft. My father suddenly leaned over in my direction and whispered, "Strangers!" An unnecessary explanation, particularly as we all knew that congregations normally never amounted to more than about twenty regulars. The curl of his lip when he delivered the explanation however turned it into a guilty verdict, an accusation not entirely commensurate with the spirit of seasonal goodwill to all men. A moment or two later, my Father's attitude was reflected by the parish priest, Father O'Callaghan. His tall dark figure appeared and took centre stage facing his congregation. He stood there in silence for a moment or two, presumably imagining that his presence would be enough to quell the noise but there was no discernible change. Suddenly he clapped his hands. He did it only once but the quality of the acoustics was such that it sounded as a thunderclap and immediately the whole place fell silent.

"Obviously," he declared in a loud penetrating voice, "I need to remind some of you where you are. This is not a social club nor yet a marketplace." Now he paused and the quiet held well, "I would be obliged therefore if you could sit and wait for the service to begin in silence... Thank you."

It was a performance in the grand tradition of the likes of Benito Mussolini. The swaggering sarcasm of a patronising despot. To complete the image, all he needed to have added were some instructions for non-Catholics to sit apart from true believers and the ecumenical movement would have been set back another hundred years. However, if their self-satisfied smirks were an indication, his statement obviously pleased my parents.

The Mass began on time and followed its usual proscription in its process. This was a high Mass with three priests in attendance, a ritual made the more impressive by the flash of gold and the complexity of pattern on their vestments. The altar had been dressed in similarly ornate decoration, a contrast to the black and white worn by the altar boys that attended and to the swathes of seasonal greenery along either side. Ignoring the secular preference currently popular with Rome and clearly in keeping with the bias of the local clergy, the service was a Tridentine Mass. The Latin proved once again its capacity to increase the mystical dimension of the occasion as it always had.

The word 'baroque' sprang to mind.

I must confess that, at least to begin with, I experienced an unexpected surge of nostalgia. The concentration of light on the High Altar; the perfumed incense that wafted through the body of the church; the richness of the costume and the grand tones of the organ; all contributed to a memory of occasions when I had a small part to play in the ritual. The vitality of the atmosphere was enhanced still further when the choir sang. A crystal-clear soprano voice led the twenty-strong choir in renditions of *Adeste Fidelis*, *Come to the Manger* and a whole host of other Christmas favourites. Indeed, it is true to say that when the time came for the sermon, I was actually enjoying the occasion.

I should have known it was too good to last.

At the appropriate time the organ stopped and Father O'Callaghan mounted the stairs to the pulpit. He adjusted the missal sitting on the lectern with a theatrical flourish before he spoke. "You are sinners," he boomed, "and if you do not correct yourselves by self-denial you will certainly go to Hell."

I could hardly believe my ears. The Hell-fire sermons were never preached at this time of the year. They belonged to Lent, the time of regret, anticipating the crucifixion. There was a stunned silence.

"Your Lord God sent his only son to earth, to give his life in order that you could have eternal life – that you might live forever – and how do you repay him? You wait for his birthday celebrations and stuff yourselves with food, drink to excess and fornicate without shame. Christmas is not simply party-time. The sins of the flesh are inspired by the Devil…" and so he went on.

His Christmas message, far from being one of hope, became a dire warning and the more excessive his complaints, the more inappropriate the sermon appeared. In marketing terms this was the one occasion in the Church calendar that could guarantee a congregation consisting of a majority of non-Catholics. It was therefore an opportunity for recruitment – I thought. A time when the breadth of the doctrine should be inclusive, when everyone was welcome, when the barriers came down and when the emphasis should be on generosity of spirit.

The words rolled round my mind serving to confirm my scepticism and to further entrench the criticisms I applied to the Roman way. It annoyed me like never before. This kind of exposition would only serve to alienate all those who heard it. It was out of keeping, demonstrating a complete misunderstanding of what was required. Here was the holy policeman threatening prison; the headmaster, promising detention – the Hitler describing how he would destroy his detractors.

What made the matter all the worse, certainly for those present who knew the good priest socially, was the fact that he was a hypocrite. He was regularly drunk down at the *Knights of St Columbia Club* and there had been a number of occasions when young women, some of them the wives of members, had complained of his unpriestly attentions.

But what did I care! The thought occurred to me suddenly. Wasn't I beyond all this nonsense, hadn't I rejected all of it anyway. Why was I sitting there trying to imagine ways that O'Callaghan and his imbecilic followers could increase his sphere of influence. The man was patently a moron and, if his aggressiveness turned people away from his church, then be it on his own head.

Eventually his sermon drew to a close with advice that was more appropriately redolent of a Government public information message.

"So – this year do not have a second helping of turkey, do not drink until you find yourself senseless and resist the easy access to sins of the flesh. Pray for forgiveness and offer your actions of denial to God in recompense. Be grateful for the mercy he shows you and give thanks for his indulgence…"

He stopped and looked about his church, "Finally," he added, "for those of you who are strangers to this place – your welcome here is conditional on the respect you show for our religious practices. Please make certain that you do not disturb the person next to you during the service… Go in peace."

To be entirely fair to the 'strangers' they had suffered his diatribe without complaint up to this point. However, just as he was descending the steps to resume his place at the altar, some wag from the body of the church said, "And a happy Christmas to you too." With the advantage of the total silence imposed by the priest, the comment was amplified and heard clearly by everyone. A ripple of subdued laughter followed and for a moment O'Callaghan could be seen to pause mid-way down the wooden steps. He must have thought better of making a reply and continued on his way, apparently ignoring what had been said.

Chapter Fifteen

During my childhood, the events of Christmas morning had always followed a proscription mischievously designed by my father to lengthen the wait before presents could be opened. Not for me the hasty tearing open of packages whilst still in my pyjamas. The programme was, as it were, etched in tablets of stone.

I would awake and go to my parents' room where we would wish one another a happy and holy Christmas and at this juncture I would be given some sweets or perhaps some chocolate. I would then return to my room and dress myself. Downstairs, the presents beneath the tree would be ignored until after breakfast, often a lengthy procedure involving full three courses. It was only when the table had been cleared that I was permitted to sit beneath the tree to wait for presents to be passed to me. And again, even at this stage the method was ritualised. Presumably, as I was an only child, Mam and Dad would take turns to pass me parcels. Then sweaty little hands would presage the passage of each by an announcement of the donor. Typically they might choose to say something like, "This one is from Aunt Maud, now she usually sends you a book but this doesn't feel like a book this year. I wonder what it is." By then of course, I couldn't give a fig who it was from, all I wanted to do was get it open and see what I'd acquired. Neither did I want to be told afterwards that I should remember to write a letter of thank you to whosoever my benefactor might have been – but inevitably this was what happened.

It was a tortuous process and, whilst admittedly it prolonged the anxiety of anticipation that can be so pleasant for children at this time of year, it undoubtedly created a feeling of frustration in my acquisitive little brain. One year my father, in his role of 'torturer in chief', decided that my presents should be opened at a rate of one per hour, rather than all at once. It was an experiment doomed to failure from the start and the idiocy of the notion was highlighted when a relative called round mid-morning to ask if I liked the gift they had sent. To my parents' embarrassment, the gift still lay unopened.

My memories of childhood Christmas mornings were often seen in slow motion replays in my mind's eye. Situations that would never move at anything like the speed I wished and in which the prevalent emotion was one of deep frustration.

I awoke on Christmas morning to find Celia sitting at the bedside in her dressing gown.

"Mick – come on it's time to get up," she said in an urgent voice. "Everyone else is downstairs."

Perhaps my resistance was on account of knowing I would need to 'sell' the idea of an imaginary present to my parents. Conversely, it may have been because of the fact that, after returning from midnight Mass, I had persuaded my father to join me in a couple of glasses of whisky. I'd brought a bottle of single malt from London for this express purpose and had joked with Celia, telling her I intended to get him drunk. In the event, his tolerance proved greater than mine and, by the time I'd climbed the stairs, I had been much the worse for wear whilst he had seemed unaffected.

"Okay, okay," I replied. "Get me a glass of water will you – please."

It took me some considerable time to organise my clothing, at least in part on account of an unaccountable sway evident in the bedroom floor. An uncomfortable movement that caused a feeling of nausea.

"You're still pissed," Celia declared unsympathetically.

"Delicate – that's what I am," I snapped back.

The tradition established when I was a child was apparently to be maintained and we found ourselves ushered to sit at the breakfast table as soon as we appeared downstairs. The fruit juice and coffee brought a welcome relief but the presentation of egg, bacon, fried tomatoes and beans stirred a gastric reaction that could so easily have ended in disaster. I was subsequently left to wonder why parents, particularly mothers, choose to believe that their offspring, once they have moved away from home, are inevitably underfed. A belief they will often use to justify ignoring the options selected by the same offspring at meal times. Sitting at the table, I had stated clearly that I would prefer only coffee for my breakfast. I accepted the fruit juice however and was grateful for it. Clearly this was taken as a sign of indecision and my request for toast – and nothing else – was completely ignored. My Father witnessed my hesitation when the dinner plate was presented to me and, in a rare mood of amusement, suggested that as an alternative to a fried meal, I might prefer tripe and onions. I left the table, albeit briefly at this point, for a singularly unpleasant visit to the

161

smallest room. Thankfully by the time I returned, the egg and bacon had been replaced by two slices of dry toast and no one made any further comment.

By the time we had adjourned to the sitting room and the site of the Christmas tree, I was feeling restored. The exchange of presents was however another trial. Given that they had not known I would return for Christmas and that they had no idea Celia would accompany me, my parents had made a surprising provision for us. We each had several packages, carefully gift-wrapped and tagged, and the choices they had made on our behalf were entirely appropriate and very welcome. Celia was given a silk scarf, a ladies' cigarette lighter and a pair of brown leather gloves whilst I found my parcels contained a coloured shirt, a man's cigarette lighter and a pair of black leather gloves. I was very impressed.

"We decided that the kind of present we wanted to give you was one of a different kind," I said, beginning my pitch. "We would like you both to come down to London – at our expense – stay at a hotel, which we will book for you and let us show you the sights – a trip to the theatre, Buckingham Palace, the Zoo and maybe the Tower. What do you say?"

They were obviously impressed and sat there for a moment with silly grins on the faces. Dad was the first to respond, "That's really generous of you, son," he said quietly.

"The best present we've had in years," Mam echoed.

"And we'd love to visit you," Dad continued, "but you see… we don't like to leave our town. Your mother gets worried if we travel far."

She nodded.

"But it's not that far," I said, "and we'd meet you at the station in a taxi, take you direct to a nice hotel and keep you company all the time."

By now I was almost beginning to believe the offer was real myself and the greater their resistance, the more I pressed them to accept. Celia joined in at some point and embellished the notion, describing the facilities they would find in a reasonable hotel. "They provide anything you want in these places. All you need to do is phone down for room service."

There was a point during this exercise at which they almost changed their minds. I could see from my mother's expression that she was imagining the detail of such a visit and for a fraction of a second she glanced at Dad uncertain as to her final decision.

"And you mustn't believe all the stories you hear about crime on the streets. London is as safe as any capital city," I added hastily.

My preventative measures proved the success I thought that they would. They had not considered the street crime situation and my mention of it confirmed their resolve.

"No, son," Dad said, "it's no good us pretending we'd come – we'd only cancel at the last minute and that would cost you money. No. Better we say no thank you now."

"It's a lovely thought though," Mam added, "and it proves just how generous you are, Michael. I always said you had a generous spirit, didn't I, George?"

"She did. She always said that even when you got yourself into trouble. Thank you, son."

For the rest of the day, the level of their gratitude, signified by their repeated thanks and their continuous reference to the offer we'd made, was almost an embarrassment. My feigned disappointment was made all the more convincing when I said that I would now need to find them an alternative present. An offer that was firmly and emphatically designated as unnecessary by both the intended recipients. After that nothing was too good for us and the business of the arrest and our co-habitation was put firmly to one side.

The obvious success of this idea proved to me once and for all time that making people happy relies more on giving them nice things to think about, rather than providing material gains. It was a similar philosophy to that which I believed would bring me success in my career. Ideas are the most important things in life and the public at large will tolerate all manner of privation if they are made to feel valued. My parents knew full well that my financial situation was near precarious and this made the offer I'd made all the more valuable. In their minds, if I was prepared to make the sacrifice their trip would necessitate, then I must value them deeply – and that was the best Christmas present they could hope for.

The rest of the day passed in a sequence of eating and drinking bouts. The Christmas lunch, although typically overcooked, was a feast and afternoon turkey sandwiches, supplemented by pickles, cheeses, biscuits and steamed pudding left us all exhausted. We found some respite for our digestive systems however, by drinking copious amounts of beer, wine and strong spirits. In the evening we played board games and watched an endless variety of television shows and films, most, of which we'd seen many times before. Although non-smokers themselves, my parents had provided boxes of cigarettes which were judiciously placed about the sitting room for our convenient use. Not surprisingly, by nightfall the whole household was stretched, dozing in armchairs around the television set.

Perhaps due to the surfeit of food and drink, I was minded of Father O'Callaghan's sermon. And whilst the over-indulgence I practised might well have been understandable given my rejection of what the man stood for, it was interesting that my parents had also chosen to ignore his message. Human behaviour it seemed was governed more by what was convenient at the time, rather than what might be seen as spiritually correct. It made me wonder how much else of the Christian ethic was relevant. If good people, such as my parents would undoubtedly claim to be, chose to give only a verbal agreement, one without serious consequence in their every-day lives, what price the moral attitude implied by society at large.

Beneath the veneer of civilization, perhaps we are all thieves, adulterers, and murderers even, and maybe it is only the threat of a punishment that maintains the balance of the status quo. The punishment I imagined was one that would also include the disapproval of one's neighbours, because every community likes to pretend an acceptable standard of what we call moral behaviour and no individual likes to feel ostracised. It could be that behind every net curtain in every suburban street, a hotbed of sexual deviation was festering, that the vengeance so many would wish to exercise on those who have offered them insults, was secretly being planned. And that the average citizen was hoping that the material goods they desired would fall conveniently from the back of some passing lorry.

This was a curious dichotomy. No small wonder that generally so many of the people who comprise our society should suffer from mental illness. The accommodation of such a contradiction was enough to split most personalities. As a consequence, success in such a world must therefore imply the necessary application of a level of ruthlessness that defies convention. In a sense this was an honesty that would fly in the face of fake standards. I decided then and there that I could be just such a person and I determined that from that moment onwards, I would strive even harder than ever to achieve all those benefits that were available through material success.

Boxing Day merged seamlessly into what had gone before. The only difference of any substance being that the meat was served cold and instead of hot vegetables, we were served potato salad and green salad. As far as food generally was concerned, the quantities available remained the same and the drinking continued. By now we were bored with board games and tired of television, so instead we told jokes and stories of unusual happenings. But the former were not very funny and the latter, not really more than pedestrian. Most of my father's tales from the shop floor, anecdotes about the period when he was a floor manager in a department store, had been aired repeatedly since I was a child. The same was true also for those my mother regaled us with about her childhood. Unfortunately, the best I had to offer had they been told in their entirety would have shocked my parents to their core. They needed therefore to be sanitised and this often destroyed the whole point of the telling.

On account of the limited amusement available, Boxing Day dragged past, a worm's progress in the apple of our holiday. And, as is sometimes the case in situations where people are bored witless, it did not take until much past lunchtime before arguments broke out. In contention were the following: which television programme, who should make the next cup of tea and whether the big armchair should be my father's by right of occupation. Inevitably therefore feelings were hurt and with the ending of the season of goodwill, the house returned to normal.

Chapter Sixteen

1977

Celia and I planned to return to London in time for the city's New Year celebrations. It was all well and good to visit the North at Christmas but if New Year was to be celebrated in any kind of style one had to be in the capital. There were those who argued that it did not matter much where one got drunk and, that once under the influence, one place was much like another but I knew better. In my experience at that time of year a city is inevitably more exciting than a town and the capital is the most exciting city by far.

Given the parlous state of our finances however, the mentality of this logic did not actually bear too close a scrutiny. At least in Stockton we knew we could be entertained without undue cost, whereas in London the cost could well be prohibitive. However, at the back of my mind there was also the possibility – the hope, that Manny would have returned and that I might therefore be the recipient of a substantial injection of good luck. During my stay in Stockton and despite it being the holiday period, I had rung Manny's office several times. On those occasions when Julia answered, unfortunately the news was the same. Her boss was still touring North America and still doing deals. She still had no idea when he might return.

I broke the news of our departure to my parents, two days after Boxing Day and though I was expecting strong objections, in fact they made no objection. Their silence on the subject was perhaps testimony to their patience having also been exhausted. A not too surprising consequence of our practice of late-night drinking and late-morning hangovers. With hindsight, and at those times when I feel kindly towards my parents, I can see now that our presence must have seriously disrupted the normal timetable of the house, stretching the level of their tolerance beyond what they might consider reasonable.

I decided that our return trip should not be left to depend on the generosity, feigned or otherwise, of lorry drivers and booked seats for us on the overnight train to Kings Cross. The savings we had made by lodging at my home for the holiday period made such expense justifiable and anything was preferable to the chance encounters we had found travelling by road.

We actually left on the day before New Year's Eve. The train was crowded and noisy and we spent the trip trying vainly to sleep. At Kings Cross I invested in a taxi and by eight thirty the following morning I was opening the studio doors. The place was like a fridge and as we had little or no fuel for the stove, we decided to have our egg and bacon breakfast at a local café. It was whilst we were waiting for the eggs to be fried that I decided on an impulse to again phone Manny's office.

"Give it a rest, Mick," Celia complained. "If he's back then we'll soon know about it."

"If he's back then I want him round here as soon as possible," I replied.

I went to the corner outside where there was a phone booth and dialled the number. Julia answered immediately. As soon as she knew it was I calling she told me that in fact Manny had returned the night before.

"He said if you rang – I should ask you to call him on his home number – the London house."

I didn't need any more encouragement than that. Manny answered and in less time than it takes to drink a cup of tea, we'd arranged for him to visit the studio that afternoon. God was in his heaven and all was well with the poxy world.

Manny entered the studio at precisely four in the afternoon, exactly one-hour later than he'd promised. We'd spent the previous five hours trying to make the place look as if it was an artist's workshop, a workshop that was not ankle-deep in dust and grime and one that bore some passing resemblance to living accommodation above the level of a hovel. I was therefore rather annoyed by his casual apology for being late. But what could I say? I took him round the space, talking all the while and hoping he would not ask questions that probed too deeply into the why and wherefore of the work there. He didn't. In fact he said very little. He waited until we had done a full circuit and then, standing in front of the now lighted stove, asked if I was planning anything new.

Celia and I had argued all day about this. We guessed that he would want to know about current work but could not agree on the size of the lie I should tell. In the end we'd compromised and I told him about some fanciful notion concerning what I called 'the preservation of today's ideas'. As usual, once I got started I ran away with the idea. I said that there were some things and ideas that should be remembered, needed to be remembered and that to make the point I'd like to build large glass cases: citrines, in which to show them.

"... The paradox being that some of the items shown would be ephemera, the kind of throw away things we pay no attention to..."

I don't know why but in terms of art criticism there are two words that appear most frequently, words apparently beloved of the critics, the mere mention of which sets heads nodding wisely as if they were the key to Aladdin's cave. Those words are – 'paradox and ambiguity'. It's almost as if art must, of some necessity as yet unidentified, contain a multitude of contradictions if it is to be taken seriously. These days, it seems that a painting of a figure cannot be just – a painting of a figure – it has to be 'not' the painting of a figure.

Anyway, Manny was seduced in precisely the manner in which I'd hoped he might be. He nodded his head in all the right places and within forty-five minutes of him entering the studio he was offering to buy the lot – everything. More importantly he offered to become my agent.

"I've got all the right connections, Mick." He said, "I know gallery owners and businessmen, I have access to the Arts Council and a host of other people who could really help... And I'd enjoy the involvement. By the way, not to be indelicate but what do I owe you for this lot?"

Funnily enough, even though I'd planned for this moment, the one thing I'd not considered was what price should be placed on the goods. For a moment I was gobsmacked. However, as he was to do so many times in the future, Manny came to the rescue. He took out a chequebook and scribbled a figure before he signed it.

"Would that be about right?" he asked showing it to me.

The figure he'd written was more than the equivalent of ten years of my father's salary and then some. With as straight a face as I could muster, I told him that would do very nicely.

He promised to have the works moved within the week and before he left, he invited the pair of us to his New Year's Eve party, "Very informal," he said, "just a few friends, a few drinks and some bits and pieces of snacks. Maybe some good contacts for you and maybe a few laughs. What do you say?"

We said we'd be there – with bells on.

It was only during his passage to the door that it occurred to me that it would be impossible to cash the cheque that night. The number was so large that even my mate at the pub would be unable to change it – and, after the fried breakfast and buying the fuel for the stove, we had no cash-money left. I hurried after him catching him at the door.

"I don't suppose you could let me have some cash, Manny. You can change the numbers on the cheque but a few quid in real money would…"

He laughed and took out his wallet, "No problem, Mick. Sorry, I forgot what it was like to be strapped. How's this?" He gave me a thin bundle of ten-pound notes, "There's about two hundred there, so it should see you through the night, eh?"

I took it and offered the cheque back for him to change the amount but he waved it away, "Have this one on me – a late Christmas present and an apology for keeping you waiting."

As soon as he left, Celia slipped into her second-hand fur coat and we went down to the pub to celebrate our good luck. At last we'd turned the corner and I was sure that from this point on, things would get better and better. Suddenly I had an agent; I had a monstrous cheque in my pocket and cash in my hand. It didn't bother me at all that work I'd sold wasn't mine. In a Conceptual sense, I argued, once I'd taken ownership of it, it became mine, much like the found objects that had been used by artists for years. I had made it into art by possessing it and being able to convince someone to buy it. It was the idea that was paramount, not who had manufactured it.

After a couple of hours at the pub, we decided we should go home and get dressed up for Manny's party. I wore my new pink shirt and Celia dug out a flapper dress she'd found in a charity shop. She looked stunning – all legs, nipples and beads.

We had no idea where Manny lived but the taxi driver seemed to know the road so we left it up to him. He dropped us in a quiet part of Highgate, the kind of area where the houses are set back from the pavement and boast high walls and big gardens. From the kerb the place looked like a castle. Huge trees surrounded the property and gigantic gates, accessed by an intercom, barred the entrance. We giggled a bit, arguing about who should press the button and what we should say when anyone answered. In the end I took the initiative and announced myself as Mr Hume's guest. Without the need for further comment, the gates slid silently open and we started up a long path. The house itself was Victorian and at the top of a short flight of steps, the front door was set back behind a portico. Music could be heard from open windows on the ground floor and the whole place was lit like Blackpool Tower. The front door itself was slightly ajar so we went in.

I suppose the first thing that registered in Manny's house was the feeling of opulence. I don't think I'd ever experienced it before, not in real life. I'd seen it on film of State occasions and in Hollywood blockbusters but this was the genuine twenty-four carat opulence, the kind only a lot of money can buy. The lighting was provided by a collection of table and wall lights, the furniture reflecting the deep glow on well-polished surfaces. Inches of carpet underfoot and the heavily embossed wallpaper softened the echo of music from a room on the right-hand side and the walls were hung with what appeared to be a collection of impressionist originals.

Several people were standing talking in the hall when we entered; they nodded a welcome in our direction and a moment later a dark-suited servant appeared, asked our names and then took our coats. He introduced himself as Morgan and guided us into the drawing room on the left where, he said, we would find our host.

Sure enough an admiring audience, a collection of well-dressed, heavily jewelled women, one or two of whom were very attractive, surrounded Manny. On the short journey across the room I began to recognise faces I'd seen in magazines, one I'd certainly seen on television and another who was best known for appearances on the cat-walks of fashion shows.

"Hi there, you two," Manny exclaimed as he caught sight of us, "come over here and meet some potential clients. And let me tell you, they're all art collectors of one sort or another."

Typically direct and without fear of giving offence, Manny presaged each introduction with a brief comment about the individual concerned.

"And this is Joan, you probably recognise her from the society pages. Joan is alimony-rich from two husbands living and one deceased – and a hellcat between the sheets. She eats young men like you for breakfast… Phillipa, meet Mick. Phillipa has a rich husband who doesn't keep a close enough eye on her, so she plays away from home mostly. Very tasty is Phillipa… This is Tracy, a singer with some pop group or other. Now you might as well know Tracy prefers the same kind of female partners that you do, so no dice there. However, Tracy is also very rich…" And so it went on. The women laughed at every comment without a trace of malice. They took my hand and unashamedly did a cursory inspection of the goods, murmuring how they would like to get to know me – and my work. I noticed that the women called Tracy paid rather more attention to Celia than she did to me, holding her hand for a fraction longer than was necessary. I made a mental note to tease Celia later.

As soon as the introductions were over, we were escorted to the bar and invited to drink whatever we fancied.

"There's just about everything you might imagine here, Mick," he told me, "and if you prefer cocktails, Celia, then Jose my barman will astound you with his virtuosity as a mixer and shaker."

We were then whisked into a smaller side room where a table was set with a feast fit for any sultan. A huge turkey stood centre-stage, surrounded by cold joints of pork, lamb, beef, guinea fowl and a host of other meats. There were salads of every description and large plates of vol-au-vents, pâté, and pastries of innumerable variety. A side table boasted a similar collection of puddings and gateaux, jugs of cream and chocolate titbits that were straight from the pages of *The Beano* comic. It was all too much.

"Christ, Manny," I said, "are you expecting this many guests?"

He laughed, obviously pleased at my surprise, "Maybe. Some will come and stay, others will drop in for a drink and a snack and leave. Anything left will go to the shelter for homeless people on the High Street."

It appeared that the homeless of Highgate were of a very different calibre from those in the rest of London. If they could look forward to a New Year's Day dinner like this, starving for the rest of the year couldn't be such a hardship.

I soon found that a number of Manny's guests had been briefed about my potential as an artist and, during the course of the evening, any number of total strangers came to me to talk about what I was doing. The deference they showed me was a new experience. Suddenly I was being taken seriously and several referred to the investment potential that Manny saw in my work. Celia danced with me a couple of times but it wasn't long before she was in demand by various gentlemen who clearly imagined they were some kind of Fred Astaire to her Ginger Rogers. Eventually, therefore, I was left to my own devices but not for long.

As the evening wore on I found myself being persuaded into corners by some of the better-looking women guests. Their chat-up line was always the same. Pretending to want to talk about art, they quickly found some reason to need me to loosen a strap for them; to adjust my tie; to remove invisible specks of dust from my shoulder – or my trouser front – and, not unexpectedly, their conversations quickly turned to who my latest nude model might be. When the stroke of midnight came and the champagne flowed ever more freely, I was assaulted by three admirers at the same time. And kissing-in the New Year was the least of what they wanted from me. In the end, after I finally freed myself from their fumbling fingers and removed their deliciously scented breasts from my face, I found I had only Phillipa left on my arm. She had been by far the most persistent, as well as being the most voluptuous of my attackers. She laughed at my embarrassment and kindly shielded me from the rest of the room whilst I refastened my flies.

We retired to an upstairs room a little later; a place where the invention of her versatile contortions was able to have free rein and the noisy response she enjoyed making was all but lost by the shielding of soft furnishings. Phillipa was an exceptional partner, combining sensuousness with sensitivity and, when the occasion demanded, willingness with an affectation of coy reticence. Even at the time I felt sure that this was one of those occasions that would remain memorable, a benchmark against which to measure any or all of my future adventures. In this at least I was not to be proven wrong. During the course of the night, surprisingly, the room we occupied was visited simultaneously by two other females. Both of these were keen to join in our, by then, exhausted struggles and to leave content only after their enthusiastic participation had stretched the bounds of my imagination. I was no stranger to the extent of the female appetite for sex but the episode with Phillipa and her friends extended my experience beyond that which I thought was possible. Not surprisingly therefore, when I eventually slept, although it could never be termed the 'sleep of the innocent', it was nevertheless a well-earned, deep and dreamless slumber consistent with total physical exhaustion.

I was awakened at seven the next morning by the sound of running water and when Phillipa emerged from the shower she looked as fresh as if she had been on a two-week holiday in the South Seas. By contrast, when I stared at myself minutes later in the bathroom mirror, I found I had acquired a deathly pallor, redolent of a middle-aged man about to have a heart attack. The hot water revived me but did little to reinvigorate my appearance and when I joined the others in the dining room for breakfast, I felt that I needed a blood transfusion.

The company at the table included Manny who sat in silence reading a magazine; a fresh-faced Celia who also seemed to have thrived on whatever she had done the previous night; Phillipa and her husband John; and two other couples. Everyone looked tired, content to breakfast in silence. And although there was a full range of likely breakfast food available on a sideboard, most favoured the fruit juice and toast instead of the eggs and bacon, the kippers or the cereal. I took an empty seat and Celia came and sat next to me smiling, presumably at my appearance and obviously wanting to chat. Being in a somewhat delicate state, I replied in one-word answers only and after a while she gave up on me. Phillipa also seemed inappropriately lively and talked about all sorts of things, and in a loud voice, leaving me to imagine that for females, strenuous sexual activity acted as a stimulus to their energy rather than a drain. Her continuous diatribe was, however, interrupted when a young man entered the room. His face was ashen, his hair askew and he looked worse than I felt. I'd been introduced to him the previous evening but could remember only that his name was Gerry. Without a word to anyone Gerry came up behind Phillipa and took her by the neck.

"You whore," he shouted, "you fucking dirty whore," he shouted.

At the same time he began to shake her violently, making her eyes bulge. I had no idea what the hell was happening or why he should be in such a state, but clearly his temper was roused and for some reason he was furious with Phillipa. Amazingly, no one made any attempt to stop him and it wasn't until I hurried round the table to him that he stopped. By this time his victim was all but strangled and hardly in a condition to speak. Sensing my intention, he turned to me as I approached, "Mind you own business," he snarled at me anticipating my interference. Manny looked up at this point and said quietly, "Sit down, Gerry, and behave yourself."

"But she's been at it again," Gerry replied, "she buggered off with someone, without so much as a word and I'm left like a fool..."

"You are a bloody fool," I said, "and if you lay a finger on her again I'll give you a smacking you'll remember for the rest of your miserable life."

By now we were facing one another and close to, he stank of strong drink and looked even worse than I'd imagined. My outburst caused Phillipa's husband to turn round in his chair to look at me.

"So, my wife has a new champion, does she?" he said grinning, "I think you've been replaced in her affections, Gerry. Best retire gracefully."

For a second I thought that Gerry was about to take a punch at me. His face contorted and he set himself as though ready to fight. While this exchange took place Phillipa had sat coughing and trying to regain her breath. Suddenly, without any warning, she stood up and hit her attacker full in the face. Her blow wasn't the lady-like slap one might have expected; it was a whole-hearted punch with her weight behind it, delivered to the man's left temple. Gerry dropped like a stone. Now, for the first time, there was a universal response and almost everyone at the table stood up.

"There was no need for that," Manny said rushing round to assist his injured guest. The others echoed his comment and there seemed to be a consensus that she had acted unreasonably. Gerry was duly revived with a glass of water and helped to a chair. From the comments made, I gathered that his behaviour was not unusual, however; there appeared to be an acceptance of his violence by his friends as if it were the norm. On the other hand, Phillipa's response was seen as being outrageous.

Celia left with me just after midday. We thanked Manny for his hospitality, I exchanged telephone numbers with Phillipa and we took a taxi back to the studio. On the way home, in answer to my inquiry, Celia admitted spending the night with Manny. She said he had proposed she should join him almost as soon as we arrived at his house but that she had not decided to do so until she'd seen me disappear upstairs with Phillipa. She added that unfortunately my new agent was less effective as a partner in bed than as a marketing man in the City. Apparently, although they had slept together, once between the bed-sheets he let it be known that he never consummated a relationship in the physical sense, preferring instead to 'play' with his bedfellows in an extended session of mutual masturbation. This amused me and I saw it as typical of all those who act as middlemen, making their profit from other people's efforts without ever committing themselves to wholehearted involvement.

The sale of the art works from the studio made a considerable difference to our standard of living. Now we could afford to eat out occasionally, we could pay our bills promptly and buy a few things for that part of the studio we used as living accommodation. When we had returned from Teesside, there had been a letter waiting for me from the college Bursar. In it he had expressed concern that I had left with money owing to fellow students over the holiday period and that if I did not make some firm promise of payment, he would be obliged to release the details of my new address to my creditors. In my reply I did not try to explain the reasons for the delay in making the payments. I simply told him that as soon as my cheque from Mr M. Hume the art collector was cleared, payment would made. His response was by return of post and as predictable as I'd guessed it would be. He assured me of his continued understanding and indulgence and requested that I should talk to him as soon as it was convenient.

The mere mention of Manny's patronage was enough to open doors previously slammed shut in my face and I knew the bursar was about to ask me to organise an introduction to my agent. Increasingly, colleges seek to recruit the good will of figures prominent in the marketing of art. Whereas previously they may have had more interest in artists with established reputations on behalf of their student's development, the current preoccupation with the business end of the art world implied a less than subtle change in policy.

Chapter Seventeen

I settled all my outstanding debts to my fellow students early in January, and one afternoon I spent a ridiculous half-hour in the company of the college bursar. As I'd guessed, once he knew of my relationship with Manny Hume he wanted me to use my influence to get Manny to visit the college. Normally, Mr Croft, the bursar was an austere person, deliberately far removed from the student body except when contact was unavoidable. In the common room bar he was referred to as the 'Insurance Man' and indeed his image was exactly that, a sober-suited bureaucrat whose eye was on financial administration rather than art, whose sole interest was in columns of figures rather than people. On the occasion of our meeting however, he offered a very different persona. He had coffee and biscuits served and chatted about my success as if he'd had a personal responsibility in my achievement. He dismissed any concern implied in his first letter about the money I owed to other students. He even suggested that if I should need funds in future, the college might be able to make the investment required. Throughout my visit, testimony to his change of heart, he insisted on referring to me as 'Mr Grainger'.

Consequently, I promised to bring Manny to visit the open day exhibition held at the end of the following term and to guarantee his introduction to the principal. Naturally, I took the opportunity to embellish the importance of my association with Mr Hume, claiming all manner of intimacy and familiarity with his business affairs, none of which was true. A strategy that nevertheless increased the value of my stock in the eyes of the Insurance Man and ensured an easier passage for me through the quagmire that was the administrative hub of the college.

During that spring, I was in constant contact with Manny. He phoned me on a regular basis and was ever keen to discuss my future work. It was simple, therefore, for me to suggest that I might be able to organise a formal introduction to the principal of my college and to imply that there might be a vacant position on the governing board. Manny was as grateful as Mr Croft had been and I experienced the unusual thrill that the manipulation of people inevitably brings.

Manny let me know that he was negotiating for premises in Dockland where he intended to build a new art gallery. He told me that if I could produce a sufficiently substantial collection of work, he would be pleased for it to comprise the opening exhibition. He tempted my taste buds by inferring the level of publicity such a show would demand would be huge and that it could establish me as a major figure in the British, if not the international, art world. At this point, although we had agreed the terms of reference relating to his stewardship of my career, we had not signed any kind of formal agreement. Manny always argued that a handshake was enough to cement our kind of relationship. And whilst such a loose association left me feeling vulnerable, his integrity was proven by the way he guaranteed any expenditure I might see fit to make in producing future works. The only problem left was in my lack of ideas.

It was April before I resolved the question of what form my future work should take, and it was in conversation with Celia and a friend of hers, a young student called Paul, that the new ideas were first explored.

My visits to the department at college had grown ever more infrequent and, on account of my new popularity with the bursar, no one sought to chastise or criticise me for this deficit. Celia still attended on a regular basis but whenever I required her company she would skip college and spend the day with me. On the occasion in question, she had brought Paul Thompson to meet me whilst we were on a visit to the Victoria and Albert Museum. Paul had just started his studies and having heard about my success had expressed a desire to meet me. We had morning coffee in a place near the museum and then took a slow walk round the various galleries.

"It's curious how so much stuff is consigned to glass packing cases," Paul said.

"It's curious WHY so much stuff is consigned to glass cases," Celia added.

"It's a sign that they think it's precious," I replied, "and that it's worth protecting for the future."

"But isn't it odd," Paul went on, "separating it from the visitors – making a demarcation as it were, between the live representatives of the culture and the iconography of that same culture?"

"Are you suggesting that artists should have a closer access to the exhibits than the general public?" Celia asked.

Paul paused then said, "No. All I'm saying is that it's odd. I mean – when we exhibit things, we don't put them behind glass. So, does that mean we don't think they're worth protecting for the future?"

It was a nice ambiguity echoing something I'd said to Manny and I began to think about what he implied. The glass case was certainly symbolic of a value judgement, the suggestion being it meant that a certain importance had accrued – and was accepted as having accrued. The notion took hold of my imagination and I began an internal discussion with myself about what sort of things, things representing our society, I would save for posterity. And having decided on things to save, how I would show them off. It was a theme I'd discussed with Celia some time previously but on that occasion, I'd not appreciated the possibilities.

By the time we returned to the studio that day I had the nucleus of an idea. I spoke to Manny that evening and he agreed to foot the bill for my first experiments.

The following week was spent making telephone calls. I had a clear idea of what I required but it took me several hours before I found anyone who was prepared to meet my specifications. And having reached some level of agreement with a manufacturer, I was then obliged to visit the factory where the work would be produced. Celia opted to stay at home so I took the early morning train to Liverpool where I picked up a hire car which took me to Pilkingtons Glass factory research department.

John Adams met me at the reception desk and took me on a tour of the facility. John was a senior manager responsible for production and it was in discussion with him that the practicality of my ideas was finally resolved. Being unaware of the versatility of the management at Pilkingtons, I was surprised at the enthusiasm that greeted my demands. Everyone I spoke to that day from the shop floor to the Board room, appeared to be excited by the project and willing to experiment with their processes in order to satisfy my needs. As a customer with the potential for spending a lot of money, I was treated as a VIP. However, as someone coming along with an idea that could have implications for good publicity, I was also treated with respect. It was a new experience for me but one to which I was quick to adapt.

Over an executive lunch John discussed the specifications of my project with me and on a plain paper pad drew out the calculations necessary to achieve what I required. Consequently, by three in the afternoon, we had a working model designed. I wanted them to produce a series of large glass containers, in effect boxes that could withstand a vacuum of considerable magnitude. I also wanted them to organise the purchase of some means of air extraction that could be contained but hidden within the base of these boxes. The thickness and quality of the glass was therefore a crucial element, as was also the metal structure, a skeleton that would contain the glass. Given that the largest containers would be six metres long by four metres wide by four metres high, the problem was considerable.

"To be on the safe side," John said, finally putting down his pencil, "we'll need to make a couple of test pieces. The tolerance is vital so we'll test them to destruction. Can you come back to see the results?"

"Anytime you say." I replied.

My relationship with John developed during the day we spent together. We shared a similar sense of humour, we ridiculed politics and politicians to the same degree and we enjoyed the same ambitions as one another for the acquisition of wealth and an easy life. As we got on together so well, it was not surprising that our discussions about the project eventually gave way to those concerning our various preferences for women. And, whilst in this area our similarities diverged, we nevertheless agreed that like beer, there was no such thing as bad sex.

By the time we had finished at the office, the sky was already darkening, consequently I agreed to spend the night and return the following day. John took me to a hotel in Liverpool and after making a phone call to his wife, said he would keep me company.

"Pilkington promotes good hospitality for its clients," he told me grinning, "and I happen to know some local ladies who are only too pleased to be hospitable – for a modest fee."

We made a night of it. After a better than average dinner we settled to drink in the bar where we were eventually joined by Tracy and Maureen – a blond and a brunette. The hotel was in mid-week quiet mode so we had the place almost to ourselves. An opportunity to be loud, to drink after hours and to disport ourselves to our heart's content. The party continued later in our hotel room and it wasn't until the early hours of the morning that the girls finally left, by which time we were all exhausted. On the way back to London later that morning, I decided that my new life should include such events on a regular basis. I saw them as remedial punctuation marks in, what I hoped would be, my long paragraph of fame and fortune.

Manny telephoned me that evening and invited me to dine with him at Langans down in the West End. As Celia had made other arrangements for the evening, I accepted and met him there at eight. We dined well and drank too much and then retired to Manny's club for more drinks. By then his mood was expansive and he thought it fitting to advise me concerning the investment of any excess funds I might accumulate.

"One of the best investments is property," he said, "especially in London. And if you can find commercial property – the kind that will show a good return, even better."

I must confess it was a subject about which I knew nothing. My financial life so far had been concerned only with survival. If I could pay my bills and have something left over for entertainment purposes, then I was happy. However, the idea of making money with money appealed to me and I questioned my benefactor closely about ways to find just such an investment as he'd described. He was a mine of information.

"Let's take residential property first," he said, "the kind you might rent out. All you have to ensure is that the demands on the property – the outgoings – leave a fifteen percent profit on your stake."

"Is that fifteen percent per annum?" I asked trying to sound knowledgeable.

"Yes – per annum. And given the price of accommodation in Town, that isn't too difficult. Also, over a period of two to three years, if you've chosen carefully the value of the property will have increased by as much as seventy, even eighty percent."

The figures amazed me and I wondered why I hadn't thought about this before.

"On the other hand," he went on, "should you choose a retail outlet – say such as a café or restaurant – the income can be even greater."

He detailed the kind of operation he had in mind and produced the most persuasive of arguments to support his suggestion. I liked the idea of a restaurant and although the management would involve a necessity for closer monitoring as well as a bigger cash outlay, the rewards were so much greater. We talked about property prices and discussed the advantages of freehold over leasehold and the vagaries of the mortgage system. Manny's little lecture that night was the best instruction I'd ever had with regard to money management, and although what he described to me was very much 'junior league investment', it was easy to see how he had become so wealthy.

The following weekend, during an impromptu shopping expedition in Soho with Celia, I noticed a couple of small shops for sale and decided to investigate. One of the properties was a newsagent-cum-general dealers. It was filled to capacity with magazines and newspapers, with bars of chocolate and sweets and one corner was devoted to a very limited collection of videos to rent. I could not help but notice that both the vast majority of the glossy magazines as well as the bulk of the videos were of the explicit variety. A ubiquitous top shelf boasted a collection of pornography. Presumably these publications were sited deliberately out of children's reach. I concluded that, never had so many bums and tits been crowded together in so small a space before.

"Can I help you, Sir?" the small, fat man behind the counter asked when I entered. His appearance fitted his role as a seller of dirty magazines precisely. Unshaven for several days, his shirt was grimed at the collar almost equal to the black edge of his fingernails but it was his expression that proved the most offensive. His smile was a vile mixture of juvenile precocity flavoured by evidence of sub-normal appetites and an obvious willingness to provide whatever deviant request his customers might require. And, whilst I am the first to admit that my judgement may well have been a little distorted by a first impression and an over-active imagination, it was apparent that I was in the presence of a particularly low form of life.

"I saw the For Sale notice... can you give me any details?" I replied.

"You're interested in buying then are you?"

That much should have been obvious but I was determined to be patient, "I may be – depending on the asking price."

He leaned over the counter and across the piles of newsprint there, "It's not cheap... And there'll be a fixtures and fittings fee... and I can't quit the place for another eighteen months at least... And..."

"I wasn't looking for a negotiation at this time," I said rudely interrupting him, "I just wanted to know what the asking price was."

"Then you'd best ring the agents. The number is on the board."

Clearly he'd had enough of me, so I left.

Celia had waited outside, spending her time gazing into the window of the next door delicatessen. It was a window worth looking at, filled with all manner of foreign sausage, olives, bread sticks, packets of pasta, jars of pickle and tins of tomato puree.

Celia was impressed, "Let's buy something for dinner," she said as I appeared next to her.

"Better still – let's buy the shop," I replied.

I wasn't certain if the family who ran the delicatessen were from Italy or Greece. They were dark-skinned, the women with jet-black hair and deep-set eyes, but they spoke far too quickly in their native tongue for me ever to be able to pick out a word I might identify. By contrast to the newsagent next door, they were keen to give me whatever information they had about the sale of the property, albeit in very broken English. I gathered from them that both businesses had fallen on hard times but that they still felt aggrieved at the sale of the leases. Maria, the wife of the shopkeeper, told me in no uncertain terms that she would insist that their rights were protected and that they would stay on in the shop until the last possible day of their agreement. I sympathised with her and explained that my interest at this stage was merely of a general nature. I don't know if she really understood my meaning. Alfonso, her husband, told me that the freehold was owned by a local gangster called Jimmy Barratt and that he was responsible for the demise of most of the small shops in the area, "'Ee wants to make 'is money selling human flesh – what you call de pornography. 'Ee's a bad man."

His explanation was clear and we thanked him for his honesty before we left.

Later that day I rang the estate agents. However, the figures they gave me, representing the cost of the lease for both properties, was of telephone number proportions. It would be a long time before I had that kind of cash available whatever the returns might be so I put the idea on 'hold'. Celia was relieved. She had found real sympathy with the family operating the delicatessen and did not like the idea of them being out on the street. I didn't like to tell her that, whether I bought their shop or not, sooner rather than later that's exactly where they would find themselves.

Chapter Eighteen

During the next three months I was preoccupied with plans for the 'glass box' sculptures. The decisions about what the boxes should contain were hard won and again, Celia was a great help. The notion that the interior of the containers should be free of air however, was nevertheless paramount. I wanted the invisible atmosphere that contained the objects – whatever they were – to be absolute but without obvious effect. Everyone would 'know' about the vacuum even if they couldn't see it.

My first choice for something symbolic to 'save' in the vacuum was intentionally outrageous. It was to consist of a Rolls Royce car – and the car would be cut precisely into two pieces, each half-contained in tandem glass cases. These would be mounted adjacent to one another so those visitors could walk 'through' the vehicle. I had not decided on a title for the piece, but the word 'through' would perhaps need to figure somewhere in it. And the Rolls being one of the ultimate status symbols of the last century opened the prospect of my dealing with mankind's ideal philosophy for a comfortable life as my subject matter.

And if I was to pursue the idea of man and his philosophy, as a contrast to the car, I needed to 'save' a piece of the countryside. A typical rural idyll confirming the conservationist view – reference to Turner, Constable and the pipe dream of millions of city dwellers. Besides earth, grass and weeds it should contain wooden structures such a fence or a garden hut, a gate or a tree stump.

The theme was set and the rest of my choices proved a logical, if somewhat idiosyncratic selection. The one item that I'd kept at the back of my mind during this period was chosen for another reason however. I wanted to put one of Ram's big canvases in a box, partly to have him shown in a major exhibition and also in the belief that any ideal philosophy for life would needs must include a work of art. The more I thought about it the better I liked it. A painting to be the subject of and contained within a sculpture was a neat paradox.

John Adams was in touch with me that weekend and he told me that the trial box was ready for my inspection. He also said that a certain blonde had asked to be remembered to me. I told him that I'd arrange a visit to the factory early the following week.

It was the Sunday afternoon when Mam phoned me. I was surprised to hear her voice as she seldom used the telephone. On those occasions when she did, she adopted a strange accent reminiscent of her view of the BBC of the 1940s, added to which, as she was one of that generation who thought distance equalled a need for volume, she inevitably shouted her message into the mouth-piece. Initially therefore the effect was startling and, if what she had to say had not been such a serious matter, I could have been amused. Celia picked up the phone when it rang but quickly handed it to me grimacing at the noise.

"I'm so sorry, son," Mam started, "I hate to ring you with bad news."

"Mam – can you talk more quietly? You're straining my eardrums."

"Sorry, son." Now the sound was more bearable but only just, "I hate to ring with bad news but I thought you should know first. I wouldn't like you to think that I'd told anyone else before you. After all you are his son."

"Mam – what are you trying to say?"

"Your dad died this morning."

"Died?"

"Yes, he died in hospital at five thirty. The doctor said it was a heart attack… Oh, son, what am I going to do now?"

Now her voice subsided, clouded by tears. Suddenly her resolve was gone. I didn't know what to say what to tell her. There was a part of me that felt desperately sorry – not for him but for her. With hindsight, however, the predominant feeling I experienced was one of relief. Dad – my adopted dad – had been a domestic despot. Often cruel, usually insensitive and always self-centred. On occasion he had given Mam a life of hell and if there was any celestial justice that's where he should reside, I decided. I nevertheless comforted her as best I could. I made the right filial noises appropriate to the occasion and soon she regained her composure. I told her that I would travel up to see her and that I'd leave that very afternoon. There was also a lot of talk about how she would manage financially and how much I might be able to help out with money but I was careful not to commit myself too readily.

After she rang off, I told Celia and packed an overnight bag. We had purchased a second-hand car by this time – an old 2.4 Jaguar with faulty brakes – and I decided to drive up north rather than wait for a train. Celia opted not to accompany me, claiming that funerals made her depressed, so I left alone.

I was passing Biggleswade before I remembered that I hadn't packed a black tie.

The funeral was held on the following Wednesday. The full panoply of a Requiem Mass was followed by the slow drive to the cemetery. A line of six black cars followed the hearse in a stately procession. An occasion Dad would have been pleased to witness had he not been encased in a polished, brass-encrusted box in the lead car. It is a curious fact that when funerals are organised, many of those people attending – and seeking a priority place in one of the hire cars – are precisely those same folk who never had a good word to say about the deceased during his life. Other than a couple of his workmates, our six vehicles were filled with relatives from the fringes of the family, and it seemed, therefore, that the vulture mentality was still alive and well.

The parish priest, Father O'Callaghan, had officiated at the Mass and in his eulogy had told the small gathering that he thought it was his duty to do so, in recognition of the support Mr Grainger had shown for his church. His duty however, apparently did not extend to making the trip to the graveyard. A young priest was given the task, a fact that presumably had nothing to do with the forecast of more rain and the likelihood of there being a muddy quagmire to wade through to get to the new grave. In the event all my worst fears were realised.

It was always going to be a desultory affair due to the small congregation having predictably forgotten the responses needed to the graveside prayers, but when the heavens opened, it became a farce. The priest had assembled with his three altar boys at the head of the deep hole and the coffin bearers had successfully located the coffin on the two crossbeams set across the opening for that purpose when the first rain fell.

The candles carried by the two acolytes blew out just as the priest said, "Let us pray…" and no matter how many times Uncle Derby tried to re-light them with his Swan Vestas they remained out. However, we got as far as the De Profundis – the prayer for the dead – before the downpour came. Nervous glances were exchanged and I could see most people were only waiting to see someone else make a break for the cars before joining their retreat. I felt certain that, had a more experienced priest been in charge, at least some of the ceremony might have been abbreviated, not so with our pastor. He trudged through the formalities bulldog-fashion and even when the hole began to fill with water he was not deterred.

It is, and always has been, common practice at burials for the earth removed to be piled high next to the grave. Sometimes it is covered with a mat of Astro Turf in order to make it more homogenous with its surroundings; otherwise it is left bare. Its proximity close-by is convenient for the gravediggers that replace it as soon as the service ends. Our pile of earth seemed to have a mind of its own. As the storm developed and the rainwashed across the open aspect, the earth moved. It was seen to slide forward, as if seeking to return to its original home. Very soon the sludge could be heard plopping into the water beneath, and the concern of the mourners grew ever more apparent. The young priest persevered. Eventually, it was Aunt Molly who took the initiative. By this time her wide-brimmed hat had sagged around the edges leaving rainwater to run freely across the shoulders of her new black jacket. Suddenly, just as the holy water was being sprinkled for the last time, she made a huffing sound, exclaiming, "This is ridiculous…" as she turned to leave. God in his heaven must have taken her criticism to heart. Aunt Molly had chosen to stand as close to the grave as possible in order that she might be seen to have taken the trouble to dress appropriately – and that was her undoing. As she turned to leave, the earth beneath her left foot slid away and she did a slow pirouette before she sat down in the mud. Her weight and the impact of it on the ground moved a huge chunk of turf and, as we watched, she slid gracefully – black hat and all – into the hole. Indeed, she might well have been the recipient of the young priest's final blessing with holy water before she disappeared from sight.

Chaos ensued. Various people nearest to Aunt Molly, having witnessed her slip, tried to step back. It was those behind who, apparently seeking to save the lady in black, pressed forward and caused the accident to worsen. And for a brief moment it seemed that, like lemmings, the whole assembly was about to join my underground aunt. I reflected later that had the Fates not been so generous, at one stroke I might have been rid of the whole bevy of my inherited relatives. In the event, although many came near to the abyss, only cousin Patrick and an altar boy joined Aunt Molly in the depths. Many of the others ended being severely muddied, however, due to their brave attempts to rescue the victims It was only Aunt Gemma's call to, "Form a chain…" that saved the day and, once arms were linked, a workmate of Dad's was able to haul the victims from the muddy underworld.

The prevailing memory of the occasion left an imprint on my imagination ever after. It was the sight of a black-faced Aunt Molly standing calf-high in dirty water screaming, whilst a darkly dripping cousin Patrick climbed over her to hang onto one of the cross-beams, that supported the coffin. A keen sense of survival was ever deeply ingrained in the Grainger family it seems

At this point I shepherded my mother away from the pit and we were already halfway back to the car before I realised that we were both laughing. The corollary to this tale was the refusal of the taxi firm to allow all those covered in thick mud to return home in their cars. Wallets were called for and cash exchanged hands before access to the cars was finally granted.

Due to the communal mudbath at the cemetery, the gathering at the house afterwards was poorly attended. With their dainty ham sandwiches and jam tarts, post-burial tea parties are often an anti-climax unless supplemented by a generous supply of alcohol. And on such occasions, sweet sherry never suffices to satisfy this requirement. I was therefore much relieved when the few stragglers who came to the house left early. It was only then, over a couple of large Scotches – from a bottle I'd brought with me – that my mother gave me the full rendition of my father's demise.

In his usual style, the week before his death he had volunteered his wife to help clean the church. An offer apparently made over drinks at the bar of the Catholic club late one evening. The church 'scrub' happened only once per year and was implemented by the good will of the Catholic Women's League. In our parish the League consisted of a clique of middle-class 'worthies' with nothing better to do other than raise funds for Father O'Callaghan's pet charity – namely his annual holiday. And, as this was an organisation that in the past had repeatedly refused membership to my mother, for no good reason other than to maintain class distinction, Dad's offer on her behalf was particularly inappropriate. Dutiful as ever, Mam had however, capitulated without complaint. Consequently, she spent the whole of the Friday afternoon on her knees washing the cold mosaic floors. Dad called to meet her after work and, whilst he waited for her to collect her coat, he was persuaded to help shift some of the heavy pews.

That night, during his evening meal, he complained of chest pains. Ever the homespun diagnostician in matters of health, he told Mam it was probably, "A pulled muscle." During Saturday it grew worse and an ambulance was called to collect him shortly after *Match of the Day*. Apparently he refused to have his wife accompany him and told her instead to come to the hospital only after she had finished washing-up the dinner pots. By the time she finally reached his bedside he was unconscious and he died without ever opening his eyes again.

In my view, it was not insignificant that his final words to his wife consisted of an order to wash-up, nor could I ignore the cause of his cardiac arrest. There was a curious symmetry in the fact that his volunteering his wife for scrubbing duties had resulted in him being struck down. The justice reaped may not have been strictly poetic but it was certainly consistent with that tradition.

I stayed with my mother for only one more day after the funeral. Pilkingtons were keen to have me examine the model they had produced and there were other matters associated with my work that needed my attention in London. To be fair, she did not pester me to stay on at the house and accepted my excuses without question. I gave her a hundred and fifty quid in cash and promised to try and send her some money on a regular basis. I told her that I had hopes that I might sell work from the exhibition Manny had promised and, once that was resolved, I might be in a better position to help. It was as much as she could reasonably expect. I still had a considerable sum of money in my bank account but it had been earmarked for other things. It was, therefore, easy to resist any feeling of guilt that might have been associated with what some might have seen as my apparent lack of generosity.

The drive back to the studio was largely uneventful but when I arrived, I found that Celia had gone out for the night to a party. She did not specify in her note who was holding the party or where it was to be held and this lack of foresight meant I could not join her. She returned in the early hours, by which time I was asleep.

The following morning I spoke to John Adams on the telephone and arranged to visit the factory the next day. Celia finally appeared from beneath the duvet at mid-day and seemed considerably the worse for wear. Other than to say that the party had been loud and that lots of her college friends had attended, she seemed reluctant to amplify her account of the previous evening. I put this down to her hangover. After a little persuasion, she agreed to accompany me to Liverpool the next day but claimed she needed to work late that afternoon and that I should therefore make my own arrangements regarding dinner. As soon as she left the studio, I phoned Phillipa and agreed to take her to a little French bistro in South Kensington for a meal.

After we had dined, I discovered that Phillipa's husband had bought a tiny mews cottage in Kensington that they used as a pied-à-terre. It was an ideal location, combining a sense of privacy with easy accessibility – much like Phillipa herself. I was a little surprised when my companion offered me a 'snort' of cocaine, which she served with our coffee. Not wanting to show my obvious ignorance of the drug, I followed her example and found the effect to be exceptionally stimulating. I'd often used marijuana in the past but had never experienced the delights of Coke. It was one in the morning before I left her cottage, both of us by then exhausted through our after dinner exertions. The studio was deserted when I returned. There was no sign of a note and no message left on the answering machine, but content that she would appear as promised I went to bed and slept deeply.

Chapter Nineteen

I saw little relevance in Celia's absence until the next morning. But, the fact that she did not keep her promise to join me on the trip to Liverpool was significant. However loose our understanding, it had always included a commitment to keep any promises we made to one another. I waited until ten, but when she did not appear I left for the Northwest on my own.

Unfortunately the car decided to forfeit its reputation for reliability around the start of the M6 motorway and I was stranded there for two hours whilst I waited for the RAC to rescue me. Eventually I hired another motor from a garage on the outskirts of Birmingham and left the Jaguar to have its 'big ends' replaced in my absence. It was gone three in the afternoon by the time I reached Pilkingtons, by which time my temper was spent. John met me and quickly ushered me to the shop floor where we found the first in what was to be a long line of glass boxes. The air extraction worked perfectly and if the calculations proved correct, the larger scaled-up versions would satisfy all my requirements.

Given the rigors of my journey, I decided to stay over as I had before and John agreed to join me. He booked us a room at the same hotel and made the same arrangements with the girls. There was still no answer from the studio when I rang the number, leaving me to presume that Celia had still not returned. I also phoned the garage I'd employed to repair the Jaguar and they told me that the cost would be prohibitive. Unless I was prepared to give them a sizeable deposit they said they could not actually begin the work. I decided that I could do without further aggravation and, regrettable though it was, I eventually did a deal with them, selling them the car for far less than it was really worth.

Perhaps it was due to the circumstances surrounding my visit, but whatever the reason and despite the obvious success of the glass box, I did not feel like female company. In fact I did not feel like any kind of company at all. As a result, I apologised to John, cancelled the hotel room at the last minute, and set out to drive home in the late evening.

It rained throughout the journey and by the time I reached the outskirts of London, I was tired and suffering from eye strain, irritable and not a little depressed. As before the studio was deserted. There was no sign that Celia had been back and still no message to identify her whereabouts.

On an impulse I decided to ring round some of her college friends to ask if they knew where she might be. Most of them were not at home and the only reply I was able to get was from a girl called Sally. She told me that there was a party being held at a friend's squat in Nottinghill and it was most likely that Celia was there. She was explicit: "It's one of those long, drawn-out affairs. They started a couple of days ago and they're set to run for the rest of the week," she told me.

"For any particular reason?" I asked.

Sally giggled, "I suppose – to see how many of them collapse from overdoses by Saturday."

"Do you know who organised it?"

"Probably a guy called Henry. He used to be a student – now I think he's a dealer. He lives there and he's always having parties. He calls them his recruitment drive – he's a good laugh."

I thanked her and rang off. I remembered Henry well. He was the character who picked up new female students and I'd met him first at the reception for new students when I'd arrived fresh from the North. I didn't know he was a dealer but it didn't surprise me. His work had always been a non-event and, although he had assumed a knowledgeable air in the style of the older, more experienced student, he had been regarded as something of a laughing-stock around college. How or why Celia should get mixed up with him and his cronies, I did not know. By then it was late but I was determined to get the bottom of the business so I immediately set out for my old haunt in Nottinghill.

Sally had told me that the squat was in a semi-derelict property down a side street behind Ladbroke Grove. It had long been a place under the watchful eye of local developers and I imagined that it would soon undergo a serious change into apartments for the upwardly mobile groups who seemed to be attracted to that area.

For a change the roads were quiet, I crossed London in record time and it was just before midnight when my taxi stopped before the house. It stood five stories high boasting the remnants of middle-period Victorian splendour. However, its façade had crumbled in one or two places and the plywood boarding that I saw nailed over the big bay windows did not improve the overall impression. From its appearance, clearly it had seen better days. I mounted the steps to the doorway and saw the flicker of a dim light reflected in the fanlight; otherwise there was no sign of life.

In my experience, student parties were characterised more by the noise they made than anything else and I was therefore surprised at the quiet. I glanced along the block and realised that the property was only one of two such places left untouched. The rest of the road had clearly achieved the status of 'very desirable' already and I calculated that perhaps this was the reason for the absence of loud music. Should groups of pot smokers and cocaine sniffers wish to congregate in derelict property to practise their hallucinatory deeds, and if such property were situated in the midst of a residential area, it would clearly be to their advantage not to attract too much attention.

No one answered my knock so I made my way via a side gate round to the back of the house where I found an open door. The whole place seemed to be in darkness and the warren of rooms and corridors were difficult to negotiate. Eventually I made my way up from the kitchen to the front of the house. There was a lighted candle on the stairs standing in a jam jar, presumably the light I saw from the steps outside, and someone had chalked an arrow on the wall next to it. Some indication at least that whoever was there could be located upstairs.

In fact it was on the third floor that I finally found the so-called party. I found one of the large bedrooms packed to capacity with bodies in sleeping bags. They covered the whole floor. A Calor gas heater stood in the middle of the room and the sleeping students were arranged around it. The only light-source was another candle, this one on a mantle-piece, and there was no sign of any kind of activity, legal or otherwise. It was impossible to tell who was present in the room as the sleeping bags hid most people's faces. I was just wondering if I should give them a wake-up call when a hand touched my arm.

I turned to find a small, dark-haired girl standing next to me holding a candle. Her eyes were as large as overcoat buttons and she wore only a T-shirt. The vagueness of her smile and her apparent immunity to the cold confirmed the fact that she was under the influence of possibly more than one chemical compound.

"Are you next?" she asked maintaining the silly smile.

"I don't know – you tell me," I replied.

"I think it's you. Come on, I'll show you where we are."

I followed the dimly lit, bare buttocks along the landing to another door. The pungent stink of marijuana met me at the threshold. The room was filled with it. This time the floor was covered with mattresses and in contrast to the still silence of the sleeping bags, the bodies here heaved and grunted and cried out in a crude reproduction of a scene from Dante's *Inferno*. There were two heaters and six candles, the widows were sheathed in heavy curtains and the room temperature was therefore at an acceptable level. However, in my view, the energy being expended by the half dozen or more couples present would have been sufficient to fire the boilers of a large steam ship. Most were naked and the others wore only flimsy T-shirts or cotton blouses. The dark-haired girl took my hand and indicated a space in the far corner, "Over there," she said.

I saw Celia immediately. Not surprisingly she was centre-stage and in the act of being serviced by two men, one of which was the bearded Henry. Resisting the tug of my new companion, I stood to watch. I had seen Celia in what I'd thought was every possible state of sexual excitement but this time she exceeded all my expectations. She was frenzied and entirely unaware of both her surroundings and her partners. Her state, one that could only have been chemically induced, prompted my first experience of jealousy.

I have always accepted that it is a basic human response to hit back when one is hurt. And, although in recent times my own recourse to violence had been almost non-existent, I was still conscious of a side to my personality that had the capacity for taking physical vengeance. Unaccountably, as I stood watching Celia, this was the response that surfaced most quickly. I wanted to hurt her, I wanted to hurt all of them but, even as the idea formed, I knew that, given my own history with Celia, I had no right to feel that way. Unfortunately, logic is always absent when passions rise. The more I tried to subdue the feeling, the more it took root. In the event the occasion may have passed without incident and once outside in the street, my anger may have been more manageable. If Henry had not turned and caught my eye at that moment and seen fit to grin, I might have left the room without making an obvious response. The fact that I translated his grin as one of conquest proved his undoing.

At that moment Celia was on her hands and knees, the engorged member of another student in her mouth, and Henry was in the act of mounting her from behind when he turned. I stepped smartly forward and, whilst ensuring that my left shoe crushed his ankle to the floor, I delivered a full kick to the right side of his face.

Initially, the part of my brain that perceived the intended agenda of violence had planned many more blows. I wanted to leave him for dead. However, the result of the kick proved spectacular. Henry's face appeared to explode and he dropped with a moan to the mattress, in the process smearing blood from his broken face across Celia's back. I knew his ankle was broken – I'd felt it crack when I put my weight on it – and that was enough.

I realised afterwards that no one else in the room had paid any attention to my actions. Perhaps this was some testimony to the strength of the drugs supplied by my victim. More likely, however, it was the tendency endemic in the student body to avoid physical confrontations at all costs. I did recall that in the few seconds it took to reduce Henry to a case for the accident and emergency ward, my little dark-haired companion had continued to hold my hand.

Outside on the street, I took a deep breath and hurried away to find a taxi.

It was a week later before Celia got in touch with me again. She phoned to ask if she might collect her few things from the studio and to make an unusually polite inquiry about the progress of my exhibition. She made no comment at all about her stay at the squat, about breaking her promise to join me on my trip to Liverpool or about Henry's state of health. I replied to her in a similar vein accepting the formality our new relationship seemed to demand. It was only when I put down the telephone that I experienced a sense of loss and for a moment or two, I found myself regretting my violent reaction. However, in the belief in which I had so often boasted in the past, that regrets are a waste of energy, I soon put Celia in that mental compartment where I store unhappy memories and proceeded to pursue my career.

In the weeks that followed I spent most of my time collecting those things that I wanted to mount in the glass boxes for my exhibition. In this context, I booked the services of a hotel chef and arranged that, when needed, he would produce a traditional Christmas dinner for six, for me. This was also to be one of the exhibits. I wanted a large dining table, set for a family of six in the festive season with the food in place. As I saw it, a metaphor for the whole business of the exhibition: food for the body/food for the mind both preserved literally in and by a work of art.

I went down to Westbourne Park Road one Saturday afternoon to look in the Antique shops in order to choose a suitable dining table. Clearly, the intended exhibit needed to be of a high quality and if I was to avoid the top prices of Regent Street then this offshoot of the Portobello Road market was the best bet.

I found exactly what I was looking for very quickly, a small shop in the middle of the parade with a nice range of classical furniture. It wasn't until I looked at the name above the door that it occurred to me that I might know the owner. Inside a very smooth young woman sat behind a polished desk. She made a five-second appraisal over the rim of her glasses when I entered and apparently decided I was hardly worth the effort. Accordingly she returned to the document she'd been reading previously.

I wandered around looking at various chairs and then, as if only casually interested, I stopped before the dining table and asked, "What's your best price on the table?"

Like a hunting shark the lady surfaced and gave me a dry smile, "We need to achieve two point five K," she said.

The language was almost as offensive as the price being asked. 'Need to achieve' implied that the motivation wasn't profit at all, that it was more to do with satisfying a problem she'd been set – a quest for example. I could imagine King Arthur telling his knights that they 'needed to achieve' the Holy Grail, or Sir Edmond Hilary telling Sherpa Tening that, they 'needed to achieve' the summit. Rubbish – I thought.

"Is the owner on the premises?" I challenged as innocently as possible.

"Mr Zimmerman doesn't deal in the shop."

"But is he on the premises?" I insisted.

"Yes – but…"

"Then could you tell him that a colleague of Mr Durham's would like a word?"

Now she was stumped. My statement might mean that I was a personal friend, equally it might be a ruse made by another dealer.

"I suppose – for trade – we could come down a little."

"Please."

My 'please' was added as the end to my previous sentence and, in ignoring her bid, I was indicating as clearly as possible that I knew the owner. She gave ground and rose to disappear into the rear of the showroom. A few minutes later she reappeared with a short, heavily built man in a city suit. He hurried to me scrutinising me closely as he came.

"A friend of Mr Durham you say. I don't think I've had the pleasure…"

"Grainger – Michael Grainger. We once did some business through Tony Durham."

He continued to shake his head, like he'd never heard of anyone or anything called Durham.

So I continued patiently, "In your little shop in Linthorpe Road. Now you must have heard of Linthorpe Road – in Middlesbrough. You do come from Middlesbrough don't you?"

By this time his assistant had returned to her seat wearing a smug smile. Nevertheless, presumably in order to be well beyond her hearing Zimmerman invited me into his back office. The mention of his background had had the desired effect. He shut the door carefully behind him and turned to me, "I don't know who you are young man but I've left all that behind me. I haven't been in touch with Mr Durham or his son for years and..."

"Okay, okay. I'm not trying to sell you stolen goods or asking you to fence anything. I want to buy something from you."

Now his attitude changed. He waved me to a seat across the other side of his desk and then he sat down himself. He looked relieved.

"What was it you were interested in?" he asked with resignation.

"The table. The dining table in the window. Miss snotty knickers out there said it was up for two thousand five hundred quid. That has to be a joke. What will you take for it – from an old customer from Teesside?"

After a little bartering he agreed I could have it for one thousand pounds, "...and that's a real bargain. I'm not making a penny on that," he claimed.

I laughed and we arranged to have it delivered to the studio in a few days. To his obvious relief, I promised thereafter to leave him in peace and never to refer to his dubious past again – especially in front of his employees. Naturally should the need arise to blackmail the man again, I had no intention of passing up such an opportunity. I had vivid memories of the disappointment my friends and I experienced when we found his offer for our stolen goods to be so miserably low. As a result, I felt no pity for Zimmerman and determined that I would use him in whatever way conditions might dictate.

Chapter Twenty

1978

The exhibition that Manny insisted was to change my life proved a long time in coming. The negotiations for the site were long and tortuous and the problems prompted by the building contractors, even longer. Nothing seemed to go right. The firm of architects employed to design and oversee the project was changed twice and it proved necessary for much of the structural design to be revised. The contract fell behind schedule and, as a consequence of Manny's continued dissatisfaction he was faced with the potential of a number of civil law suits, brought by some of the people he had fired. And, as time dragged on, the financial fund I had saved and with which I had been so impressed was gradually depleted.

During this period, on account of my financial situation, I began to accept occasional offers made by all manner of organisations to deliver lectures. On the strength of the promises made by Manny, I had dropped out of college. This was no great loss to me as I felt I had outgrown any help they might have been able to give. Also, the bursar, still hoping to attract Manny's patronage for the college had implied that once my reputation became a matter of fact he would persuade the powers that be to award me my degree anyway. I therefore earned a crust by talking about modern art to anyone willing to pay me. I was able to add to this modest income by a careful manipulation of the expenses I claimed from Manny in the process of producing the work for the exhibition.

It was fourteen months before the gallery was ready to open, fourteen long hard months. Fortunately by then the work planned was ready to be installed. Pilkingtons had been fabulous. They had satisfied my every requirement without complaint or question and, months before the gallery was ready, I was able to view the work, which was then sited in an annexe of their factory.

One weekend, John Adams invited me to see the outcome of his labours, promising me that I would be delighted with the results. I made the drive and arrived midday to be greeted by several members of the Pilkingtons Board who had also come to see all that their factory had produced. In the event, I believe they were startled to see the extent that an artist was prepared to go in order to achieve his artefact. They had no idea what the work was really about and no amount of explanation could persuade them of its value. Nevertheless the scale of the pieces and the diversity of their content left them to question their initial judgements.

As John had predicted I would be, I was pleased with the results. He promised to organise the specialist transportation necessary to move the sculptures to London and we agreed a schedule for the delivery. All that I was left to do was to decide on titles for the works, a matter that I had been delaying as long as possible – or at least until I'd actually seen the finished pieces. I drove back to London the same day and spent the evening poring over reference books trying to design or discover suitably obtuse but appropriate titles.

In all there were ten major pieces to be named, all contributing to the chosen theme. Some were easier to title than others. The dining table set with a Christmas dinner with all the trimmings I called: *There is no longer a consensus that human action involves mental capacities radically unlike those found in animals.* (A quote from a philosopher I'd been reading.) Due to the vacuum in which it now existed, it was a celebratory feast that would last as long as 'The Last Supper' by Leonardo da Vinci. In similar vein it contrasted the normally limited life of such a meal with a quality of permanence. However, it also made reference to appetites for over-indulgence that we humans share with animals – them through the constant need to ensure survival and us through a memory of the same. Ram's painting was a difficult one to settle a title for and I finally chose the last line from Nicholas Nickleby which states, 'And they spoke low and soft of their dead cousin'. I liked the allusion to something long since passed. Ram was dead and gone and the practice of traditional canvas painting also fitted the bill perfectly.

One of my boxes contained a huge mound of rotted food. I'd persuaded a local restaurant to save their waste for a couple of weeks and then arranged the stinking pile in one of my glass containers. I'd been surprised and pleased when the air was driven out of the box to find that, unknown to me, several rats had established themselves within the mound. They died of asphyxiation in prominent places and in the process added a further dimension to the piece.

I called this one, using a truncated quote from the Rubaiyat of Omar Khayyam, ... *the wine you drink, the lip you press, end in the Nothing all Things end in* – Yes... Again the references were to over-indulgence as well as outmoded art forms

I worked through the night on the problem of the titles and the morning light shone through the end windows before I'd satisfied myself. The task had left me feeling energised and, keen to see the matter resolved, I took the list round to a local sign-maker just as he opened for business.

*

My first major exhibition opened with a private viewing on a Friday night in the middle of July. The preceding weeks had been a busy time for me. The glass boxes arrived as promised but their installation proved to be as difficult an engineering problem as spanning the Mississippi. Due to the size of the exhibits and the delicacy of their contents, moving them from the back of an articulated lorry was a nightmare. Arranging them in the sculpture hall that occupied most of the ground floor of the new Hume Gallery therefore took days of careful manipulation using hydraulic lifts and a team of a dozen men.

Most of the gigantic glass containers were mounted on black plinths that raised them almost to average eye level. Once situated they looked monumental, towering over the viewer and making it necessary for him to look up at them. This section of the gallery had been opened to the roof five floors above ground level, leaving access to a number of smaller gallery spaces via staircases to landings on either side. The sculpture hall could also therefore be viewed from these landings and the impression was one similar to that which might be found in gothic cathedrals. A huge space in simple but enormous proportions that was occupied by ten equally sized glass boxes arranged in pairs along the length of the ground floor and one box, twice as big as the others located at one end.

The additional container, one that, as it had been an afterthought, was the last to be produced, was my special pride and joy. It had been made deliberately at twice the proportions of the others and stood alone at one end of the big hall. In it was my landscape sculpture. It comprised a grassy/muddy mound, on top of which was mounted a farm fence. There were rocks strewn about the lower edges with the remnants of a footpath implied leading to one end of the fence where a gate was situated. To one side there was a huge tree stump on which my initials had been carved. This one boasted a quote from Wittgenstein as its title, reading, *A fact-value distinction is necessary*. The notion of a landscape 'preserved' was traditional enough not to need justification except that this was the real thing and therefore not open to interpretation.

Naturally Manny had designed the publicity himself and for weeks before the opening, posters showing a large photograph of the 'dining table set' had graced the walls of tube stations throughout the capital. My name was prominent in the marketing programme, second only in size to the name of the gallery a fact that, although it annoyed me, I was ready to accept. Suddenly I had a taste of the celebrity status I'd sought for so long. Letters arrived from institutions and people I'd never heard of before. Telephone messages were left inviting me to functions, to deliver lectures and to address all manner of organisations associated with the arts and offers of sponsorship were made sufficient to make any professional sportsman happy. Needless to say, Manny's office collated all the incoming offers and he was increasingly delighted at the success of the campaign.

On the day of the private view, I surveyed the guest list Manny had designed. It contained names of politicians, businessmen, artists, and gallery owners; it included Pop stars and actors, foreign dignitaries and people from every aspect of public life. Names, many of which prompted memories of press and magazine articles both from the hard news sections as well as the society pages. It was a list that would have done credit to any Oscar ceremony and for the first time I began to get 'first night' nerves.

I had submitted a collection of names to be included in the guest list myself. A few of whom were from Teesside, from a previous life. Invitations had gone out to Tony Durham and his wife, to Bruce and some to my first college to Joss Pruitte, to Mr Bernard the principal and to Ruth Menzies and her boring husband. I also invited Ram's parents and Miss Winterness from the Studio Club and last but not least I sent one to my mother. I knew she would not attend but I knew also that receiving the invitation would be enough to keep her content for months to come.

In the time since my break-up with Celia, I'd heard through mutual acquaintances that she'd begun to take her studies that much more seriously. She'd exhibited some work in Munich, apparently at some international show and had received good notices for her efforts. By all accounts she now shared a studio with one of the lecturers and maintained a rigid regime of work, one that she refused to interrupt. This was a side to my ex-girlfriend that I'd never seen. She had always been helpful in promoting new ideas to me and in finding solutions to my problems but as far as her own work was concerned, she always seemed to lack genuine interest.

I missed Celia's company. I missed her sense of humour and her constant flow of ideas. Most of all I missed her companionship in bed. To some large extent she had been the kind of seminal experience all young men need to have, prior to reaching full maturity. Naturally, I'd included her in the guest list even though I suspected that she would not come.

Manny had also taken the responsibility of putting prices on the work. He argued that as he had laid out the investment money he needed to guarantee a good return. A claim he made – he said – for both our sakes. I had no quarrel with this. Once I saw the prices that he'd placed in the catalogue, I began to appreciate that valuing my work was best left to him.

On the night of the opening, Manny sent a stretch limousine to collect me, the driver having been instructed not to arrive at the gallery until forty minutes after the doors opened. My agent instructed me in his reasoning saying, "How and when you arrive is as important in the eye of the public as the work they've come to see."

As ever his view was cultured by the appearance of the project rather than its content and who was I to complain. He'd also taken the precaution of buying me a new wardrobe for the event, fashionable clothes the like of which I never imagined I would wear and, in paternalistic mode, he'd warned me not to drink too much before nor during the course of the evening. Of late I drank little – little that is for a lad from the North – but that evening I needed all the Dutch courage I could muster. Consequently, by the time the car arrived I was just finishing the third tumbler of Scotch and the third line of coke of the evening. Suitably fortified, I set out for the most important night of my career.

My arrival was greeted by crowds of well-wishers, making me feel like a Roman general arriving in Rome after a successful conquest in foreign lands. Hands shook mine in quick succession, my back was slapped and shoulders gripped and the prominence of white dental porcelain aimed in my direction was enough to dazzle if not blind me to the real reason for my attendance. I entered the gallery to an enthusiastic round of applause and the accompanying flash of cameras and by then my own smile was fixed rigidly as if rigor mortis had set in. It was nevertheless a welcome I could never have imagined.

I have since found that on such occasions as this when actuality transcends that which one imagined might be possible, my inclination to doubt increases in almost direct proportion. As I stepped across the threshold that evening therefore, I found myself wondering if it was simply Manny's stage management that I was witnessing rather than a genuine response to the work on show. Naturally, I then began to listen to that secret inner voice, the one that told me I was a fake. Did the work have any significance other than the price it had cost and the price being demanded to purchase it? As king for the night was I about to be shown as being naked? Were the ideas behind the works superficial? And the questions ranged across the full spectrum of my insecurities about my lack of talent.

Fortunately, the doubts were soon swept aside by the atmosphere. Manny took charge of the situation and, in a loud, specially-designed-for-the-press-voice, he congratulated me on the quality of my products as if he'd had no idea what I'd been doing. Shorthand pads were the subjects of many scribblings and recording machines clicked as his words were registered for the readers and listeners of broadsheet speculators. And then the introductions began. I met more household names in the space of one hour than I'd met in the whole of my life to date. Many of the faces were easily recognisable and those I could not identify, I knew by their titles. Manny was at my side constantly prompting, advising and informing me about the proper mode of address for those guests whose role made it necessary politeness to refer to them as 'Your Grace,' or 'Sir', or any of a litany of other nonsense.

It was two hours before I had a minute to myself. Two hours before I had a chance to wander round and see the exhibition in its entirety. Even then, whenever I stopped to look at one of the sculptures I was accosted by small groups of visitors asking about the piece I was scrutinising. The catalogue had made it clear that the glass containers held a vacuum and that was the most usual bone of contention, the subject of most questions. The one exception to the vacuum rule was the box that held the goldfish. This box stood the last in one line, immediately adjacent to my 'landscape'; I thought, a fitting juxtaposition in the concern both exhibited for the natural world. However, the significance of the siting of my goldfish apparently went unnoticed.

In fact I was standing looking at the fish when Joss Pruitt approached me. He congratulated me on what he said was the thoughtfulness of the exhibition and then asked if I still practised drawing. Before I could frame a suitable answer Celia emerged from the crowd and said, "He could never draw, Joss. No good asking for the impossible."

I was pleased to see her despite her crack about my lack of technical skill and we kissed and hugged one another like old friends should.

"So – you two are still together then?" Joss asked grinning.

Another voice, this time from behind me answered saying, "In fact no. They're not still together. Celia finally developed good taste and chose an older and wiser partner."

I turned to find Ken, our old painting lecturer standing there. He grinned and patted me on the shoulder, "A nice show, Mick – well done."

I could never resist a challenge so I replied that my success was entirely due to his influence whilst I was a college. My sarcasm was deliberately obvious, "I think it was those two afternoon each week when you managed to attend that made all the difference. You must remember – it was those days when there was no horse racing on the TV."

The target of my attack prickled noticeably and snapped back immediately, making some weak comparison between Manny gambling on my success with his own betting on horses. I suppose I might have let the matter drop at that point, except that I saw Celia smile. It was all the encouragement I needed. I turned to Joss, "A pity you didn't have his job, Joss. He took a senior lecturer's salary for teaching part-time – and even then all he could talk about were the pasty-faced Impressionists. No wonder he had the time to chase girls young enough to be his daughter."

Ken changed colour but obviously thinking that discretion was the better part of cowardice, he turned and stomped away without another word. Celia still had her arm linked through mine and as her new boyfriend disappeared, she whispered in my ear that I was the same bastard that I'd always been.

"He could never resist a battle of words, could he?" Joss offered.

In the company of Joss and Celia, the evening improved immeasurably. We toured the show and talked about the work, occasionally making fun of some of the ideas, sometimes disagreeing and usually having a good laugh. Drinks from the waiters who ranged constantly through the gallery with trays of wine and spirits for the guests stimulated our comments and observations. Consequently, as the evening wore on the observations we made became louder and coarser and we soon attracted a small coterie of followers. Each time we stopped to observe a piece of sculpture, the followers would also stop. When we laughed they laughed and when one of us became ruder than usual, we heard their intake of breath and real or imagined, there was a sense of supreme power in having responses echoed by all those nearby. As we progressed around the room, we were continuously supplied with drinks and this fact ensured my somewhat hazy recollection of much of what followed. Afterwards I recalled only snatches of conversations, fragments of our arguments and odd, disenfranchised moments of amusement. There was almost a confrontation with Manny over my behaviour and a virulent disagreement with one of his business colleagues about technology versus art. I remember briefly, much later, being on top of the exhibit containing my 'landscape', attempting to sing a Beatles number from the *Sgt Pepper's* album but I have no recollection whatsoever of falling. All I know is I was in an ambulance shortly afterwards.

I suppose it was also due to my ingestion of large amounts of alcohol that I do not remember talking to Tony Durham. However, according to his letter, apparently he was responsible for suggesting that I sing to my guests. I can only suppose that it was also he who proposed the site from which the singing should take place. He was always a malign influence but I was nevertheless sorry to have missed him. My left arm was in plaster for six weeks, an inconvenience to me but, by all accounts, a badge of courage according to the letters I received from students.

Fortunately the concerns expressed continuously by my agent were not reflected in either the critical write-ups in the press or the sales record. The exhibition sold out in the first week.

On account of its immediate success, the exhibition became a focus for visitors to London. The newspapers made reference to its sensational aspect almost on a daily basis and Manny's office could hardly cope with the requests for catalogues. In his usual fashion and in order to enhance the profit margin, Manny came up with an idea that each of the exhibits should be advertised as being from a limited edition. We could then reasonably reproduce the works, number them and sell them all over again. Indeed, it proved to be the only way we could satisfy all the potential purchasers. The money flowed, in a hitherto unimagined dimension. Suddenly my bank manager was on the phone offering me credit and investment advice and I was being courted by a host of galleries from around the world offering me exhibition space. I felt that I'd arrived.

As some testimony to my new 'secure' status, I bought a house. Always having been impressed by Phillipa's little mews cottage, I found one similar and clinched a deal. Intent on placing my own individual stamp on my property, I employed a team of fashionable interior decorators, Angel Interiors, to do their magic. The results were an amazing, hand-finished collection of rooms that any of the crowned heads of Europe would have been pleased to boast of.

I also bought the studio and paid off the debts my mother had accrued. I put a down payment on a Rolls Royce and paid for a city 'runabout' jeep outright. Life was good. All the things that characterised the VIP were now obviously apparent. I had often read about the preference given in famous restaurants to honoured guests, the deference of head waiters, the easy availability of concert tickets and the best hotel rooms, and the never having to queue for anything ever again – now it was all mine for the asking.

On a casual visit to the Studio Club for example, a spontaneous round of applause greeted me and Miss Winterness showed me off to all her foreign visitors throughout the evening. If I showed my face at college, even my contemporaries treated me as a famous artist. I travelled in style, often in the new Rolls Royce; I dressed in expensive clothes from the best and most fashionable shops and the most beautiful women courted me. It seemed that in the course of just a few weeks the whole tenor of my life had changed.

I realised nevertheless, that in most instances my new status owed more to my recently acquired wealth than it did to my creative abilities and that it was money that opened doors. However, I was intrigued to see that many of those who recognised my name actually knew little or nothing about me and still less about the world of Art. I concluded therefore, that past a certain point, fame needs no justification and that the public is ignorant of the reason why many well-known historical figures are known to them. This realisation made me more determined than ever to confirm my reputation in such a way that even the most badly informed person could not ignore.

It was shortly after my first exhibition that I took an assistant to work for me. I badly needed someone close to hand to organise my social life. Julia, as Manny's secretary, had enough on her plate dealing with him; besides which, her administration was one step removed from my control. Also, I wanted a sympathetic intellect with which I could discuss ideas and I wanted them available on a twenty-four-hour basis. Eventually I employed Paul. Ever since Celia had introduced us, he had kept in touch. He was willing to listen, willing to dispute ideas and he had his own slant on things. I'd found him to be a very creative person and someone I felt I could trust. He took the spare bedroom at the mews house and immediately lifted the weight of administration duties from my unwilling shoulders. His presence also provided me with company; something that was sadly missing since Celia had left.

Chapter Twenty-One

1980

Needless to say during the next two years there were still those in the art establishment who sought to decry my work. The traditionalists, jealous of the all the attention I received, wrote articles for magazines and published letters in the press arguing that what I did was spurious. They said that my sculpture was trite, the ideas superficial and that my reputation had been gained simply through a marketing scam. They even accused Manny of designing the publicity only in order that his investment in the work would increase in value. I replied to the letters that were published but my replies were equally scorned as being sadly uninformed and, for a short period, the sales suffered. Manny came to me one day saying that I should make a live broadcast to refute the accusations and answer the criticisms. He told me he had organised an interview on Radio 4 on my behalf and that I would be given every opportunity to say my piece.

I had very mixed feelings about the broadcast. Secretly, I still harboured the fear of being found to be less than I seemed. My old insecurities about the relevance of the work remained just beneath the confident surface of my public face. There had been cases in the past of people being too proactive in defence of their reputations, too keen to accuse the accusers and on occasion it had cost them everything. The last thing I needed was to be found by consensus to be a charlatan. And for all his art collection and his bluster about taste, Manny was ignorant of the depth of the arguments about modern art. His presumption that I was the genuine article was far more to do with his business acumen than his understanding of the issues. If he'd known just how great my own deficit was in this regard, he may not have been quite so keen on having me interviewed.

There was no doubt, however, that British art was in a state of flux and this provided me with some encouragement. In February Graham Sutherland, the artist some chose to believe represented the best in English painting, had popped his clogs. I thought he was crap. He was best known for his portrait of Winston Churchill – the same portrait that his wife had later destroyed; its continued popularity, despite its non-existence, provided an ambiguity that was far more interesting than the work itself. In my book – that was art.

The morning of the day before the radio broadcast, I was awakened early by an insistent ringing and knocking at my front door. When I dragged myself down to answer it, I found Speedy standing there. Speedy was a young man, possibly still a teenager, who made his living by delivering a door-to-door service for the local drug dealer. Polly Masters, his employer, had developed an exclusive list of clients over the previous five years, all of whom were partial to the added stimulus of that exotic white powder known as coke. Now, whilst it would be wrong to describe her customers as addicts, there were one or two who showed a greater dependency than the rest of us and who needed the reassurance of a constant supply – hence Speedy. However, certainly in my own case, I never allowed him to actually deliver to my door, the risks were too great. Instead, when I wished to enhance my sexual performance, I arranged to meet with him at some obscure location and did our dealing in private. To find him on my doorstep was therefore a shock and my first reaction was to close the door in his face. Instead, I glanced along the mews then grabbed him by his collar and dragged him into the hallway.

"What the hell are you up to, Speedy?" I snapped, still holding his shirt. "I've told you a thousand times not to come here."

He wrestled his collar from my grip and said, "Sorry, Mick. It's an emergency. Polly sent me."

"An emergency?"

"Yeah – she wanted you to have first option on some very cheap stuff. She's got more than she can handle and she's selling it off at less than half price."

This was interesting for a number of reasons. I'd never heard of a dealer having too much 'stuff'. The more usual complaint was that they couldn't get enough. And the prospect of buying at less than half price was equally unheard of. Also, even accepting the story as being kosher, why would I be given the option of a bargain purchase? I was a small buyer by comparison to some of the pop stars she supplied.

I tried to cross-examine Speedy but he wouldn't say anything more.

"Look, Mick – all I can tell you is what I've already said. Now – are you interested and how much would you like?"

"How much has she got?"

"How much do you want?"

It was an intriguing idea to buy a large quantity of cocaine. I was certain that I could sell it on to various associates for a good profit but I knew that drug-dealing had a risk factor much greater than anything I'd tried in the past. On the other hand it was easy money…

"I'll have half of what she has for sale."

The boy looked hard at me, "That'll be more than a kilo and that's a lot of money…"

"I'm good for it. She knows I am. Anyway, I'll bring cash."

He nodded still obviously surprised at the size of the order.

"Just one more thing, Speedy," I added as an afterthought, "if we're to do business, I want to know the inside story. If you can't answer my questions when we meet next time then the deal's off. Okay?"

We agreed a place to meet and he left.

I began immediately ringing round to let my friends know I could supply them.

*

The interview was to be a live broadcast at eight in the morning, part of a popular magazine-cum-news show. The more usual format was to have a member of the Government, a minister or other prominent politician, cross-examined by an informed specialist. And, whether the subject concerned health, economics or the farming industry, the question and answer session often tended to highlight deficiencies in the politician's understanding. It was only very occasionally that this model was changed in favour of news items that had caught the public's imagination. My work, proving to be as controversial as it had, was considered to provide just such an opportunity for change.

On the morning in question, I arrived in good time and was duly supplied with BBC coffee and a stale croissant. As such a modest offering could hardly be described in terms of bribery, I presumed therefore that it was normal practice. During my breakfast, I was introduced to the presenter, a pleasant, erudite man with a reputation for tenacity and a low tolerance for bullshit. He was polite and businesslike. Allowing little time for chit-chat however, he described the form the session would take and told me that whilst he could chair the period, the questions would be asked by Clive Farquenhart-Smythe.

My interrogator would not be present and his comments and questions would be relayed from a studio in the West Country. I was well aware of Mr Smythe's antipathy towards the Conceptual movement and had, on occasion, heard him express his views on television. He was a professor of the history of art at a lesser-known university and had first attracted media attention by way of a book he'd written about Picasso's love-life. He was an eighteen-carat sensation-seeker with his own agenda, the focus of which was his own image. The kind of academic who did not allow the establishment of fact to interfere with his prime purpose in life, namely the further development of his own career. He was nevertheless well read and knowledgeable, and I knew then that I was in for a hard time.

The broadcast began with my making a statement about my philosophy. In this, I laid claim to my work being simply punctuation in a sentence about art philosophy today. This was followed immediately by a sarcastic tirade from Smythe. He described what he said was the paucity of the intellectual content of the work and then he went on to question the motives of employing a marketing man as my agent. Naturally he was well prepared for the occasion and was able therefore, to call on quote after quote from all manners of different sources to support his hypothesis. I was furious and had to struggle to maintain a reasonable level of polite behaviour. At some point I dredged up the only reference of any significance I could remember. A quote from one of Paul Cezanne's letters, in which he said, "The artist must scorn all judgement that is not based on an intelligent observation of character… He must beware of the literary spirit which so often causes the painter to deviate from his true path – the concrete study of nature – to lose himself too long in intangible speculation."

"Odd that Mr Grainger should choose to quote from a real artist," Smythe quipped back, "odder still that the quote chosen actually supports my argument and not his own. The basis of the problem with his work – and those others who pursue similar devious ends – is simply that in terms of content, it can never be profound. It can never transcend a level higher than the banal."

"I think you're missing the point," I snapped back, "the nature I choose to study is the nature of man's thinking – I don't try to be profound and the notion that it should transcend the obvious is outdated. It is what it is."

"Manipulation of semantics is insufficient. Can't you say precisely what you mean?"

We went on for some time in this vein drifting further and further from the point of the interview until the presenter interjected, reminding us to talk about the work currently on exhibition.

Smythe switched tack with the speed of a snake, "Thank you, John, I suspected Mr Grainger might try to move us away from the real issue. I wonder if he can explain what kind of significance he associates with – say for example – cutting a Rolls Royce car into two pieces, or in a glass container filled with garden refuse?"

I bit back my annoyance and tried to keep my voice on an even keel, "Even Mr Smythe must have heard of the Dada movement or the Surrealists. The point being that my pieces makes reference to those kinds of beliefs. Nothing drastically new except in extent. Duchamp was doing things like this years ago."

"So much for Mr Grainger's claims of originality. Yes I know about Duchamp, I also know that his shock tactics were the considered development of ideas from an artist who was already an established authority in terms of art philosophy. He had a record of significant achievement and was therefore, able to offer new ideas without fear of anyone questioning his integrity. This is not the case in the instance of Mr Grainger."

"Is there a suggestion then that only those artists with established reputations are able to shock the public. What about the young Picasso?"

"Picasso moved comfortably in a traditional mode long before he applied his innovations. He could draw – some say – as well as Raphael and his work demonstrated a profound understanding of the history of art in all his creations."

I was quick to respond, "But why should any artists today want to draw as well as Raphael and what is so important about observing the conventions found in the history of art. The world has turned. Mr Smythe needs to get with it. The culture evolves."

My adversary paused and then answered quietly, his transparent stage management technique hoping to imply deep thought, "Sadly that only illustrates Mr Grainger's poor grasp of the subject. If his product has no meaning other than a very limited ability to shock, then history will judge it to be something other than art, something of less value and less importance. A foible of the commercial bias found in the art business rather than a true creation."

And so it went on. The whole slot was filled with a bickering argument in which we both tried to score points at the other's expense. To make matters worse, Smythe was allowed the last word. I'd just protested that culture was always in a state of flux; that artists in the present were a new breed with new thinking and new ideas, and that was what I represented. This was a favourite argument and one I'd employed in the past to credit myself with a carte blanche. Unfortunately Smythe decimated it.

"The word 'evolve' suggests development, that is it takes account of what has gone before and the equally the word 'change' necessitates a previous state. We therefore have change – from something, to something else. And for Mr Grainger's further understanding, notions concerning 'culture' generally imply a value system based on or derived from previous practices. The development of culture therefore suggests that society draw on the best from the past in order to make progress. It may take time but periodically, society also rejects that which is evidently spurious and superficial – and I put it to you that work we are discussing today falls into that category. If, as Mr Grainger claims, his works were punctuations in the life of the art sentence, I would see them only as parentheses bracketing a simplistic addendum. The kind of addition that could easily be omitted in the cause of a more sophisticated understanding of the grammar employed."

The presenter quickly terminated the discussion at this point and I left the studio.

I was offered more coffee but chose to leave without it, my stomach felt delicate and I needed some time to myself. I took a cab to a coffee shop I knew in Nottinghill Gate and sat for a while commiserating with myself about the interview over a good-quality Jamaican blend – very black and very sweet. Although I couldn't quite identify the precise occasion when it happened, I knew I'd come off second best. The Smythe creature had upstaged me, in effect winning the argument. It rankled but there was nothing I could do about it now. I tried to mitigate the injury to my pride presenting myself with various arguments. I told myself about the low number of listeners tuned in at that time day; about those in the audience likely to have switched off as soon as they heard the word art and about the low level of understanding amongst a group more used to hearing political discussions. Unfortunately, none of this helped me and I was left only with my feeling of failure.

As a consequence of the early morning battle of words, I added Smythe's name to my secret hit list, determined that, if the occasion should present itself at some time in the future, I would do him as much harm as possible.

Chapter Twenty-Two

The interview on early morning radio provided my critics with ammunition sufficient to start the rumour that I was a sham. Later, even Manny was critical, accusing me of unnecessary aggression and of being ill-prepared for the discussion. He was, however, the first to contact me. Fortunately, his news was not all bad. He baited me and waited until I was almost at the height of my fury before he told me that he had begun negotiations with Tate for a one-man show.

"The Tate!"

"Yes, Mick – the Tate Gallery would like to show you."

"But – the radio interview…"

"Fuck the BBC," he said laughing. "What the hell do they know about art? This will give you an opportunity to prove you're not just a piss artist – so make it good."

I could hardly believe my ears. A retrospective at the Tate was the pinnacle – it guaranteed a level of acceptance that other galleries around the world could not. Now the prices could really soar – the money would roll in. There was nothing I could not achieve. However, whatever it was that I intended to show would have to be special. This was the peak I'd always hoped for, an acceptance by the establishment in a public forum none but the philistine could deny. Manny had ended his call by telling me that a formal letter of invitation would follow in the next few weeks and that, until I received it, I should keep the matter confidential. I began to telephone my friends immediately.

Phillipa was still in bed – lazy cow – but even despite her hangover, she was suitably impressed. Before she hung-up, she suggested meeting me at the Ritz for lunch, promising it would be her treat – a little celebration, she said. I tried to contact Celia after that but without success. She and I had shared a few laughs at the exhibition and had almost fallen back into the kind of relationship we'd enjoyed previously. Sadly, as our past was so dependent on a physical association – and that was missing – things could never be quite the same. Celia was always hard to find these days. Since she had begun to show her work, she had become obsessive. Her creative endeavours had acquired the status of a vocation and she seemed to spend every waking moment in her studio. A boring phase, I thought, but one entirely understandable in one so new to the international art scene. I left a message and made it as temptingly cryptic as I could. She may well have devoted herself to her work but her insatiable curiosity was still one of her dominant characteristics.

Finding myself in Oxford Street and having a couple of hours to kill before meeting Phillipa, I decided to pay a visit to Soho and to have another look at the site I hoped would become my trendy new restaurant. With my new wealth intact, I'd made an offer on the two premises and it had been accepted. It was still occupied by a delicatessen and a small newsagent. However, albeit to the irritation of the leaseholders, both these businesses were due to close as their leases were not being renewed.

The delicatessen was still run by Alfonso and his wife Carla, and by Carla's elderly parents Maria and Tony. They were a nice crowd, typical of their culture but hopelessly out of date in commercial terms. Initially they had proved to be completely ignorant of their rights and would have remained so, had it not been for Johnny the newsagent next door. He was a 'barrack-room lawyer' sort who appeared to be prepared to go to any lengths to secure a new lease and if that failed, to cause as much delay as he could to my take-over. Johnny's prevarication was eventually sweetened by my offer of a substantial sum of money paid into a Jersey bank. The last time I'd talked to him, he was concerned that the Inland Revenue did not get to know about his windfall, "It's gotta be kept quiet," he'd insisted, "else the deal's off."

A curious demand on two counts. In the first instance, he had no control whatsoever over the 'deal' so he could not assume his disagreement would, in any way, affect my acquisition of the property. The offer to him had been made simply to ease the transition and to enable the legal side to be enacted without delays. Secondly, whilst he was ready to try and impose restrictions on who got to know about the payment made to him, he was nevertheless prepared to alert his neighbours to the fact of my indulgence. Carla and Al had already been in touch, demanding similar treatment and this had caused further complications.

Maria was serving from behind the counter when I entered the shop. She was in the process of parcelling a large chunk of Parmesan cheese when she saw me. Her look was poisoned and without pausing in her task she called back into the small room behind the shop for her son-in-law. She spoke in Italian. Alfonso appeared almost immediately. His smile was limited to his mouth, "Ah, Mick – nice of you to pay us a visit. To what do we owe the pleasure of your company today?"

"Just passing, Al – thought I'd pop in and see how things were…"

My justification sounded weak even to me. Carla appeared at the inner door and snapped something in her own language at her husband. She ignored me and as soon as she'd had her say, she vanished again behind the beaded curtain. The customer took her Parmesan and left the shop leaving me outnumbered.

"Did you instruct your solicitors yet?" Alfonso asked.

His question betrayed the instruction given him by his wife.

"I asked him to negotiate with you," I replied.

His face flushed, "There's no room left for negotiation, Mr Grainger. All we want is a fair deal – like you agreed with Johnny – that's only right – yes?"

"How long is left on the lease?"

"Fourteen months or so. Why do you ask?"

"Perhaps we could do a better deal if you were prepared to leave early – do you think?"

The old man must have been listening beyond the curtain, as I'd no sooner made my offer, than he stormed into the shop shouting in Italian. He came round the counter and stood before me firing a continuous tirade in my face. Al tried to calm him but without success, so we waited until he finished.

"I'm afraid dat Tony sees this request as an insult to the family… Okay Dad, leave it to me."

Clearly there was a lot of enmity felt and I decided that little progress could be made by further discussion. Finally out of steam, the old man turned and stomped into the back room.

"Can we talk cash?" Al asked. "How much is the offer, if we go – say – in a month's time?"

Effectively that implied my buying thirteen months of the lease and, given the extortionate rates of the ground rent, I knew we'd be talking large numbers. Fortunately, I was able to accommodate large numbers.

"Name your price." I said.

He did and he made it obvious he was talking retirement money. The figure was ridiculous. I kept a straight face and promised to tell my lawyers what he'd said.

"Thank you, Al. You'll hear from them within the week," I promised.

I stood outside on the pavement and looked back at the shop front. It was painted in garish colours and the window space was filled to capacity with sausages, hams, cheeses, jars of olives, purees, mustards, packets of dried fruits and a host of other continental foods. Typical, I thought. Next door the small window of Jimmy's newsagent shop was used as a magazine rack and like the window of the delicatessen, every inch was occupied. It was a foretaste of what was to be found inside. The thin, cork-covered counter-top was crowded with newspapers piled high. Periodicals, magazines of every conceivable size and kind, filled the walls. Well-known titles crowded alongside those that were less salubrious. Pictures of women were everywhere, some exhibiting naked parts and in various poses that were obviously meant to entice the customer. The aromas experienced next door were now lost. No longer could I detect the rich smell of coffee or salami, the pungency of cheeses or the vinegar of pickles; here the environment was musty, a dry foetid smell that suitably complimented the bored, facile expressions worn by the girls on the covers of the saucy magazines. It was a seedy place, the kind that should have had a health warning on the door. The atmosphere was made all the more wretched by the wording of the suggestive small advertisements exhibited on the face of the glass of the door.

Needless to say, Johnny was at home in the shop. His appearance and character were entirely appropriate for his surroundings. He was the kind of man, I decided, who gave heavy-breathing a bad name. I had spoken to him several times over the last six months or so and I'd swear that he wore the same collarless shirt on every occasion. Due to him being a chain-smoker, the shop was hung with stale nicotine clouds providing him, in his seat behind the counter, with a grey halo.

"Good day, Mister Grainger," he wheezed at me, "and what brings you to Soho today?"

"Just passing – I thought I should call by and say hello," I replied.

"Did you talk to Al?"

Now given his broken promise, I thought this remark was more than a little provocative, so I took him up on it, "You shouldn't have told him about our deal, Jimmy. It was a special agreement between you and me…"

"Be fair, Mr Grainger. Me and Al are in the same boat – about to lose our livelihoods – we have to stick together."

"Unfortunately, now that he has been told, I've got to renege on the deal. No cash for you or for him."

That brought him to his feet.

"You can't do that. I've made arrangements… I need the money. It was a deal…"

"The deal was just between you and me, Jimmy. You broke your word – so it's off – sorry but that's the way it is."

Suddenly he was sweating. Little droplets appeared, shining down into his stubble and his breathlessness became more pronounced.

"Look, Mr Grainger, I've got commitments I must meet – outstanding commitments, [in plain English he meant debts] and all I did was mention to Al that we had an understanding. I didn't tell him the figure we'd agreed."

I shook my head and shrugged my shoulders, as if the matter was now out of my hands. I had never liked this sweaty little unkempt man or his smelly little shop. And I didn't give a toss about his debts or what might happen to him if he couldn't settle them. As far as I was concerned, he had broken our agreement and that was that.

My silence in the face of his pleas turned his mood. Now he adopted an aggressive stance.

"If there's no sweetener in it then I'll have to fight you," he said glaring at me through his National Health specs, "and I could drag it on for months."

"Fine. I can afford to wait – I'll see you in court – after your lease has expired."

I turned as if to leave and he raised his voice at my back, "There are people… friends of mine that'll stand up for me. You fucking developers are all the same – but you should be careful – no one is fire-proof."

I replied from the doorway, "Friends you no doubt owe money to – they can suck a lemon too."

I took a taxi from the corner and sat thinking in the quiet of the back seat as I was driven to the Ritz. It had been a reasonably productive visit. Now they had shown their hand – a greasy, greedy palm in either case – they would get nothing. I'd give them nil – zero, not one red cent. They could huff and puff as much as they liked but the fact remained that as soon as their leases expired they had to vacate the premises. I made a mental note to remember the strategy should I need to employ a similar negotiation in the future.

*

Phillipa was late – as usual. However, when she finally arrived she looked delicious. Despite the cold she wore a see-through top beneath a smart three-quarter-length jacket and her skirt was split high enough to tease a view of inner thigh when she strode through the long room. It was a vision that tempted the stares of every male at every table. The image of uncaring nonchalance was, nevertheless, a performance staged for the viewing public and in fact when we settled down to talk, it was obvious something was bothering her.

"It's money of course," she said replying to my query, "there have been some silly debts – gambling debts and now they've been called in. Don't know what the hell we're going to do."

I could see the next phase without trying and sure enough she went on to ask if I had any spare cash available.

"It would only be for a short while and," she added hurriedly, "we could probably pay reasonable interest – eventually. What do you say, Mick?"

"What sort of money are we talking about, Phillipa?"

She paused and I could imagine the cash register in the back of her head rolling the figures round.

"Well – seven-fifty would do it…"

"Is that…"

"Seven hundred and fifty K, darling. Hardly the price of one of your sculpture thingies."

She knew I'd amassed a sizeable nest egg but most of it I'd invested in safe stock overseas. As the money rolled in, I'd learned to channel it into a number of off-shore banks, making sure that my tax returns reflected only a tiny part of my true earnings. It nevertheless amused me to have Phillipa, undoubtedly one of the landed gentry – if not minor aristocracy – asking me to lend her three quarters of a million pounds. I noticed also that whilst she was pleading poverty she ordered the best champagne from the wine list and the most extravagant items from the menu, and she topped this between courses by openly sniffing coke from a silver 'snort' box. I liked Phillipa. She was a wonderful fuck and a good sport by anyone's standards but – point seven five of a mill – no way. My money had been hard to come by; unlike her I'd not married into a fortune, neither had it been inherited from a rich daddy. However, in order to let her down lightly, I said I would have to consult my accountants.

"The numbers are too large for me to be able to agree it over lunch." I told her and this seemed to satisfy her for the time being.

As ever the food was excellent and by the time we'd finished a magnum of the best fizzy, we were both a bit merry and, especially in her case, a good deal more relaxed. Despite her promises, I settled the bill, of course, and at her suggestion we went back to her town flat for an afternoon shag. In her view, a reasonable return for a meal costing more than my parents earned in two months.

During the course of our fleshy pursuit, at least during one of the rest periods, I mentioned the possibility of my obtaining some good quality 'best white' at less than usual cost. We discussed price and once an agreement had been reached she said she'd take half an ounce – every week. I was in profit already.

It was late afternoon by the time I reached the car park. I found Speedy skulking at the boot of a Land Rover, pretending to be sorting out some tools. The 4x4 was jacked-up as though he was about to change a wheel. I was an hour and a half late.

"Christ, Mick, I was just about to go," he muttered as I approached him, "I can't stand about with all this stuff all day. Have you got the money?"

We exchanged the money for the goods and he promptly released the car-jack and jumped into the driving seat.

"Polly says to tell you to take care who you push this stuff onto. She says she's retiring due to the kind of competition she has been faced with – very violent competition – her words. So to take care."

He revved the engine.

"And you, Speedy – how about you. Are you retiring too?" I asked.

"Like hell. Wish I could. No – I got fixed up with the competition."

Before I could comment he was gone in a cloud of petrol fumes.

Back at my house, I tried to invent a foolproof place to hide my newly acquired goods. I'd often been advised that it was best to move any quantity larger than a few grams as quickly as possible. In the past this had never been a problem – I'd never had more than a few grams in my possession at one time. The usual places, like under the loose bedroom floorboard or in the toilet cistern were too obvious; the fridge would also be a first place to look, as would the bookshelf. In the end I settled on a standard lamp with a hollow, domed base. The package fitted the space like it had been tailor-made.

The notion of being a dealer was still new to me but it added a much-needed frisson to my daily life. I enjoyed excitement and thrived on any venture that tested the rule of law, particularly if there was an opportunity to make money. And, whilst those juvenile efforts made in a car-park in

Stockton all those years ago had met with predictable failure, there was every likelihood that selling drugs would succeed without detection. I was no longer a nobody, a kid without contacts; now I was established and a force to be reckoned with.

I felt pleased with myself and when Paul arrived home, we sampled the goods before going to bed.

Chapter Twenty-Three

Ever since Manny had informed me about the exhibition at the Tate, I'd been thinking about what I should show there. It was the opportunity of a lifetime and I wanted to really 'sock-it' to them. Whatever it was, it would have to be sensational – completely off-the-wall; something to shock the establishment; to render the fat of traditional art down to a sticky, glutinous mass of aesthetic jelly.

That evening I talked to Paul about it and tried to point him in the direction of 'extreme shock unlimited'. Normally he provided a fund of ideas but that night his ideas were pedestrian. Eventually, he went out for a drink with friends leaving me to try and invent something by myself.

I started by listing the social taboos – always a good starting point for things 'shocking'. But having written down incest, cannibalism, rape and murder, I came to a halt. In terms of violence at least, it would be difficult, if not impossible, to compete with real life. I'd just watched a newscast in which the SAS had stormed the Iranian Embassy in London. Better than any James Bond plastic adventure, these were real bullets, real bombs and real heroes. It was real life imitating art!

I decided instead that it was the intellectual taboos I needed to explore – those that implied a rejection of traditional values, much in the same vein as the things I'd become known best for. I recalled Ram's painting stored like an antique in a glass case – and the piece, *the dining set*, the crockery lined with shit – that was the sort of thing. Body excrement was usually a winner. I remembered that Manny had made some crack about me being a 'piss artist' and the nucleus of an idea began to germinate.

Just after midnight Phillipa rang, asking if I'd had an opportunity to talk to my accountants regarding her loan. I adopted a regretful voice and said unfortunately that the bulk of my funds were tied up in long-term investments. I told her I could raise about two hundred and fifty thousand in cash in the short term but that was my limit. She was upset. She said that she had been relying on my help and did not know where else to turn.

"Can't you sell something?" I asked, "You've several houses full of expensive goodies – furniture, paintings and the like. You must be able to capitalise on something."

Then she admitted that the debts were her gambling debts – nothing to do with her husband, "And if he finds out how much I owe – well, things could get sticky. So you see I can't go about selling off stuff. He'd know immediately."

How the hell she'd managed to lose quite so much was anybody's guess and I almost began to feel sorry for her.

"How long have you got – before the money is due?" I asked.

There was a long pause then she said, "He wants it within four weeks."

"Will he take something on account?"

"Probably my arse."

I laughed, "Well that wouldn't be a bad deal."

"It's not funny, Mick. This guy is heavy-duty."

"So who is he, anyway?"

She paused again, obviously reluctant to tell me too much, but eventually she said, "I owe the money to James Barratt – have you heard of him?"

Jimmy Barratt was a name I had only recently been told about. He had been highlighted in connection with my property deal; the message being that he was one of the new breed of London gangsters who believed in a return to the bad old days with violence as a remedy for failed contractual obligation.

"You'd be well advised to settle with the man," I said, "I'm told he's very bad news."

"There's no need to tell me that – but I don't know what to do."

"Let me think on it and I'll get back to you. I can often come up with creative solutions and…"

"This isn't a fucking work of art," she snapped back, "he could put me in an emergency ward. If that's all you can offer – thank you for your trouble."

She smacked the phone down.

And this was the same lady who had promised to buy a thousand pound's worth of cocaine from me earlier in the day.

Early the following morning I spoke to my solicitor and asked him to speed up the acquisition of the two properties in Soho. I didn't mention the visit I'd made there, but instead left him with the impression that my programme had speeded up.

"And are you prepared to sweeten the deal?" he asked, "If you offer the current occupants a few quid, they'll go much more happily."

"I don't care how happy they are and I have no interest in making them happier still. Just get them out ASAP, Okay?"

My instruction was as clear as I could make it and so I left him to do the business. I didn't give a flying fuck about the 'current occupants'. They'd had their chance and blown it.

Paul was still in bed when I left the house. He'd arrived home in the early hours, probably the worse for wear and was enjoying a sleep-in. I left him a note telling him that he could ring me if he needed to talk. He had been somewhat distant and uncommunicative of late, less useful than he'd once been, and I was beginning to wonder if I needed to keep him on the payroll. I determined that once we had agreed the list of works for the big exhibition, I might send him on his way.

I took the Jeep and drove down to Hackney to the workshop to see what progress had been made on the multiples being made there. The idea of making a limited edition of art objects was not a new one but it was nevertheless one with obvious financial attractions. Manny had first suggested it to me and it had not taken me long to devise a suitably economic rendition of my own.

I had reckoned that, given the current interest in painting, it would be profitable to produce an artwork that the buyer could have a hand in making himself. Consequently, I had a team of students stretching and preparing canvases in one of three flat colours. These I would sign but whoever bought them would agree a contract in which they promised to use only two extra colours, and these would be determined by me. The grey background could therefore only include images in pink and/or white; the blue, an image in grey and/or purple; and the black, an image in white and/or grey. The plan was to market these in a signed edition of two thousand with an asking price of eight hundred pounds sterling each. If I sold out, the 'take' would therefore amount to £1.6 million. We had advertised the series in several Sunday glossy magazines and already had a customer waiting list amounting to nine hundred buyers. The series was entitled, 'AYCD' (Anything You Can Do). A kind of 'painting by numbers' exercise.

I had four assistants working on the canvases, students who needed to make some extra cash. Needless to say, three were attractive young women with a young man in charge of them. Manny liked to joke that the workshop was in fact my harem and whilst my predominant interest was in the girls' productiveness, I had to admit to having sampled the physical delights of each of them during the period of their employment. I'd made it clear when I employed them that sexual compliance was expected, and none had so-far complained at the arrangement.

From my earliest days as a student there had been a whole succession of females, willing to share their favours. However, since the further development of my reputation, the process had become even easier. If I attended a conference, or delivered a lecture, inevitably there would be a number of art groupies present who were only too eager to jump into my bed. Admittedly there had been times when I had made use of professional working girls. The call-girl service available in London was, as ever, prolific. Unfortunately, even with top-of-the-range models, there was always a feeling that the transaction was one rooted in business rather than pleasure, and I much preferred the willing amateur to the practised professional.

Sam showed me the finished works when I arrived at the workshop and it was clear the production was on schedule. Dorothy (Dot), Mary and Susie were all hard at work and I spent a couple of hours adding my signature to the blank canvases. Privately it amused me greatly to think that each time I signed my name, I was earning eight hundred quid. It was like printing money.

At the rate of about four canvases each per day, I knew it would take the four of them a hundred and twenty-five days or so to complete the work. The first seventeen days therefore, had seen two hundred and seventy-two canvases completed. It was an efficient operation and even allowing for the on-cost of Manny's percentage and the wages bill, I was still likely to make a handsome profit. Not surprisingly, I liked the idea of an art production line and had been thinking of another project that might produce a similar result.

In fact it had been Paul who had come up with the idea. He argued that I should produce a three-dimensional multiple – a sculpture, as a compliment to the painting series. Initially there was no simple answer, however. I did not want to involve myself in expensive equipment that might be needed to manufacture a solid object and neither did I want to pay for more expert assistance to produce such a thing.

"But there's no need," Paul had said, "you could choose a ready-made object – something cheap to buy – and simply add on something of your own."

He was right of course. But what that 'ready-made' might be was another concern. I had finally settled on tomato ketchup... Plastic bottles of tomato ketchup were easily available and relatively cheap to buy. They were recognisable and in common use, so why shouldn't they be art. Didn't a certain American artist make Campbell's soup into a ready-made image! Accordingly I coined the phrase: 'Real-time, hand-made Art dwells in the Public domain.' An expression that was both descriptive and one that conferred the desired status. The bottles would be only half full (illustrating an 'Art in progress' theme), the label would be removed and each would carry a green rosette bearing my signature and its number in an edition of one thousand.

Before I left the workshop, I talked to Sam about the idea and he pointed out that there was still plenty of room available in the studio in which a production line might be set up. He also suggested that, if I were prepared to wait until the canvases were finished, the same team could organise the new project.

"The girls would be glad of the work," he said, "and at least now you know them – you know who you're dealing with."

It was a proposal well worth considering and I promised I'd let him know as soon as I decided.

My phone rang. It was Paul.

"You've had a call from someone calling himself Jimmy Barratt," he told me, "left his number and asks will you ring him as soon as possible – something about your property deal."

I rang the number and a woman answered. She had me wait a moment and then Jimmy came on the line, "Ah, Mister Grainger," he said in a South London accent, "I've been meaning to talk to you for some time. D' you think you might call round to my place and have a chat?"

I started to say how busy I was but he interrupted, telling me it would be in both our interests to meet face to face and that a meeting may enable the property deal to be settled all that more quickly. Naturally I agreed.

*

Jimmy Barratt's house was situated in Iver, a smallish community just outside Uxbridge, and quite close to the movie studios at Pinewood. Given his business interests in London I found this location not a bit surprising. The same was true of the man himself. A maid answered the door and I was asked to wait in a book-lined study, a room, I thought, more appropriate to a university office rather than the headquarters of a gangland boss. I was studying the titles on the nearby shelves when Jimmy made his entrance.

"Can't say I've read many of them," he quipped, when he saw me looking, "they're more for atmosphere than education."

He was a short man with a surprisingly large head, the eyes were deep-set beneath jet-black brows and he sported a sun-bed tan that resembled teak. He approached with a hand held out and I took it, returning his smile as I did so. He had the grip of an exhibitionist and the shoulders to match.

After asking my preference he poured two large brandies into bubble glasses and invited me to sit in one of the leather armchairs that acted as sentinels to the huge fireplace. The atmosphere was one of casual friendliness, not at all what I had expected and the man himself was quite different from what I had imagined he might be. Raised on the fantasies invented by Hollywood, I had expected a sleazy setting populated by swarthy, cigarette-smoking continentals with bulging jackets. Jimmy was none of these. He sipped his drink and invited me to stay for dinner.

"It's about time we met," he said, "recently our paths seem to have crossed several times." He paused and sipped his drink, "They tell me you're an artist?"

"I suppose. But not in the tradition of any of those you might recognise."

He laughed, "You may be surprised. Tell me – do you show a profit?"

Now it was my turn to laugh, "If I didn't, I shouldn't be able to pay so much for those Soho properties."

"Even though you seem to want to 'stiff' the tenants?"

I felt the colour rise in my cheeks. So that was what this was all about. The little sod in the newsagents had obviously gone running to Jimmy to report on me.

"The contract I agreed was broken. I don't feel any responsibility to offer more cash. If people want to gossip to their friends that's their business and they have to bear the consequences. Fuck em' I say."

He studied me for a moment and then smiled, "My sentiment exactly. However, it may interest you to know that a certain scruffy little man, also called Jimmy, who sells cigarettes to school children from his newsagents shop was relying on your handout to pay off a debt to me."

"That's surely between you and him."

"True – but I wondered if we might manage a quid pro quo concerning your friend, the lovely Lady Phillipa."

"In what way?" I asked.

225

He reached into his inside pocket and produced a small notebook which he opened, "Let's say I extend her credit – not her credit limit I hasten to add – she's a poor gambler, destined to lose continuously. But if we say she has a further six months' leeway to settle her debt – would that help?"

"In return for me paying the sweetener to our friend the newsagent?"

"Exactly."

It didn't take much thinking about. If Phillipa was given another six years to settle she'd still be in debt. And anyway, why should I be inconvenienced to help her. Stupid cow.

"And what about the family in the delicatessen?" I asked.

"They don't owe me anything. Do what you like about them. Is it a deal?"

I shook my head, "No. Phillipa will only get herself into more trouble. She spends too much and pushes too much 'happy-powder' up her nose. She's a great fuck but unreliable. Sorry no deal."

I was surprised and relieved to find that my decision pleased Jimmy. He smiled a big grin and congratulated me at what he called my shrewd estimation of the risk factor. He said that had I not been so committed to the world of culture he could have found a niche for me in his organisation.

"Too many people would have been swayed by friendship," he said, "or too influenced by my reputation as a bad man. I'm delighted to find a kindred spirit. Let's have something to eat."

I followed him to the dining room where we found a table already laid and a butler standing by to serve us.

I didn't leave Jimmy's house until the early hours of the morning. He was a great host, attentive and generous to a fault. I even began to doubt the stories I'd heard concerning his ruthlessness. In any event, by the time I took my leave of him we'd agreed a suitable sum in compensation for the Italian family. We'd also agreed that the sleazy newsagent should get nothing. As a consequence Jimmy promised that all the property would be vacant within two weeks.

When I got home that night there were a couple of messages on the answer-phone. Phillipa had rung again, sounding more distraught than ever and asking me to ring her back and Paul had also left a message telling me that he would be away for a few days. Phillipa I could understand but Paul was a different matter. He didn't say where he was going or why and there was not even the suggestion of an excuse. Thinking about it, I came to the conclusion that I had been too soft with Paul and that he was apt to take advantage of my good nature. I determined to have words with him when he returned and re-establish an employer – employee relationship.

The following morning I was up and about very early. I spoke to the gang at the studio and found that production of the 'multiples' was still on schedule and I spoke briefly to Manny about the Tate exhibition. He was just as excited at the prospect as I was but I resisted his inquiries about what the nature of the exhibit might be. I wanted this show to be as much a surprise for him as it would be undoubtedly for the rest of the art establishment and the public alike. This was to be my pièce de résistance, the biggest nose-thumbing exercise I'd yet undertaken.

In that same context I spent the rest of the morning talking on the phone to various officials from the Council of Sanitary Health and the Engineers departments.

They were opposed in principle to my suggestions and warned me, unnecessarily, about what they described as the health hazards that might accrue from my proposals. Stuffed shirts without a modicum of imagination. Appreciating that they would not easily change their minds, I spoke instead to my local councillor. As I suspected, the offer of a better than modest donation to the party funds was sufficient to convince him and he promised to put the wheels in motion for me. In my view, happiness equals getting your own way, accordingly I was happy.

Later I spoke to one of the larger, nationally known building contractors and arranged to meet with one of their directors the following morning. He assured me that, based on the brief outline of my needs, he could see no problem in doing what I wanted him to do – as long as the Council did not object. I promised him that Council permission was – as it were – in the pipeline.

I went out to the club for dinner that evening. Spending quite so much time on the telephone is about the most boring activity I could imagine and I fancied some company. Miss Winterness greeted me literally with open arms. It was noticeable however, that she had fallen back into her old ways and she sat at the bar with a continuously full brandy glass throughout the evening. After I had eventually extricated myself from the voluptuous embrace of the club secretary, I went round to the kitchens and said hello to Mrs Barnes. She was just the same as ever and promised me a first-class meal. I exchanged gossip with a number of other members before settling down to enjoy the chicken cacciatore that was the highlight of Mrs Barnes' menu.

About nine thirty, I took a seat at the bar but before I could place an order, Charlie Bonphiro appeared and bought me a drink. I had not seen Charlie for some time; we did not mix in the same circles anymore and from the look of him, he was in poor health.

"So – are you well, Charles?" I asked. He liked to be called Charles in preference to Charlie and, as he had just bought me a large Scotch, I was in the mood to indulge him.

"Not so good, my boy," he replied, "I'm waiting for a hospital appointment. Something wrong with the old kidneys they say."

"Bad blood?" I offered mischievously.

He smiled faintly, "If it is – it's of my own making. A surfeit of pleasure and an excess of comfort will do it every time."

We laughed. I liked Charlie, he had been instrumental in my early success and I suppose I still felt I owed him a debt of honour. He drained his glass and I ordered a refill immediately. He thanked me and then to my surprise asked if I knew where he might be able to purchase a supply of cocaine. His request shocked me. Obviously it was not that I had any conscience about ingesting that substance or still less about selling it, only that he was a most unlikely participant in any such practice.

"Who do you want it for Charles?" I asked, needing to be absolutely sure about his intentions.

"Me, dear boy – it's all for me. I've found that a snort now and then does me a power of good… Makes the colonel stand to attention when he is more usually suffering the 'droop'."

Sexual stimulation was the most common reason for snorting cocaine but Charlie was the last person alive I would have thought would admit to such a reason.

"I may be able to help you out myself. What sort of quantity are we talking about?"

He paused, the glass half way to his lips, and studied me, "I had no idea you could supply, Michael. Didn't know you were into that sort of thing."

I grinned, "Well it is a fairly new venture to be honest – but I do have access to some very good stuff. Not cheap – but high quality."

"Well isn't that a turn-up for the books, just when my regular supplier has gone out of business. Should we say a quarter of an ounce – for starters?"

The price was agreed and I promised to deliver him his order before lunch the following day. He was delighted.

As a consequence of our association, we spent the rest of the evening together. We drank too much and laughed too easily at one another's jokes. However, it was just before we parted outside the club to take our individual taxis home that he surprised me again. I'd been describing some of my recent works to him and, as usual, he'd been scoffing at my efforts and heaping scorn on modern art generally when Paul's name was mentioned.

"He's a dear boy, young Paul, and if what Manny says is correct, he has a lot of talent."

"Does Manny know Paul that well?" I asked.

"Indeed he does. In fact they were dining together this evening unless I'm very much mistaken."

I felt the cold hand of suspicion grip my neck and a doubt began to form. Paul's absence and his resistance to discussing ideas were perhaps explained by what Charlie said.

"Probably talking about his exhibition, eh?" I said, trying to tease a little more information.

"Possibly – mind I think it's not planned to go on until the spring."

Charlie's comments gave me food for thought on the way home. What price friendship? What kind of treatment was this – by a friend and employee and by my agent? More importantly, what were they cooking up together and how would it affect me? If I found that the bastards were using any of my contacts – any of my ideas or facilities – God help them both.

Chapter Twenty-Four

The suspicion of treachery by such a close associate as Paul made me depressed. Consequently, the day after my meeting with Jimmy Barratt, I could not settle to do very much of any importance. I could not however, avoid the meeting I'd arranged. I delivered the cocaine to Charlie and at ten a.m. I met with the managing director of the building firm I'd contacted to discuss the detail of my special requirements. It was to be largely a plumbing procedure, one associated with several of the public toilet conveniences found around the outskirts of the local authority and, although it was an unusual request, the contractor did not make spurious inquiries about my motives.

It was a simple enough exercise. Once the permission was granted by the Planning and Public Health Departments, the men's urinal outflow was to be tapped at four locations and the waste to be pumped into zinc containers that would stand alongside the buildings. These would then be emptied on a daily basis over the period of two weeks and the ensuing cargo delivered to my studios where they would be stored in huge closed vats specially built for the purpose. The detail I left to the contractor and once a fee had been agreed, I promised to be in touch with him as soon as the red tape had been satisfied. Later I spoke to my friends at Pilkington's Glass and ordered a variety of clear glass containers. All this business was completed before lunch.

There were two more messages left by Phillipa on my answering machine, neither of which I responded to. After a lunchtime burger in a fast-food shop, I went over to the studios and invited two of the girls from the assembly line back to the house for dinner. I was determined to give myself a treat. I needed cheering up and the indulgence of two young women to act as overnight 'belly-warmers' was just the thing. However, my fortunes continued on the same downward path and, later in the afternoon, they telephoned to say that they would not be able to make our date as arranged. By then it was too late to visit the college bar – a favourite place for picking up stray girls. However, just as my mood was dropping through the floor, the doorbell rang.

I knew she was an art student immediately. The hair was long, the jeans were torn and the pupils of her eyes were somewhat larger than is normal.

"It is… it is Mick Grainger. Isn't it?" she asked.

I nodded and continued to examine her details, keeping my reply as non-committal as possible, "Yes. What can I do for you?"

"I'm sorry to bother you, especially at this time of day – but…" she was breathless with excitement. A state I preferred to imagine caused by my presence rather than the inducement of some chemical source. "But… would you have a look at some of my work – sometime?"

I gave her my most friendly grin and asked if "now" might be convenient. Twenty minutes later Jade Hagan was sitting alongside me in the lounge peeling sheets from her sketchbook and talking at a rate of knots that would have done justice to an attempt on the land speed record.

She had just arrived from Huddersfield to study at the Royal College of Art on the postgraduate Master's course. And having succeeded in gaining one of the few places at the RCA she had clearly experienced her first taste of glory – the promise of a career in fine art. I knew the feeling well. You develop a belief in yourself despite the odds against success and then you get hoisted onto the first rung of the ladder. You can hardly believe it but the taste lingers and suddenly you are doing all kinds of things to further your ambition – even things like knocking on the door of established artists and asking them to help.

Under most normal circumstances, I would have shut the door in her face. I mean why the hell I would help someone who might prove later to be the competition? This evening was different, however. I needed company. Who better, I thought, than an admiring student to share the night with? Jade was just eighteeb years of age, a well-formed natural blonde that, if my perceptions were on target, had been round the block a few times already. Her thin shirt did little to disguise the fact that she lacked a bra and the instant familiarity she assumed sitting knee to knee with me, was just the encouragement I was looking for. I poured her a large vodka that she took without complaint and we settled to look at her folder.

We spent a turgid hour or so looking at her ideas, photographs of her work and some drawings, and then I invited her to stay for something to eat. My suggestion made her bloom. It was almost as though she'd just won the Turner Prize.

"I really didn't expect… I mean… Well I thought you'd probably chase me…"

"If you like to be chased, Jade, then I'll chase you later on," I answered quickly, giving her a wink.

To my surprise she blushed and for a moment she looked confused. I did an immediate reappraisal. Perhaps after all she wasn't the 'girl-about-town' I'd imagined her to be. The idea of her being innocent gave me an erection it was hard to hide. Suddenly the evening looked far more promising than I could have hoped for.

After consulting with her about her favourite food, I telephoned the local Indian restaurant and placed an order, and whilst we waited for its arrival I laid the table in the kitchen. I then gave my guest a guided tour of my little house, ostensibly to direct her to the bathroom; however, I took care to open the door to my bedroom and to demonstrate the hi-fi system I'd had installed. She was clearly impressed and although the blush persisted, I could tell she was considering all her options.

With the meal we drank lager and afterwards I opened a couple of bottles of red wine. We talked arty talk and exhibitions, we discussed the politics of the gallery system and the prejudice evident in the London colleges, and we drank copious amounts of alcohol. We sat close together on the big settee and at some stage Jade even rested her head on my willing shoulder, but it was only later when we sat watching a semi-pornographic 'art' film together that I made my first pass. I had just promised to introduce her to Manny Hume when the question of her staying over was raised.

"You'd have one helluva job getting a taxi at this time of night," I said, "why not stay over?"

She giggled and the blush came back, "I'm not that kind of girl, Mick," she said coyly draining another glass.

I assumed a shocked expression, "What on earth do you think I was suggesting?" I asked – like butter wouldn't melt in my mouth. "I'm not in the habit of trying it on with students – not of course, unless they're willing."

It is no wonder that so many primitive civilisations laid such importance on identifying and safeguarding the virgins in their society. Once they were kept for use as handmaidens or offerings to the Gods in temples, for purposes of guaranteeing trade agreements with allies and sometimes as an elixir of restoration for old men. And whilst the emphasis today has clearly changed, the attraction felt by mature men for much younger women remains consistent. The texture of youth is found as much in resilient skin as in sparkling eyes, neither of which can be actually counterfeited. No matter what the advances made in the face-lift surgery of the celebrity sciences, genuine youthfulness is unmistakable. It is the quality of naiveté, however, that best characterises the young. A sense of half-informed curiosity always apparent in young women's eyes, their doubt combining with an innate willingness. The tantalising prospect of playing Svengali to Jade's Trilby was the kind of challenge any red-blooded man would find irresistible. And I was nothing if not red-blooded.

Now she was embarrassed – just as I'd intended – and to give her time for her confusion to grow, I poured more drinks and allowed a silence to develop. After a moment or two I added something patronising, something about her being very young, very immature, "… And clearly you don't have much experience… not that that's a bad thing… just that it shows."

Within half an hour she was almost begging me to let her stay the night. A request to which I reluctantly agreed. We took a shower together and then retired to the king-sized bed but it was just when I was about to mount her that she froze-up. Suddenly she was resistant, beginning to try and hold back.

"What's the matter?" I asked, pretending a patience I did not feel.

"I… I don't want to," she said.

Now it should be understood that by this time we were laid naked together on the satin coverlet and by then she'd allowed the most intimate exploration of her very ample body and appeared to enjoy every minute of it.

I laughed quietly, in the character of a Victorian melodrama cad, "That's what they all say, Jade. That's what you're supposed to say."

But the attempted humour had no effect and she tried to heave me off her, muttering something about it being her choice and not mine. I laughed again and held her down. Her struggles became more agitated. Now I was annoyed. I'd devoted a whole evening to this little chit of a girl; the least she could do was to submit with style. There was no way I would allow her simply to walk off without settling her debt. So I fucked her anyway.

She was strong and she put up a good fight but I was stronger and the booze had sapped her co-ordination. In the end she was a good screw and once a rhythm was established her struggles stopped and she joined in with some enthusiasm. I must admit there is a side to me that takes extra pleasure when the subject of my attentions puts up a fight. Celia used to fake her objections sometimes, just in order to amplify the enjoyment for me. Moreover, there is a pattern to the behaviour of women who are initially resistant to sex. The verbal objection comes first followed by an appeal to the man's generosity; when that fails the struggles start. Depending on the energy, if not the bravery, of the victim, she will then make a real effort to dislodge her companion, and it is only after penetration that she finally submits. Oddly enough after the first good shagging they are apt to become completely compliant and at this point you can do anything with them. Jade soon reached this stage and even when I took her from behind she did not object. I played with her until the early hours of the morning, giving her the benefit of all my years of sexual invention including a modicum of violence. I'd introduced her to fellatio and to sodomy, and when she began to look tired, I had her sniff a line of coke. Eventually, just as the dawn broke, we lay together and fell into a deeply satisfied sleep.

I was awoken at eleven a.m. by the telephone and it was only after I had picked up the receiver that I realised my partner of the previous night had left the bed. The voice on the phone introduced himself as a CID inspector. He told me that he had received a complaint from a young woman that morning accusing me of rape and he would like me to go to the police station immediately.

The next twenty-four hours were a nightmare. Dressed in a sober business suit I duly appeared at the police station and answered the questions put to me. It was only when things began to get ugly that I insisted on my statuary phone call. Naturally I telephoned Manny and within half an hour he had a lawyer at my side. On his advice I refused to answer any more questions and after a lengthy session with a chief inspector, I was allowed to leave on my own recognisance. The solicitor, a Mister James Belling, advised me to accept the fact that there would most likely be a court case to answer. It transpired that my little friend Jade was the daughter of a Presbyterian minister, a gentleman I was to discover with significant connections amongst a variety of London politicians as well the hierarchy of the Middlesex police. It was the beginning of a long and tortuous legal situation that almost resulted in my imprisonment. Fortunately, in the final analysis, Jade was disarmingly honest and when we eventually got to court, she admitted that she had agreed to stay the night, that she had drunk fairly copious amounts of wine and that she was the one who had initiated the first contact. The chief magistrate – a woman – was clearly biased in Jade's favour and looked more than a little annoyed at her confessions. She demonstrated her feelings by addressing me at the end of the hearing, as if I was a habitual rapist. Happily I left without any blame on my part being proven and with the threat of a full-blown trial having been lifted.

The evening of my resurrection I went to dinner with Manny. It proved a desultory affair. He behaved like he was half ashamed to be seen out with me and by the time we were having coffee, he was suggesting I should make myself scarce for a while.

"Take a long holiday," he said from behind a cloud of cigar smoke, "or if you wish, I'll organise a lecture tour in the States – but whichever, you should keep a low profile."

"Why the hell should I go into hiding?" I snapped back. "Wasn't I found innocent."

My agent looked at the floor for a moment or two, then he said, "Being found innocent as you were – doesn't mean a thing as far as polite society is concerned. You knew you were guilty, the magistrates knew you were guilty and, take it from me, all your society friends know you were guilty. If it hadn't been for that little girl's innocent admissions you'd probably be behind bars tonight. Also, you may well find that her parents will bring a private prosecution. "

I drained my cup and snapped my fingers for more coffee before I answered him. I had imagined he would be pleased at my escape from justice and to find him adopting this 'holier than thou' attitude irritated the hell out of me. It wasn't as though he was without experience of young girls. I knew he had a constant stream of sexy young things staying over at his house in the country.

"Hypocrisy isn't becoming, Manny," I said, "you should think hard about yourself before you start claiming sainthood and…"

He turned on me, interrupting in a loud voice, "You silly bugger," he snarled. "It's not me that's been shown-up to be a criminal. It's you. And for what? It isn't as though you're short of a bit of 'Totty' – but you have to go and screw some bit of a kid just because you were bored. The tabloids have the story and over the next few weeks you will be torn to shreds… Give it up, Mick. Disappear for a while and let things blow over." He paused and then added, "This is just the sort of thing that could jeopardise your Tate exhibition."

The news that the gutter press were about to pursue me was depressing and I finally agreed to take a holiday.

By the time I got back to the house that night I was thoroughly down in the dumps. The accusation itself had been depressing enough but the promise of having my face all over the newspapers was completely debilitating. What happened to the idea that any publicity was good publicity? The lights were on as I approached the house and when I entered, I found Paul sitting before the drawing room fire drinking my best Scotch. He turned and grinned at me, "Aha – the rapist returns," he said.

I poured myself a large drink before responding. I needed something to distract me else I would throw this ingrate out of the house. I sat opposite him, "And where, pray tell, have you been?" I asked trying to keep the anger out of my voice.

"Oh – I took a few days break. I needed to get away for a while. Stress I suppose."

"The only stress you suffer is trying to decide how much whisky you should pour into your glass – my whisky incidentally. I hope you don't imagine that I'm going to pay you for the last few weeks."

"Of course not."

Now he was arrogant – still grinning and apparently unperturbed by my accusations.

"And when were you going to tell me about your exhibition?" I asked, firing my secret missile.

He was still unmoved, "Tonight, as it happens – if you ever give me the chance to get a word in."

"Too little, too late, Paul. I employed you on the understanding that you worked exclusively on my stuff. There was never any agreement that you should use my contacts, my manufacturers, still less my own agent to further your own career. I think it's time we parted company."

My comments this time hit the desired mark and he sat forward in the chair staring at me.

"Are you serious?"

"Never more so. I'd like you leave these premises tonight."

He stood up and put the glass on the mantle, "I never thought you'd turn on me like this. I've seen you turn on other people," he started, "and we've all known for ages what a bastard you are privately, Mick – but this is uncalled for. I thought you'd be pleased that I wanted to show my work."

I looked at my watch, "And if you could be out in say – the next hour, that would be most convenient."

He turned and stormed to the door but before he could leave I added, "Incidentally, I am having my lawyers study the circumstances and if they find that you have breached our contract, I'll sue you through the courts."

He left without further comment and some thirty minutes later I heard the front door slam. It was a pity about Paul, he'd been useful at times but I couldn't have him operating a private agenda at my cost – so good riddance. I checked his room, just to make certain he hadn't helped himself to any of my belongings. All I found was a rude message scrawled on the wall behind the bed in felt tip pen. An act of irrational vandalism one might have expected from the likes of an ungrateful sod like Paul.

As expected, the following morning the tabloids were full of derisory comment about my court appearance and I answered a knock on the door at eight thirty to find two reporters wanting to interview me. I slammed the door in their faces and immediately made telephone reservations on the noonday flight to Paris.

Before I left, however, I made calls to Jimmy Barratt and to Phillipa. Jimmy wasn't at home so I left a message on his answering machine telling him that I'd ring him that evening. Phillipa was at home but the tone she adopted was distant and it was only when I offered her the financial assistance she had asked for that she became a little more friendly.

"I'm sorry I didn't get back to you sooner," I lied, "but things have been rather hectic – as you no doubt appreciate."

There was a long pause before she answered, "Yes. I heard about your problem. What a pity you didn't apply your lust to people who might understand you. I'm told that Jade's family are going to bring a private prosecution."

"Really," I said. Now this was news to me – unwelcome news and it irritated me to hear it first from Phillipa, "Then I hope they can afford to lose as I will defend the action, whatever it takes."

I heard her smile into the mouthpiece, "I'm glad to hear it, Mick. Despite your strange appetites, I never saw you as a child rapist."

"Well thank you for that. Now – how would you like this money transferred?"

"Actually, there's no need for you to bother now Mick. I've made other arrangements."

Now it was my turn to pause. I couldn't imagine who else would stump up that amount of cash to cover her gambling debts. "Oh – and who was your knight in shining armour this time?"

"It's complicated. I'll tell you all about it next time we meet."

"That may not be for a while," I replied, "you see I'm off on a holiday today – shan't be back, probably for a few weeks."

"Excuse me one moment…" she said and she must have put her hand over the phone to talk to someone else in the same room, however I heard her say, "It's Mick Grainger… he's doing a runner by all accounts…"

In the distance Manny's voice replied: "The world isn't big enough," he said laughing bitterly.

I hung up without waiting for her to answer me further.

Chapter Twenty-Five

1984

I was not to know it at the time but the journey I began when I set out for Paris was to take me well beyond the European Continent, although in the beginning that was far from my intention. Indeed, to tell the truth, I did not want to leave London and never intended to be gone for long. Testimony to this fact was evident in the small amount of luggage I took with me. I packed quickly, taking only a medium-sized suitcase and a shoulder bag. However, conscious of my likely need to contact people in England as Christmas approached, I made certain that I included my telephone address book.

There was still so much to do with regard to my restaurant, that and the large environmental piece that I was planning for the Tate. And I feared that, no matter who I left to represent my interests, those interests would not be secured in the manner in which I would have wanted them to be. I felt that there was no one I could trust and it was actually in the taxi that took me to Heathrow that I decided to contact Celia. She was the only person I felt confident would never betray me. Fortunately I caught her on a day when she was not embroiled in her studio and we talked for some thirty minutes. She said that whilst she would have nothing to do with any negotiations involving Jimmy Barratt, she would agree to organise the engineers I'd employed and to maintain contact with Pilkington's Glass. Her antipathy concerning Jimmy was a subject she would not discuss further and I gathered from her attitude that either she had had dealings with him in the past or that his reputation was known to her through friends.

I enjoyed talking to Celia and felt a sincere nostalgia for the days when we were together. She had always been honest with me – well nearly always – and I knew she was someone who could be trusted with any of my secrets. There was no doubt however, that she had changed. Now she was brimming with self-confidence and certain about what she wanted out of life but despite her new maturity, she remained one of the sexiest women I'd ever known. I found myself smiling at the memory of a night on the beach at Marske car park, the occasion when an energetic policeman and his shy friend joined us. A night to relish and one that served as a trendsetter for much of the sexual fantasy that we enjoyed afterwards. On the Paris shuttle later, I also found myself wondering why it all went so wrong. I hadn't neglected her; I hadn't mistreated her yet she'd deliberately started an affair with a group of dead-beat, no-hope druggies. The kind of human dross she'd mixed with gave personal affront to all my aspirations for her. I supposed therefore that, however justified, it had been my injured pride that had caused the rift.

I was eventually delivered to a modest hotel on the Left Bank by a taxi driver who, whilst apparently keen to earn a few extra Francs for his advice, gave a typical demonstration of Gallic stubbornness by refusing to understand the English language. My schoolboy patois nevertheless proved sufficient and I was quickly settled in a room overlooking the better part of the city. Not having much to unpack, I spent most of my first evening on the telephone organising the details of my affairs concerning the restaurant. I left my address with Manny's secretary Julia, with Jimmy and with my solicitors. But it was not until I settled for an evening meal in a little café round the corner from the hotel, that I remembered my cache of drugs. Stupidly, I'd left the package in the base of the standard lamp, probably the first place anyone, particularly any housebreaker, might look. And if that were true, then it would be undoubtedly the first place any inquisitive policeman might look also. I remembered then that I had promised to sell a quantity of the cocaine to Phillipa. She would be furious if she did not receive it so I rang her from the café and asked her to collect the package. I told her to collect the spare key from Manny and to use whatever she required – but that she would need to pay for whatever was taken when I returned.

I slept badly that night, disturbed by crowds of late-night drinkers outside my window. However, I suspect my sleeplessness was also partly to do with having reservations about Phillipa's honesty and my concerns over Paul. They both knew rather too much about me and whilst Paul had been effectively annexed, Phillipa certainly had not. Regrets about asking her to collect the drugs began in the early hours and by morning I was already formulating a plan to have someone else secure the package. Being in a strange place also troubled me. Not that strange places bothered me *per se* only that being one-step removed from London, I wondered how I might spend my time most profitably. Consequently, after my coffee and croissants I went to a bank and, after paying for a call to be made to my London branch, managed to organise a line of credit. Afterwards I took a taxi and spent most of the day sightseeing. I kept telling myself it was a holiday but an inner voice insisted that, having run away from possible prosecution, I was only fooling myself.

On my tour I visited the usual galleries, taking the opportunity privately to heap scorn on the daubs and scribbles of a, thankfully, now passing generation of artists and their imitators. Most of what I saw would have been better used as wallpaper for a children's nursery, or as wrapping paper for presents to a tasteless girlfriend. The accidental splurges and splashes exhibited under the Impressionists' banner could be seen now as the mindless doodles of intellectual dwarfs. Any relevance they might have once had was long since lost; leaving only their frayed pattern-making as a residue. No small wonders the photographer's art prospered. It occurred to me that there might be some mileage at a later date, in making my observations public. An article – or a series of articles perhaps – in one of the newer arty type magazines. With that in mind, when I returned to my room, I made some caustic note about what I had seen, seeking to find some suitably recriminating expressions to fit my mood.

Around eight that evening a maid from the hotel knocked at my door. She had messages for me, one of which asked that I should telephone Manny and another, my solicitors. I did so immediately, in Manny's case only to find the recording of his answer phone on the end of the line. I left rude remarks and hung up. My solicitor had left his home number so I disturbed his evening meal. He said that Jade's family was prepared to settle out of court, should I wish to prevent a scandal. The sum they asked for was clearly cultured by a newly acquired knowledge of what they imagined to be the value of my current estate. They didn't want only a pound of flesh – they wanted half the torso as well. I said I needed time to think about their kind offer and instructed my representative to make a lower bid.

"I explored that possibility," he told me in his most serious voice, "but I suspect they may have made up their minds."

"Nevertheless," I said, trying to maintain my patience, "I do not wish to donate such a large part of my capital to pay for the services of their daughter in, what was after all, only a one-night-stand. What are our chances of winning the case if the case should be brought?"

"I'm not confident."

Now whether one's legal representative should be quite so blunt, I do not know. Equally, his reply prompted a question in my mind as to the professional loyalty of someone who was taking a considerable quantity of money in fees and yet promising failure rather than success in return.

"Excuse me," I snapped back, "but are you paid to represent my interests or do you work for Jade's family?"

"I beg your par…"

"Because if you work for me, the least I expect from you at this point is a list of possible strategies that promote my chances of winning. I do not – repeat – do not expect you to simply say you're not confident. If you cannot manage that then I'll seek another lawyer."

In respect of getting one's own way, without doubt, the possession of money is the most effective catalyst in the civilized world. And the more polite the society then the more efficient the effect of intolerance by those that are wealthy. Typically, my lawyer quickly changed tack and in no time at all he was reassuring me of the likely outcome in my favour.

I do not like, nor do I trust anyone with who has anything to do with the legal profession. In my view they can be relied upon only to act under the guise of propriety, a stratagem simply designed, I believe, to hide the depth of their acquisitiveness. They possess a devious nature complimented by the most cunning of personality characteristics and usually act according to a private agenda far removed from that of their client. To make matters all the worse, the system of Law in this country is so hide-bound, that their employment is as mandatory as their fees are outrageous. It has long since been my belief that any person of average intelligence could represent themselves before a judge and plead their own case with as much chance of a successful result as any of the legally trained and accredited lawyers in the land might achieve. Needless to say, by the time my own legal representative rang off that evening, he had been left in no doubt about my feelings with regard to his trade.

It was therefore with a degree of justifiable self-satisfaction that I treated myself to a substantial dinner in one of the better restaurants. And, after several large glasses of brandy to compliment the bottle of fine burgundy I drank with the meal, I made my way to bed where I slept like a baby.

The following morning was bright. Sunshine flooded my room and, despite a headache, I rose with a feeling of anticipation. On such a day nothing could conceivably go wrong. After the visits I had made the day before to those museums and galleries exhibiting more traditional works of Art, I made up my mind to try and view some work representing more modern thinking. Despite its apparent dependence on art that was steeped in the banal preferences of the nineteenth century, Paris was once at the forefront of new ideas. There had to be places where new, young, modern artists were working and places where one might see work of real significance.

I considered this over my coffee that morning and was obliged to admit to myself that my motives were, at least in part, to look for good ideas that I might use myself. Since my first successes my reputation had increased as steadily as my income; however, I could not deny the occasional voice of my conscience that still told me I was a confidence trickster. And in this respect, although a significant percentage of critics and other cultural observers of different sorts supported the beliefs I proclaimed in public, secretly I still remained unconvinced myself. To be entirely honest, whilst I had learnt to play 'the game' I had little understanding of much that I claimed. I knew the work could be more shocking, more controversial, possibly more original than most of my contemporaries, but I remained uncertain as to whether that constituted art as most people understood it. Indeed, was it any kind of art at all? Fortunately my moment of honest self-doubt did not last long and I quickly put such questions to one side.

My taxi driver, usually the sort that proved a fount of all knowledge, was of little help in directing me to artist's studios and I found myself wandering the back streets of the Left Bank by myself. The street artists' productions were predictably biased to the tourist trade but I was surprised to find that many of the private ateliers I stumbled upon were of a similar ilk. Various scenes of L'eglise de la Sacre Coeur (The Sacred Heart Church) and the Paris roof-scape seemed to be the preferred subjects for the painters. Despite the one or two who were found to be showing video installations and text messages, there was little that truly represented the modern movement. Consequently by the middle of the afternoon, I had started back to my room, disenchanted with the Paris art scene and missing London all the more.

I stopped for a café cognac at a restaurant and sat outside for a while people-watching and enjoying the thin sunshine. There was still a magic about the city of Paris and despite my disappointments, I felt that the style and attitude of the French was more attractively liberal, more adventurous, even more creative than those one might witness in a typical London street. I was just beginning to notice a particularly attractive streetwalker across the road when my mobile phone rang.

"Mick, I've got some good news for you."

It was Manny and he sounded excited, "How do you fancy a trip to the West Indies all expenses paid?"

"Are you really that keen to see the back of me?" I replied.

"Seriously. After a bit of wrangling I've persuaded the University of the West Indies to offer you a Fellowship – just for twelve months. What d'you say?"

The offer took me completely by surprise. Fellowships were few and far between and those awarded in exotic places were generally reserved for well-established, respectable figures.

"The West Indies... I must admit that sounds like it could be interesting... what would I have to do?"

"Don't be so pedantic you lazy sod; this could be a good break. They'll supply housing and a modest stipend, a studio and materials. All you have to do is to hold a few seminars with local artists give the odd lecture and at the end – maybe hold an exhibition at the national gallery."

"And where in the West Indies would I be based?"

"The island of Trinidad – Trinidad and Tobago actually."

The vision of sun-drenched beaches and beautiful black women suddenly filled my imagination. And twelve months would pass in the blink of an eye. Moreover, as I'd seen in France, the art scene in Europe was stale.

"Okay," I said, "I'll do it. I'll take a flight this afternoon and meet you at..."

"No. No need to come back. I'll send you the details and the airline ticket and you can leave from Paris. No point in coming home first. The contact numbers are all listed, all you have to do is give the University a ring and that's it."

Remembering one of the niceties he liked to insist upon, I remembered to thank him before he rang off – Manny preferred to leave an impression of an old world charmer, a cultured person who observed the manners of a bygone age. It was an act but I indulged him on this occasion.

If he sent the details by courier, I knew I'd have them by the following morning so, instead of going back to my room, I spent the rest of the day shopping for clothing suitable for the tropics – and more suitcases. Clearly I was to spend the Christmas season in a hot climate and, if the guide books I'd purchased were an accurate representation of fact, during the following February I'd witness the carnival. My reservations slowly ebbed away and thoughts of palm trees on hot nights and black flesh on cool cotton sheets took their place. I had no idea what to expect of the Tropics, most of my imagined images were rooted in those black and white Hollywood movies from a previous generation, but if only half of it was true, then this was an opportunity not to be missed.

Chapter Twenty-Six

1985

I landed at Heathrow airport on October 25th 1985, a birthday date I shared with Picasso. In fact the one hundred and fourth anniversary of his birth. A cold windswept day under the greyest skies and the heaviest most threatening clouds I'd seen for quite some time. It was a world away from Port of Spain, a different planet from that which I had grown used to. Symptomatic of the prevailing climate, the people also appeared to be grey, monochrome shadows without substance, dull in nature as much as they were miserable in their attitude. No one smiled, there were no impromptu greetings and there was a resistance to pleasantries apparent even amongst those employed to assist the travelling public. The word anti-climax stuck in my mind.

None of this was too surprising in the context of the current political climate in the country. In February that year 51% of the infamous striking miners were still on strike. Only a couple of years earlier the same workers had complained bitterly when unemployment had reached the three million mark. Yet here they were again – still on strike. Not surprisingly, the pound dropped to its lowest level yet almost equalling a rate of one for one with the dollar and typically riots had broken out in left-wing Toxteth and Peckham. I found it increasingly difficult to understand the mentality of the so-called working classes. They'd seen Thatcher win the Falklands war, a victory that had pulled the country together and given the Argies a bloody nose into the bargain. Her popularity had never been greater and when she applied the same ruthless technique in her defeat of the unions, the spirits of the business community rose. But the mood of optimism had soon evaporated and here we were again with all kinds of industrial and social unrest. There were lots of jobs advertised in the London papers and all those seeking employment had to do was make a trip south to restart their miserable lives. But making that kind of effort was much more difficult than sitting back and bemoaning their fate. Great Britain was again in a mess.

Progress through passport control was slow, not so much due to the arrivals from the tropics than, on account of the pedantic cross-examination to which the officials subjected them. Consequently, a huge cluster of black faces blocked the area making ingress by British citizens almost impossible. The same was true a little while later near the luggage collection point however, whilst passport control was characterised by worried looks and an air of depression, as the cases came round the mood lightened and everyone appeared to be relieved. A Jamaican who stood in front of me was actually singing, leaving me to wonder how anyone could be so happy to leave the sun behind them in preference for the cold damp of England. No doubt he'd find work doing a menial job for less money than his British counterpart. The poor sod didn't know what he was in for.

It had been fourteen months since I left the UK and, although initially there had been a certain level of concern on my part, especially with regard to the unknown working conditions and the reception I might expect, everything had turned out well. The ethos in Trinidad was casual almost to the point of being sleepy and totally without the familiar emphasis on timekeeping that is so much a part of the British culture. No one fussed about incidentals and holiday time was stressed just as equally as work time. Needless to say, it was a culture with which I found immediate sympathy and one in which I was quickly absorbed.

In the beginning I had tried to keep abreast of my business interests in Britain but found that the soporific influence of the climate and the people and the normal slow rate of living increased the feeling of distance from that reality. Eventually, I had been content to let events take their natural course without my interference. As regards my work, all my good intentions had soon evaporated and, although I carried out my Fellowship duties, I did little else. I discovered that the West Indians turn socialising into an art form. They are never happier than when they are in a crowd, drinking rum, singing calypso, and persuading females into bed. They party with style and truly know how to enjoy themselves. Most impressively, their tolerance for extramarital affairs is remarkably liberal and it seemed that almost everyone had several mistresses. It was my kind of place. There were drugs on tap, booze was cheap and the women easily accessible. Moreover, the small cohort of white women in evidence, some of whom had accompanied their husbands on short-term contracts to the university, proved to be just as susceptible to the culturally deviant morals as was the local population.

Anticipating the difficulty of transport from the airport, I had written and asked Phillipa if she might meet me on my return. However, although she had agreed, when I left the concourse she was nowhere to be found and I had to bear the unnecessary expense of a taxi.

The first omen of bad times came just as we were leaving the tunnel at Heathrow. Another cab paused nearby momentarily. It was facing the opposite direction and I was able to glimpse the passenger – it was Jade. Only a year and half later and suddenly she appeared to be a mature woman – a very attractive mature woman. In another life – or a Hollywood movie – I might have jumped out and greeted her. I might even have suggested that I accompany her to wherever she was going. The thought that stopped me however was that she was obviously going off on holiday to spend some of the funds her family had extorted from me. I couldn't tell if she travelled alone but for the rest of my journey, my imagination conjured a variety of faces of men who might well have sat next to her. Even when it's only in the mind, revenge is sweet and the worst fate I could wish for her was to spend her holiday with Mr Bonphiro, or Manny or still better with Speedy. This at least made me smile.

Almost as soon as I turned the key in my front door, I knew something was wrong. Inside the entrance there was a strong smell of cooking and several unidentified coats hung in the cupboard. Entering the lounge I found a young man stretched across my settee reading a novel and the sounds of activity coming from the kitchen. I must confess my first thought was that squatters had invaded me, until Paul appeared at the kitchen door with a glass of wine in his hand.

"Mick!" he said looking as surprised as I felt myself.

In an instant I realised what the scenario represented, "Paul!" I replied, imitating his tone and dropping my suitcase.

Now his face was flushed, "Sorry about this Mick but... well ...the place was empty and going wanting and I didn't think you'd mind us looking after it for you. I told..."

I didn't let him finish, "How long have you been here?"

"I told Manny and he said that..."

"How long have you been here?"

The youth on the settee then took an interest and I found him scrutinising me like I was the intruder. "Who the hell is this, Paul?" he asked aggressively.

"This is the guy who owns the place," I answered, "the one you and your boyfriend here have clearly been ripping off. Now I'd be obliged if you'd get your feet off my sofa."

"There's no need to get nasty," Paul said adopting a hurt look, "there's no harm done. This is Tim by the way."

Tim got to his feet and stared at me.

"Well – I'd like you and Tim to be out of here within an hour. As far as I'm concerned you are squatters. You didn't have my permission to use the place so I want you out otherwise I'll call the police."

My statement created exactly the shocked looks I'd hoped it might and Paul began to make plaintive sounds, talking about being reasonable and willingness to negotiate and the like. Tim on the other hand became truculent, "The police can't do a thing," he said, still staring at me, "okay so we're squatters – but squatters have rights. So fuck you."

By then we were almost nose to nose, with him trying as hard as he could to intimidate me. I hit him almost before I realised that was what I was going to do, a short twelve inch punch, just below the breast bone with as much force as I could muster. He bent towards me gasping and, in the words of my northern friends, I stuck in the nut. I headed him on the bridge of his nose. The resultant sound of a sharp crunch was satisfying and a moment later Tim was on the floor. It had been a long time since I'd exercised my talent for violence and a feeling of physical superiority swiftly overtook my relief at its success. These two were just southern softies. I turned to Paul as if expecting him to come to his friend's aid but he showed the flat of hands, "Easy Mick," he muttered, "no need for any more of that. We'll be out in half an hour."

He helped Tim to the bathroom and applied a cold compress to his bloody nose before quickly packing a couple of bags. I looked on throughout this operation and although I could not quite catch the whispered conversations between the two of them, my imagination filled the gaps. They thought they were on a good thing living rent free and, judging by the fact that at least some of their belongings were already packed, had obviously planned to be on their way before my return. Tim was the first one out of the door but Paul stopped on the threshold for his parting shot.

"There was no need for the rough stuff, Mick. We'd have left anyway."

I grinned, "Whoever told you when I was coming home cocked-up then – I'd like to bet it was my dear friend Phillipa."

The look on his face told me I'd scored a bullseye but he turned without confirming or denying it. Once outside he called back only once, asking me to send on any bits and pieces he might have left behind. I assured him I'd send any of his stuff I found, to the rubbish dump.

For an hour or so I toured the house examining all the cupboards, even the linen basket, looking for things to complain about. To be fair – not that I felt any need to indulge myself in that way – I discovered nothing untoward. Indeed the place was clean and tidy. Even the drinks cupboard was just as I'd left it. There were two nice sirloin steaks in a frying pan in the kitchen accompanied on the hob by a saucepan containing a clutch of new potatoes. Not wishing to see good food wasted, I opened a bottle of Burgundy and treated myself to a lavish homecoming dinner. It was a good feeling.

There was a mound of mail laid on my desk and I spent the rest of the evening sorting it into stacks according to its priority. There were three letters from Jimmy Barratt and after reading them I was forced to conclude that neither Phillipa nor Manny had been in touch with him. The notification from my solicitors, however, confirmed the fact that I had acquired the Soho property some three months ago. This left me to wonder if the previous tenants had been paid off as I'd promised Jimmy they would be. There were letters also from various colleges inviting me to give lectures and one or two from Galleries inquiring about recent works. The rest comprised a collection of bills, none of which had apparently been paid despite my unwelcome tenants.

I woke early the next morning and for a change the weather was bright with a trace of sunshine under the usual grey clouds. I needed to talk to Phillipa about my cache of drugs, to Manny about the exhibition plans and to Celia concerning the 'wet' project. As expected, Phillipa was still under her duvet when I rang. She was surprised to hear from me, she said, and had obviously confused the date of my return with some other item on her social calendar.

"No," I told her, "I was due to arrive yesterday – as I told you but never mind all that – what did you do with the powder?"

There was a long silence then she said, "Which powder was that?"

A sinking feeling started in the depths of my bowel. If she was about to deny all knowledge of the cocaine then things could get very difficult indeed. There was a lot of money tied up in the stuff, an investment I could not afford to write off.

"The cocaine that I asked you to look after for me," I replied, trying to be patient.

She giggled nervously, "Oh that powder. I used some of it myself and sold some to friends – just like you said I should. There's still some left though..."

The sick feeling persisted, "So how much is left?"

"Oh – I suppose – about – maybe a quarter of it."

"Okay," I said trying to sound unconcerned, "so how much do you owe me... for the stuff you sold?"

"I couldn't say exactly... it must be about two or three thousand but..."

"Don't worry, I'll come round this morning and weigh it out – then you can settle up with me."

"I'll be going out later so it may be better to call tomorrow."

I agreed but determined secretly to visit her within the next hour. Her excuse was clearly to put off the final reckoning. I'd been a fool to trust her with the cocaine and regretted it deeply but there was little use in recriminations. Bearing in mind the profit margin was normally four times what had been spent, with luck, there would be sufficient left at least to recoup my investment.

Neither Manny nor Celia answered my call so I dressed immediately and called a cab to take me to South Kensington. I'd decided not to mention the business of Paul and Tim to Phillipa, preferring to keep that information as a coup d'état should the argument over the drugs prove greater than I expected. If Phillipa had used my stash to settle her debts, as I was beginning to suspect, she would have only transferred the debt – and no doubt she already owed me a considerable sum for the stuff she'd used herself.

Phillipa now occupied a small mews cottage, a little pied-à-terre in one of the side streets near the tube station. It was somewhat down-market for her and, although she denied the fact, she admitted it was her husband's response to her increasingly dubious lifestyle. A move that presaged a divorce, or so most of her friends assumed. It was nevertheless beautifully furnished and had been decorated by one of the top interior designers; however, she was able only to employ a part-time housekeeper as her help.

I rang the bell and waited. It was some time before Phillipa opened the door. It was immediately clear when I saw her that she had become more than a casual user of hard drugs. Her eyes were swollen and bloodshot and her concentration was fragmented. Initially she did not recognise me and kept me standing on the step like a stranger. However when recognition dawned, she became nervous and told me my visit was inconvenient, suggesting that I should call another time – as if I was a tradesman. In the end I ignored her and pushed past, striding along the passage and into the drawing room. The first thing I noticed was the smell. The room had an aroma of being unused, the kind one experiences in a house that has stood empty for a long time. It was tidy enough but it was not the neatness accrued by daily care, the probity of a thorough housekeeper, rather it was that found by remaining untouched.

She slammed the front door and followed me.

"What the hell do you think you're doing?" she asked loudly.

Her voice was steeped in cigarette smoke and her tone high and superficially aggressive. The sound matched her appearance exactly: a skimpy night-gown under a towelling robe, both looking as if they had been slept in, her hair unkempt and her leftover make-up smudged. She was a wreck.

"I think that's a question I should ask you," I shouted back. She calmed momentarily and I continued in more reasonable mode, "Just look at yourself, Phillipa."

She paused as if the words had difficulty sinking in and then she began to cry. She cried like a baby for half an hour and nothing that I said or did had any effect. She tried to talk but could not manage more than an odd phrase without interruption. Eventually, hoping that shock tactics might work their usual magic, I took her back upstairs and shoved her in the en suite shower in her bedroom. Minutes later I stripped her and wrapped her in the warm thick bath sheets that hung on a rack nearby. I felt sure that the ambiguity of the situation was not lost on either of us. My appearance that morning had not been as a comforter, still less someone offering practical help, far from it, but here I was playing doctor to her act as the helpless patient.

It nevertheless took most of the morning before Phillipa was properly *compos-mentis*, or at least sufficiently so, to hold a reasonable conversation. Gallons of coffee contributed to this process plus packets of sweet biscuits and numerous cigarettes. Despite my good intentions to keep well away from her bed, there was also a brief sexual encounter. Indeed it wasn't until afterwards, as we lay side by side, belly to belly under the duvet that she tried to explain her condition.

It seemed that a whole string of circumstances had tipped her over whatever edge she had fallen from. Firstly the forced estrangement from her husband, then the accumulation of her debts. This was followed by the feeling of hopelessness prompted by not being able to pay or even to borrow the money to pay and finally, after the help promised by Manny had not manifested itself, the method her creditor, my friend Jimmy Barratt, had used to exact payment.

"I had to sleep with whoever he told me to," she whispered, "sometimes three or four of them at a time."

He must have marketed her like a dirty magazine and no doubt many of his less reputable acquaintances would pay dearly to have sex with a genuine 'Lady'. Not surprising, therefore, that her use of cocaine had steadily increased, or that its use was magnified tenfold by her sudden access to my store of the drug. As I suspected, once she realised the quantity involved she had sold the majority of it to help settle her debt. She had rented my house to Paul for the same reason. There was a side of me that felt sorry for Phillipa but, given her theft of my goods and the manner in which she had exploited my trust, the degree of my sympathy was severely limited. She had caused me a financial setback and that was almost unforgivable. Before I left therefore, I made it crystal clear that now she was in my pocket and that if she imagined the consequences would be any better than those imposed by Jimmy Barratt she was sadly mistaken. I left her just after lunchtime and went home to try and calculate how my affairs stood.

Obviously I was annoyed and upset. However, the other side of the coin left me with a feeling of perverse pleasure. I quite enjoyed the notion that Phillipa could be used as and when I saw fit. I might even charge for her services – a way of recouping my losses. In some sense there was new satisfaction in my acquisition. In the past I'd often controlled the women I'd used but it was the first time I'd actually owned one.

In the last few years I'd obviously made a lot of money. However, the purchase of the Soho property and the setting up of the studio production line had tapped deeply into my capital. To make matters worse, the settlement arranged by my lawyer, a sum agreed with Jade's parents to make the charges of rape go away, would compel me to sell off some of my assets held abroad. The loss of the drug money was therefore just the final straw. I still owned my property as collateral but didn't want to get into debt myself by borrowing against it. That way lay disaster. Basically, although it was simply a cash flow problem, the cause, I decided, was my own lack of production. It had been quite some time since I'd made or exhibited any art-work of any kind. Clearly it was time to take the show on the road again. Accordingly, I rang Manny.

"So – you're back," he replied. "We thought you might opt for a longer stay. In fact some imagined you might stay out there permanently."

I ignored the sarcasm, "Yes, I'm home – and, what's more important, I'm ready for work."

I could see him smile in my mind's eye.

"Good. I'm delighted to hear it. Your pieces have slipped in price at auction lately and I was beginning to think I might have to unload them… but, if you're full of new ideas then who knows – you may be able to take the initiative again."

The question in his voice shocked me. It was almost as if he had been expecting me to retire and I was certainly not ready for that – I couldn't afford to. I told him about the production line at the studio. In my absence they had completed all three projects I'd set: the 'paint your own picture' idea; the tomato ketchup bottle multiple, now listed as, *Common Taste Art for Tables*; and a new one that I'd devised and sent the instructions for, whilst I was away. The latter was intended as a pastiche on a coffee table book, the kind one sees casually displayed in the drawing rooms of the rich. Usually this was exhibited proudly, almost like an art object and visitors might glance through it with a similar kind of reverence. My rendition was made up of a collection of paper sheets each of a different texture and thickness. There was brown wrapping paper, tissue paper, silver foil, crêpe paper, white card, coloured card, cartridge paper and a whole host of others, and on every sheet the number of the page was printed in a complimentary colour to its location, and in very large type. I'd called this *The Taxonomy of Number For Those Wishing to Question the Photograph*. This had been an expensive production, beautifully bound in a hard cover, each copy to be signed, dated, and numbered by me.

Manny appeared to be impressed, more so when I estimate the total value for him, the sum of the three collections amounting to well over three million. "I thought the Tate exhibition might be the place to launch the collection," I said, "– maybe through the book shop. What do you think?"

"Ah, the Tate…" he replied and I knew immediately that it had been aborted.

The excuses were reasonably convincing and the tone my agent adopted was one of genuine sympathy but I knew then that I'd been screwed. He described the failure only as a delay. He said it was still only a matter of time before I was offered the space and added that his own gallery was, as always, still open to me.

Now I was brought up in a hard school. I knew about people fucking you over when they got the chance. I also knew that moaning and groaning to them only increased their pleasure at your position. The secret was to do it back – only twice as hard and twice as quick. I was furious but I hid my feelings well.

"Not to worry then, Manny. If the shits don't want me then I'll show my stuff elsewhere."

"Okay that's fine, as I said you can book time and space in my gallery anytime… naturally you'll have to talk to the exhibitions committee – but there won't be a problem."

This was the deepest cut. Now I'd have to justify myself in front of a group of failed artists and stupefied administrators. Like hell I would.

"Have you been down to the gallery since you got back?" he asked innocently.

"Hardly, I was on the plane this time yesterday. Who have you got down there now?"

"Would you believe it – Paul – your friend Paul, he's come on a treat in the last year or so – and selling like ice cream does on a summer's day. You should take a walk down there."

I promised I would visit the place and then made some excuse to ring off.

I sat at my desk and pondered the situation. I was not aware of any offence I might have given to Manny, any word or deed that would have upset him. Consequently, I could only assume that his 'cold shoulder' had been a business decision. He must have decided that my potential sales in the immediate future did not warrant his further investment. Fine, I thought, fuck him. If he wants to play hardball then that's how the game would be played. I took a card from my wallet and made the transatlantic call to New York to the offices of Carl Jonathan Schwitters. His secretary put me through immediately and the big man seemed pleased to hear from me. I'd spoken to Carl only once before and on that occasion I'd turned down his offer to be my sole agent. He had not taken offence at my refusal but had insisted on giving me his card arguing that I may want to make a change at sometime in the future. Now I did.

We chatted for an hour or more and he told me finally that he'd be over in London at the weekend and that we could finalise the details then. Fortunately there was no love lost between Carl and Manny and rules of ethical consideration had no place in either of their working practices. His terms were similar to those boasted by Manny with the exception that he still saw a rich future for both of us via my art work. Naturally, we agreed that until the deal was signed, we should keep the matter entirely confidential. That same afternoon, I telephoned Manny's gallery and booked an appointment to talk to their senior exhibition officer.

My first twenty-four hours home were proving to be a very busy time indeed. However, there was still one piece to the jigsaw that I needed to find and after speaking on the phone to his assistant, I went over to talk to Jimmy Barratt in person.

Chapter Twenty-Seven

There was a bill on the mat from the engineering firm I'd employed to do the piss collecting. Another lay alongside from Pilkington's, this one for the glass containers. I'd been down to the studio the previous evening after Sam and the girls had gone home. I went to inspect the collection and found three huge cylindrical containers made in clear, hardened glass and each had been filled almost to the brim with human piss. Fortunately they were each capped with slightly domed glass lids, with rubber seals. I was informed on the delivery note that the base material had been delivered in a tanker and pumped into the cylinders from the doorway. Piss delivery was a reversal of the accepted sanitary proscription with the added potential of being deeply offensive, like something from a Breugel painting.

They'd stood there catching the light and reflecting a mid 'bladder' yellow onto the white walls when I opened the door. The whole room was infused with the yellow light – an excellent effect. I was well pleased. However, when I saw the bill I was less well pleased. Unless Carl could be persuaded to stump up some funds that weekend money was still going to be a problem, at least for the immediate future. The other glass containers stood along one wall; they were carefully packaged in bubble wrap and stored in heavy cardboard containers. These would need to be tested for balance and checked for damage before I could accept delivery. I'd designed them to be stand-alone structures, their bases being considerably heavier than their walls. They had to be guaranteed against leaking or instability. If a gallery – any gallery – were flooded with human piss the effect would be catastrophic… if perhaps fitting.

There was also a hand-written letter amongst the bills and I found this to be from Celia. During the process of supervising the engineers, she said, there had been minor decisions that needed making on the spot, these she had made on my behalf. There were also some sundry expenses – as she described them – amounting to several hundred pounds and although she did not ask outright for prompt payment, her description of her own constraints implied that repayment would be appreciated. I sent her a cheque immediately.

I spoke to Celia briefly on the phone and found her in poor health, suffering from flu. She was depressed, she said, on account of her latest lover leaving and also because her work was not selling as she'd hoped it would. I told her about my stay in the West Indies and advised her to make a visit to those islands, "… they are the best place on earth to find a relaxing environment," I said. Typically in return she asked if, as she'd heard, the men there had larger than average cocks. It was nice to know that she hadn't changed and I said I would call round and take her out to dinner one night. The idea seemed to please her.

I still had a special place in my affections for Celia and I was delighted that her 'serious artist' phase appeared to have come to an end. I knew, however, that she continued to apply herself almost exclusively to her work and therefore did not wonder that she could not maintain a relationship with anyone from the opposite sex. During our conversation she had again made one or two derogatory references to Jimmy Barratt and, despite my asking, she continued to refuse to say why. Naturally this made me all the more curious and I determined to seek an answer from her during our dinner date.

The thought of Jimmy reminded me of my second visit to his house the previous evening. To begin with it had been an uncomfortable occasion. His attitude this time had been brusque and business-like. He wanted none of my small talk and clearly had the impression that I had reneged on our agreement. At some point he told me that the previous owners of the deli now found themselves with serious money troubles and this he blamed on me. It was only after I explained the circumstances of my hasty departure following the rape hearing that his attitude softened.

"So you were screwing little girls, were you?" he said with a smile. "I thought you had access to plenty of big girls for that – like the Lady Phillipa. How is she by the way?"

Jimmy was quite shameless about his exploitation of people about him and I felt his reference to Phillipa – after all he'd made her suffer – was a little unnecessary. Also, it was all well and good him blaming me for Alfonso and Maria's plight but it had come about initially by his money-lending operations. However, I told him that I would pay the couple what I'd promised to pay them as soon as I had sold on the property in Soho.

"But you've only just bought the place," he said, "I thought you were going to go into the restaurant business."

"I was," I replied, "but suddenly I need the money. Things have become rather tight – a cash-flow problem."

"Do you need a loan?"

His inquiry was made in the most sympathetic of voices but I'd seen what chaos his rate of interest could cause and there was no way that I wanted that kind of relationship with the man.

"No thanks Jimmy, but perhaps you might know someone who would want to buy two nice properties in Soho?"

He smiled, "You'll need my permission to sell them this soon, Mick. You see I own the freehold."

Now this came as no big surprise to me, my informants had told me long ago that Jimmy was the actual owner. I came back at him quickly, "Fine – so give me your permission and we'll all make a profit without any problems"

"Are you suggesting there might be problems if I don't agree your sale?" he asked.

"There will be – at least for me. If I don't recoup some money quickly then I may have to go bankrupt."

He studied me for a moment then, with a straight face, suggested he buy back the lease from me for twenty percent less than I'd paid for it. It was one of those offers I felt I could not refuse. However, I negotiated the deficit down to fifteen percent before I agreed. Fifteen percent and half of what I'd agreed to pay Alfonso and Maria. Given the circumstances it wasn't a bad deal. To try and find another buyer, given Jimmy's involvement, would have been difficult if not impossible in my time frame.

We had a drink to celebrate the agreement and by now Jimmy's attitude had become rather friendlier – or so I perceived – but, almost in the next breath, he put me on the defensive again.

"Friends tell me that you've set up in business recently, Mick?" he asked. I raised a questioning eyebrow, uncertain what he was referring to, "Have I?"

"Something to do with the drugs supply business?" he said quietly.

My laugh was nervous, "No – not really. I just happened to come by some gear and thought I might show a modest profit by selling it on."

Jimmy shook his head like a disappointed parent, "You're either very ignorant or a crafty sod," he said, "didn't you know that the drug franchise in West London is mine – and – any deal involving large amounts of – say cocaine – need, to be cleared through me. Where did you get the gear from?"

"It belonged to some woman called Polly."

I had no hesitation in telling him about Polly. On the one hand I did not want to fall foul of this man and probably end up with broken legs, and on the other, I didn't owe her anything.

"I thought it might have been Polly. She should have known better – how about your friend Speedy?"

"Speedy. Oh – he was just the delivery boy."

"I see. Well thank you for being so honest, Mick. It makes a change for people to tell the truth without encouragement. It may interest you to know that Speedy has set himself up as an importer now. Currently he's trying to form his own network in competition to me. Silly boy. So – how much profit did you make on the coke?"

"Actually I lost money on the deal. You see I left Phillipa to look after it whilst I was in Trinidad and…"

"And she shoved most of it up her nose."

"That's right."

Jimmy sat back in his chair and smiled. "Phillipa sold what was left of your stuff on to me. It helped settle her gambling debts – crafty cow. She said it was your stash but I didn't believe her at the time." He looked into his glass for a few minutes and then added, "I reckon you owe me a share of your take on the drugs. Kind of a license fee for dealing in my area. I'll settle for – say ten grand."

"Christ, Jimmy, if I pay you another ten thousand, there'll be bugger all left from the lease money and I'll be back at square one."

Now his smile was very tight, "It's a hard life, Mick – but you're getting off lightly. Under normal conditions you'd be having a long stay in hospital for doing what you did. I'll tell you what I'll do – I'll pay you back the whole of the lease money, I'll settle your debt with Maria and her husband and I'll forget about the drug money… in exchange for a half share in the profits from your next two exhibitions."

And that's how we left it. I had a new partner but I also had enough ready cash to enable me to operate without financial duress.

As I sat paying my bills that morning I calculated that if Jimmy took half of my profits and Carl took his twenty-five percent agent's fee, I'd be left with only a quarter for myself. I'd been done over and there was little I could do about it.

That Saturday evening I met with Carl in the piano room at the Dorchester. It was an expensive place to drink and the gaudy décor of mirrors and gold leaf was not to my taste, but that was where Carl was staying and naturally the place he wanted us to meet – so we met there. Fortunately it was not one of Manny's regular haunts, so there was little or no possibility of bumping into him by accident. We took seats at the bar and Carl bought the drinks. He was every inch an American, wearing the loudest tuxedo in the room and the largest gold watch, ID bracelet and rings I'd ever seen on a man. I was not surprised therefore when he told me he had been born in Houston, Texas. Having said all that, he was certainly much more obviously generous than Manny had ever been. He would not let me pay for anything and before the night was out, agreed to give me a cheque for fifty thousand pounds to help pay for the manufacture of my next piece of art.

"Take it as a down payment, son, "he said grinning at me, "a token of good will if you like. I feel it in my water that we're going to make a lot of money together."

Carl was like no other agent I'd ever met. He never talked about art or what my philosophy might be and he never referred to the significance or the importance of what I might be doing, all he wanted to discuss was money. I saw him as a man after my own heart, an impression that was further amplified when, at the end of the evening, he invited me back to his suite where he said we could enjoy the company of four young ladies hired specially for the occasion.

In the lift going up to his rooms, he commented that, "These English girls certainly know how to keep a guy entertained and if you have them in pairs, the sky's the limit."

He was proved correct in every detail and I began to believe that I had found a soul mate in my new agent.

At Carl's invitation I agreed to make a lightening trip to the USA. It could have easily turned into a holiday but as there was still so much to do back in London, it was limited to a weekend. We flew out on the early morning Concorde and by mid-day we were enjoying a heavily biased liquid lunch in Manhattan. I saw the gallery, I met Carl's staff, once or twice we even discussed details about transporting the sculptures, but most of the time we drank, joked and screwed with a delightful bevy of willing starlets. By the time I made the return flight, I felt like I needed a week in a sanatorium to recuperate. I was not to know it at the time, but the notion of needing medical care was in fact well founded. It was during this visit that I contracted a dose of venereal disease.

The following day, despite my hangover, was spent at the studio signing the collection of mass-produced artefacts Sam and the girls had made. By now they were almost ready to start packing them in large cardboard boxes, ready to be shipped. None of them knew about my change of plan regarding their destination; that was to be kept as a secret between Carl and me. There was a lot of comment about the piss containers but I told them nothing about that either. As far as they knew, the glass cylinders contained only yellow-dyed water, a foible of the creative mind. It was a productive day and by four in the afternoon, after Dot and Mary had left, Susie, Sam and me sat around sharing a bottle of single malt whisky. I was still a little tired and hung-over from the previous night but when Sam suggested that we might enjoy giving Susie a fucking on the office settee, I could hardly refuse. As far as Sam was concerned, easy access to his three assistants was a perquisite of the job and so far none of the girls had complained. It was his practice to sweeten the agreement with a twenty pound note each time he indulged himself and this served to increase their take-home pay, often by as much as forty pounds per week. When he told me of this arrangement, I was shocked that he would spend so much of his salary on pleasure that was so easily obtainable elsewhere for free. In the event however, Susie proved such a willing and enthusiastic participant that I agreed to subsidise his daily shagging by increasing his salary.

It was eight o'clock before we were done with Susie. A most enjoyable four-hour fucking session that left me drained completely. I went straight home to bed and slept, like babies are reputed to sleep. The next morning I stayed under the duvet until gone ten, a rare treat for me, as I am usually an early riser. I did not sleep late however, but used the time to cogitate on my life-style and the direction in which I seemed to be proceeding.

In a general sense, there was no doubt about my good fortune; I was the luckiest sod alive. And despite the occasional hiccup in my plans, most things seemed to go my way. Money was the only problem but having said that, my money problems were nothing as compared to those my parents had experienced. By their reckoning I was wealthy. I decided that the whole money conundrum hinged on what or whom one compared oneself with. A good example was apparent in the state in which Phillipa currently found herself. No doubt she would claim to be hard up despite the mews cottage, the car and the leisurely life of ease. I had often thought how fortunate I was to be able to make objects that were so valuable and that it was almost like printing money, like having an investment that repeatedly paid high dividends with a minimum of effort needed.

Naturally at this point my mind turned to the work I had currently under consideration and I tried to analyse the reasons why it was so easy to shock society. There are three basic taboos in most civilized communities and these relate to a further group of things that frighten/surprise/shock/appal the general population. Cannibalism for example is one of the prime shockers and thereby all matters associated with eating things that are entirely foreign to our diet. Then there is incest – not a nice subject at all, but one also relating to all matters concerning deviant sexual practice, the production of sexual icons and any implication of perverse sexual interests including the focus on the human waste system – shit and piss. A whole folklore has been built around this essential function – one that, especially in the English psyche, has become a major part of the culture. We appear to be so ashamed of having to crap and to wipe our bottoms that we shut ourselves away in 'the smallest room' so that there are no witnesses. We advertise toilet tissue on billboards without ever commenting on what it is used for and we insist on the most extensive sanitary practice and potty training for our children but allow many of them to reach adulthood before they recognise words like faeces, anus or even penis. Even our history is suffused by stories concerning the use and misuse of what have become known as 'Water Closets'. And the stories in this context are many and varied. For example, the exclusive reservation of swans for use only by the Royal Family, apparently, once included the king using the swan's neck as an arse wipe. Not surprising then that so much of our English humour is dependent on anecdotes about bowel movements. What is surprising is that a section of the public is still shocked by such stories. But this is a paradox entirely consistent with modern society, much of which remains in a state of denial about so much of their human condition. Consequently, the main mass of the public is easily offended and I suppose this is why so much art today is about the shock factor. The final taboo was of course that which is associated with death.

*

I was pleased with my conclusions, satisfied that I had confirmed the things that motivated my work and, although the other voice in my head continued to scoff, I was nevertheless satisfied that I could justify what I did.

As I was feeling so good, I arranged to take Celia out that night and, although she was reluctant initially, I finally persuaded her that we should dine at Langan's, one of my favourite eating places. I had the cheque in pocket from Carl plus one from Jimmy. The latter representing what was left from the sale of the property in Soho. Moreover my creditors were prepared to wait for payment and I was at last in a position to repay Manny for the bad treatment I'd received.

Before I left the house I arranged to talk to Garry Hislop after lunch. Garry was the exhibition officer at Manny's gallery. Once upon a time he would have come cap-in-hand to me, begging me to show work there. Now, however, things were different. His attitude was patronising and he left me with the impression that I'd have to crawl over broken glass before he would permit me a one-man show. I dressed in a dark three-piece suit and a crystal white silk shirt for the meeting. First impressions are everything. And although I knew he would assume the upper hand and be unpleasant, I didn't want the little 'shit' to think I'd fallen on hard times.

At two o'clock sharp I entered his office and was asked to wait by his secretary. Typically for an unimaginative man, he had chosen an elderly woman to front his operation. She sat crouched behind her desk like a latter day Quasimodo in the bell tower, a crone without presence or personality – a fitting image, I thought.

Garry kept me waiting thirty-five minutes. An ill-mannered ploy designed to establish a hierarchy and one so old-fashioned that it had become meaningless. When he did appear, I was pleased to note that his suit jacket was crumpled and his shirt creased.

"Hello, Mick," he said feigning enthusiasm, "sorry to have kept you so long – busy, busy – you know how it is. Come on in."

It was the first time I'd been in this office. Manny had set up the gallery administration service sometime after the gallery had opened and wanted to keep it quite separate – a business arm. As a result it had been situated in a newly renovated block just off Berkley Square. Pretension it seemed followed pretension.

Once we were seated, me in a low hard-backed chair, he behind a monstrous desk, he applied the executive concern.

"So – good to see you. You haven't done much lately have you?"

"Enough – enough to keep body and soul together."

"That's good. Now what can we do for you?"

The assumption that he was suddenly a 'we' and that I might have any interest in whether he thought my progress was good or not made me smile – but I persevered, "I want to book the gallery for a big show," I said, "sometime in the autumn – if that's convenient."

He pulled a face as if he was constipated and suffering with haemorrhoids; "You mean the coming autumn, next year – of course?"

I nodded and he began to shake his head slowly, "I'll look in the diary of course – but I know we are fully booked." Then, as if the idea had just struck him he added, "I could include you in a joint show though – I've got a group of older artists showing at Christmas. Now Christmas is a good time for sales as you know and…"

"No, Christmas is out," I interrupted, "How about the spring – say late February early March?"

He pulled the face again and rose from behind the desk, "Best I get the diary," he said and he went to the outer office. There was a whispered conversation and I heard the old crone mutter that she'd never heard of Mick Grainger. I doubt she'd heard of Michelangelo either. Garry returned a moment later carrying a large appointment book, which he laid reverentially on his desk. He flicked the pages slowly, running his finger down each as though it was an account ledger and shaking his head as he went. I could not imagine that Manny had barred me completely from showing in the gallery. His investment had already been too great. I assumed instead that Garry had been instructed to make the situation as difficult as possible for me but that eventually he would relent and make a booking.

Garry looked up over the top of his glasses, "What sort of time period for the show, were you thinking of?" he asked.

"Well nothing less than a month. My stuff tends to be big and it takes a lot of time to install."

"Ah – yes – big art can be a problem."

"But the gallery was set up to show – big art as you call it. Wasn't it?"

He didn't respond but instead went back to his cod search. After a while he looked up again, "How would January suit you?" he asked.

So that was the game. Usually January was a dead month for sales, the dealers had all gone home and the gallery-going public stayed in front of their central heating radiators. I was to be condemned to January.

"Four weeks?" I asked.

"Only three I'm afraid. I can squeeze you in between a couple of American artists but it would have to be three weeks only."

I pretended to look disappointed. I sighed and shrugged my shoulders, "Okay – I suppose if that's all you have. But I'll need a couple of weeks for the installation…"

"Seven days only – and seven to take it out afterwards. Sorry – that's all I can offer."

There had been times in the recent past when I would have smacked his face for even daring to constrain me like this but now my agenda was different.

"Okay. I'll take it. Can you organise the posters and the private view – obviously you can bill me but it would save me a lot of hassle?"

He smiled, struggling not to grin. I suppose he was already imagining the praise he would get from Manny for screwing me down to such a tight deal. And of course he could organise the posters, the catalogues and the private view – and of course he would charge me three times the actual cost, that was the name of the game. The bastard really thought he was onto a good thing. He even had the audacity to ask me for a small deposit on account. However, I didn't mind paying him a deposit of one thousand, as I was about to cost him at least twenty-five thousand in return.

We parted on what appeared to be amicable terms but I knew he could hardly wait to get me off the premises before telephoning his boss. In the taxi I began to wonder if Manny might smell a rat. He was a cute businessman and he knew me well enough to know I wouldn't take this kind of treatment – certainly not from Gerry Hislop. But what could he do? He had no knowledge or evidence that I was playing a double game and he would never think of accusing me outright – that wasn't his style. I would make all the arrangements, order large amounts of publicity, get Manny to place national advertisements and to pay for the catalogues, and then at the very last minute, I'd cancel. By then all my things would have been shipped to New York and I could honestly claim that I had no work to show. The coup de grace would be when I informed him that he no longer represented me – and that would come at the end. I was beginning to enjoy myself all over again.

On reflection I think that the prospect of vengeance is probably one of my prime motivators. Almost as soon as I had set up the situation with Manny's gallery, I began to have new ideas for new work. I seem to need the edge that such aggression brings to stimulate my creativity, as though the prospect of upset and the generation of anger spark my imagination. I decided that I must get hold of some of the printed material produced for the exhibition, in that I could use it in the New York show. A piece of work describing an exhibition that never took place was a compelling idea. I could even include photographs of Manny and maybe Garry as well. A collection in a glass case – a parody on my own work. The more I thought about it the more I liked it.

The fact that the art produced by an artist is essentially about him seemed to fit. Perhaps a series of glass cases again, each one dealing with an episode in my life and, like the severed Rolls Royce of my first show, the episodes would be kept for posterity – a three dimensional diary.

My mood was so good that afternoon I went shopping for a present for Celia. She had sounded as though she needed cheering up and I knew how she liked to receive presents. After a lot of discussion with the manager of a well-known jeweller in Bond Street, I purchased a locket on a gold chain. A nice piece, inlaid with red and white gold, it opened to hold a small photograph and I had the inside engraved with the words, 'Memories of Marske from Mick'. I hoped it might make her smile. I liked to see Celia smile. Once upon a time I could often make her smile.

Still feeling generous, I telephoned Sam that evening and told him to go round to Phillipa's place and screw her.

"It's all kosher, Sam," I said, "Phillipa is on the payroll and she'll do it because I say so – and if you want to take a mate then feel free."

I then had the pleasure of informing the lady, telling her to expect an overnight guest and that she should entertain him without any reservation on her part. She was surprisingly docile about it and hardly made any objection at all.

Chapter Twenty-Eight

1986

The work went well. In November I paid another visit to the New York gallery. It was a grand affair with more than enough room for my pieces and when I returned, I completed the third in the series of 'diary' works. Already I had enough to complete the exhibition but I intended to carry on producing more. There was a point to be made to Manny and those dealers in London who seemed keen to write me off and I intended to make it as forcefully as I was able. I would flood the market with 'Grainger' works and then no one would be able to ignore me ever again. For the moment I discharged my staff at the studio sending them off on a long Christmas holiday just to get them out of the way for a while. The logic was simple; I didn't want any witnesses to the preparations I was making. I set up the glass cylinders as I wished them to be shown and made the studio into a mini exhibition space. It was difficult handling all the materials on my own but the results were well worth the effort. Turning the studio into a showcase reminded me of my first attempt to impress Manny – the occasion when Celia and I were still living together in the studio – happy times. Jon Adams from Pilkington's had been a real treasure. He produced the new glass cases in record time and had them delivered within two weeks. His advice had been invaluable and when the show was over, I intended to reward him with a nice cash bonus. Carl appeared to have the details of the exhibition well in hand, the posters were printed and the catalogues were already on site; apparently therefore there was nothing to concern me.

Perhaps on this account I found that returning to the studio after my trip to the USA made me strangely nostalgic for the North again and I began to consider a trip back there over the holiday period. It is not unusual I suppose for migrants to wish to touch their home base again, especially after a long spell away. As I get older, I begin to appreciate the significance of my roots and the influence they have exerted on my character. However, it was on an impulse that I actually decided to make the journey and to invite Celia to join me.

Since I'd given Celia the little locket we had seen one another on several occasions and, although none of these had resulted in the kind of intimate meeting we once enjoyed, we had become close again. Consequently, we spoke on the telephone at least three times each week and she joined me for dinner twice per month. She was fully apprised of the situation concerning Manny and me and knew something of my intentions.

One afternoon she invited me to visit her place of work to look at the things that she was making. Her studio was out in the sticks, a renovated warehouse near Heathrow airport. It was a big space and I was surprised to find it almost full of very accomplished pieces. There was no doubt that Celia had a talent, all she needed to achieve the success that she so obviously deserved was a new agent. I suggested that she should allow Carl to represent her and promised to get him to ring her as soon as possible. She was impressed and, as she was in such a good mood I told her about my plans to visit Teesside at Christmas.

"How if I came with you?" she asked with a cheeky grin.

"Believe it or not I was about to invite you."

"On one condition," she added. "I don't want to hitch-hike in lorries."

Later that evening I took Celia for a sneak preview of my exhibition. She had not been back to the studio in some time and was pleased to see the improvements. She was less pleased with the work however. She said she thought it was superficial and that I was capable of better. She criticised the 'shock' philosophy as being the kind of incidental idea best belonging in a sketch book, the three dimensional diary for being self-absorbed, and the *Piss-works* for its obvious bad taste. She was about the only person I knew who would state her opinions quite so openly and with such disarming honesty. Naturally I disagreed with her but didn't mind at all that she didn't understand what I was about.

Celia had worn well. She never tried to appear younger than her real age, nor did she try and dress in the style of younger women. She had kept her figure and her looks and I still found her very attractive. Consequently, before the evening was over, I suggested she might like to stay over at my place. To my delight and surprise, she agreed.

*

Stockton had not changed much since my last visit. This time however, we arrived in style, driving the Rolls. In anticipation of a family reunion I'd spent an afternoon shopping for Christmas presents in the West End and the boot of the car was therefore full of expensively wrapped parcels. Celia was probably correct when she said I was just showing off and that my generosity might be taken as being patronising by those it was aimed at. But I didn't care. I was determined that my mum and the coterie of relatives, who were bound to attend for Christmas afternoon tea, would experience a glimpse of my success.

When we arrived at the house the street was deserted. It had snowed the night before and the ice was still a hard glow on the evening pavements, somehow helping make the scene more than ever one from my childhood. I parked the car and went to the front door; to my surprise it was locked. After a short delay Mum opened it and it took her a moment to recognise me. When she did, however, her welcome tears were all that I expected and in minutes we were all three of us sitting before the kitchen fire, drinking mugs of strong tea. The welcome was thrilling; everything I'd imagined it might be – the tears, the roaring kitchen fire and two of my favourite women attentive to my every need. I always felt more successful back in Stockton, perhaps on account of the possible local comparisons and this also added to the thrill. Here, I wasn't just another face amongst a crowd of similarly successful faces – I stood out as being different. And the jam on the bread was that everyone in my hometown accepted that my success was entirely on account of my own, individual effort. There had not been a silver spoon in my mouth at birth, no legacy of property and nothing that was handed down worth a fig. This was true even with regard to my genes; being adopted meant that my DNA had been inherited from persons unknown. I was all my own work.

Given the satisfaction I experienced at my reception, one incidentally that was echoed tenfold by the admiration of those relatives with whom I came in contact during our week's stay, it was all the more disconcerting to find that the Christmas holiday I'd thought would be such a good idea, was such a failure. But perhaps failure is the wrong way to describe it – disaster would be more fitting. A total disaster at every level.

Firstly there was the total cock-up over the presents. Outside of a West End farce, it would be difficult to conceive of getting things quite so wrong. I'd gone to some trouble to choose presents for everyone and, unlike my normal practice, had ignored the price of the items chosen in favour of, what

I thought was, an appropriate selection for the individuals concerned. Of course, I was not to know that Uncle Derby and Aunt Molly had stopped smoking and that therefore, the heavy-duty table-lighter in onyx and gold would be a useless addition to their living room and a seductive reminder of the pleasures they'd so recently given up. Equally, although I'd been assured in a Bond Street store that the Moroccan leather handbag with matching wallet that I chose for Aunt Gemma was an exclusive designer product, the fact was that she was already the proud owner of exactly the same handbag – bought in a department store in Middlesbrough – and probably for half the price. And to some degree the same sad story was true of every gift I'd had so carefully wrapped for every person present on Christmas day. The silk nightie and dressing-gown for Cousin Patricia was being opened by her, just as she was telling the assembly of relatives an anecdote that included the information of how she had always preferred to sleep in flannelette pyjamas. The monstrously expensive, hand-knitted sweater in pure wool I'd bought for Cousin Billy was apparently the single most offensive material affecting his skin allergy other than sandpaper. And finally, I was told by my mother that the gold wrist watch I'd given her that she knew had cost me a king's ransom was beautiful – but that she would never dare to wear it for fear of attracting thieves.

The presents were therefore, hardly the success of the year. However, I consoled myself with the thought that, in normal circumstances I would not have cared a jot about the feelings of my relatives, so their disappointments on this occasion were actually incidental. My only concern was that I'd spent a lot of money to no good effect.

In anticipation of Celia's company, I had been looking forward to the resumption of the kind of intimate relationship we'd once enjoyed together. Indeed, in the two days before we set off on the journey north, we had slept together and, whilst the quality of our coupling was clearly influenced by the nostalgia it prompted, there was no doubt that, at least in this respect, we were good together. Unfortunately we had been in my mother's house only two hours before Celia began her monthly bleed. And as she is one of those people who suffer attendant cramps and profuse loss of blood for five days, although I was willing to overlook the inconvenience she was not and any thought of sexual intimacy had to be abandoned.

I must confess that this blighted the holiday for me from day one. Nevertheless, had that been the only blot on my Christmas landscape, I might have been better able to contend. The Fates however, work traditionally in threesomes and, whilst I might previously have scoffed at such a notion, I am now inclined to give the idea some greater credence. The coup de grace was delivered with the Christmas dinner. As I have explained previously, my mother was never what one might describe as a cordon bleu cook. She had always had difficulty preparing the simplest of meals and, in terms of culinary prowess, what she lacked in skill, she lacked even more in imagination. These were shortcomings that could be tolerated, however, if only because at least the food presented was usually prepared observing basic laws of hygiene. I was to discover to my cost that, since my father's death, even those precautions had been forgotten.

Some health enthusiasts might argue that undercooked vegetables are better for the constitution than those boiled to formlessness. The same folk could no doubt present convincing arguments in favour of undercooked beef and lamb – but no one, certainly in my experience, has ever promoted undercooked turkey. The doctor that was called on Christmas evening endorsed this belief and instructed the worried assembly that, if fowl was not cooked thoroughly, it could communicate a range of stomach bugs, including salmonella. And even though his confirmation would have been satisfying for me, by the time he delivered his verdict, I was in no condition to rejoice in his agreement.

The details of my three days confined to bed are hardly worth describing, sufficient to say only that, after my initial award as the gold medallist in the projectile vomiting competition, I came a close second in both the 'most sweaty-bodied' and the 'diarrhoea' finals. For twenty-four hours I was delirious, reportedly making the most outrageous statements about my sexual prowess and even on one occasion, propositioning my own mother. Once my faculties were restored sometime on day two, I concluded privately that if, as people around me claimed I had been close to death, when the time came for me to pass on, I would prefer to prompt the event myself. The natural causes one hears of are, in my opinion, anything but natural. Perhaps on account of my previous scepticism, on this occasion the Fates decided that my troubles should arrive in foursomes rather than three at a time. And the fourth was to prove even more of a trauma for me than any of the others.

On my first day out of bed I went out to inspect the car. It had stood untended all that week in the street outside the house. And, whilst the area in which we found ourselves may not have ever been the most salubrious location in the civilized world, it was far from being a slum or the kind of place where one might expect mindless destruction of private property or even casual vandalism. Having said that, it is also true to say that Rolls Royce cars are relatively few on the ground near my childhood home. Perhaps such an ostentatious sign of wealth proved too great a temptation for local graffiti artists, or maybe it was the finding of such large areas of unblemished white paintwork that inspired the emergent artist. Whichever it was, the product of the confused, if not diseased mind of some passer-by was a message, scratched into the coachwork – through more than ten layers of high quality cellulose paint – simply to inform me that I was a 'fuck face'. It was a legend that, on the one hand would cost a ridiculous sum to obliterate, and on the other, might prove an encouragement to those low-life denizens of dark places claiming redress against, what they perceived as, the unfairness of my acquisition of wealth. And although I am often heard to preach the gospel of tolerance and understanding, had the artist concerned been present, I would have cheerfully removed his liver with a broken bottle.

This was the final straw. The homecoming I had planned had resulted in one catastrophe after another. I excused myself to my mother, packed my case and my still delicate constitution, took Celia on my arm and set out to return to London.

It was not until we were well into the return journey that I thought to compare notes with my companion regarding her impression of our visit. Surprisingly she said she had quite enjoyed herself.

"It's what I miss the most," she told me, "the people are genuine up here. There's no edge to them. They say what they think."

Eager to be agreeable, I didn't want to dwell on the 'honest' response my presents had engendered or the 'honesty' of the message scratched into my car, instead I changed the subject. However, I could not resist saying, "Honest they might be, but cordon bleu chefs they are not."

Chapter Twenty-Nine

This was to be an important year for me, a year that would see major changes in my life. One in which the further establishment of my reputation as an international figure of repute in the art world would be confirmed. According to my plan, it was also the year when I would wreak my vengeance on Mr Manny Hume and on those 'brown-nosed' associates of his, the ones for which he had shown preference.

The single signed edition of coffee table books, the Heinz sauce bottles and the blank canvases had all been dispatched to New York by the end of January. The following week the glass cylinders and the huge container of human piss followed. The remaining glass containers – my autobiography – were still in production but were due to be shipped by the end of February. All was going well. The bonus still waiting to be cashed was the fact that no one knew that the exhibition scheduled to take place in February at Manny's gallery was to be cancelled. Garry Hislop had been in touch just after Christmas to inform me that my show would need to be delayed another four weeks and that I would have only ten days to mount the exhibits. Under normal conditions this would prove an almost impossible task but the delay also meant that the exhibition would be held at a more fashionable time of the year. Whether this signified that Manny had relented in his persecution of my career I did not know. The fact was, I did not know and did not care. He would have a four-week period with an empty gallery whenever it was. Fuck him!

By February 15th I was being petitioned daily by Garry to let him see the pieces I intended to show. He would phone each evening and, after polite inquiries about my health, he would suggest that he came round, "…just for a quick look." Unfortunately it was never convenient. There were other social functions that I could not miss; there had been a power cut, leaving me without lights and there was the bout of flu that I had mysteriously contracted. I knew Garry had been checking on the progress of my work at Pilkington's. My contacts there had told me as much. Consequently, as the pieces were actually in production he must have felt secure that I would deliver as promised. As the date for the installation approached, I approved the posters and collected a quantity for my own purposes and it was not until the day before I was due to arrive at the gallery, that I broke the news.

In keeping with the cavalier attitude he had shown me, I did not speak to him personally but at eight o'clock in the morning I left a message with his secretary instead. I simply told her to tell him that unfortunately, the exhibition would need to be cancelled as I was rearranging my affairs abroad. An hour later Manny was on the telephone.

"Mick," he said in his most business-like voice, "I think there's been a mix-up. Garry's secretary has the mistaken view that you cancelled the show."

I allowed a silence to develop before answering. "Yes," I replied.

"Yes – you know she has misunderstood – or yes – it is?"

"No. I mean yes, the exhibition is cancelled."

There was another silence. When he spoke this time his voice was soft, almost menacing.

"You can't do this, Mick. A lot of money has been laid out already. We stand to lose… well a significant investment – and you agreed to the show and…"

"I don't recall signing any agreement," I said interrupting, "I don't even remember agreeing the dates. Garry has been pestering me for days but I didn't make any commitment. So yes I can do this. I'm sorry if it's going to cost the gallery – but that's life."

"Are you serious?"

"Serious as I get."

"I'll sue."

"Sue away, you'll lose."

"But, Mick, I'm your agent…"

"That's something else, Manny. I've changed agents – there's a letter in the post."

Now I was really enjoying myself. The sleights I'd suffered, the insults flung casually in my face and all the insecurity his attitude had engendered – now the boot was on the other foot.

"Sorry, Manny, but you did get greedy – and as you apparently don't have any respect for what I do any more, I thought it was the best for everyone concerned."

The line went dead. Clearly he wasn't about to enter into any kind of discussion about the matter. He was probably onto his solicitors immediately.

Sure enough there was a letter on the mat the following day threatening a lawsuit, according to them, through my breaking a contract. My own lawyers had been well primed and I had them reply to the effect that any such litigation would be defended energetically. The following day I left with Celia for New York.

America's most important city was a joy by comparison with London. We were entertained royally every night for the first ten days. Nothing was too good for us. Carl had organised a suite of rooms at one of the best hotels and had guaranteed me three weeks in which to mount my exhibition. He had assistants standing by to make and take telephone calls; there were people to schedule and receive deliveries from England; secretaries to deal with the public and a personal 'executive' secretary at my beck and call twenty-four hours each day. This was celebrity status of the first magnitude and we used it for all it was worth.

The gallery was enormous and teams of men were constantly on hand to satisfy any alteration I might conceive of, to change the layout of the place. Partitions were erected, decorations were changed and best of all and the sculptures were sited without my having to lift a finger. The arrival of the work and its final installation went without a hitch. My secretary assured me that in the week following the opening, I was booked to appear on a number of TV chat shows and interviews and that a request had been made for me to deliver lectures at two of the premier colleges. It was like a dream come true.

Carl would contact me every afternoon, often just to see if I was happy. He called round one day to show me the catalogue – and the price list for the items on show. The number of noughts after each figure left my head spinning – we were talking millions of dollars. He said he could guarantee me a six-figure income for life and all the fame I could handle. He also said he had received a letter from Manny.

"He's very upset, Mick, says you did the dirty on him."

"I treated him – like he treated me. Do we need to worry?"

He laughed his deep Texan laugh. "Fuck him, son. Just remember that any publicity is good publicity. If he sues, we defend ourselves in kind. This could run longer than that show of yours in London – The *Mousetrap* wasn't it called?"

"But could he win the case?"

"In this kind of confrontation, the winner is always the one with most money – and I have more money than him."

The night before the opening, a pre-exhibition party was to be held at Carl's town house in Manhattan. He sent a stretch limousine to collect us and the driver had instructions to take us on a tour of the billboard sites around the city that boasted the poster advertising the show. It was startling to see the lines of monstrous forty-eight sheet posters showing a picture of a line of urinals in a men's toilet. It was an image designed to shock conservative America and the legend stated, 'Mick Grainger, English Piss-Artist.' As unequivocal a message as it was possible to send. We laughed all the way to Carl's house.

The party was as much a marketing exercise as were the posters. Everyone was there – at least everyone worth more than a couple of million dollars. There were film stars, sportsmen and women, Pop stars, politicians, people from the business world, art dealers and even one or two other artists. There were faces I'd previously seen only in the newspapers, faces from record covers and those from the silver screen and to some extent, they were all there to pay homage to me – Mick Grainger, the lad from Stockton-on-Tees, the adopted son of a cripple from a rented house. It was a dream come true. Given such a gathering, naturally the press crowded the entrance, which, by the time we arrived, had become a sea of popping flashguns. Carl met us at the door and began the ritual of the introductions. I shook hand after hand, kissed cheek after cheek, and grinned until the smile froze on my face. Once or twice I even had my bum pinched. And, whilst I chose to believe those doing the pinching originated from amongst the bevy of attractive young starlets present, I was also conscious that several well-known men's faces were rather more effeminate close-to than they appeared to be on television.

It was a night of excitement, a night when I at last achieved access on an equal basis to the glittering set. It was also a night spent talking. Indeed, I was held in conversation of one sort or another from the moment I entered Carl's home until the drive back to my hotel. And by the time I made the return trip, I had pockets full of invitations. I found that Americans are a generous people, only too eager to ask English visitors to stay in their homes, on their boats, to their dinner parties and to whatever celebration they may be about to host. I also received a number of propositions. There were those who offered to sponsor me alongside those asking to buy a share in my business; there were a few who wanted to become my agent and several more who proposed deals in which I would endorse their fast food chain, their fizzy drink, their soup or their sporting goods empire. As expected there were also those who offered the more usual, and the more unusual carnal pleasures. And, whilst those suggestions concerning money were referred to Carl, those involving free flesh were noted privately for future reference. America was certainly a land of opportunity it seemed.

At some point during the party Carl slid alongside me and whispered that the evening was a great success and he had every hope that the exhibition would sell out on the day it opened. He did not say so at the time but I discovered later that evening, that he had also received notice that Manny's lawyers were applying for an injunction to stop the opening of the exhibition from taking place.

I did not miss Celia until well after midnight. I had been so busy that her absence went completely unnoticed. As far as I could remember, she had certainly been at my side during the first hour or so but then she had disappeared into the crowd. Not being proprietorial however, I thought it best to give her whatever freedom she required. Instead of looking for Celia I spent some time talking to a tall brunette. Bernice was the wife of a merchant banker, she told me. Her husband was new on the art-collecting scene and had been persuaded that it was a good idea by his very attractive wife. More importantly she had convinced him that he should specialise in modern art rather than collect Old Masters. She was my kind of woman.

Typically Bernice was hungry for information. She wanted access to personal anecdotes, the kind of juicy stories she could tell her friends back in Oklahoma that would confirm the fact of her meeting with the artist. She even intimated that, if her meeting with the artist became rather more intimate and a friendship was formed, it would not offend her. If ever anyone was asking for a good humping this lady was – in spades. However, before our friendship could properly blossom, Carl sidled up to me, followed incidentally by a group of witnesses to suggest that we adjourn to the gallery.

"I think it would be nice to let these good people have a pre-preview of the show. What d' you say, Mick?" he asked in a stage whisper.

Now in principle, I had no objection to showing my work, especially not to a band of wealthy – potential customers. But it was already three o'clock in the morning and even in New York, people have to sleep some time.

"Great," I said, "but who are you going to get to open the place at this hour?"

"Leave that to your Uncle Carl. I'll make a telephone call and – hey presto."

I don't know who he telephoned, what he said to them or how much money was promised but five minutes later he announced that anyone wishing to see the exhibit now should follow him in their cars. We left in convoy. And, as promised, when we arrived at the gallery there were two men there ready to open the doors. This was madness but by then I was beginning to get used to crazy things from Carl. He was the complete opposite of Manny – Manny the control freak, the same Manny who would need months of preparation before he would act 'on impulse'.

We all entered the gallery together and the 'we' by now consisted of some forty people. They represented a residue of party guests who were still able to stand unaided despite the alcohol and other narcotic substances that had been freely ingested. Initially, the place was in darkness. It wasn't until we were all standing in the Great Hall, the first exhibition space that the light switch was pulled. The consequences were pure magic.

I had spent recent weeks in the gallery arranging and rearranging the exhibits, leaving instructions about the positioning of the works and tuning the finer detail. However, at Carl's suggestion I had agreed to leave the detail of the lighting to a lighting designer. I hadn't even met the man. But when the lights came on that morning, I knew whoever he was, whatever he was being paid – he was worth every cent. The effect was startling. The lights added just the right degree of drama, an ethos of sophistication I had not appreciated was possible and the gasps of my audience told me that they were also similarly impressed.

Everyone spread out to view the exhibition separately, a fact for which I was grateful. I preferred to see the work by myself – first time round. In the entrance there was a grand display around the reception desks showing my multiples in all their glory. The sauce bottles, the AYCD canvases and the coffee table books were stacked, surmounted against a background of life-size photographs of yours truly. It was like an advertisement for a movie. I hardly recognised myself and my skin began to tingle with excitement. This was the first time in my career as an artist that I began to believe that my work might really have some significance. Even the secret voice in my head, the one that always told me the truth about my motives was in awe. The Great Hall was filled with my 'diary' pieces and the catalogue described them as 'the life and times of Michael Grainger'. Various exhibits of different sizes were all shown in custom made glass containers courtesy of Pilkington's. Some were fixed to the walls, some on plinths and some were floor mounted.

The first, entitled, *One Summer in Italy* consisted of an underpants' tree and claimed to be the personal undergarments that I'd worn on a working holiday in Rome. The catalogue added in small print that they had not been laundered. Another was labelled as the, *Time Distractions to the boredom of a developing psyche.* This one included a long shelf containing a whole series of toys. It started with the rattles and teething rings of infancy and ended with the primitive electronic games preferred by twelve-year-old boys of the period. There were forty-five exhibits in this section and I'd used photographs, newspaper cuttings, letters, old clothing, diary entries, junk that I'd picked up on my travels and even some used condoms. None of it was my own. Art could not be more personal or introspective.

At the far end of the Hall was a smaller chamber and here I'd sited a group of pieces representing previous exhibitions. Pride of place went to the Rolls Royce in two parts and this was mounted, as before, on gigantic plinths with the glass cases at eye level. I'd included here the case containing Ram's painting. It had appeared at each of my shows across the world and although there had been offers, I'd always refused to sell it. It was a talisman, a good luck token and a memory of a good friend.

The third gallery, not quite as big as the Great Hall was off to one side and it was here that I expected to shock conservative America. This was my most important work to date I told myself. The lighting was lower in this space but sufficient to catch the columns of yellow in the forest of glass cylinders making them, as one critic had said, a verticality of sunrises. The room was crowded with glass cylinders of differing heights in columns of varying widths giving a first impression of a mid-spectrum colour exercise. In the distance was the sound of running water, not obtrusively just sufficient to register in the sub-conscious. By the time visitors reached the far end of the room, they were most likely persuaded of an aesthetic experience far removed from reality. The two cubicles on the far wall however, would disabuse them of such esoteric notions. These were two pissoires, designed to allow the visitor an opportunity to make the same kind of art as that which he had just witnessed. In other words to piss and to have his/her piss stored in glass containers as mine had been. Transparent plastic tubes ran from the cubicles to a large glass container where the fluid discharge was to be stored. The containers were hermetically sealed so that no accusations about a danger to public health could be levelled and the exercise, as far as visitors were concerned, was to do with influencing the colour of the fluid in the container.

I had finally called the piece, *Discharging the duty nature insists, during a decade.* The text describing the work claimed that the urine was all my own and had been collected during the preceding ten years. Like the other claims made for the 'diary' pieces, this was not true. Many of the bits and pieces in the glass cases in the other room had been obtained from Charity shops and jumble sales and of course the piss collection was from a public toilet in London. None of this mattered, as the importance lay in the idea not the product.

I was the first of the party group to reach the far chamber, so I stood to one side to watch the reaction of the others when they entered. If my plan worked as I'd intended there should be a transition from various levels of interest and appreciation to shock and disgust. I was not disappointed. However, one or two of the more adventurous amongst them even chose to christen the pissoires and the consensus was one of approval. Carl was delighted. He told me quietly that almost everyone there had taken an option on one or more of the pieces on show and that the profit margin would be fantastic when we did the final calculations.

It was a very successful evening and by the time I returned to my suite at the hotel the morning light was already in the sky. Celia had caught up with me at the gallery, excusing her long absence by claiming she'd fallen asleep in an armchair. I ignored the fact that I found she was knickerless when she arrived back at the hotel, glad that it was a sign her appetites had not diminished.

The official opening of the exhibition was set to begin at seven that evening and this allowed us to catch up on the sleep we'd missed through Carl's party. I didn't wake until well after noon and Celia slept until three. We had a meal served in the room and spent the rest of the day preparing for the next bout at the gallery.

I knew that this exhibition was special. This would be the one to establish both my reputation and secure my financial future. If all went well there would be no need, from this point onwards, for me to concern myself with the trivia of balancing my account. With the level of projected sales promised, I could rest on my laurels. Anything I produced now would be collectable only if the purchasers were exceptionally rich.

My father often used to paraphrase Burns, saying that the best laid plans, particularly of men, often go awry. It was an expression of which I was reminded that day. At six o'clock precisely Carl called round. His face was ashen and he clutched a bundle of documents when he entered.

"The show's off," he announced in a husky voice, "I've talked to the lawyers and they say we cannot proceed."

To begin with I thought this was a joke – that he would just as quickly say he was pulling my leg and that we should hurry so as not to miss the opening but that was not the case.

Manny had successfully applied for an injunction to stop the opening of the exhibition. He claimed that the work in the gallery was his property and that I could only exhibit it with his permission. Needless to say, such permission was not forthcoming. So much for Carl's boast that his money would protect us from litigation.

This was the beginning of a nightmare, a disaster of gargantuan proportions.

Chapter Thirty

1987

For those used to intense public scrutiny, some say there is a relief in anonymity. The same people tell me I should be glad at the absence of media intrusion and be pleased with the quiet opportunity for reflection that privacy brings. They describe the importance of, what they see as, the necessity to understand the new intimacy that accrues between oneself and the creative urge when solitude is possible. In the main however, these are people who have never been blessed with the attentions of the public nor the recognition that celebrity brings. I accept that the intimacy they describe may well be found for those dwelling in a rural setting, down some leafy backwater in Devon at the edge of a village where time might appear to be stilled. Not so however, if the taste of recent fame and the flavour of lost riches remain fresh; not so for those obliged to live in two sordid rooms in the middle of a city; not so either should the ideas for which one might justifiably claim authorship, now become common currency. Given my circumstances since my professional disaster, relief in this context is therefore not a word within the scope of my vocabulary.

My new friends are apt to make tentative but pressing inquiries about my material worth. They are polite but they remember press stories describing how a piece of my sculpture was sold for a million pounds. Generally I make no comment however, on those occasion when I am inclined to talk, I explain that £1 million was not an unusual price to pay for my works. This leaves them to believe I am still wealthy. I can see it in the looks they exchange. They imagine that my penury is a charade, my appearance deliberately contrived, affectations made for unwholesome private reasons. Nothing could be further from the truth.

And on the subject of friends – particularly old friends – I'm now forced to admit they have become an outdated currency. The face value of many has been devalued, apparently subject to inflation equal to a Third World economy. Few seek my company or wish to socialise with me. Fewer still attempt to help. Even those who in better days owed much to my generosity choose to ignore my telephone messages. In fairness I suppose that, given the opportunity of my contact, they fear I might try to borrow money from them. Given the opportunity they are of course correct. I suspect however, that my lack of popularity is more likely to do with my loss of face after my court appearance: a deliberate disassociation for fear of the infection spreading.

I never imagined that Manny could or would be so vindictive. I knew he was successful in business and, I suppose, that should have alerted me to his potential as an enemy but it didn't. As far as I was concerned, Manny was simply a big, clumsy oaf with a lot of money and little taste, particularly in modern art. I'd seen him be generous and I'd witnessed him being tight-fisted. I recognised that his preoccupation with deal making was his obsession and I realised he was insanely possessive about his acquisitions. But I did not know then that he had a vindictive bone in his body. I learnt differently on the day my New York exhibition was due to open.

With hardly a word of warning, Manny's American lawyers successfully applied for an injunction to halt the show. I was furious. Carl was furious and even Celia was furious. We held an impromptu council of war in my hotel suite and, after much discussion, we decided to fight. Carl reckoned that whatever the outcome, the inherent publicity would be worth millions of dollars in future sales. Consequently, we immediately employed one of the largest law firms in the city and instructed them to bring Manny to his knees. Posters were printed telling the gallery-going public that Manny Hume had stopped the show through his greed. The small print explained that it would nevertheless go ahead after a short delay. It was a strategy designed to ridicule my ex-agent but in the process it also provided him with a different public persona. After a few weeks he became almost as well known as I was.

For a while my name was on everyone's lips. Like a pop star, I was in constant demand for chat shows and interviews, my photograph appeared in popular magazines, and I was quoted in the press every time I opened my mouth in public. Suddenly there were never enough hours in the day or days in the week to satisfy all the invitations I received. I found myself giving talks to politicians, to women's groups, to college students; I awarded prizes at high schools, judged beauty contests and even opened a new department store. And, whilst this was all great fun and a superlative sop to my rapidly enlarged ego, during this period there was no real money coming in. On the contrary, there was a lot of money being paid out. Initially I had not appreciated the extent of the injunction. However, I soon found out that, pending a legal decision on ownership, it stopped the sale of any of my works, anywhere in the world.

If I had known that the litigation might endure for fourteen months, I may have been more inclined to try and reach a settlement with Manny. But no one can ever say how long these cases will run for, not even very expensive law firms whose lawyers wear button-down collars and two thousand dollar suits, who bill by the minute and charge for every incidental – even taxis. Fourteen months was a long time to go without any kind of income, certainly longer than my cash base could comfortably sustain and, for the first time, I began to appreciate what my running costs actually amounted to. There was the studio in London with four employees – reluctantly, I fired them all; there was the property – I sold it, the cars – I sold them too. All that I had left of any value was a modest deposit account in the Channel Islands and a collection of work that I wasn't allowed to sell.

Nine months on, shortly after the first full hearing (and the first disappointment) I rented a small studio intending to make some new pieces. I argued that if all the other stuff were under an embargo, new works must be exempt and selling them would allow me to pay my bills – at least. Again Manny was way ahead of me. As his lawyers told me when I tried to trade some drawings through an auction house, the injunction claimed that through our contractual agreement, Manny was solely responsible for the sale of all or any of the work I produced. And that meant ever! Or at least until a judgement was handed down.

We tried to negotiate a deal – but deals were Manny's special province and he didn't want just an arm and a leg – he wanted the whole cadaver. Try as we might there was no hope of compromise.

The appeal was heard just before Christmas and our legal representatives, seeking to elicit sympathy for a young artist from England trying to make his way in the labyrinth of art world big business, decided I should give evidence on my own behalf. They rehearsed me to perfection before I took the stand. I knew every answer by heart. Unfortunately, the opposing counsel had other ideas and I found that I was not familiar with any of his questions. It was another nightmare. Manny's men had done their research and in order to counter the claim made by my representatives that I was a person of integrity and unimpeachable character, they raked over my past with a toothcomb. They produced sworn affidavits from students with whom

I was once at college, testifying to my deceitful intent in purchasing their work. The work was described in detail and then compared to photographs of that which Manny had first bought from me. Clearly it was one and the same. They brought Ram's parents across from England to swear that the painting shown in the big glass case currently exhibited as my work, was in fact an art work produced by their late son – my friend. And the coup de grace when it eventually came (and by then I was half expecting it) presented evidence alleging my involvement both in thefts from cars and the statutory rape of a minor. Little attention was given to the fact that none of these charges was ever brought successfully to court still less, proven. The accusations grabbed the headlines and the mood changed. That day I learnt a hard lesson about American justice.

Up until the time of the appeal, the press had been largely on my side. It made good copy to stand up for the underdog. And when that underdog was a young English artist trying to show his stuff in a major gallery in New York – against all odds – public empathy was almost guaranteed. In their eyes at that time, Manny represented a suspect aspect of the British establishment. He was the grasping profiteer with all the traditional signs of pompous British superiority that the American public hated. As taxi drivers were wont to tell me, the Yanks had kicked them and their sort out years ago. However, when selective news of my past was released, public opinion swung completely against me. Suddenly I was the foreign confidence trickster trying to break his contract with a legitimate businessman; biting the hand that had fed me. The mood became aggressive. The headlines screamed for justice, for legal recourse, demanding I should be deported and that the exhibition should be dismounted.

Manny's fondest wish was satisfied and, by the time the lawyers had been paid, I was bankrupt. I avoided the potential of claims from Carl – for entering into an illegal contract, deception and misrepresentation simply because I had nothing left to take. Celia paid for my passage home and, although she remained my friend, I was never again to be welcome in her bed. She had known full well about the strategies I'd employed on my way to the top. In fact she had been partly to blame having been responsible for suggesting some of them herself, but none of that made any difference.

On my return home, I found a two-roomed flat just behind the train station in Hayes, Middlesex and tried to kick-start a new career. Sadly it seemed that in the applied arts, such as advertising, those traditional skills that I had always scorned were precisely the ones required. For a while I became a window dresser but after only a short time I discovered that to succeed in that career meant changing my sexual preference from women to men: unlikely possibilities even given my proclivity for survival. One afternoon, I even went back to the Studio Club to see if my friends there might find me a niche. It had closed twelve months ago, according to the new owners, an event presaged by the death of Miss Winterness who had suffered a fatal heart attack in the bar. I tried to contact Phillipa, after all she still owed me a considerable sum of money but she was untraceable and had apparently sold her pied-à-terre and moved to an unknown address.

Deeply frustrated, I finally got in touch with Jimmy Barratt. He was the only person other than Celia to offer me more than sympathy. He invited me to his house just as if nothing had happened and received me in exactly the same way that he had previously.

That afternoon, we sat in his luxurious study, in the same deep-buttoned armchairs as before drinking the same excellent single malt whisky.

"So, Mick – hard times are upon us I hear?" he said smiling.

"It's a temporary situation," I lied.

"Really."

"Look at it like this, Jimmy. Manny Hume invested a lot – and I mean a lot of money in my career. He owns a massive collection of my work, so it can't be in his interest to see me disappear. Sooner or later he'll want me back."

Now Jimmy was smiling more openly, "One of the things I always liked about you Mick was your optimism," he said, "you're the most gullible man I ever met. Surely if Manny has all this work, he doesn't need you. He can feed it into the market a bit at a time and reap huge profits. All he needs now is to market the work instead of marketing you."

The truth of what he said was obvious and it made my one remaining hope leak away. He must have seen the change in me.

"But that's not the end of the world," he said quietly. "You have talents – other talents, some of which I might be able to employ myself. How would you like to work for me? On a freelance basis if you like?"

It was a lifeline and he knew I couldn't afford not to grasp it.

"Doing what exactly?"

"There are lots of things you could do – how does being a courier suit you? Failing that you could recruit couriers?"

The idea of ferrying illegal substances across national borders was déjà vu. I recalled someone else years ago, the night of my inauguration at my

London college, trying to recruit me for the same purpose. But that was a lifetime ago, a time when I had other options.

We went on to talk about the relative cash rewards that might be enjoyed if I was to be employed in the various positions Jimmy had described. Clearly, if I were to recruit lots of innocents to do the run to Holland or Eastern Europe, the money would be fantastic. I knew this was a difficult assignment however, and although the courier's wage was less, that seemed the most immediately profitable. Seeing the way my thinking was biased, Jimmy amplified the proposition.

"It's piss easy actually, Mick. You take a run over to Amsterdam and collect a package. You bring it back and I pay you... Let's say four hundred quid, seeing as how it's you. The only tense moment is coming through customs"

Now it was my turn to grin. We both knew that importing drugs was an offence that could land me in prison. But Jimmy ignored my smile and went on, "The secret in getting through customs is always to look ordinary – and if possible, to be accompanied by a wife and kids. That never fails. How you do this is of course your own business. Needless to say, however, should you get picked up, you stay schtum."

What could I say? I badly needed to earn and no one else was queuing up to offer me employment – so I signed up and became a drug mule.

It was a bit like starting out all over again on a new career. So many people to meet so many places to go and so many new skills to acquire. My first trip to Holland was effortless. Dressed in a 'straight' dark suit, I flew to Amsterdam and took the ferry back. I returned with a large suitcase of various pills and powders and delivered these to an address in Slough where I was promptly paid in twenty-pound notes. Other trips to the same destination were equally without incident and for a while I began to think that the customs authorities were just as stupid as everyone would have me believe. Fortunately for me, the first time I was 'pulled', the suitcase I was importing was located in the boot of a car belonging to a friendly couple I'd met on the ferry and who had kindly offered me a lift. I didn't overplay my innocent act and as a consequence I was let off with a light search. The officers went through my briefcase and an overnight bag I was carrying and then 'patted' me down. Finding nothing worthy of their efforts they apologised for the inconvenience and allowed me to go. A senior customs officer advised me to beware of carrying other people's luggage and told me that it was the frequency of my visits to Holland that caused their suspicion.

I telephoned Jimmy that same evening and requested a different target destination.

"Better that I'm not seen going to Holland too often Jimmy, they're suspicious."

"If you were to stop going now Mick, they'd get even more suspicious," he said, "but I take your point. I'll find somewhere else for you in a little while – just be patient."

And that was his last word on the subject. The Amsterdam run was to remain my exclusive province for some considerable time to come. To be fair, there were occasions when I was sent to other European capitals to make collections but these were few and far between. During the next two years, my regular two-day trips were made each fortnight and the money I earned proved just sufficient to maintain the basic essentials for a life-style only one step removed from that of a homeless person. Truth to tell, had I not been able to organise a small business of my own on the side, I could not have maintained a base in London. The small package of cannabis resin I purchased on my own behalf every two weeks produced a profit, enough to provide me with a small taste of life's luxuries. Needless to say, Jimmy had no idea that I was also in business for myself. Had he been aware of my entrepreneurial activities, I imagine that our association might have been terminated abruptly – and possibly with a certain amount of violence followed by a long stay in hospital for me.

I couldn't help but think that had the US legal system not been so vindictive, it might have obviated the need for my involvement with Jimmy Barratt. The worst effect of the court decision was to reinforce the contract with Manny Hume. In their wisdom, the judges decided that, given the level of his investment, it was only fair and proper that he should have exclusive control of any of my products for a decade. A ten-year embargo that precluded my dealing with anyone else concerning the sale of my Art works. I suppose I could still have made a more than reasonable living despite Manny's fees but I was determined that for ten years, he should reap the dividend only to the letter of the law – I would make nothing else. In other words, my agent would have a fifty percent share of nothing new.

My share of the sale of the works in the abortive New York exhibition plus various sundry purchases made by collectors had been added to the list of my assets in settling my bankruptcy. The multiple sculptures and paintings (the blank canvases, the ketchup bottles, and the coffee-table books) all sold out within days of the court's resolution and despite Manny's requests, I was not prepared to produce more. Naturally, once he began to appreciate my strategy, he was furious. However, whilst the Court could insist that anything I produced would be partly owned by Manny, they could not insist that I produced anything at all. I decided I would have a ten-year holiday from the visual arts, I was confident that I could earn my living doing something else and Manny could go fuck himself.

It was only after I'd been a delivery boy for Jimmy Barratt for two years that I discovered the existence of 'skunk'. Skunk is a virulent variety of marijuana, fast growing and many times stronger in its effect. It is best grown in conditions where light, heat, and irrigation are strictly controlled and, due to the abominable smell of the plant, in a place where the air supply is carefully filtered. It should be explained that, although there were numerous producers of marijuana in the UK, for the most part they were small and insignificant. And whilst some did sell small amounts to friends, usually the garden crops they produced were for the benefit of their own habit. The fact was that they could not grow enough to satisfy the increasing market for a 'quiet smoke' and this necessitated the import of huge quantities from the Continent. Skunk changed all that.

Skunk was developed with the assistance of a couple of scientists who had access to laboratory facilities. A hybrid, in which the content of a certain chemical was hundreds of times more concentrated than anyone had ever thought possible. The only disadvantage was its smell. During the growing process, it generated a noxious aroma, sufficiently pungent to permeate large areas around the production site. And, although the sensory organs of local policemen are not known to be their greatest attribute, the smell was such that it was impossible to ignore.

In a relatively short period of time a number of new growers sprang up only to find themselves, on account of their activity being so easily detectable, subject to serious fines and occasionally to jail sentences. In an effort to dissipate the effect of the prevailing stench, some of these tried to locate themselves in far-flung places in the open countryside but largely without success.

It was one of my Amsterdam connections that first offered me one of the new plants. He told me that by careful husbandry I could propagate the original within a month or so and eventually enable a sizeable crop. He explained that, although the mother plant was expensive, once I had grown a couple of dozen shoots, I could look forward to a crop every six weeks. A crop that could easily sell on to dealers for as much as six thousand pounds. In one bound I became a horticulturist.

The plant I purchased lasted precisely ten days and although initially it shown all the signs of the rapid growth I'd been promised, I was left with a withered stump through lack of water. Clearly I needed expert advice. Not having easy access to such expertise, I started to spend some time at a local garden centre where I struck up a friendship with one of the gardeners. It seemed like the obvious place to start. Steven, the young man in question, was just out of college, away from home and very hard up. He was a mine of information and only too pleased to impart it when I treated him to a pub lunch. The garden centre where he worked paid him only subsistence level wages and he said he was keen to earn more – doing almost anything. As a result of my inexpert questioning he quickly deduced what I was about and although he knew nothing about skunkweed, he was full of ideas as to the best ways to propagate it.

Fortunately there were a number of small industrial sites around the Hayes area where one could rent premises without attracting too much attention. Consequently for a modest sum, I took a small unit at the back of one such site, a place immediately adjacent to a railway line. It was the last unit in a row of old warehouses and although it boasted the basic services, the security was almost non-existent. With the promise of suitable cash compensation, Steven worked with me for two weekends to provide the necessary alterations and although the result was nevertheless a little makeshift, he said it would make possible the conditions required for my needs.

There were three basic requirements. The first concerned the constant supply of water for the plants, the second a controlled environment for light and heat and the third, a filter system to get rid of the smell. Accordingly, we built two rooms inside the warehouse, fabricating the walls, floor and ceiling from marine plywood and sealing the joints to make the spaces as air-proof as possible. Inside each space we put together a series of waterproof troughs filled with vermiculite and lined with pond-liners. Our irrigation system was primitive consisting only of pumps to keep the water circulating and plastic bins filled with water to act as top-up reservoirs when necessary. For the lighting we installed a series of UV lamps controlled by a time switch and the same switch was set to operate two extractor fans fitted with dense filters. Theoretically at least, we had provided a completely controlled environment that would be undetectable and almost maintenance free. All that remained was for me to buy more plants.

On my next trip to Amsterdam I found that typically, whilst the plants were still available, the price had doubled. Instead of the six I intended to buy, I could therefore only afford to bring three back with me. This time, however, I had qualified help on hand to ensure their continued good health. Inside ten weeks we had a complete collection. In one space the larger plants were allowed to grow to fruition and in the other, the cuttings were left to develop. Another six weeks on and we were ready to crop the product.

The shortcoming of the scheme was the fact that the only client we could possibly sell to was Jimmy Barratt. Jimmy was the 'Mister Big' of the West London drugs world and trying to bypass him would have been a recipe for certain disaster. On the other hand there was no way that I could represent myself to Jimmy. I was already his employee and once on the payroll with Jimmy there was no room for private enterprise. I needed a middleman and there was only Steven to choose from.

I consoled myself by arguing that in June Mrs Thatcher had been returned for a third period in office and she was known for her admiration of the entrepreneurial spirit. If I was nothing else, I was certainly an entrepreneur. Unfortunately in October the bottom fell out of the stock market and some fifty billion pounds was wiped off the value of publicly quoted shares. It seemed that I was not the only 'chancer' who was suffering. I only hoped and prayed that Manny Hume had been caught in the disaster.

Chapter Thirty-One

1997

My ten-year isolation from the world of art and artists affected me only in two respects; it represented a loss of status and a loss of relatively easy money. And if the money had acted as a lubricant for the engine of my career then the status was certainly the fuel that fired it. I enjoyed the celebrity and revelled in the attention it brought and although, during the interim period, I had found alternative ways of making money, the lack of comparable status removed much of the joy. Much of the time it felt as if I had been demoted.

Having said all that, the fact remained that there was still a body of work the origins of which no one could deny represented me. I had made it and no one could take that from me – not even Manny Hume. I appreciated that, in some sense, I had through my own actions conspired to annexe myself. It was my own decision not to work – as long as my work was to be represented by Manny. However, I suspect even if my decision had been otherwise, the consequences might have been the same. The art world, particularly in London was ever a fickle creature and had reacted badly to the disclosures in the US Court. It saw the exposures as an apparent loss of control on my part. Paradoxically, the work was still popularly controversial but its maker was no longer acknowledged. It was almost as though I'd died and been sent to limbo.

On the occasion of the tenth anniversary therefore, I promptly made an application through my solicitors to be released from the court injunction binding me to Manny Hume. The response was automatic and suddenly I was again free. The anvil Manny had placed on my shoulders was at last removed and I was able to resume my true vocation. Now it was time for me to have my 'pound of flesh'.

My lawyers immediately demanded an itemised list of all the art property of which I'd been responsible that was still held by Manny. A move intended to re-establish my ownership and to allow me to re-evaluate my financial position. The list was a long time coming. When it did arrive, it was a masterpiece of double bookkeeping. It took my accountants four weeks to analyse the detail, only to conclude that currently none of the works was held by Manny, they had all been sold. And in respect of my share of the profits after Manny's expenses were paid, I was sent a cheque for one hundred thousand pounds. As I'd been led to expect a return of more than 1.8 million pounds, this was yet another disappointment. There was little I could do without engaging in a protracted legal wrangle, the fraud was seamless, the joins invisible. The bastard had done it to me again.

I had long since planned that at soon as I was free of Manny, I would take whatever opportunity that afforded itself to irritate his business and to ruin his reputation. During the period of my self-imposed exile, the fashion for Conceptual art had surged and the value of pieces I'd made previously had reached ridiculous proportions. Even the Ketchup bottles were fetching high prices. I knew therefore that my reappearance on the scene would cause a renewal of interest, hopefully one from which I would benefit as before.

On the morning of my 'freedom' I received two cards, each to varying degrees offering me congratulations on having served my term. The first boasted a sea view with a gull in the foreground and inside it said simply, 'Well done. Fuck art – let's dance!' It was from Celia. The other was from Steven and had been posted in Detroit. Steven was much more sentimental and filled the available space with turgid expressions of good wishes. By all accounts, he was still in the throes of a hero-worship-cum-gratitude syndrome and obviously still regretful that I had never accepted his homosexual overtures. His card gave me pause to recall our long business association. A partnership that had almost cost him his life, leaving him with a 'stripe' the length of one cheek. The scar was Jimmy's response, a punctuation mark in the negotiation he had carried out with Steven concerning the supply of skunk weed.

Steven had agreed with me that the best way to market our product was through Jimmy. He'd been sympathetic when I described my own difficulty in this regard and, without any prompting from me, had offered to 'front' the deal himself. The plan we hatched therefore was that he would tell Jimmy the project was his alone and that the location of the skunk factory was out in the Buckinghamshire countryside well beyond the M25. The site of our operations was especially relevant in that anything on the London side of the motorway would fall within Jimmy's administrative region.

Typically Jimmy's immediate response to Steven was to suspect him of undermining his authority. To begin with he wanted to visit the factory and when this request was refused, he asked for details of the way the scheme had been financed. Steven was adamant and argued that the integrity of his operation was his business alone. The deal was eventually struck but unknown to either Steven or myself, Jimmy had my partner followed.

The money rolled in and life became easier. After a suitable period of time, I resigned from Jimmy's employment, claiming that the stress associated with my part in the illegal import of hard drugs was too much for me. He took my retirement amicably and even made me an ex-gratia payment of a thousand pounds for my faithful service.

All went well for a year or so, Steven continued to supply the product and Jimmy continued to pay well for it. Naturally I stayed in the background, spending at least some of my time monitoring the growth of the plants, taking cuttings and ensuring the semi-automated process ran without fault. The problem arose when one of Jimmy's minions reported to his boss that Steven had been seen loading boxes from a warehouse in Hayes. The warehouse was put under observation and in no time at all Jimmy realised that our factory was actually on his turf. Fortunately for me no one at that stage had seen me visiting the site and I was made aware of the impending crisis only by a chance conversation with one of Jimmy's associates. I telephoned Steven to warn him and immediately moved our production site to another warehouse on the outskirts of Reading. The move was a complex operation and, even with paid help, to re-establish the conditions necessary for a healthy product took several days. We took the precaution of leaving several boxes of goods at the Hayes site providing the argument that it was used only as a staging post before delivery. This did nothing to assuage Jimmy's bad humour and on the occasion of the next delivery he cross-examined Steven. Clearly he did not believe our concoction of lies and had my partner beaten. He said that as the factory had been inside his territory, he was due fifty percent of the profit from day one. To make his point he introduced Steven's face to the sharp edge of a cut-throat razor and gave him three days to raise the cash.

There was no doubt in anyone's mind that should Steven prove unable to meet Jimmy's demand, he would end up floating face down in the canal. Steven had to vanish; it was the only option. Neither of us wanted to pay Jimmy and, more importantly, neither of us had sufficient capital available to satisfy the extraordinary amount of cash he demanded. We'd been making in excess of two thousand pounds per week profit but, without regard to the future, we'd been spending it almost as fast as we made it. Consequently, Steven left the hospital that evening with thirty stitches in his face and took the first available flight from Heathrow to New York. I guaranteed him a twenty-percent share in future business and sent him on his way with my blessing.

I was glad that my partner had escaped his fate but was left with a twofold problem. I could not operate the production and distribution of the skunk without help and I could not approach Jimmy to offer the drug for sale without exposing my involvement. I did not appreciate however, that as we had created such a market for our product supplies could not be simply cut off without repercussions. A week later, in the midst of my ruminations about what I should do, I had a call from Jimmy asking me to call on him. Dutiful as ever, I travelled to his home that same evening. I found him in an irritable mood and looking to me to find a solution for him.

"I'm in a bit of a fix, Mick," he said once we had settled with drinks in his study, "a supplier has done a runner, and I need someone to be a producer for me."

"Producing what exactly?" I asked innocently.

He studied me for a moment over his glass and smiled, "Like you hadn't heard eh? Like you weren't aware that my skunk-weed producer had hit the road leaving me in a hole?"

I tried to maintain my poker face and after a moment he continued, "Let's cut to the chase, Mick. You know all about skunk don't you?"

"Some…"

"Well you certainly know more than most. You cross-examined old Jasper over in Holland about it – or so I'm told, so you'd be the ideal person to grow it here. How if I was to set you up and cut you in for – say twenty-five percent. Interested?"

I pretended to think about it. The cheeky bugger wanted me to reduce his on-costs and I wasn't having any of that.

"How if I set myself up and became your new supplier – exclusively of course," I said.

That made him laugh, "I thought that's what you might come up with – a clever sod like you will always see the wrinkles. Okay. But not on my turf. If you set up on your own you must do it beyond the M25, you take all the risks yourself and… and you put up the cash yourself. A deal?"

"A deal."

"Also – as you said – you supply only to me."

"Who else round here would buy."

So once more I went into business with Jimmy Barratt. This time, however, I made all my own decisions. We agreed a price and the estimated delivery dates for each six-week cycle, shook hands on the deal and I left a happy man.

It had been the revenue from my 'factory' that had eventually restored my financial fortunes and allowed me to begin thinking again about my art. As a result, the remainder of the ten-year isolation had been served without undue financial embarrassment. The earning potential was great and, even when I paid Steven's share into an offshore bank account, there had still been plenty left over to furnish a comfortable life-style. I nevertheless realised, however, that the money was only part of what I'd missed. In drug dealing any notion of celebrity is necessarily anathema to the dealer. The last thing he wants is to be identified. Indeed, if the dealer is to retain his freedom, much of the effort involved is to do with maintaining his anonymity. My conundrum therefore was caused by an uncontrollable if not capricious desire to be famous again.

When Steven had helped me set up the factory and even when it had been relocated, I'd made certain that it was his name that was used in any or all of the transactions involving outsiders. As far as the world outside was concerned, it was Steven's operation and I was just a nameless employee. Originally this strategy was designed as a safeguard against discovery by Mr Barratt but, in the new context, it also provided me with a whipping-boy should the police ever take more than a passing interest in my activities. And in order to confirm the subterfuge, I kept records of all the money paid into Steven's account. If I were ever found to be culpable therefore, it would be only as a helper rather than as the originator of the scheme. I was proud of the way it had all worked out so well. Unfortunately, I could not boast of the plan to anyone and had to content myself only with the rewards that the profit brought me.

On the morning of my tenth anniversary I was therefore pleased to hear from Steven, more so because he was still satisfied with his share of the business and content to live abroad. His return, should he choose to come home, could herald all manner of complications especially if Jimmy had the chance to cross-examine him.

By that time, I had employed two ex-art students to run the growing side of the skunk farm. My only actual involvement then was in delivering the goods and collecting the cash. As a safeguard against eventual discovery by the forces of Law and Order, my employees had also been led to believe that an American called Steven was the ultimate authority responsible for the decision-making side of the business. And to reinforce that idea and to provide me with independent witnesses, occasionally I asked one or the other of them to bank Steven's share. It was a sound project and as safe as it could be under the circumstances. From that point on, however, I was determined that life was about to get better still.

I telephoned Celia to thank her for the card and in the process, made arrangements to take her out to lunch. By now she was well on the way to establishing herself as a 'name' in the art market. Since winning a prestigious award the previous summer, the sales of her work and the demand for her appearance at all kinds of public events had increased tenfold. Celia however remained much the same as ever – thankfully.

We met at the Ritz where I had booked a table for lunch. Although we had remained in contact on a regular basis, I had not actually seen Celia for some time. Her appearance was therefore something of a surprise. The naturally golden hair was now bleached with streaks, the generous figure had become a little over generous and on closer inspection her face was beginning to bear the signs of her past over-indulgences. The laughter lines were more deeply engraved and the pouches round her eyes, that much more pronounced.

"Hi, sexy," she said kissing me.

"Hi, yourself. You look good enough to eat – as ever."

We took a moment to scrutinise one another. An honest appraisal with critical awareness only close friends could tolerate.

"You don't change, Celia," I said diplomatically.

She laughed and shook her head, "Mick – if you intend to bullshit me I'll leave right now. Get me a drink and tell me how my wrinkles suit me – but don't tell me lies."

We took our drinks to a table and exchanged our respective news. She was planning a major exhibition in California and was full of tales about the sunshine state and its crazy inhabitants. She said she had seen Manny in the USA recently and that apparently his business was not doing quite so well. I knew differently and took this as a sop to my continued antagonism to the man but let it pass without comment. She also told me that, if I was interested, her gallery in England was prepared to represent me. This was good news indeed. My only concern during my lay-off had been how to find an agent once I made my return. Agents are inclined to close ranks on such occasions and, like the parasites that they are, prefer to suck the blood of only those with a recent history of success. There was also a tendency for them to ignore anyone who had demonstrated an antipathy to others of their kind.

"Maurice Clare-Jones is the man you want to see," Celia told me. "He's okay but he'll try and screw a high percentage from you."

"But is he willing to invest anything?" I asked.

"Do you need investment? I thought you were solvent – more than solvent?"

"I'm sound enough financially but…"

"Don't start to wheel and deal with these people, Mick. I recommended you highly and if you fuck up this time, it will reflect badly on me."

Suddenly it was clear that Celia had twisted a few arms to get me this new start. I was being courted only on account of her recommendation. The thought rankled – but what the hell. I needed representation in order to increase exposure and once I had re-established myself they could go for a trip up their own arses.

We had an excellent meal and inevitably imbibed too much drink. When we parted late in the afternoon, I put Celia in a taxi to take her back to her studio. Before she left, however, she gave me Maurice's home number and suggested I ring him as soon as possible.

Within the week I was signed up with one of the more prominent West End galleries. This time, possibly as they were aware of my previous encounter in the American court, the contract was specific. They would handle all my publicity, arrange exhibitions, and negotiate sales including commissions in return for a forty- percent stake in profits. In return, I would pay for the production of all my works and settle the transport costs within the UK. I agreed to make use of the gallery's accountants and promised to keep receipts for any or all expenditure.

I found Maurice to be more like a market trader than the representative of a major art gallery. He spoke with a pronounced East-end accent, smoked like a chimney, and was forever cracking dirty jokes. Having said all that, there was no doubt he had a profound grasp and understanding of the art market. He could recite the optimum price fetched at auction houses around the globe for most of the major art works sold in the last five years; he knew most of the artists concerned on a first name basis and all the gallery owners and their directors. He was fully apprised of my own background and the catalogue of works for which I was responsible. And, whatever his idiosyncrasies there was characteristic evidence of both professionalism and style in his presentation, and despite myself, I found that I liked the man.

After the negotiations had been settled we had a drink together and he inquired about the arrangements for my working conditions. The studio in Hackney had long since gone, a victim of the bankruptcy, and as I had not worked since then I was currently without a workspace. Our discussions in this regard led to him asking how long it might be before I could produce a collection of work. This was the rub. I explained that the major part of my previous productions had been manufactured for me, mostly at Pilkington's factory near Liverpool, and that it was only the multiples – such as the sauce bottles, the canvases, and the coffee-table books – for which I'd had any hands-on responsibility. However, I told him that I was brimming with new ideas, none of which I was prepared to discuss in detail at that stage, but couldn't wait to get started. This seemed to satisfy him but he said he would expect to see some results within two months.

In truth, I'd hardly given the subject of my art too much thought during my long absence. My time had been too busily engaged in the production of marijuana and in re-establishing my financial base. I knew that in the interim period, a large number of younger artists had jumped on the bandwagon. Their products filled the art magazines and caused frequent debates both on the radio and the television. It was apparent therefore, that if I were to rise once more to the top of this ménage, I would need to be more inventive, more creative and possibly more outrageous than ever before. The shock factor had now been well established and the tolerance levels of the public as well as those patronising the arts had been raised beyond what had once been thought possible.

Also, by now my erstwhile assistant Paul had made a name for himself in his own right and by all accounts his work could command prices far beyond his previous expectations. He had hit the headlines earlier in the year with, what he called his 'Prairie Schooner'. This comprised an exercise in topiary in which he manicured the hedgerows along a twenty-mile section of a motorway. The result was a series of primitive forms; some reminiscent of animals, some human figures that, according to some critics, 'danced' along the side of the dual carriageways. It was a theme that he was currently employed to repeat for a number of local authorities in a variety of different situations. Patently, it was also a mindless exercise providing nothing more than an exterior decoration and a dangerous distraction for motorists. It was nevertheless a real money-spinner as the need to re-cut the shapes would be a mandatory requirement annually. Trust that little shit to have come up with such a scheme.

On the same day that I signed up with Maurice, I found and purchased a studio in Shepherds Bush. The space was only a fraction of what I'd been used to in the past but property prices had increased exponentially in the last few years and it was as much as I could afford. The next thing I needed was to hire some assistants and, bearing in mind my previous reservoir of labour, I called round to my old college. By the end of the day I had recruited three young women who were as keen to earn a few extra pounds for their time and effort as they were to entertain the sexual demands of their new employer.

I never knew how he discovered that I was planning to exhibit work again but on the same day that I signed the contract with Maurice, Jimmy Barratt telephoned to remind me about an agreement we'd made ten years before. He said he recalled that he was due a large percentage of the profit from my next two exhibitions and that he was prepared to forget about his long wait and not charge me interest on the loan he'd made me. To some extent this took the shine off my new-found enthusiasm but there was little to argue about. I had promised him his share and he had waited – like a spider waits for the fly.

*

In all honesty it isn't fair to say that throughout the whole of the ten-year period I hadn't given any thought to art. In fact as the time of my freedom grew closer I'd found myself increasingly considering possible alternatives. The most troublesome part of such considerations, however, was the potential cost. Whereas in the past Manny was always there to foot whatever bill that might be presented on my behalf, from this point on I would need to be able to settle my own accounts. Clearly this had implications regarding what I could make – or have made. The wild excesses of the vacuum glass cases were over and any expense account I ran up then was one I would need to pay myself.

As a consequence of such considerations, I began to wonder what kind of materials I could use that could prove both sufficiently economic and yet still sufficiently unusual. I remembered the piss sculpture and smiled to myself, and the sauce bottles and the blank canvases. It was finally one morning on my daily visit to the bread shop that I had an idea. I had given my three assistants the job of decorating my studio only in order to occupy their time whilst I ruminated about the next project. As a consequence, it had become my practice to deliver a breakfast to them each day, one consisting of bread rolls, butter and jam and coffee. That particular day, feeling generous and having scrutinised the baker's window display, I had decided to treat them also to a gingerbread man. It was that day we began to make body casts.

To start with, as the girls were as unfamiliar with casting techniques as I was myself, we employed a professional to help. He took a plaster cast of Judy. She posed nude whilst Marian, Ruby, our instructor and me covered her well-greased anatomy with fine white dental plaster. We made a piece-mould of twelve parts, each fitting neatly alongside its nearest neighbours. A process designed to enable the whole assembly to be taken apart and re-made for each individual casting. Initially the cast was of a standing figure.

The following morning I spent a fruitful hour with the local baker persuading him that the idea I had was practically possible and within the week my studio began to fill with figures made from a biscuit mixture with a chocolate veneer. In the beginning there were some difficulties. The plaster moulds needed to be cooked more slowly than those in the usual tins are and the hot chocolate needed to be poured to make hollow figures that were joined by chocolate welding afterwards. But the results were a startling mixture of confections – edible art. It took a little while for us to guarantee the results but in the end all was well. Three weeks later I telephoned Maurice and he came over to view the new pieces.

Maurice came over at three in the afternoon. The girls had spent the morning adding some finishing touches to some of the sculptures. The ones made from a biscuit mixture were easily decorated with coloured icing and now nipples were red, eyes were green and pubic hair a golden blond. We were experimenting with a fine spray in order to try and provide a surface colour but there were difficulties and when Maurice arrived we were carefully removing the icing from an effort that had failed.

He poked his head round the double doors and gasped, "My God." was his first comment. I suppose that at first sight the collection was quite impressive. The big room contained thirty figures in a variety of poses. They were mostly female forms but one or two were from the cast the girls had taken from me.

"And they're edible," I said before he could comment.

*

The first showing of the Edible Art Show took place in the atrium of an outer London building belonging to one of the largest supermarket chains in Britain. By then the production process had been refined by the manufacture of metal moulds in which the bread/biscuit/chocolate figures were made and, although this proved a more reliable guarantee of good quality, it was still nevertheless labour intensive. Fortunately the base material was infinitely more economic than bronze, stone, fibreglass or stainless steel and, even given that the cost of the metal moulds was high, the fact that they were reusable mitigated the cost of my investment.

The occasion of the private view was in no way as prestigious as had been those organised by Manny. However, the reaction of the media and thereby of the public was just as startling. I suspect that my new agent had been doubtful about the validity of the work and had therefore, resisted spending for a high society 'bash' in favour of something more akin to a private party. Accordingly, Maurice was surprised and pleased by the publicity. I had arranged that after one week, visitors to the show should be able to eat the exhibits and this had been a marketing 'hook' on which to catch the attention of the non-gallery going public. A ruse that proved enormously popular. One tabloid newspaper gave the show a headline that read, 'Fat Art turns to Edible Art' and underneath questioned if I would eventually produce, 'Fat Edible Art'. It was all good fun but it served to re-establish my name and that had been the prime purpose

The following morning Maurice called on me to tell me that the gallery was delighted and that I should begin to plan immediately for another show, this time at the gallery itself in central London.

"Do you have any ideas for a follow-up?" he asked casually.

I was aware that he had reservations about the temporary nature of the pieces. After all, art that does not last is not a good investment and the galleries are only there to sell the goods on show. However, I had planned for just such a contingency.

"Yes, I have. For a start we could have some of the figures cast in bronze, a limited edition of course – temporary art made permanent – so to speak. And I am considering putting one or two into the same kind of vacuum containers that I used in the past – preserving temporary art! Eh, what do you think?"

He nearly wet himself with excitement. It was only then that I realised he must have been under some degree of pressure from his board. Clearly he'd been sent to persuade me to make things that had a longer shelf life than chocolate nude figures.

"I wouldn't want to turn the gallery into a cake shop," I added tentatively, "but we might also want to consider doing some miniature figures. The kind of thing parents might buy for their children. 'Art gingerbread men'. Obviously they'd sell for considerably more than your everyday version…"

He wasn't certain if I was pulling his leg so he maintained a very serious expression and before he left he promised to present the idea to his directors and I was left to chuckle to myself. There was not a chance in a million that the directors would accept such a hare-brained scheme but the idea of a smart, sophisticated gallery selling cakes for kids amused me. I telephoned Pilkington's that afternoon and ordered six life-size glass containers. John Adam was still with the firm and he was pleased to hear from me but, as he explained, without the backing of Manny Hume, I would need to pay up front for the order. Apparently my credit rating was suddenly questionable.

I had made sure that Manny received an invitation to the private view. I wanted him to see that my ideas were just as fresh and just as creative as they had always been and for him to regret his lost opportunity. In the event he didn't turn up. I had a note from his secretary a few days later saying that he seldom attended such occasions if they were outside the centre of town. I made a mental note to forget to send his invitation when the new show opened in Cork Street later in the year.

Chapter Thirty-Two

I don't imagine that the slogan 'Death can be fun' would ever win any advertising award, still less persuade the public. But there have been occasions when I've almost been inclined to believe it myself. Death is still one of the great unmentionables. In polite society we talk about 'the departed', those that have 'gone before' or 'passed over', we say that someone 'left us' or more popularly that someone has, 'popped his clogs' we seldom say they've died. Death, it seems, is so undesirable, so frightening a prospect that we want to describe it only in euphemisms – and then quickly move on to a more acceptable subject for conversation. Not surprisingly, therefore, grief and notions concerning the loss of those near and dear to us are consigned to the privacy of our homes, often to the further privacy of our own bedroom. Is it any wonder that our society is fraught with so many psychoses?

Conversely, in my experience there is nothing quite like a funeral to brighten the weekend. My father's funeral was a good example and the vision of mourners slipping down the mudslide into the grave will stay with me all my life. I suppose the exception was that of my poor unfortunate friend Ram and to a lesser extent my mother's cremation.

Mam died shortly after I returned to this country from America. Apparently the attendant publicity from the court case, especially the references made to the charges of rape, had made her into a hermit. Whereas previously my reputation, however avant guarde was acceptable and had fostered a pride in her son's achievements, it soon dissipated in the light of the gossip she was obliged to hear from neighbours about my personal life. Her next door friend, Mrs Carson, told me that once the press began to intrude with their stupid questions, Mam seldom left the house. She said, "She would often wait until late afternoon before daring to go to the shops. And then she would creep about with a scarf covering her face like some film star trying to avoid being recognised."

The thought annoyed me. That anyone, no matter who they might represent, should subject an old woman – my mother – to such treatment was infuriating. And significantly, it was as a consequence of her long and deliberate absences that she wasn't missed. When Mrs Carson finally thought to use her spare key, she found her neighbour sitting in Dad's old chair in the kitchen, a cup of tea in her hand and by then the hand was as cold as the tea. The doctor said she'd been there for several days. Naturally I travelled up for the cremation.

Only a small crowd collected to see her off, one or two neighbours and some old friends, no more than eight in total. Due to the death being so unexpected and me living so far away, I'd been unable to organise any kind of reception afterwards. Instead therefore, I took the little band of mourners to the local pub and bought them a ploughman's lunch and a pint or, as most were elderly women – a glass of sherry. Not an ideal solution but one I thought would be perfectly adequate and acceptable given the situation.

I had once been familiar with all the local hostelries and, on account of the frequency of my custom, had even known most of the landlords by name. Unfortunately by then I was out of touch. However, even allowing for the unusual number of men that crowded the bar that day, I could be forgiven for not knowing that on Friday afternoons, that particular pub hosted live entertainment. My intimate little gathering of elderly folk had just settled in a convenient corner to exchange anecdotes about the life and times of their friend, my mother, when the first stripper appeared only yards away from our table.

Although there were few pretensions of gentility amongst my mother's friends they nevertheless lived by a strong moral code. And whilst it was capable of ambiguity allowing a blind eye to be turned if one pinched stationary from work or told the occasional off-colour joke, women taking off their clothes in public was never to be tolerated. Mrs Carson grabbed her husband's arm at the first sign of dimpled flesh and, muttering something about my typically scandalous behaviour, led the furious exit team to the street. Consequently, by the time the first raunchy tune had run its course and the well-worn performer had reduced her tired costume to the ubiquitous G-string, I was left alone with only several plates of cheese and pickled onions for company.

Mam had left instructions that her ashes were to be spread over Dad's grave, a request I chose to believe that was her final revenge on him. He'd always suffered from asthma and any suggestion of air-bound pollution had always brought on an attack. It wasn't her style of course but I like to imagine that she'd ensured by her dusty presence that he would continue to suffer a shortage of breath throughout eternity, an appropriate quid pro quo for the way he had always stifled her behaviour.

Her solicitors telephoned me shortly after the funeral to tell me that I was her sole heir and that the sum total of her assets amounted to two hundred thousand pounds. This came as a surprise given her threadbare life-style. It was also rather annoying to realise that, at a time earlier when I could have done with financial help, she had maintained pretence of penury. At the time of her death the money meant nothing to me. Subsequently I blew most of my inheritance on a Stock Market gamble that didn't pay off.

For a short while then, my financial affairs seemed to blossom. The money from the skunk factory was more than sufficient to pay for the production of my sculpture and the profit made from the sale of the work, even after paying off Jimmy Barratt, equipped me with the kind of expense-account life I'd always dreamed of. However, although there was a degree of publicity attendant on the exhibitions in which my work was shown, nothing I did now seemed to attract the public's attention as it had in the past. Not surprisingly, as a consequence, my efforts became more and more bizarre. I recalled those conclusions I had once preached about the taboos that would inevitably shock society, namely: incest, cannibalism, and murder, and planned to demonstrate one or more of them in the new works.

In the meantime, my production team at the new studio was busy reproducing the limited edition of edible figures I'd promised Maurice and installing them in the glass cases provided once again by my friend John Adams The income from this collection was substantial, assisting me to live high off the proverbial hog and establish a sound business relationship with my new gallery. The potential however, was limited. Those who purchased the figures found that they needed to show them in an environment where the temperature was rigidly controlled and this proved an impediment to sales. Equally, those we had cast in bronze defeated the originality of the project, as they were no longer edible. Sales of the bronzes were therefore even more limited. I badly needed a new angle and sought it in one of Her Majesty's prisons.

I interviewed a notorious serial killer at a high security prison, a man whose crimes had fired a public reaction that had almost succeeded in the restoration of capital punishment. We exchanged letters and I visited him several times. I tried to explain to him that my purpose was to make him and/or his activities into art. He listened attentively but, unfortunately, his experience of art was limited to those sickly romantic works popular in the nineteenth century. Although he cooperated with me, it was very much with 'tongue in cheek' and the unlikely hope that his cooperation might help persuade the parole board of his possible rehabilitation. It was common knowledge that his chosen method of dispatching a number of his victims had been through the violent use of a ball-pin hammer. As a result of this I made a trio of double life-style sculptures employing the cruciform shape of a hammer. The exhibit was titled *On Golgotha the dawn brings redemption*. I made them deliberately reminiscent of the crucifixion on Calvary. In these giant ball-pin hammers, there was a cast of the killer's face and the handle equated to a monster-sized phallus. The outcry from a variety of religious and lay bodies included objections from the Muslim and Hindu communities as well as criticism from all the political parties.

I found it amusing also that the most serious objections came from Jimmy Barratt. Suddenly aware of the investment potential in the art business, he had taken a more than casual interest in what I was doing. He tried on several occasions to buy a share in my activities with the offer of substantial funding. Naturally I resisted. Paying him his percentage had been difficult and I wanted nothing more to do with him. Predictably, his reservations about my intentions for the new work were similar to those expressed by the gallery – arguments concerning good taste and possibly adverse public reaction. However, now that I was no longer in his debt, I could afford to ignore his comments. Moreover, as far as the gallery was concerned, I had proved the viability of my product through a better than average sales record and they could not therefore object too strongly.

The argument that I made public to justify the work included the fact that Christ himself was a convicted felon. Also that the hammer had been used repeatedly as an image associated with war and that the structural composition of the cross was sufficiently similar to that of the hammer to warrant comparison of two diametrically opposed icons. In an interview on a television arts programme I said that, whilst I was in no doubt about the murderer's guilt, there must always be a question as to the certainty of the verdict – as there had been with Christ. The sale of ball-pin hammers signed by me as multiple art objects was surprisingly good despite the fact that the interview only increased the degree of my unpopularity.

Despite a sell-out at the gallery, the reaction of the press inspired a lot of criticism by the public and my friend Maurice suggested I should seek less high-profile subjects on which to concentrate my efforts. Clearly the gallery wanted to enjoy the level of profit the work brought but to protect its good reputation at the same time – equating with one having one's cake and eating it at the same time. They failed completely to appreciate that it was the notoriety I'd achieved that caused the sales record to rise or that the public reaction – if not outrage – at the product that drew the attention of the Media.

Undaunted, I turned to the subject of cannibalism. This time in order to allay the fears and objections of the squeamish, I made sure that tickets inviting critics to the private view contained a clear summary of the materials used. A similar instruction was highlighted on the posters. This one was described as a 'Feast of Fine Art – Critics can devour a sense of the ridiculous without blame.' In fact it was a dinner invitation. The event was to be filmed and the film shown on a screen situated above the remains of the dinner after the event.

We took over one of the larger rooms in the South Bank complex and laid a table for some two hundred diners. The menu was a masterpiece starting with 'Blood' soup, a surprisingly difficult concoction that sought to reproduce the exact density and texture of human blood. It was served from plastic bags resembling those used as hospital 'drips' and the croutons appeared as gelatinous lumps to further the illusion. The next course was described as, 'Finger and Avocado salad with Tarragon' and appeared to consist of human fingers mixed with the avocado and crunchy French beans in a bed of bushy sprigs of tarragon, leaf parsley and a handful of rocket leaves. The dressing included olive oil, white vinegar and just enough tomato puree to guarantee an impression of gore.

The 'fingers' were a construction invented by a London chef and were derived from bleached pork spare-rib, shaped to resemble digits in which the fingernail was a piece of soft bone. They were very realistic and initially the cause for much amusement. It was the main course that caused the upset however, the innocence of its title disguising the intention. I called it, 'Albondigas' (Spanish meatballs). Scallops were shaped in an imitation of testes and cooked in a fine 'scrotum' mesh made from thin streamers of pasta. These were served on a bed of appropriately thick white sauce strengthened with slices of yellow peppers and seasoned with garlic. The pieces of tripe that decorated the plate had been dyed with herbs to make it more closely resemble human skin and a similar construction was used to reproduce the shrivelled penis that was the garnish with each platter. This section of the menu was served with black rice 'maggots'. It was a public relations disaster.

By the time the last diners were served their main course, many of those already served were on the point of leaving. Several of the female guests became nauseous and one actually vomited. Those with stronger stomachs that remained seated received a chocolate roulade for their pudding but this time the sponge had been adapted to form a turd shape and the cream yellowed, like strong piss.

As before, although the sales record of miniature 'scrotum bags' in plastic boxes and 'groups of fingers' also in plastic boxes exceeded all expectations and seemed to imply some level of approval, generally the comment was derogatory. The critics tore me to pieces, insisting that my credentials were exposed as being fatally flawed, a sentiment that was echoed tenfold in the tabloid press. A film had been made of the occasion and it was meant to be shown at the Cannes Film Festival. Unfortunately the gallery, reacting to save its reputation, withdrew it at the last minute.

Both of the taboos explored so far had proved the strength of society's resistance if not its abhorrence and, whilst there was an element of predictability in their unreasoned response, the result in terms of art appreciation was nevertheless disappointing. More to the point, it had been a costly exercise. Maurice explained that although my ability to rattle society's cage was appreciated and that there was no doubt that my work had successfully aroused the interest of the media to a hitherto unknown degree, the level of repugnance and disgust that characterised the public's reaction was unacceptable. Accordingly I was left to foot the bill.

My *Feast of Fine Art* had other repercussions that were more difficult for me to accommodate. For the first time it caused me to be alienated from my oldest friend and collaborator, Celia. Naturally she had been one of the diners. She always received invitations to my shows and in the past, even when my popularity was at its lowest, she was always the one to encourage me to further efforts. This time however, the realism of the image proved too much and Celia had been the one person to regurgitate her dinner. The following day she called me and told me I was sick in the head, "There's a limit, Mick," she said, "and you went over the edge this time. God knows how you could imagine the project qualified as any kind of art event…"

It was a reaction for which I was totally unprepared and in the heat of the moment, I responded in kind. In no time at all were hard at it, criticising one another's work and even name-calling. In the end she slammed down the receiver.

Celia's betrayal had a salutary effect, and for days I replayed our conversation over and over in my head. For the one person who knew me so well to fail to appreciate what I'd done was catastrophic. Obviously she'd lost the thread. She'd been sucked into the hypocrisy perpetrated by the 'good taste' merchants and forgotten where we came from. More sadly and more significantly she'd apparently lost her sense of humour. Once I had digested her complaints however, I was more than ever determined to continue with my experiment.

Partly because I never believed that I would need to employ its horrors, I'd left the most contentious taboo until the last. And I knew long before I began to consider a method of interpretation that incest/child abuse was probably the most sensitive of all issues. In recent years the publicity associated with paedophilia had raised the public's consciousness of the crime. The number of cases involving cohorts of perverts had multiplied exponentially. Those found guilty, on occasion even after they had served their respective prison sentences, were forcibly ejected from communities by groups of vigilantes. There were calls for a register of child abusers to be made publicly available, for sentences to increase and for the details of their offences to be placed in the public domain. And, quite rightly, when the perpetrators were relatives of the victims the indignation was that much more voluble and the retribution called for, that much more extreme.

Nevertheless, whilst I shared the consensus view, I also appreciated that it was only on account of modern communications technology that the issue had been identified so clearly by the public. It was my belief that child abuse had been a part of our society for as far back as the institution of the family existed. It was only now, in our age of freedom of information and our provision for social services within the National Health Service that our awareness had been heightened. I also chose to believe that the fashion industry in its misuse of children's images was at least partly responsible for encouraging the practice. The incidence of child 'beauty contests' particularly prevalent in the United States was a typical catalyst.

How exactly I might engage with this particular taboo was therefore a difficult and potentially dangerous problem. I knew that by involving myself at a level similar to that of my other projects, I would run the gauntlet of social propriety and leave myself open to all manner of accusations, however unjustified. Clearly therefore, I could not in conscience argue for more tolerance for the perverts, I could only contribute to the call for more openness and better information. I could of course refer to the abuse to which I myself had been subject: the constant and pernicious religious ritual especially as it was manifested at meal times, but I finally decided such references might defray the shock element. What was needed was a more direct statement – something more shocking.

Around this time money, or lack of it, once more became a problem. The *Feast of Fine Art* despite the sales had cost me dearly and I had committed myself to the purchase of a very expensive motorcar. In desperation, I was obliged to sell my skunk factory to Jimmy Barratt. Steven had long since decided that he would settle in California and although he continued to receive monthly cheques the value of these had been steadily reduced since he left the country. It had been a conscious decision on my part to gradually limit Steven's share of the business. And whilst this might appear mean on my part, his importance, in terms of what he might tell Jimmy Barratt should they ever meet, grew less significant as time passed. It was therefore only reasonable that the money he received on this account should also be reduced.

It had been a good investment, producing in the region of several thousand pounds profit per month but Jimmy paid a fair price and I was again solvent. I resisted his offer of another deal involving him being a partner in my ventures and relied instead on the money he paid for the factory. However, if I was ever to regain the financial strength I'd known previously, I realised that the art projects would need to pay considerably better than they had recently. With this in mind, I planned the *Incestuous Art* exhibition, subtitled, *Would you like a sweet little boy?*

From its first inception there were problems Maurice and his Board of Directors would not agree the title. They said it was pornographic – consequently it had to be changed. If I were to reap the benefits of the gallery's protection and enjoy the indulgence of its publicity machine, I'd known from the beginning that I would have to compromise – if only a little. Unfortunately their objections went deeper than the title.

They had expressed reservations about the idea continuously ever since I'd outlined it and this necessitated my appearing before them, to justify myself. I prepared a short talk to be illustrated with slides and delivered it, dressed in my best suit and wearing my most beatific smile. I showed them pictures of historical importance, many of which might well have been seen as pornographic at the time. Some of these by artists who were now regarded as Old Masters. I led them visually on a path that demonstrated the changes

310

in public taste simultaneously making the argument that such work had been responsible for the increased tolerance evident today. Finally, I went on to describe my own motives and listed the taboos I had sought to investigate ending with incest.

So far so good. The questions aimed at me were manageable and the atmosphere thus far, surprisingly supportive. It was when I began to talk about how I intended to explore this subject that the objections started. I said that I would publish a series of life-size photographs of naked children bound hand and foot. Each would have the face of the subject obliterated and a portrait of an adult superimposed. The point being those children become grown-ups and that perhaps the same respect should be given them as one would adults. More importantly still, with the passage of time many of the children portrayed would become parents themselves and that the cycle of abuse could only be broken by society's attitude reflecting the way they were treated.

Someone asked, "And all that is supposed to be apparent and achievable, simply through these – these photographs – is that what you're saying?"

I shook my head, "No the pictures are only the first stage. I intend that everyone who comes to the show will be given a miniature child-doll and that there will be larger, child-sized dolls on sale as multiples. This will offer the possibility of surrogate parenthood, or at least a pastiche representing it. Much like the Japanese 'Furbee' toys that were so popular. I also hope to have miniature electronic children produced for sale, again as a limited edition."

The arguments went on for several hours. In the end I had to agree to finance the production of the photographs, the palm-sized dolls and the life-sized dolls myself. The gallery would provide the space for the show, the publicity including the private view and would take responsibility for the 'Furbee' type toys. We finally agreed that the exhibition should be titled, *Come to Daddy*.

It took six months hard work and the investment of most of my capital before the exhibition was ready. Significantly, the technical side proved easiest to organise. There were photographers aplenty willing to take the commission and several manufacturers prepared to design electronic toys to my specification. The biggest difficulty was in finding children whose parents were prepared to allow them to pose nude. It seemed that no matter how many times I gave my assurance concerning the underlying motive of the exhibition, or how often I explained my intentions to individual couples, the same questions, the same doubts, cropped up time and again. Never having had children of my own, all my attempts to empathise were met with incredulous disbelief and my promises of anonymity for their offspring, with scepticism. Indeed, it was not until I offered to pay fees, considerably greater than those paid for professional models that I succeeded in recruiting a large enough group for the pictures.

I learnt two lessons from this exercise. I came to appreciate that, in so far as their children are concerned, parents are undoubtedly the arbiters of public morality – but only in proportion to the profit they might accrue from using them. I concluded that it was therefore reasonable to assume that, given sufficient financial incentive, the same parents might well prostitute their children. And if such a statement were not fuel enough for a heated debate then, in my opinion, nothing would ever suffice to prompt one.

As part of my research programme I logged onto a number of Internet sites that offer child sex. In my defence, I can argue – hand on heart – that these forays into the depths of pornography were carried out for the same specific purpose as that of the exhibition. I needed to know – first hand – what the degree of the infection might amount to. The Scotland Yard investigators, to demonstrate my depravity, however later used this. The exhibition opened in a blaze of publicity – all of it bad. Apparently, not a single member of the press was prepared to believe my motives and the main focus of all their articles was an examination of my lack of moral fibre. They dredged the bottom of my ethical barrel, citing instances and quoting references that spread as far back as my days on the dole. Phillipa, with whom I had not had direct contact for several years, was photographed getting into a taxi and described as a woman of questionable morals whose marriage I had destroyed. Tony Durham (of all people) was quoted as saying that as a young man, I'd been responsible for leading him into a life of crime. My rape case – brought by an underage girl – was listed as evidence of my propensity for child-abuse and Manny Hume described what he claimed was my depraved behaviour at several of his parties.

The exhibition opened on a Friday morning and was closed by a vice squad injunction on the Monday afternoon. I was arrested on the following Thursday, charged under the Lewd Publications Act and accused as a child pornographer.

Chapter Thirty-Three

1999

It seems to me that there are three criteria by which one can assess the impact of a life's work. The three big 'Rs': (1) Recognition by both the establishment and one's peers of one's place in terms of the historical hierarchy. For example one might ask, 'Am I more important than say – Henry Moore, or Barbara Hepworth?' (2) The quality of one's reputation, as it might be identified by the virtuosity/originality apparent in one's work, and (3) remuneration. That is the fortune accrued by the value placed on the work. The trick is in accumulating all three at the same time and, as recognition inevitably enhances reputation and reputation always increases wealth, which in turn cannot fail to increase the recognition one receives, it's a merry-go-round. A carousel of success.

I'd been fortunate enough, on occasion, to enjoy all of these. And, despite the ignorance of the public, the jealousy of my fellow artists and the sharp practice of the gallery owners and agents, I am sure I'd secured a place for myself in my own lifetime that will not be forgotten.

Recently however, the vagaries apparent in the practices of auction houses have caused the price achieved for my work to fall. A situation not helped when my old enemies in the tabloid press got hold of my medical records and discovered my history of venereal disease. Apparently, it's all well and good to read about Gauguin or Toulouse Lautrec having had similar complaints. The public chooses to believe their infections were obtained in the cause of their creative endeavour, but if a living artist should contract such 'dirty' diseases then there must be something seriously wrong with him. I reckon that selling art as an investment is much like selling insurance. Clients will not only want to be certain that the product itself is worthwhile but they will also need to be reassured that the producer of that product is bankable; that their history of trading is unimpeachable and that their future is assured.

Paradoxically, in the case of living artists, if the work offered for sale is by someone who is obviously at death's door the value of that work may well be enhanced. The fact is that immediately after the death of an artist, the value of his work will suddenly surge. This equates with the emphasis on complimentary remarks made at funerals generally. We seldom hear a eulogy in which the deceased is criticised and never witness one that describes the dearly departed as a 'right bastard'. For example, whilst admiring his tenacity and the quality of his effort, no one at Vincent van Gogh's funeral described him as, 'a mad bugger who really needed psychiatric help.'

The hope therefore, is that the lull in price-fixing will eventually pass and all those stalwarts who invested in buying my work will reap the dividend they so richly deserve. Significantly, this is a conclusion I could never have accommodated as a young man. The ability to take the longer view is undoubtedly one of the benefits of the ageing process. I appreciated that I was no longer at the cutting edge of latest thinking; equally I knew that the art world is subject to pendulum swings in terms of fashion. I did however, choose to believe that the significance of the work I produced was far and above that of most of my contemporaries and that, as such, it will increase both in its relative importance as well as in the cash value attributed to it.

Unfortunately, no matter how sound my reasoning, it was of no great value in affecting my situation. As a consequence of the trial and the antipathy of the popular press, it would not be an exaggeration to claim that my stock was at an all-time low. The reports of my venereal disease was as grist to the mill for those who continue to believe me to be a pervert. And, even though eventually I was found to be not guilty of being a child pornographer, the photographs themselves were found to be pornographic and I was therefore guilty of publishing lewd material. Consequently, the exhibition that was to restore my fortunes did not reopen and bankruptcy again reared its ugly head.

In that respect at least I feel that I had come full circle. My first accommodation in London all those years ago was a mean little room just off the Portobello Road and I found myself again in similar circumstances. With the passage of time however, I could no longer afford any kind of little room in Nottinghill, the area had been developed – gentrified by upwardly mobile pimply-faced youngsters earning salaries that read like telephone numbers. The gardens were full of decking; the windows clad in John Lewis fabrics and the cars that lined the streets were entirely responsible for the trade gap with our European partners.

By dint of circumstances, I was forced to rent rooms again in distant Hayes, the last refuge of those sharing the benefits of the scrounger's charter with the refugees that fill the council housing lists. It was a sombre place boasting only a railway station, a snooker club, some nondescript supermarkets, and a bingo hall. Not surprisingly, there were numerous places in which one can drink – after all, what else are the dispossessed supposed to do but imbibe alcohol. The crime rate was high, commensurate with, and I suspect occasioned by, the vast number of pubs. Significantly, in my little room on any night of the week, although secure in my appreciation that I had nothing worth stealing, police sirens nevertheless serenaded me before I slept. Locally, the highlight of the social calendar was watching strippers perform desultory moves twice per week in a local hostelry. Sad young women and some not so young, trying to eke out an extra income by exposing their stretch-marks and dimpled cellulite to the unsympathetic gaze of an audience representing the flotsam from various war-torn countries from across Europe and Africa. A gathering that seemed to believe calling out, "Gerr 'em off." is a sign of appreciation. These, the representatives of a variety of religions, appeared to me to find a unification of purpose that had escaped them in their countries of origin, by the apparent novelty of witnessing women remove their clothing to the accompaniment of canned music. This paradox almost qualified as art. Otherwise however, notions concerning the visual arts were as remote and unlikely in Hayes as they were in Stockton a lifetime ago and the local benchmark for creativity was judged only by the limited originality of the car thieves and burglars.

The coterie of friends and associates I'd once enjoyed was now even more seriously diminished. I still had some limited contact with Celia but suspected that she still bore a grudge over my poor performance with her gallery. Very occasionally she telephoned and invited me to a private view of an exhibition but I always claimed to be otherwise engaged. She refused to loan me money and told me without hesitation that no agent in Britain will ever touch me again. She said that, instead of trying to get back in the art world 'swim', I'd be better employed, looking for a regular job. As if the pursuit of art was not a regular job.

As far as my financial situation was concerned, I found myself in a curious position. On the one hand I had no regular income worth mentioning and my assets column was empty. However, there were considerable sums of money still owing to me. The continued sale of my works by Maurice's gallery was considerable. Naturally he claimed that the outstanding amount was negligible due to the expenses he said he had incurred and the level of his original investment. The only way I could challenge his accounts would be through the courts and, as he would defend himself from a position of financial strength, such action would inevitably prove costly. I was therefore left at his mercy with little hope of ever receiving that, which was rightfully my due.

To make matters worse still, the effort I made to establish myself in the public eye as someone who had the ability to question society's value system had rebounded on me. The media seldom referred to me but on those occasions when my name cropped up, I was described as, 'the artist of bad taste who was charged under the Obscene Publications Act'. Usually these presaged comments culled from old newspaper articles in which my not guilty verdicts are suppressed and the emphasis is inevitably placed on the misinformed observations of my detractors. A priest once shamed me. A man prompted by my parents who once announced to my local community that I was a sinner. The same message was now nationally accepted. I was lampooned by cartoonists, scorned by previous colleagues, and ignored by a public that once queued to see my latest work. And my response – fuck 'em all.

Clearly this world was a place where genuine creative ability was no longer valued, where integrity was made light of, where hard work went unrewarded and where the double standards practised by the most influential people left society moribund. Small minds could only manage small thoughts, I concluded, and small thoughts never conquered new worlds.

Sometimes I remembered my stay in Trinidad, the heat, the rum punch and the girls. I recall the sculpture workshop that I operated in San Fernando, a desolate place near the docks and the bus terminus where, no matter what the time of day or night, there always seemed to be a group of local guys playing cards. Most importantly of all, however, I remember the casual ease evident in that society no matter what the issue under public scrutiny. An attitude that proved to be the antithesis of that I experienced in Britain. It is also odd that in a manifestly Christian country such as England, notions of forgiveness and redemption figure so low on everyone's agenda.

The work I once described as my 'Landscape' was sited that year on a promontory facing the River Taw in Devon. The huge glass box containing the fence, the shed and the earth looked magnificent but only one critic had the temerity to laud it. His comment that it echoed the work of Turner was ridiculed to such an extent that the local authority was eventually obliged to have it removed. What price the appreciation of art now?

*

The telephone call was most unexpected. I'd been led to believe that the gallery represented by Maurice had lost interest in my affairs and consigned me to some culturally inaccessible back burner. As the call was from Maurice himself, I was therefore agreeably surprised and, after the usual polite pleasantries, he told me that he had recently had an inquiry from a lesser-known town in the Southwest.

"You probably aren't aware of the fact Mick but our Chairman is from that neck of the woods," he said, "and although he doesn't spend much time down there anymore, he maintains an interest."

My ignorance of this fact hardly equipped me to comment at this stage. And, I must confess the information was hardly the kind that I might have thought to be 'riveting'. Indeed, I could have quite easily spent the rest of my life quite happily without ever having appreciated that the gentleman in question had his roots in the Devon and Cornwall peninsula. Nevertheless, as telephone messages of any consequence at all were few and far between at that time, I listened politely and waited for the punchline. I was surprised when it came.

"The thing is, Mick, someone down there must have been impressed by something they've seen that you did, because they want to offer you a commission."

"Are you certain they have the name correct?" I asked sceptically.

"Absolutely sure. The guy who wrote to us listed some of your achievements, quoted chapter and verse, and said you were the choice of the arts committee."

I was subjected to a small thrill of excitement at this news. The qualifying degree of this excitement being governed by a well developed cynicism if not suspicion that anything I attempted would inevitably meet with the public's disapproval. Perhaps all my efforts hadn't been in vain after all, I thought. I was aware that that the Southwest of the land was known as a centre for the arts but had wrongly assumed that their taste ran only to seascapes, sunsets, and cute little ceramics. Clearly someone down there must have been paying attention to the London art scene.

"And what kind of money are we talking about?" I asked.

Maurice laughed, "Don't worry, Mick, they've had funding from the Lottery and they can afford you."

This was brilliant news and I gradually began to feel the stirring of an optimism I'd long since abandoned. Maurice gave me the name and number of the County councillor responsible for the inquiry and suggested I make contact with him at my earliest convenience. He went on to remind me that the gallery would expect its usual percentage, for which it would provide the usual services. I didn't argue the point but made a mental note to keep a complete record of their involvement in advertising/marketing and administration, assuring myself that this time they would not take the lion's share for doing nothing. Clearly in light of the offer, the gallery had had second thoughts about my earning capacity and Maurice ended by saying that there was a cheque in the post that would settle what they owed to me in respect of outstanding sales.

Later that morning I sat thinking about the possibilities of the new opportunity. It was a chance to redeem myself, an occasion to guarantee my reinstatement. It nevertheless took me some time to work up the courage to make the telephone call. The failures I'd experienced had had their toll on my confidence and for the first time in my life, I was fearful of another catastrophe.

Phil Dunn answered my call and in just a few minutes convinced me that we were on the same wavelength. Besides being a county councillor, Phil was employed in a small advertising agency. As a consequence, he was familiar at least with the background to public art. More significantly, he claimed to have been a fan of my work as far back as the first exhibition in Manny's gallery.

"I always admired the cheek," he said, "– the balls it must have taken to lampoon the art world like you used to do. I always enjoyed seeing what you did. Believe it or not I travelled up to London on more than one occasion just to visit your exhibitions."

Phil was a revelation. He did more for my flagging ego than a win on the football pools could have done. The punchline however was the real payoff. As a result of his heartfelt admiration, he said he was prepared to clear local authority red tape and fight the good fight with any opposition on my behalf, in order that I could have carte blanche in deciding the form that the commission might take. It was almost a return to the good old days. Suddenly I was in the presence of the converted. To make matters better still he had negotiated a six-figure fee for the work with an added expense account to cover manufacturing costs. I was back in business. Early the following day, shortly after depositing the cheque from the gallery in my bank account, I took a train to Exeter and then onwards to Barnstaple. Phil met me at the station and promptly took me to meet his committee.

Unlike the officialdom to which I had become used, these were administrators with heart. Moreover, after they'd listened to what I had to say and looked at a few slides of my work they asked sensible questions. There was no edge to their inquiries, no displays of town hall righteousness or spurious moral argument. They were prepared to admit openly that they hoped my work would attract visitors and that whatever its significance otherwise, that it would help their tourist trade. I did not see this as any kind of limitation and welcomed the expectation of maximum publicity. They took only five minutes to decide to offer me the commission officially.

There was only one request regarding the piece I was to produce and that was a plea that it in some way it should be site-specific. As the deputy chairman put it, "We'd like to think that whatever you decide to make, it would take account of its location. After all it's the location that we're trying to market to tourists."

The key phrase in this was the fact that it was described as a 'request'. There was no onus placed on me, any regulation governing my actions and no clause designed to inhibit my thinking. I liked these people. Their appreciation and understanding led me to wonder why I had not spent more time in that part of the country before. Clearly there was a different attitude evident, one of open-mindedness, of freedom from preconception, one in which they as sponsors were prepared to demonstrate that rare commodity known as trust. I stayed over at Phil's home that night in order that, on the following day, he could show me some of the sites where my work might best be located.

The next morning we went out in his car. That was the day I discovered Exmoor.

It was only on the train on my way back to London that evening that I began to realise the enormity of the opportunity I'd been offered. This could be the West Country equivalent of the *Angel of the North* – a national monument, an icon representing all that might be seen as fine in that pleasant rural society.

As soon as I got home I began to try and find out something more about the history of the region. I was excited and the excitement fired my enthusiasm. I wanted to know as much as possible about the place that had shown me such respect. I read all I could about the smuggling trade, once such an important contributor to Devon's economy. I looked at the record of achievement in the arts throughout the region and I examined evidence from the community of artists that settled there. I researched the history of tin and clay mining, the shipbuilding and fishing industries and last but not least, I studied the impact of farming. In this last respect I was surprised to discover that, nationally, some twenty-five percent of cattle and sheep farmed in England hail from the West Country. It was this last activity therefore that I finally decided was the most significant and consequently, the one that should bear most significantly on the work I was to produce.

Given that I had been so impressed with the wonderful space of Exmoor, my concentration on farming as a stimulus for a sculpture was appropriate in every way. Also, as an industry, it was clearly an important source of revenue for the region. Given the numbers of beasts farmed there however, it was also a major industrial player on a national scale. The local interest therefore being reflected on a countywide basis. Needless to say, Exmoor would be the site I chose, and farming would provide the stimulus and some of the iconography.

During the next six weeks I spent as much time as possible in and around the moor. I tramped the fields, talked to the inhabitants and photographed innumerable locations in order to get a feel for the project. I imagined huge configurations set starkly against the landscape; I tried to perceive linear structures that would snake across the skyline; I experimented with natural materials such as willow, stone and even soil and I began to build scale models in which valleys were bridged, rivers forded and hillsides spanned. But it was all too usual. It was the Henry Moore School of landscape sculpture mildly adulterated to suit my purposes or a type of Richard Long walking-memory-piece adapted for Devon. None of that would do. This time the work needed to be entirely original. I wanted the shock factor – but on a grand scale, I searched for the kind of universal statement that would be a magnet containing a must-see factor that would attract visitors from all over the world. Unfortunately, the inspiration was a long time in coming.

Suddenly it was Christmas again and even Hayes Town made the effort to symbolise the season by the appearance of gaudy lights, tinsel and Father Christmas, a vain attempt lacking in any kind of conviction. The weather turned and a cold North wind swept in leaving the temperature in my bedsit to resemble that more normally found in my fridge. And although for the first time in ages, my finances were now on a more reliable footing, I had prudently chosen to maintain my frugal life-style until such time as the publicity (that I knew would accrue from my project) demanded my recognition again. The typical rags-to-riches story is ever the meat of the popular press – 'the artist living in squalor suddenly hitting the big-time' – the headline designed to sell papers. And if the artist in question is one needing rehabilitation then so much the better. I had long since decided that on this occasion, I would organise my own image making as well as the most appropriate time to project it.

The nub of the idea came to me one Saturday evening when, despite being fortified by a bottle of good Scotch and a couple of risqué videos, I found myself flicking through the pages of an old sketchbook. It was the first of its kind in my career – the one I deliberately fabricated to take to my interview at Middlesbrough College of Art all those years ago. I stopped at the page with a drawing of a large hole and recalled the argument with Joss Pruitt. Briefly – I had argued that it concerned negative volumes: why do we always have to have something built in solid terms when a well-defined space is just as significant? Of course one cannot have a space defined completely else it becomes the interior of something and can't be seen. But a hole? Why not a hole?

If a hole was big enough and there was sufficiently interesting things going on in it, it could surely attract as much attention as a solid. And how many monuments does anyone know that consist entirely of – a hole?

I liked it – I liked it very much. It was just the kind of conclusion no one would ever expect. It could easily be justified in relation to landscape – and hadn't I first been awed, if not inspired, by the space I recognised on the moor. What better then that a space within a space.

The hole was the first step. I went to sleep that night quietly giggling to myself.

Chapter Thirty-Four

2000

Perhaps on account of the number of miserably disappointing Christmases I'd experienced as a child, I never paid too much regard to the festive season. And with the absence of my parents there was no good reason to change that view. As a result, that year I confined my celebrations to a meal in a London hotel, a visit to a cinema and the self-indulgence of a new wardrobe and a pair of walking shoes. I suppose to some extent I was preoccupied with thoughts about what my 'hole' might contain and therefore paid little attention to my immediate surroundings. Being distracted I was surprised therefore when, as I was strolling towards Oxford Circus late on the evening of Christmas Day, I heard someone call my name. A car had pulled over to the kerb and a woman's head protruded from the driver's window.

"Mick," she called waving a hand in my direction, "Mick Grainger... here."

It was only when I drew closer that I realised the woman was Phillipa. It appeared that she was pleased to see me.

I'd had no contact with Lady Phillipa for a number of years and our last association had left me to believe that any future meeting would be both unlikely and probably unwelcome. After she'd sold her little mews cottage she had all but disappeared. My attempts to locate her had been hampered by the fact that (a) she owed me money and (b) by then I was persona non grata. Equally, her friends were determined that she should be protected from, what they saw, as my malign influence.

The passenger-side door swung open and she said, "Mick, get in and I'll drop you... It's been ages."

I forced a smile and took the seat next to her, "Well – this is a real surprise," I said.

From her appearance she had either just left, or was just about to attend a party. Her outfit was full of sparkle and see-through silky materials and her make-up – the full war paint. She had worn better than I'd imagined she would and the years had been kinder than she deserved. As she drove, I scanned her with sidelong glances, discovering in the process that her jewellery was the real thing and as ever, abundantly evident. Clearly she had been restored to something resembling her former status and her confidence also reflected the fact.

"So," she whispered in that same croaky voice she once employed to seduce her men-friends, "what are you up to? No one has set eyes on you for ages. Where on earth have you been?"

"Travelling – mostly," I lied.

My well-practised subterfuge was one I'd constructed to disguise my situation and although, given my isolation from the society I'd once enjoyed there had been little opportunity to rehearse it, I was glad that it came so easily. I did not want anyone who had known me previously to know how far I'd fallen or how spartan the conditions in which I found myself. My story satisfied her immediate curiosity and typically then, she began to talk about herself. She let me know that she was divorced and that the settlement from her ex-husband had enabled her to have a comfortable life-style, in keeping with her 'need' for, "a reasonable level of luxury."

"I'm going to Paul's Christmas party – over in Hertfordshire," She told me, "Why don't you join us?"

I smiled, "I doubt I'd be made very welcome at Paul's home."

She glanced across at me and I recognised the look. It was a survey made to assess if not actually enumerate my financial status.

"You've changed, Mick," she said, "are you sure everything's okay?"

"Everything's fine."

"Are you still working?"

"Yes. As ever."

"Anything in particular?"

I paused. I knew that anything I said to Phillipa would soon become public knowledge. She had always been a gossip. And whilst I wasn't keen for the details of my project to become too well known, there was some kudos in leaking the scale of its importance. I told her that I was being commissioned for a national monument and that the project was taking all my time at present. I would not however, say more than that despite her questions.

We continued to head west and were soon approaching Ealing Common. Phillipa continued to petition me about the party and just as we passed into

Southall she pulled over to the side of the road, stopped the car and took out her cell-phone.

"I'll ring Paul and tell him you're with me. You'll see that he bears no grudge and I'm sure he'd be delighted to see you again."

Apparently Phillipa was proven to be correct. At least superficially and in front of a whole collection of people I'd once claimed as friends, Paul welcomed me. We'd driven out into the far reaches of Hertfordshire to a village not far from Much Haddam, the place where Henry Moore had once settled, to a grand manor house set in some twelve acres of beautiful rolling fields. It was a wonderful setting, every bit as impressive as those I'd imagined myself occupying – when my fortunes returned. The long drive was lined with sweet chestnut trees and the car park filled with a dozen or more equally 'sweet' limousines.

Forewarned of our arrival Paul met us at the door. His greeting was theatrical, his hug an unnecessary gesture copied from an American movie about male bonding. He had put on weight since we last met – a noticeable amount of weight – and, although his tuxedo had been carefully tailored, the strain ripples around the button-holes and across the back of the jacket betrayed his obvious over-indulgence. Now he sported a double chin as well as the obligatory, South-of-France-tan of which many celebrities likes to boast in mid-winter.

The guests included a variety of faces, ghosts from a past era, all older and showing the signs of dissipation I might have expected. Many of the people there however, seemed genuinely pleased to see me and my back was slapped and my hand shaken by one after another. The last person to greet me was Manny Hume.

I'd often conjectured about my reaction should I ever meet with Manny again. Initially, the plan had been to smack him hard in his ribs and then to put in a well-placed boot once he hit the floor. Alternatively, I'd thought, I might just ignore him or turn my tongue on him. Manny had never been the fastest wit in the world and had admired my ability to ridicule those who'd crossed me. It would have been easy therefore to cause him serious embarrassment – but I chose not to do so. For the moment his nervousness was sufficient recompense. In fact I took the hand offered to me and grinned like an idiot, answering his polite inquiry with an equally polite response.

I was pleased to see that the years had not been kind to Manny. He looked ill. His belly sagged and the fine thread veins in his face, a mark of over-indulgences, showed red and purple against his thin skin. I noted also that although he had amassed an extra few stones in bodyweight, in contrast, his face appeared to have grown thinner leaving his nose even more pronounced and his voluminous lips ever more inappropriate. His escort that night was a woman I knew as Judy and we exchanged nods of recognition without engaging in any real conversation. She was still attractive although considerably thinner and I made a mental note to telephone her soon.

Suddenly I was glad that Phillipa had persuaded me to attend the party. On account of the hard times I'd experienced, I was thinner than before, sleek by comparison to most men present and whilst my hair was rapidly greying, at least I still had hair. Manny was all but bald and Paul, along with most of his contemporaries, sported a disguise of thin gossamer strands. John Adams shook my hand and asked if I was active again but, as by then I had a small audience ringed around me, I chose to be enigmatic in my answer. All that I told them was that I had been commissioned to produce an extraordinarily large work and that it was to be funded by Lottery money due to the prominence it was to achieve. With a sly grin Manny asked if I was represented by an agent in the matter. I answered quickly that representation had never proved a problem for me and that on one occasion I'd even had two agents. The shocked reaction to my quip ended with laughter – mostly at Manny's expense and I used the occasion to excuse myself in order to get a drink at the bar.

The drinks were located in a small room behind the main reception area; a quiet place with only one or two drinkers mostly seated at tables in the shadows. I asked for a large Scotch but before the young barman could respond, a voice to my left added, "Best make it a single malt." I turned to find Jimmy Barratt sitting on a barstool, his immaculate dinner jacket complimented by a huge smile.

"I'm delighted to see you about again, Mick," he said, "seems like it's been a long time."

"It has," I said, "too long."

"How's the bank balance?"

"Promising."

He laughed, "Good to see you're still the optimist. But if you want any help, you know my number."

We spent an interesting hour exchanging news and, at my request, he was able to provide me with some information concerning a girl I used to know before we parted company.

In some respect Paul's Christmas party was my reintroduction to the world of art and artists and to the business of selling art. The welcome I received indicated to me that my period of exile was over and the past, if not forgotten then certainly laid aside. My only regret concerning the evening I spent at Paul's home was that Celia was not present. She had seen firsthand how the estrangement forced on me had affected my life; she had also been one of the few to offer me help, it was unfortunate therefore that she was not present to witness my reinstatement.

*

As I did sometimes during that period of my life when I was closely associated with Jimmy Barratt, occasionally I still visited an exclusive brothel at Cowley House in North London. The exclusivity I refer to was of course one qualified only by the size of the clients' bank balances and there were no prizes offered for knowing who owned the premises. Jimmy had property all over London. Originally it had been set up as a recreational centre for his business friends but seeing the potential for profit, he was quick to capitalise on its assets and, as it were, opened it to the public.

One of the more attractive girls on staff at Cowley House was a girl called Judy. She worked from a front room on the first floor overlooking a small park and for a while her services were in great demand, not least by me. For a period of around five years I was a regular visitor to her front room at least once each week. Unfortunately in 1983, during my then latest attempts to re-establish my career, we lost contact. To be entirely honest my absence was probably more to do with my renewed access to female students. At that time, I reasoned that if I could find satisfaction from willing amateurs, then why should I pay a professional.

It was not until 1994 that I met up with Judy again and this time we met by chance in one of the larger department stores in Oxford Street. I was pleased to see that she looked as good as ever – almost. She was thinner and her sparkling green eyes had lost some of their liveliness but that didn't surprise me as by then I knew she'd been diagnosed HIV positive. Jimmy had kept me informed, telling me finally that he'd had to let her go due to her condition. He wasn't one for running a charitable establishment and naturally, there was no private health care provided with the job. Over coffee that day she told me that she now operated from a small flat just off Edgware Road and that if I cared to visit I'd find the same level of service as I'd enjoyed at Cowley House. Apparently as an afterthought she added cautiously that currently, due to a, "small health problem" I'd need to take precautions. Her warning was an unusual generosity given her circumstances and it prompted the solution to an idea that had been bothering me for some time.

I took Judy to lunch. In the belief that treating one's friends to an expensive meal at a premier restaurant always proved as therapeutic for them as it was a guarantee of their gratitude, I telephoned the Dorchester and booked a table. I ignored her protests that she wasn't dressed for the occasion and whisked her off in a taxi. In Judy's case the gratitude was immediately made obvious when she told me the truth about her state of health.

"I wasn't trying to con you Mick, honest," she whispered to me in the cab, "just that – well things haven't been so good – and you were once a favourite customer…"

She accepted my reassurances and for the next hour or more we enjoyed a first-class meal and fine wines together.

It was only once she'd relaxed that I put my scheme to her. After she'd heard me out she looked pensive, "That's pretty evil, Mick," she said uncertainly, "you must hate this guy. Are you sure this is what you want?"

"Absolutely."

"Okay – I'm game but what's in it for me?"

Judy's years as a working girl had sharpened her business sense and even though her position was hardly one of strength, she made a good case for a sizeable reward. We finally settled on a series of phased payments. A deposit would be paid immediately, followed by a second payment after contact had been suitably established, followed by a final much larger settlement as soon as the objective I defined had been confirmed.

*

The winter was a very busy period. I spent considerable time travelling between London and Devon, organising contractors and negotiating with local authority representatives. I employed a firm of engineering contractors to do the excavation work and in the process became very friendly with one of the partners; a man called Guy Peppard. And, although they were more used to building structures that reached skywards than those that delved into the earth, Guy's firm quickly produced calculations that would ensure the integrity of my proposal. His help proved invaluable and although he expressed reservations about my intentions, once the excavation began to take shape, I was able to persuade him of the seriousness of my intent. It was Guy's suggestion that we have a metre-high wall built around the perimeter. He argued that this would provide both a definition to the rim of the hole as well as a safety barrier for viewers. The cost was substantial but, given the scale of the expenditure already agreed, there was little realistic opportunity for my sponsors to change the decision.

In the end the excavation occupied five acres. The hole, some seventy-five feet deep, was a crater worthy of a moonscape. A guarantee was needed that the walls of the hole would remain permanently free from vegetation and, in order that this was achieved, the strongest, most concentrated defoliant available was used. The ground lining the hole was thereby killed to a depth approximating seven feet. Next the structure occupying the centre of the hole was constructed. Originally I had thought that a support would not be needed but after the structure had collapsed several times under its own weight, I decided to form the shape firstly with earth, and this enabled it to stand. The next and by far the most difficult stage was in the transport and manipulation of the detritus which was to cover the sides of the hole and provide a two feet thick surface on the central structure. Suffice it to say that every major town in the West Country peninsula contributed tankers filled with both human and animal excreta. They lined a route daily, often over six miles long to discharge their cargoes into the hole and the workers – each clad in environmentally closed suits – then set about the task of spreading the material according to my instructions. This last task took five days and fifty workers to achieve the desired result.

When I had first conceived the work, I'd imagined that on completion, it might be covered with a huge tarpaulin; this in order to enable a ritual uncovering on the day it was opened to the public. The plan was impracticable. Not only would the cost of such a canvas cover have been immense, but the feat of engineering needed to make the tarpaulin pull back would have far exceeded the cost of the project itself. I need not have worried. Once the piece was ready, it became apparent that the 'uncovering' would be one graduated by the smell. As the guests invited to the opening approached the site, the aroma from the hole grew steadily stronger. A far more appropriate sense of discovery than any that might be governed by a sheet of canvas.

On the day in question the representatives of the media arrived in droves, outnumbered only by those from local councils and from organisations such as the Arts Council and various community organisations. A huge crowd lined the perimeter of the excavation, many choosing to wrap scarves or handkerchiefs around their noses and as each new contingent approached; their arrival was marked by a communal sigh, a sound reflecting some degree of shock or horror. Cameras clicked and whirred and reporters vied for positions each trying to get as close as possible to the committee members or myself. The board from Maurice's gallery was represented in their entirety and at some stage, I even saw Manny Hume amongst the viewers.

Later that day, I gave a press conference. I knew there was the potential for all manner of silly questions and so I tried to preclude the possibility by making a detailed statement and refusing to answer questions.

I explained that, the vegetarian diet of cattle and the complexities of the digestive system they employ are both reflected in the constitution of cow-shit. "Initially, when it is first excreted, although the texture is often rough, the detritus is exceptionally moist. However, after only a little while particularly if the temperature is high and/or it is subject to sunshine, it sets as hard as concrete. Consequently the nature of the substance produced is similar to many of those materials used traditionally in the making of sculpture. Characteristics such the malleability of modelling clay; the change witnessed in cement as it hardens and the surface negotiability of stone or plaster when cut by carving tools are all evident in cow-shit. It can be modelled or fabricated on an armature, it can be cast in a mould or it can be carved. Moreover, although the pungent aroma readily associated with cow byres is generally thought to be unpleasant if not offensive, as the material hardens the smell is considerably reduced. And whilst the resistance some artists exhibit to the use of this material is understandable in terms of hygiene, the versatility available in its use should be acknowledged by all. This is art shit!

Clearly there is also another dimension needing consideration when choosing sculpting material, namely that of its intrinsic form. This point is best illustrated by a quote from Michelangelo. He once said, "If a stone-carving is rolled down a hill, any parts that break off are only those that are not needed." His meaning, founding the 'Truth to Material' movement, was that stone contains innate qualities of structure affecting the form produced and that they are quite different from those found in other materials. Therefore a human hand carved in stone is of necessity a stone hand and not one of flesh and blood. It would also be true to argue that, for example in this instance, stone has relationships and ramifications that far outweigh its actual physicality. It was the material of the pyramids and that used extensively by the Greek sculptors; it helps form the mountains of world-wide landscapes and is represented in molten form whenever volcanoes erupt. There is therefore both an historical and an emotive resonance in our appreciation of how we might employ this material.

Considering that, since the birth of time, we all have a hand in its production and are so much closer if not dependent on the process of its production, how much truer this is in respect of shit.

Animal life on this planet has been manufacturing excreta ever since animal life first existed and significantly, the process is one shared also with other life forms. Shit should not therefore be misunderstood still less misrepresented. In some communities it is still used as part of the building process, in others as a fuel. And even the social mores that incline society towards a sense of revulsion when shit is mentioned provide another strata of significance in relation to its possible use in the making of art.

My decision therefore in making this sculpture and in so doing to focus exclusively on this material is founded in the same fine tradition of creative originality similar to that of the cave men when they first ground natural earth colours with which to paint their walls. And whilst I accept that some may find it shocking, I know also that the *Shit Hole* will open yet another door for artists struggling to find an alternative means of expression."

The journalists listened in silence, far more patiently than I ever imagined they would. And when I finished, although a few cameras flashed, no one tried to question me further.

Chapter Thirty-Five

It's difficult to believe that I'm now close to the grand age of fifty years. I don't feel any different than I did at twenty-five. Indeed it seems almost that one day I went to bed a young man and in the morning I was suddenly middle-aged. Faced with the same conundrum, so many people ask "Where did it all go?" – meaning how did their life pass so quickly. Usually their confusion is appropriate. Most of them could never boast much more than getting a job as their life's achievement. Inevitably therefore, their passing is without note, their impact on their environment minimal and their lives largely without significant consequence. Not surprisingly, the history of the planet remains ignorant of their presence. Fortunately, having always kept myself busy and at the hub of things within my specialist area, I can chart the periods of my life with some degree of clarity. In this context without fear of contradiction I can lay claim to a significant effect.

In my own instance, I quickly discerned that society's bias was one that saw ambition as being laudable. It recommended those who strove actively to improve their lot; it admired the ruthless amongst us and paid due respect to acquisitiveness. And although some of the less successful members interpreted such liberal attitudes as a period when greed became legitimate, it was nevertheless in the finest traditions of the English entrepreneurial spirit. The same spirit as that which tempted Drake to piracy defined the British Empire. I realised that to play the game was not enough and that it was unnecessary to legitimise one's actions. Winning had to be the sole objective.

Almost from the first day I attended art college, I knew exactly what I wanted. I could suddenly see a way through the jungle of social mores and proprieties and was able therefore to take a direct path to celebrity status without any qualms of conscience. As an artist, I claim immunity from the ethical norm. I believe that artists are the people who set the agenda for tomorrow by ignoring that which is set for today. And whatever the cost to those who become victims of progress – the necessary flotsam cast aside to lighten the load – it is through the efforts of people like me that our descendants will be enabled to bridge the chasm of traditional ignorance. In so doing the perceptions of the majority will be enhanced.

I am not alone in being accused of using those around me, particularly my female friends, for my own ends. But isn't that merely the nature of most human interaction? Even in the best and most altruistic relationships, don't most people seek their pleasures and satisfactions independently – often at a cost to those near to them? The profit we achieve in any sphere is made by making our personal needs central to those considerations that define our actions. It may well be therefore, that as this philosophy was always at the heart of my thinking in my formative years, my rejection of the new 'touchy-feely' selflessness as exemplified by the juvenile efforts of do-gooders today is understandable. I have no sympathy with such institutionalised hypocrisy and no patience with those who propose it.

My personal popularity as with that of my work has varied over the years. On occasion it dropped like a barometer with a storm approaching but it always surged again, often to even greater heights than before. Consequently, the claims I make for the new ground I have explored in the visual arts are unimpeachable. I have redefined new boundaries regarding the constitution of art and, against considerable odds, I have created a body of work that can stand alongside the best seen in the twentieth century. Significantly in this context, the powerful resonance created by what has become known as Devon's Millennium *Shit Hole* is now seen as a major contribution to the development of public art and reputedly, it attracts over half a million visitors each year.

New offers from America indicate the likelihood of similar commissions being offered there and my old friend Carl Schwitters is in the process of negotiating them on my behalf.

In the meantime, the world of art has changed immeasurably. And although some artists and their tame critics continue to complain about what they perceive as a lack of skill, the fact remains that the world has turned since manual skills were a basic necessity for making art. Cell-phones, computers and digital communication systems have opened everyone's eyes and increased perceptions; the world village can share a global joke and the art of today need not be hidebound by the code of good taste or the morals of a previous century. The public applaud celebrity particularly in the arts and treat those who attain it as role models. The notion of celebrity, however it might be achieved, forms a fundamental aspect of our culture and an aspiration of the majority.

As far as the rest of my associates are concerned, mainly they appear to have reaped whatever rewards they were due. Phillipa remarried, this time to an Argentinean millionaire and Paul finally came out of the closet and spends his time in the company of a bevy of young men equally inclined. Celia continues to live alone, making obtuse abstract pieces that sell selectively to buyers mainly from the European continent. According to close friends, my first agent Manny Hume is apparently stricken with HIV. The fashionable killer disease of AIDS has blossomed and hopes for his recovery are few. I cannot pretend to be too upset by this news and can only express the hope that he lingers for a long time.

I sent the last cheque in final payment to Judy as soon as I heard the news.

END